Praise for *The Broken H*

"A mother's love is powerful beyond measure in a world where domestic violence touches every circle of society. With colorful intensity, Ann Marie Jackson speaks truthfully of San Miguel de Allende: its impressive traditions and cultural strength as well as the inevitable frictions within a community formed of people from every corner of the world who face the excruciating pain of loss. This novel makes the reader feel emotion with every fiber of their being."

— CAMILA SÁNCHEZ BOLAÑO,
Editor-in-Chief, *Newsweek en Español*

"With vivid and colorful descriptions, Ann Marie Jackson renders a vibrant literary canvas that transports the reader to Mexico's treasured San Miguel de Allende. While there, we witness the transformation of a woman who, surrounded by the strength of her close friends and community—as well as through her own focused determination—is able to rise above the pain of a broken marriage and restore her spirit to what it once was."

— JESSICA WINTERS MIRELES, author of *Lost in Oaxaca*

"Women from two worlds, coexisting in San Miguel de Allende, are empowered in different ways while depending on each other far more than one might suspect. Jackson provides a richly detailed depiction of place as well as close, careful study of tragedy and triumph in these women's lives."

— LUCINA KATHMANN, Vice President emerita of PEN
International, representative to the United Nations
Commission on the Status of Women, and author of
Para Que Nos Escuchen/To Make Ourselves Heard

"This story beautifully illustrates the power of connection. The author's deep love and respect for the culture of her adopted country shine through in her writing. Bravo!"

—DEANNA SINGH, author of *Actions Speak Louder, Purposeful Hustle*, and *A Smart Girl's Guide: Race and Inclusion*

"With visually rich prose, Ann Marie Jackson tells a moving tale of a woman's resilience and reinvention through the eyes of an expat in the beautiful but complicated city of San Miguel de Allende, Mexico."

— BRIAN CREWE, award-winning film director

"A deep, delightful read! Spanning the parallel worlds of privilege and poverty in San Miguel de Allende, Ann Marie Jackson's *The Broken Hummingbird* captures the heartbreak of a dissolving marriage alongside the joys of making a difference in others' lives as well as one's own."

— LUCIE FROST, satirist published by *Slackjaw, NextTribe*, and *The Belladonna*

THE BROKEN HUMMINGBIRD

THE BROKEN HUMMINGBIRD

A Novel

Ann Marie Jackson

SHE WRITES PRESS

Published 2023
Printed in the United States of America
Print ISBN: 978-1-64742-559-3
E-ISBN: 978-1-64742-560-9
Library of Congress Control Number: 2023904922

For information, address:
She Writes Press
1569 Solano Ave #546
Berkeley, CA 94707

Interior Design by Kiran Spees

She Writes Press is a division of SparkPoint Studio, LLC.

For my beautiful boys,
Rowan and Tristan

"The daily hummingbird assaults existence with improbability."
—Ursula K. Le Guin
No Time to Spare:
Thinking About What Matters

"Some of my old memories feel trapped in amber in my brain, lucid and burning, while others are like the wing beat of a hummingbird, an intangible, ephemeral blur."
—Mira Bartok
The Memory Palace

We invite our beloved dead to visit. The thin veil between worlds dissolves one night a year so the lamented may come home to their families. The angelitos, those souls who died in childhood, appear one night earlier. The days and nights before that, we prepare.

JANE URGES HER SON FORWARD as a thousand dancers shuffle around them and spin up Calle Hidalgo under a darkening sky, their faces hidden behind paint depicting the dead they will become, with skull-white skin, black nose and eye sockets, and skeletal grins stretched wide. Women soften the ghoulish effect with glitter, gems, or floral designs around the eyes. They wear long gowns while the men sport top hats and suits, and children master the look in stylish miniature.

She wants to dance, but Liam holds back, his hand in hers transmitting the weight of his fear. As thoroughly as he has adapted to Mexican life, he still shrinks from the loudest mysteries. So, at first, they walk. After a couple blocks, he begins to recognize friends and teachers under layers of makeup. Jane senses that he's still jealous of his big brother for being tapped to march at the front of their group with the school's banner, but he allows himself to be charmed by the huge mojiganga puppets that move through the crowd. Nervous giggles erupt when one of them leans over him, her twelve-foot frame tilting at a crazy angle. The man inside looks out through a hole in the puppet's skirt and suggests a dance. Wide-eyed, mute, Liam shakes his head. The mojiganga straightens up and whirls away.

A block later, Liam lets go of Jane's hand and joins two seven-year-old girls from his class. The girls' urging has more impact than his mother's. Hands on hips, Liam stomps out a pattern learned at school. The girls match his steps, and a handsome father Jane recognizes from the drop-off line approaches with approving eyes and joins in.

They arrive at the heart of the city and circle the central plaza where several bands compete to be heard. Above them all looms the façade of the famous church, a pink marble confection with elaborate spires. Friends jump in line, cameras flash, and Liam still dances.

Then it's over. Drifting away, Jane shouts her goodbyes to fellow parents and corrals her boys. It's time to meet their father for dinner.

On the restaurant's terrace, where other elegantly dressed skeletons enjoy their arrachera or carnitas with an enthusiasm belying their deathly appearance, Kevin waits for them, tall and coiled, intensely alive, his chiseled face just beginning to soften with age. Even after all these years and despite the current tensions between them, Jane feels a potent tug of the attraction that has sustained them. The boys run to him.

Connor arrives first. "I wish you could have seen me carry the school banner. It was much more fun being in the parade this time. You know, instead of just watching it like last year when we first got here."

"I almost got head-butted by a mojiganga," Liam adds.

Throughout the meal, Jane makes an effort to keep the conversation light. Kevin follows her lead. Together they focus on their children, who soak up and radiate the magic around them.

At home, though, after scrubbing stubborn makeup from the boys' faces and tucking them in, their eyes dreamy with the evening's alchemy, she has a harder time tamping down her frustration. She had tried earlier to convince Kevin to join them in the parade, but when she offered the tin of face paint, he refused to take it, flaring his nostrils as though it stank.

"The boys are ready," she prompted.

"So go without me."

"They want you to come with us, and so do I. We need to start doing normal things as a family again. Normal-for-here things. It's been a year. How much longer will you freeze me out? You're punishing them in the process."

That didn't go over well.

She distracts herself now by looking for an inch of space on the family altar she constructed earlier in the week with the boys' help. Someone gave another sugar skull to Liam tonight, and she wants to find a spot for it.

Bright orange marigolds alternate with wine red cockscombs whose folds resemble the human brain and whose color, she was told by a flower vendor, represents Christ's blood. Behind the flower border, a dozen candles stand guard around the photographs. Jane glances at her father's formal portrait in his army uniform. At twenty-five, he'd been a real heartthrob, even with his wavy black hair, like Liam's, cropped short. He was still quite handsome in his forties, the way she remembers him. She murmurs an apology for his proximity to the candids of her boys' recently deceased guinea pigs, as he would never have approved of sharing altar space with rodents. While he might not have minded a portrait of the purebred mare she'd loved as a girl or one of his prize bulls, her sons' furballs would not have made the cut. *Sorry, Dad, you'll have to bear it. It's been twenty years since you made the rules.*

Interspersed among the photographs, candles, and flowers stand delicate, handmade sugar skulls, sugar lambs in whorls of sugar wool, and sugar donkeys laden with tiny bottles of tequila. She and her boys were so impressed by the artistry that they bought more of the sugar sculptures than necessary. She wedges in the new skull, with its clever use of colored foil behind the eye sockets, next to one of the candles.

She didn't realize they were funeral candles when she bought them in a shop off Calle Mesones last week. She had already paid for the selection of tapers when she saw, on her way out, coffins for sale in an adjoining storefront. At the center of the display sat a small, white box lined in pink satin. She shudders at the memory.

From the sofa, Kevin notices. "You OK?"

"Just a chill."

He compliments the altar. Jane studies his face, currently sprouting salt-and-pepper stubble below the defined ridges of his cheekbones and guarded eyes. Sensing a peace offering in his words and the relaxed set of his lips, she smiles. "Thanks. I like how it turned out, even though we didn't follow the rules."

An ofrenda is supposed to include particular items, like the favorite foods of your dearly departed, on various levels, she almost explains but doesn't. He's not that interested.

"You've had fun this week," he says.

"Yeah, the art installations are amazing. Apparently there's a little controversy, though."

"Oh?"

"About the holiday, that it's gotten touristy here in San Miguel. Some people feel there's too much focus now on dressing up as a Catrin or Catrina. It wasn't meant to become a party costume." The elegant skeleton, she learned this week, was originally intended a century ago as a critique of elite vanity and greed. "This day of remembrance should be serious and respectful."

"So I was right not to do it."

"Very funny, like you knew that. But anyway, yes, it's been fun." He smiles again, so she uses the opportunity. "Have you thought more about joining the Thanksgiving beach trip? It's so nice that the school's giving time off for the sake of the American students. If we're going, we need to pay the deposit this week."

"No. I have to work, and it's too expensive."

"It's really not. We can caravan with the others, not fly, and the hotel's not bad."

"I said I don't want to spend the money." His body, powerful though subdued by middle age, tilts forward an inch, enough to convey impatience.

She doesn't take the hint. "Don't I get a vote? It'll be good for the kids, and we can get to know the other families better. I'd like to do this."

"Make your own damn money then."

She must stay calm, or she will lose any chance of convincing him. "Hey, be fair. We decided together that here I'd focus on the kids, and you're fine with me not earning for a while, remember? The trip won't be expensive, and anyway, it feels like this isn't about money."

"Whatever. I'm not doing this." He shrugs and walks away. He does that now, drops his dictates and goes, assuming he's won. The only thing worse is when he stays to fight.

A HUMMINGBIRD, HER SECOND IN as many days, appears near the back wall of Jane's garden. She freezes so as not to frighten the delicate creature. Iridescent green wings flutter at an impossible rate as it darts back and forth. She recently read somewhere that a number of indigenous peoples, such as the Yaquis in Sonora, the Mayans of the Yucatan, and the Purépechas of nearby Michoacán, believe hummingbirds to be divine messengers sent by the gods or souls of the departed. The Mexica or Aztecs saw hummingbirds as the reincarnation of fallen warriors. She wonders whether this one carries a message and if so, for whom. Eyes squeezed against the sun, Jane watches the tiny, uncageable bird until it flits beyond the wall. Then she goes inside, grabs her purse, and steps out the front door onto her street's cobblestones, still enthralled by the aviator's dizzying movements and peacock glory in pocket size.

Jane's route takes her through Parque Juárez, where she notices a girl, perhaps eight or nine years old, sitting at the end of a bench, swinging her legs. Scuffed black shoes appear and disappear beneath her. She wears a school uniform that Jane doesn't recognize. One of the girl's hands grips the scrolled ironwork of the armrest while the other rests in her lap. She chips off flakes of black paint with her thumbnail. Jane offers a cheerful buenas tardes, but the child returns neither the greeting nor the smile.

Leaving the park, Jane turns onto another narrow lane edged in high, bougainvillea-draped walls painted warm shades of red, orange, yellow, rosa mexicana, and the occasional white or sky blue. While her eyes focus on the uneven stones as she passes one elegant home after another, she wonders about the girl. The child appeared well looked-after, her uniform neat with shiny ribbons entwined in long black braids, but she was alone. Jane should have stopped and offered help.

She worries until she arrives at her sons' school and turns her attention to the sea of children flowing down the steps. Jane and other parents swim against the tide. She soon spies her own boys within the bilingual chaos.

"I saw another hummingbird," she tells them. "He was gorgeous but as nervous as the one yesterday." The first visitor was white-breasted and grey-winged with patches on its head and throat as red as the blood spilled by Huitzilopochtli, the Aztec god of war often depicted as a hummingbird. It had lingered over the blossoms on the lime tree in her garden but fled at her too-obvious approach.

"Mom, you know it's not their fault they can't hold still," says Liam.

"That's a myth," Connor corrects him. "They don't die if they stop flying. Otherwise they'd never be able to sleep or sit on a nest."

"I just wanted him to relax for a minute and tell me why he'd come. Some people believe they bring good news, you know, and good luck."

Connor shakes his head at her sentimentality, swinging the mop of tousled blonde hair he has for weeks resisted her entreaties to cut, but nonetheless offers a sweet suggestion. "We should get a humming-bird feeder again, Mom, since you like them so much."

Liam agrees. "Yeah, like back home on the balcony. I remember you said only a couple kinds make it to New York, but there are tons here, right?"

Jane looks from the vivid green of her elder son's eyes, the exact shade of a new, still coiled stalk on the rainforest ferns she'd known in childhood, to Liam's even bigger, deep brown ones. Back home. She wonders how long they'll live here before considering Mexico home. It's been more than a year already. "Yes, tons. Let's do it."

On the return walk through the park, in the company of her own children, Jane looks for the girl, but the bench is empty.

As soon as she pulls her key from the lock, the boys shoot through the door ahead of her. Jane sets out snacks, supervises homework, and starts dinner, with half her mind on her tasks and the other half once again chewing over how her family came to be living in San Miguel de Allende.

Twenty years ago, it was "Watch out, New York City." She and Kevin moved there from a small, wet town in Washington State when she was all of eighteen and he twenty. Awestruck by the city in its frenetic allure, they knew their lives were beginning for real.

There she charged through her college classes. In her sophomore year, she tried painting for a required art credit and discovered how much she enjoyed it. Kevin had developed a talent for drawing in childhood. Sharing this interest in interpreting the world became another potent way of being together.

Then she marched into law school. His college career, meanwhile, was haphazard, but he got by on charisma, first bartending and then falling into a job in software sales, soon making too much money to go back to school. He still said then, on occasion, that what he really wanted to do was to be an artist.

After law school, Jane went to work for an underfunded children's advocacy organization. Kevin made considerably more money selling customized software than she did as a lawyer. They still found a few hours together on weekends to create art, shutting out their harried weekday worlds, and when they were too busy even on weekends, well, that was a sign of how successful they were becoming, wasn't it? Of how far they'd come. They thought still that they were happy.

Looking back, the pattern is as clear to Jane as if it were spray-painted on the walls of their Brooklyn apartment. First, he resented that college came more easily to her. Then he resented that she drew more satisfaction than money from her career while it took them years to pay off her student loans. He even begrudged her painting on the side, especially when she actually sold a few pieces, no matter how sincerely she urged him to pursue his art, too. Somehow, she'd stolen it. Later, he hated paying so much for childcare when, as he put it, she made as little as a full-time lawyer in New York possibly could. Eventually he even came to resent their chosen home, deciding the city was too expensive, too hard, too much.

This creeping, insidious metamorphosis unfolded silently in the untended corners of their marriage. Disappointments lingered and multiplied, but for a long time, they shared an assumption that those frequent slight wounds were inevitable, ordinary costs, unfortunate but worth enduring.

After all, there were happy times, too. The babies became the crux of their relationship, filling them up with love and wonder. That was how it was supposed to be.

Then came her mistake, the fascination that honed and justified Kevin's accumulated resentments: David, a lawyer she worked with. She put in long hours with him on a case targeting abuses in the state foster care system, even as her jealousy of the young nanny spending more time with her own children than she did festered and chafed. Over those months, David applauded her legal mind, and he came to understand what she was thinking often before she articulated an idea aloud. Talented and driven, he radiated a worldview far more optimistic than Kevin's, despite the horrors of their work.

As with the roots of a seedling brought into the sun after long struggling in shadow, the attraction grew slowly at first and then deepened with urgency. They were discussing the case, as usual, one late night when David stopped mid-sentence. A look surfaced that she had glimpsed once or twice before. This time, he didn't hide it but let his eyes fill with invitation. She saw that he recognized the matching hunger in her. The connection was so full of possibility it shook her, waking up places inside her she'd nearly forgotten. Like hot black coffee to her brain after restless nights, so that look was to her soul. She stepped away, guilt warring with desire and winning by the slimmest of margins. Every day at work after that was a skirmish with herself. Kevin sensed her turmoil. When she admitted to him her attraction to a colleague, his trust in her broke so definitively that he simply wouldn't believe the betrayal hadn't been thoroughly consummated. Appalled by his accusations, she understood the harm she had caused.

Hope arose when Kevin agreed to take dramatic measures to save their marriage. They decided to leave David, Jane's long hours, and all the other pressures and expenses of New York behind. They would move for a year or two to San Miguel de Allende, the beautiful, improbable city in the highlands of central Mexico where they had dreamed of someday retiring ever since they discovered it as back-packers one summer during college. Kevin would work remotely while Jane cared for their boys herself, better than any hired help. Earning dollars while spending pesos, that was a ticket to the good life, so why wait for retirement?

"You're doing what?" family members and colleagues had asked. "With children? Isn't it dangerous?"

"San Miguel is safer than New York," they answered.

Their friends said better things, like "We're jealous" or "We're coming to visit."

Mexico would help them come back together. It would also give Jane much more time with their soon-to-be bilingual kids and inspire both of them to develop their artistic passions. These were the cheerful explanations they gave everyone for the move.

Jane pulled Kevin to marriage counseling when they first arrived, after assuring him that the counselor was another transplanted New Yorker and they could do it in English. But holding up their frustrations to the light seemed only to make things worse. They should try again, they decided, soon, with a different therapist. Neither of them has looked for one.

After a year, despite Jane's apologies and another hundred assurances that the almost-affair never became physical, despite her date night plans and regular invitations to explore their new world together, Kevin's anger still simmers. He finds new reasons to resent her. For having much more time now with the kids than he does, and for having time to paint, volunteer, and study Spanish. For what he calls being on an unearned extended vacation.

He just needs more time to heal. With effort, they can patch enough of the smaller, older cracks in the edifice of their marriage, as well as the big David-shaped one. Maybe then she can forgive herself, too.

Jane has to make both the marriage and the move work for Connor and Liam's sake. Her boys need reassurance and stability. While she gives Kevin the time he needs, she can at least enjoy San Miguel and help her sons get the most out of the experience. Jane throws herself into their new community with her usual fervor.

JANE CAUGHT A RIDE WITH her friend Meghan twice before, but she's confident now that she can make it to Pueblo Nuevo on her own. Stylish and seemingly hypercompetent at expat life, Meghan is the mother of a child in Liam's class at the international school. They met on the school steps on the first day of classes last year, and since then, Meghan has been a regular source of good advice. So when Meghan suggested that Jane get involved with Casa Mía, she didn't require much convincing. "It's like Habitat for Humanity. We change families' lives. You'll love it," Meghan had said.

The road changes abruptly after the third luxury development, a place called La Buena Vista. Cobblestones and islands of palm trees disappear, leaving only dirt, endless rocks, cacti, and huisache. Jane weaves back and forth across the rutted track to avoid potholes capable of shattering an axle and thinks about the times she visited homes in those upscale neighborhoods without giving a thought to what lay behind them. Not long ago, she blithely attended a pool party and a brunch, and just last week she was thrilled to be invited to her first posada, a traditional pre-Christmas celebration, at a beautiful home in the best part of La Buena Vista.

Now, thanks to Meghan's recommendation that she fill a vacancy on Casa Mía's board, Jane knows what's back here. Pueblo Nuevo begins at La Buena Vista's back wall, where all city services end. The neighborhood consists of cobbled-together shacks and one- or two-room brick homes, often unfinished, where residents survive without city water, sewers, electricity, trash collection, or real roads. The government's excuse, Meghan explained, is that the land is private ejido property. In reforms following the Mexican Revolution, the new leaders divided up huge swaths of hacienda lands and gave them to the campesinos as self-governing farming collectives. To this day, many still operate under their own laws, in an arrangement somewhat similar to that of Native American reservations in the United States.

Now, more than a hundred years after the revolution, some ejido lands have been subdivided among descendants to the point that many a person's property is hardly large enough to build a small home on, let alone cultivate productively. Jane looks around. As Meghan told her, this neighborhood really should be regularized, which means losing its special status so it can be incorporated into the rest of the city. These people deserve access to public utilities as much as any other citizens.

In fairness, she knows the government doesn't deserve all the blame. Meghan also warned that the current ejido leader resists any change that might diminish his power over his fiefdom. For years, he's been collecting his own taxes from ejido families to pave the roads and bring in water, yet somehow the pavement and water never arrive. While some ejidos run successful collective businesses, this one seems to provide very little to its members.

Deciding not to push her luck any further, Jane parks her car on the side of the road. She'll walk the rest of the way. When she opens her door, the sounds and smells of the place flood in. Dogs barking, dust swirling, children squealing, smoke, sunbaked earth, sewage, chickens.

She sees Meghan a little farther up the road walking with Rocío, Casa Mía's long-serving executive director, and a photographer recruited for the day. Jane calls to them. They turn as a group, wave, and pause to let her catch up.

"So nice of you to volunteer." Jane shakes the photographer's hand.

"My pleasure. Meghan here was very convincing. How could I say no?"

"I know the feeling." Jane grins.

Meghan makes an innocent face while Rocío focuses their attention. "So, portraits of the family and candids of the crew at work. What else?"

After thinking for a moment, Meghan responds. "We could use some good shots of Juanito—"

"Sorry, excuse me. Hola, Nayeli," Rocío calls as they approach an open, muddy area. The pungent odor triggers a strange sense of familiarity in Jane.

A slender woman bending low over a row of raw bricks straightens up. Her hands, coated in slick mud, glisten as she responds to Rocío. "Hola Señora, buenas tardes, ¿cómo está usted?"

"Bien, ¿y usted?"

"Muy bien."

"¿Y tú, Dulce, how are you?" Rocío addresses a young girl standing nearby whose smile is shy but magnetic. "Why aren't you at school today?"

The girl looks at her mother. "Oh, there's no class," Nayeli answers for her. "The teacher is not there. She's sick."

"Oh? That's too bad. Well, I'm sure you'll be back in school tomorrow, right?"

Dulce nods, eyes still sparkling under Rocío's attention, before looking down. Jane follows the girl's gaze toward her feet, buried in soupy earth. Then she sees from the corner of her eye that the photographer is taking pictures of the child and wonders whether to stop her. It feels wrong since they haven't yet asked for the girl's or mother's permission, but calling attention to it at this point might be more awkward. Jane is spared the decision when Rocío moves the group along by saying goodbye to another even younger girl whom Jane hadn't yet noticed sitting in the dirt on the edge of the work site. "Hasta luego, Lupita."

A chorus of "hasta luegos" echoes among the women and girls, and the group walks on.

The photographer exhales heavily. "That breaks my heart."

Jane agrees. "I'd heard that women and sometimes children do backbreaking work out here making bricks, but I hadn't seen it myself until now."

"You don't know the half of it. That mud Dulce was standing in?" Rocío's voice carries frustration and pity. "It's part manure, I'm sure you could smell it. They're barefoot because they have to feel for the perfect consistency. It's actually very technical, and it takes hours. Those girls should be in school, keeping options open for their future, not losing their chance already."

The joy of the day leaches away.

"I'm from here." Rocío smooths her already sleek hair. "I've seen poverty near wealth my whole life, but these kids, they still get to me sometimes."

"God, of course they do," says Jane. "Weirdly, I recognized that smell from my childhood. I grew up on a farm, and when my dad fertilized the fields, for a few days we had to smell a similarly potent combination of manure and mud. I hated it, but I could just go inside my house and keep the windows closed."

"Look." The photographer proffers her camera's viewfinder at the person closest to her, which happens to be Jane.

"Oh, wow." The photo is stunning. Framed from above, a world of mud surrounds a beautiful child. There is nothing else, only girl and mud, every detail vivid. Something in the child's eyes leaves Jane uncertain as to the emotion she witnesses. The photographer clicks forward, and the younger sister appears, sitting in the dark orange dirt, raw bricks stacked behind her, bare toes protruding from caked jeans. The barest hint of a smile warms her features.

"These are incredible, look." Jane hands the camera to Rocío.

When Rocío looks up, she passes the camera on to Meghan. "You are clearly the right person to do this. They're amazing."

The photographer shakes her head as though to clear the images from her mind.

Rocío continues. "The mother works from about eight in the morning until eight at night, six days a week, and those poor girls are with her far too much of the time."

"Twelve-hour days?" The photographer blanches. "Doing that?"

"Yes," says Rocío. "And they still only make a few hundred pesos a week, which is not a living wage. Plus, if they don't reach their quota, sometimes they don't get paid at all."

"Seriously?"

"Yes."

"Where are the men?" asks the photographer.

"Some have gone north, and the ones still here, their jobs are worse. At the kilns, firing the bricks. These aren't traditional adobe bricks, they don't just dry in the sun. They're considered better, stronger, more modern, but you don't want to know how they make the kilns burn hot enough."

Somehow Jane knows. "They burn plastic."

"Right. So toxic, the carcinogens, can you imagine? No respirators, no protection at all, breathing in chemicals all day, every day but Sunday."

"It must take years off their lives. Do we have any statistics?" Jane drafts a fundraising appeal in her head.

"Statistics? No. And they're glad to have the jobs. When some snowbirds built them an environmentally friendly oven a few years ago, they tried it but quickly abandoned it because it didn't burn hot enough to work."

"Major fail," interjects Meghan. "The way I heard it, those guys just swooped in and built the damn thing. They did almost no consultation with the people they expected to use it. Totally in white savior mode, thinking they knew better."

Rocío shrugs. "They had good intentions, but yeah, that's pretty much what happened, with predictable results."

The photographer looks concerned.

"Casa Mía's not like that," Meghan says hurriedly. "Not at all. We've always had a bicultural board and—"

"Me," says Rocío, "doing plenty of community consultation."

Meghan grins. "Rocío saves us from our truly bad ideas."

"The moderately stupid ones get by me sometimes, though."

"Hey—" Meghan starts to protest before they both crack up.

"What's that about?" asks Jane.

"Oh nothing." Rocío smiles. "Casa Mía's one of the good ones, I promise. Really good."

"I can tell." The photographer smiles but continues in a somber tone. "But the kilns sound like a nightmare. Isn't there anything that can be done?"

"The state environmental agency has tried more than a few times to shut them down over the pollution, but they never stay shut. I heard once the inspectors were met with knives. It's the workers' livelihood at stake, so you kind of understand."

Jane observes Rocío testing how much the photographer is prepared to hear. Should they tell her about the untreated medical needs in the community, or the rampant domestic violence, alcoholism, and glue-sniffing ten-year-olds? Jane can't tell. As Rocío warned her, she's finding it difficult to judge how much truth a visitor is ready for. Sometimes learning the full spectrum of problems motivates people to volunteer or fundraise, but other times, Rocío cautioned, if you tell them too much too soon, their eyes glaze over and they never come back.

"That's awful," says the photographer. "It sounds hopeless."

Meghan jumps in. "It's not hopeless—that can be an excuse to do nothing—but yeah, the odds are seriously stacked against these people."

Jane feels a gnawing sense of dread for the girls in the photos. The sparks in their eyes seem terrifyingly vulnerable, at risk of being extinguished by a never-ending pile of dirt and manure, the toxic flames of a brick oven, the alcohol- and desperation-soaked urges of a neighbor, or simply by frequent absences from primary school. With the limited education they're getting, the brickyard may be the only job they have access to when they grow up and have children of their own to provide for.

The women continue to walk in silence along the rutted track toward the construction site.

"I was just thinking about those girls," the photographer says slowly. "Isn't one of your rules that the kids have to be in school for a family to receive a house?"

"Yes." Rocío nods. "But that family isn't getting one."

Jane stops walking. "Why not?"

"Because they already have one, but only sort of. They live in the husband's uncle's house while he's working in the States. It's not much, just one small room, but with a functional roof and concrete floor, they don't qualify. We help people in worse situations."

"Is the uncle coming back?" asks the photographer.

"Maybe." Rocío shrugs. "He's been there a couple years, and he has a steady job and a family there now and everything, but they're afraid, you know, with this new American president building his wall. So I brought Bob, another board member, out a couple months ago to accept the family's application. But he said no."

"Then they're screwed," Jane concludes. "We're about to vote on family selection for the coming year, and then after that we're moving to another community, so if the uncle and his family get deported and need his house back any time after the next board meeting, it'll be too late for Bob to change his mind."

"Exactly," says Meghan.

All four women look up at the sound of rapid footsteps. A young boy runs toward them from the construction site just ahead, a huge smile lighting his face.

"That's our Juanito," Jane tells the photographer, feeling a little better.

Juanito heads straight for Rocío, who opens her arms. The boy slows only slightly before launching himself at her. She barely manages to stay upright as she catches him, and then she spins, his legs outstretched, shoes showering them all with orange dirt.

"Ay, qué grande eres, Juanito."

"Hola, Juanito, mucho gusto." The photographer introduces herself. Juanito just smiles.

"He doesn't really speak yet," Rocío explains. "He's never been to school or physical therapy, no special services for his Down syndrome, nothing. But we're working on that, even though it's way beyond Casa Mía's mission."

"I imagine that photos of this handsome young man will help. May I take your picture, sir?" The photographer and Juanito grin at each other. Then the women greet other members of the boy's family who have approached at a more restrained pace.

As the photographer works her magic, Jane moves out of the way and finds a seat on an upturned bucket. A member of the construction crew looks up from the wall taking shape before him. She waves. That's a bedroom wall. For the first time, this family will have bedrooms. Juanito, his two brothers, and any future brothers will share one, the two girls and future sisters will use the second, and the parents will finally enjoy a room of their own, with a door for privacy and dignity.

The photographer arranges the mother with a baby in her arms, the husband and Juanito at her sides, and the other three children at her feet, in front of their tarp shack. In the photographer's hands, Jane expects that the green tarp and blue sky will be crisp and bright, and this family, already beautiful, will look truly striking. The resulting photos should be fundraising gems. The backdrop is a bit of a lie, but Jane doesn't tell the photographer that they don't sleep in that shack, that Rocío told her she believes most of them continue to sleep the way they always have, all seven members of the family crammed onto one ratty mattress on the wife's brother's floor. They put up the shack only recently to comply with Casa Mía's rule that they live on-site during their house's construction to guard the building materials at night. Rocío suspects that only the husband sleeps here, meeting the requirement effectively if not to the letter.

Jane watches the photographer capture Juanito loading clumpy sand into a sifter. The boy glows with pride at helping to build his own home. Joy at being a small part of something so unequivocally good radiates through Jane, and so does the heat. Even in December, the sun is strong in the afternoon. Rivulets of sweat form on her scalp and under her bra. Fifteen minutes later, the photographer joins her for a water break, her face flushed. Jane considers the toughness required to perform strenuous work in the intense sun all day and then freeze in unheated homes through the winter's cold nights.

Rocío and Meghan walk toward them, escorting a tiny, stooped woman with grey braids coiled regally around her head. The woman laughs at something Rocío says, further crinkling her skin, and Jane instantly takes a liking to her. She stands up as they approach.

"May I present Doña Carmen," says Rocío.

"A pleasure, Doña Carmen." Jane extends her arm. The woman's papery hand is weightless in hers.

"Welcome, Señoritas. May God bless you for the work you are doing." Carmen looks penetratingly at Jane for several seconds and then shifts her gaze back to Rocío. "Maybe this one will decide my granddaughters are as deserving of a better life as those other children."

Jane takes the bait. "Would you tell me about your granddaughters, Doña?"

Rocío interjects in English. "Actually, you just met them. Be very careful not to make any promises."

The conversation continues in Spanish. "Dulce and Lupita? Nayeli's your daughter?"

"They're good girls. They need a chance. What I had and what I could do for my own daughters isn't enough anymore." Carmen's eyes, as well as her words, are compelling in their intensity. "They should be in school every day, filling their minds."

"We agree." Jane hopes her smile comes off as polite but noncommittal.

"Are we still on your list?"

"Yes, your family is on our waiting list for future consideration," Rocío responds, clearly choosing her words with care. "But as you know, the board determined that other families currently have greater need."

Carmen continues without acknowledging the obstacle. "We came here from Chiapas two years ago," she tells Jane. "My daughter's husband heard about a job in construction through his Uncle Carlos.

Carlos has a small house, and he's not using it while he works in the north. So my son-in-law brought us here. The construction job didn't last, though, so then he found work in the kilns. My daughter thought she'd find good work here, too."

"Doña—" Rocío tries, but fails, to intervene. Even she appears slightly awed by the tiny, formidable woman.

"Our lives are no better here, and we'll have nothing when Tío Carlos returns."

"I hope your granddaughters spend more time in school—every day counts—even if a house is not possible." Rocío's voice is again resolutely cheerful.

"Yes, but God willing, I will see them in a real home before I leave this world."

Jane remembers Rocío's warning. "May you be with us for many years."

Doña Carmen smiles and stops lobbying the women. Jane suspects it is a temporary concession. Rocío offers to walk Carmen home, Meghan joins them, and the photographer returns her attention to the Casa Mía builders at work. Jane sits down again on the bucket.

Something about those girls pulls at her, inciting a protectiveness distinct from the everyday fears of a mother. Nor does this response seem triggered solely by her professional instincts. This is subtly different, something long dormant.

A pleasantly cool breeze lifts strands of damp hair from Jane's neck, but the air carries the scent of the brickyard. She wrinkles her nose. It truly smells like the fertilizer she hated as a child on her dad's ranch, a very particular stench resurrected. Other memories begin to rise, too.

They sat together in their usual spot on the second-from-the-top stair. Jane wanted to watch her parents' faces, but she knew that if she and Thomas were to move down even one step, Mom and Dad would see and yell them back to bed. So they stayed where they were, silent and still despite scratchy carpet fibers reaching through worn pajamas. She was twelve years old, so he was nine.

Jane heard the distinctive gurgle of tepid liquid encountering ice. Mom's voice rose half an octave, but Dad's held steady. He just wanted to enjoy a little peace at the end of a hard day, he said. "Haven't I earned it?"

Something broke with a woody snap. Her brother's chin took on a tremble.

"Let's go up," she whispered. "I have an idea."

She pulled him to his feet and over the top stair. They passed by his room to get to hers. Jane eased the door shut, and they both climbed onto her bed, sinking into the extra-thick comforter Mom made for her the winter before last. Thomas looked at her expectantly.

"Let's run away, just for tonight. To the hay shed. It'll be an adventure."

"We can sleep in the big fort." He got it.

"Pack your sleeping bag and flashlight, and your bear if you want."

"And Sam."

It didn't take long to pack. Then, leaning from the usual stair for quick glances, she scouted their escape. After a few minutes, Dad disappeared into the hallway and her parents' bedroom door hit its frame. Mom turned toward the bathroom.

Jane glanced over her shoulder at her brother. "OK, now. Let's go."

They made it to the back door unseen. The night sky was unusually cloudless, so dozens of stars took the edge off the dark, but they still needed their flashlights to unlatch the door to Sam's dog run at the edge of the lawn. "Shhh, buddy, you're coming with us."

They followed their long driveway, a gravel road as straight as the railroad tracks it once supported, past a muddy corral and looming barn toward the hay shed. The large structure, just a roof on poles, was only half full, leaving plenty of space to move the bales around.

They crawled through the tunnel entrance, pushing their sleeping bags ahead of them, into their best fort. At four bales high, it was so tall they could stand up inside.

Jane pointed her flashlight into every nook to look for mice and snakes. "All clear."

She didn't have to remind Thomas to check the bales underfoot before unrolling his sleeping bag. He made sure the baling wires' sharp ends were folded down into the hay, not sticking up. They took off their shoes and climbed into the sleeping bags. Sam circled, scratched at the hay, and settled between them. They both rolled toward him.

"Janie?"

"Yeah?"

"Are they getting divorced?"

"I don't know."

"If they do, can I live with you?"

"Here?"

"Yeah."

"I don't know."

"Oh." A pause. "Can we leave the flashlights on?"

"Sure." Then, "No, they might get hot and start a fire, Mom said so last time."

"But—"

"I'll wait until you fall asleep, OK?"

"OK."

Jane watched the gaps between the bales, imagining young mice going about their lives. Dad once told her that thanks to the barn cats, snakes, and his mousetraps, there probably weren't many old mice on the ranch. She tried not to think about snakes at all.

Thomas's breathing deepened, and his face relaxed. She was about to click off the flashlights when Mom's head poked through the tunnel. Jane counted six pieces of hay caught in Mom's perm, but she still looked pretty.

"Hi honey. Thomas is out? Then we're staying. Move, Sam, you're in my spot."

Mom lifted the dog in her strong arms and settled him into

a corner. She zipped her coat up to her chin and lay down in the vacated space between her children. Up close, in a flashlight's glare, Jane saw the sting in her mother's eyes. Mom could do anything—help a cow birth a calf, dive to the bottom of the river and bring up the prettiest rocks, bake the best bread in the world, grow every kind of vegetable in her big garden, and even teach calculus and physics at the local high school—but she looked scared, like maybe now there was something she couldn't do. Jane shivered at the idea, and Mom pulled her close.

They woke cold and stiff to a gray glow filtered through narrow gaps between bales. Thomas sat up suddenly. Jane watched his face cloud over with confusion and then clear. He lay back down and scooted toward Mom, who wrapped an arm around each of them.

Jane broke the silence. "You guys hungry?"

They quickly rolled up the sleeping bags, crawled through the tunnel one after another, and then started back up the driveway, Mom holding Thomas's hand and carrying most of their things.

In the now pink light of sunrise, Jane felt her family's farmhouse belonged in a fairy tale. Before her birth, Dad had converted the building from a rural railroad station on a long-abandoned line. The house stood proudly among a grove of Oregon White Oak trees, and from the second floor, her bedroom windows and Thomas's looked out into a sea of branches. Planted over a decade ago, Mom's roses, ferns, and rhododendrons thrived in the cool, damp climate. Some of the climbing roses now reached Jane's windows. Dew sparkled on the plants as though every flower, leaf, and vine were encrusted with jewels. First Mom, then Thomas and Jane, entered quietly. Jane was careful not to let the screen door slam the way it always wanted to. Mom set to work on breakfast. Frying bacon brought back a sense of normalcy, and it brought Dad out of the bedroom.

They all acted as though nothing was wrong. Dad didn't mention that his wife hadn't been by his side all night. Jane wondered whether he knew that she and Thomas hadn't slept in their beds, either, but there was no reason to point it out. While Mom passed the platter of corn cakes to Dad, Jane plucked a piece of straw off Thomas's shirt and held her index finger to her lips for a second. Her brother nodded his understanding.

Jane looks around. Meghan and Rocío haven't returned, and the photographer is no longer in sight, either. She supposes she had better find someone. When Rocío and Meghan left with the grandmother, they seemed to be headed in the direction of the brickyard. Doña Carmen's house, or rather Tío Carlos's house, must be nearby. If she walks in that direction, hopefully she'll run into Rocío and Meghan coming back. She watches for dog and chicken droppings, cactus thorns, and snakes.

When she reaches the edge of the brickyard, stacks of raw bricks taller than a person block her view, so she hears the voices before she sees their owners.

One belongs to Carmen. "—no, this one's different. You and the girls made an impression on her."

"Mamá, why would you think that?" Nayeli's tone is sharp. "Don't get the girls' hopes up. What does she want?"

"She seems sincere, but we need to convince her now before she gets trapped in rules like that stubborn man."

"Maybe. But don't tell Pablo or the girls until it's real, which is probably never."

"My daughter, are you so tired? You can't show such hopelessness to your children or they'll give up before they truly start."

Jane peeks around the end of the row. Nayeli flips her braid over her shoulder and rubs her knuckles into her lower back. "You know I want a better life for them. We didn't bring them here for this. But I'm not pinning their hopes on some güera because you talked to her for five minutes and liked the look in her eyes while she spoke bad Spanish."

"That's not kind, daughter."

"That's the road to disappointment, that's what it is, and we'd be fools to walk it again. Telling my children they deserve more will only breed resentment. You know, you watched it fester in me."

As Carmen pulls her daughter into an embrace for the brief moment the younger woman allows, Jane retreats, stepping as quietly as she can. She finds Rocío, Meghan, and the photographer back at the Casa Mía construction site.

"Where did you go?" asks Rocío. "I can't lose any of you out here."

"I was just looking for you guys, exploring a little."

Meghan shakes her head. "Maybe don't."

Jane changes the subject to the photos. Only later, nearly back at their cars, does she bring up Doña Carmen. "What do you think of her? She's a feisty one, isn't she?"

Rocío nods. "She's more open and direct than anyone else in this community, I suppose because she's an outsider and so old. She has nothing to lose and much to gain for her granddaughters."

"You know," Jane says, "my husband and I brought our family to San Miguel for a better life, too, and on arrival we basically had it handed to us."

Meghan agrees. "You got the historic architecture and great climate you'd read about, and of course, the lower cost of living."

"Exactly." Jane thinks of her sons' private school tuition, which is a steal by American standards, and the fact that she now employs a maid and gardener for the first time in her life. "Because we're here, I can afford not to work now, while Nayeli can do nothing but work, and Carmen dreams not of colonial-era architecture but a concrete box with a bathroom—" Jane's eyes flip to Rocío's. "She knows the water won't even run all the time, right, since on ejido land the house won't be connected to city pipes?"

"She knows, of course. They'll only have water when the water truck comes and they can afford to fill the tank."

"And we'll give them a couple solar eco-lights, but they won't have actual electricity unless they tap the line from a neighbor who's pirated it from La—" Jane looks at the photographer. "You didn't hear that. We know nothing about it."

Meghan rolls her eyes. "Smooth."

"Carmen and Nayeli and the husband, Pablo, understand all that," Rocío continues, "of course they do, but an indoor toilet and septic system will improve their lives, even if they have to pour a pitcher of water in the tank every time they want to flush."

The photographer's gaze slides back and forth between them. Jane fears they're exceeding the woman's limits, but she can't seem to stop herself. "Privacy and safety instead of squatting in a field. Those girls risk injury and even rape whenever they go out in the dark to pee. Can you imagine living with that fear? What's wrong with this world?"

"Plenty." Darkness flickers through Rocío's expression. "So yes, I like Carmen. She's making it her mission to get them a house before she passes. Says she's too old to be patient."

Jane makes a decision. "I want to help."

"I already tried." Rocío's shoulders lift and drop. "But if you think you can convince Bob and Eleanor to bring it to a vote, go for it. I'll back you as much as I can without risking my job."

"No, I got this. Board members are just volunteers, so I'm not risking anything."

"We can try." Meghan's smile does not convey confidence, either. "I have to warn you, though, it's a long shot. So many other families need help."

That night, up to and beyond the moment sleep takes over, Jane's thoughts turn again and again to Carmen, her daughter, and her granddaughters. If she were Carmen or Nayeli, what wouldn't she do to give those girls a chance at a better life?

They remind her in some raw way of kids lost in the foster care system whom she encountered through her job. More disconcertingly, they remind her of her little brother, too, slipping through the cracks after her parents' divorce. Be rational, she chides herself, that was twenty-five years ago in utterly different circumstances. Why obsess over these girls in particular? Hundreds of other kids in the same neighborhood, let alone a thousand other neighborhoods, have similar fates. What about them? Well, she can't help everyone, but she can start somewhere. With these two.

In the morning, when she rises toward consciousness, Jane re-inhabits a body weighted with intention. Suspecting that she doesn't fully comprehend her own motivations but trusting them anyway, she concludes that Dulce and Lupita's family is worth picking a fight for. The girls deserve a real home they're not in imminent danger of losing. Bob was wrong, and she'll tell him so at the next board meeting. After Christmas.

"WHERE SHOULD I PUT THIS?" Jane, with her arms under a bowl of spinach salad, looks to her hostess, Alejandra. They scan the table set for fourteen, the sideboard dominated by a floral explosion that would do a hotel lobby proud, and a slab of granite insufficiently described as a kitchen island. It's a full continent, like Australia. Between the caterers' creations and dishes brought by guests, there's no available surface left. Rich smells comingle appealingly, and Jane feels a carnal anticipation for the Christmas meal.

Alejandra lifts a cheeseboard and calls to her husband, Enrique. "Mi amor, find room for this on the kids' table, would you? Jane, your salad can go here." Before a smiling Enrique has taken two steps in her direction, a maid relieves Alejandra of the platter. "Never mind," she says, and "Gracias." Enrique turns back to his conversation.

Jane deposits her bowl, kisses Alejandra on the cheek, and then greets everyone else, ending with her closest friends, Meghan, Gabriela, and Lindsay. The latter two are as usual teasing each other in rapid-fire Spanish Jane still struggles to follow, something about a double date gone hilariously wrong twenty years ago. Both grew up in San Miguel, although as Lindsay explains on the rare occasions when she forgets a word, she got a late start because her family moved here from Houston when she was seven, while Gabriela can trace her Sanmiguelense roots back through many generations to Spanish aristocracy whose New World fortunes, she admits, came from the depths of Guanajuato's silver mines on the backs of indigenous miners.

The dinner guests, like their broader social circle, are a lively collection of Sanmiguelenses, Chilangos from the capital, Americans, and Europeans. Jane credits San Miguel's position as a hub of art and culture far from a beach for attracting well-traveled and well-educated expatriates, many of them creative and artistic with nicely indulged bohemian streaks, and she has found that the Mexicans who choose to befriend these immigrants tend to share such qualities in abundance and are also impressively patient with the new arrivals' frequently poor Spanish and limited knowledge of Mexican culture. *How lucky we are*, she thinks, not for the first time, *to have landed here among these people.*

After the toasts, the feast, the children's whacking of a traditional star-shaped piñata with seven points for the seven deadly sins, and a decidedly less traditional Dirty Santa present exchange, Jane settles in beside her friends on the long wrap-around sofa on Alejandra and Enrique's terrace.

"How's the painting going?" asks Meghan.

"Well, I've started taking classes at Bellas Artes. It's been years since I've had time to paint consistently, what with work and kids, so I'm pretty rusty, but it's great to be at it again."

Lindsay looks up from the toy she's assembling for one of the children. "So we shouldn't ask to see your work quite yet?"

"Not yet."

"And how's Casa Mía? Meghan here signed you up, right?"

"She did, yes, and I love it. I need to keep from getting too sucked in, though, or that's where all my time and too much of our money could go."

"I'm sure."

"As Meghan knows, I've fallen in love with this one family in particular, a mother with two daughters and their little powerhouse of a grandma. I haven't met the dad yet. They were turned down last year for not being poor enough."

"Seriously? How poor do they have to be?" Lindsay asks.

"We focus on the families living in those awful shacks, while this family has a house already, but barely, it's just one room with no electricity, no water, and no bathroom. It's not even really theirs, it belongs to an uncle in the States."

"He's returning?" Alejandra asks.

"Well, that's the thing, who knows? He's been there a couple years, has a job and a family, but apparently he's increasingly worried, what with everything that's going on. Anyway, that family just got to me. Little girls standing barefoot in mud and manure helping their mom make bricks by hand instead of going to school."

"That's heartbreaking," agrees Lindsay.

"It's almost time to choose the ten families for this coming year, so Jane will get the board to reconsider their application." Even as she says it, Meghan's voice betrays her doubts.

"They'll vote with you if they know what's good for them." Alejandra beckons Kevin as he walks past carrying, to Jane's surprise, a bundle of sparklers, the extra-large kind she'd never seen before San Miguel. "Your wife has always fixed the world, hasn't she? Now our town."

Kevin smiles. "You know it. When she sets her mind on something, it usually happens, I can testify to that." Jane enjoys the flicker of pride in his eyes.

"Hey, I have an idea," says Lindsay. "Why don't we all clean out our kids' closets? We can buy toys, too, and give the Casa Mía kids a nice Three Kings Day."

"That's when they get presents, right? Not at Christmas?" asks Kevin.

Gabriela nods, and so does Alejandra.

Meghan loves the idea. "We can ask friends who went to the States to hit the after-Christmas sales and bring stuff down. They should all be back by the sixth for Three Kings because school starts the next day."

"Great! Spread the word, toy drive, we're doing this."

"Doesn't sound like we have a choice." Kevin pretends to grumble.

"How about blankets, too?" suggests Gabriela.

"Yes, totally, toys, clothes, and blankets." Jane looks around the circle of people who have so quickly become like family. "You're amazing, all of you. Thank you."

A few minutes later, at the first sizzle, the adults stand and move to the edge of the terrace. In the street below, Gabriela's husband and Kevin light the huge sparklers and pass them out as fast as they can until each child is holding a three-foot-long, hissing, sparking rod. The children whirl like banshees, shrieking, laughing, and looping fiery trails, some writing their names in the air. Several neighbor kids get in on the action, and soon there's a pack of twenty wild souls running up and down the block, going back to the dads for more whenever their wands fizzle out. Through some Mexican magic, no one gets poked in the eye, nobody sets anyone else's hair on fire, and not a single child trips on a cobblestone and lands on a sparkler. Several approaching drivers stop, take in the scene, and without complaint back up to go around the block. Jane shares nerves and enchantment with the other parents but keeps to herself her surprise and delight at Kevin having instigated the craziness. She watches him grin and push more huge sparklers into more small hands.

At home, after they put their happy, exhausted kids to bed, Kevin gives his seal of approval to the outing. "Well, that was fun."

"Certainly different from any Christmas we've ever had before, but the boys seemed to love it, didn't they? The sparklers were awesome." She has an idea. "I know it's late, but I'd like to paint for a little while. Join me on the roof?"

"I don't know. Do you really think we might still have it?"

"What?"

"Talent. Anything real."

The question draws a twinge of sadness, but she covers her reaction with chatty enthusiasm. "Only one way to find out. Here we are in San Miguel like we dreamed, why not try? Even if it turns out we're all washed up, it can just be for fun, who cares? Hey, I'm going to bring up some tea. Want some?"

"No thanks, and I care, I guess. I don't want to find out I never had much. Talent."

Having taken a few steps toward the kitchen, Jane turns back. "But you did. You still do, of course."

"Don't play dumb. You know my dad, for one, was never convinced I could make a living as an artist. My youthful confidence wore off a long time ago, so now I think maybe it's better not to risk it, in order to protect my idea of what I could have been if I hadn't had to give it all up to support a family, you know, my alternate life as an artist, the life I could have had—as long as I actually had talent."

Although she finds it encouraging that Kevin is being unusually forthcoming, his rendering of events still stings. "That's not fair. You didn't have to give up your art to support us. Do you really believe that? You quit, mostly, even before we had kids, remember? It's not my fault or the boys' that you barely gave it a go to begin with. Blame your parents if you want, but they didn't actually stop you, either. I didn't make you sell software, and you still could have drawn and painted on the side like I did."

"I know, I know, let's not fight, but I like my version of the story. I'm a hero who gave up his dream for his family, a hero with loads of untapped artistic talent, obviously, who could have been a big deal."

"You still could be. Come on, you're not that old. We're here in San Miguel, for God's sake, and we're not that old." She's forgotten about tea.

"You think I just pick up charcoal again at forty and magic happens?"

"You never know."

"Yeah, right." He shrugs but follows her up the stairs to the roof terrace, where she's created a quirky and, now that she's seeing it through his eyes, rather pathetic makeshift studio. City lights, one overhead bulb hanging from the palapa roof above her easel, several strands of cheap fairy lights strung thickly, and two floor lamps poached from the living room, while far from ideal, provide enough light to work.

On the easel, under a plastic drape, sits her current project, a rough portrait of Nayeli. Well behind their mother stand the girls, orange mud sucking at their legs. The reference photos she pulled from the family's Casa Mía file are clipped to the side of the canvas. She'll return them when she's done. She thinks about how to explain the painting to him. The conversation plays out in her head. That's dark, he'll say, the mud's a bit much. Too on the nose, maybe? What are you planning to do with it? Nothing, just practicing.

But he doesn't say anything when she uncovers the canvas and prepares to work.

She thinks about why she invited him up. Should she go ahead and offer him the gift or not, given what he's just shared? Will it be received as a vote of confidence in his ability or backfire? Well, she's come this far. From the dark but recently cleaned closet in the corner of the terrace near the stairwell, which previously held a collection of worn-out brooms and other household orphans left behind by the prior owners, where she now stores her paints and canvases, she collects a wrapped package with the logo of the local art supply store stamped in red ink.

"Here." Jane finds herself holding her breath.

When Kevin pulls out the pad of thick, creamy paper and box of high-quality charcoals, he grins. "Oh, I see. Thank you."

She smiles back at him with relief. "You're welcome. Merry Christmas."

She tries not to be too obvious about watching him. He pulls a chair up beside her under her crazy lights and starts drawing. Look at this, she thinks, we're making art together for the first time in years. Progress, for sure.

A memory comes to her of the two of them finger-painting with the boys. Liam, just a toddler, had ended up with red and blue all over his body. When she put him in the bath, the water turned a royal purple. The best part had been later that night when Kevin was inspired to fingerpaint on her body, too.

The next time she glances over, Kevin's face has taken on a focused look that could almost be described as contented.

MEGHAN AND ROCÍO START HAULING bags out of Jane's car as soon as she turns off the engine. Rocío pours out the contents on the front steps of a small church at the feet of waiting women and children. Piles of donated clothing, blankets, housewares, and toys spill down the top three stairs.

Jane is certain that this scene is not what her friends envisioned when, cozy on Alejandra's terrace on Christmas night, they made plans to collect donations for Casa Mía families. Well, she won't share the details. At least they'll end on a more civilized note when they present a new wrapped toy to each child.

"Oye, ¿estás bien?"

Jane responds to Rocío in English. "This feels disrespectful. I imagined something more organized, with tables at least, not dumping everything on the ground and making them root around."

"It's fine," says Rocío. "Why spend hours sorting this stuff when there's no point? How would we ever make it fair? Besides, this is concrete, it's clean. They don't mind."

Meghan agrees. "It would take forever to organize everything, and then what? Make them take turns? Better to have a fun free-for-all done in twenty minutes."

"All right. You guys know best."

Jane sees Nayeli spot something among the piles and follows her gaze. There. Delicate fabric flutters, and sequins sparkle like broken glass along the highway. Nayeli edges around several of her neighbors, clearly trying not to appear too eager. Apparently sensing Nayeli's mission, one of the women scans the piles with heightened interest, and her eyes light upon the sequins. The woman's hand snakes out and rakes in the prize. When she holds it up, the blouse is even prettier than Jane expected. Red satin, the color of ripe sandía, shimmers below the woman's fingers. Ruffled cap sleeves, a deep V-neck with inset lace, and tiny embedded sequins. Most of the women stop digging to stare.

Doña Carmen tries to help her daughter. "Too bad, it's tiny," she says to the woman holding the blouse. "But I think it would fit little Nayeli."

"Do you think so?" Nayeli reaches out for the shirt, but the woman's fingers do not loosen their grip. Nayeli lowers her arms. The other women and even some of the children fall silent. Nayeli's next words matter. She'd better come up with something clever and be quick about it. Jane holds herself back from grabbing the blouse and pushing it into Nayeli's hands.

Another woman swoops in. "Actually, it's so small it'll fit my daughter. She'll look beautiful in this," she says, snatching the shirt out of the first woman's startled grasp. Just like that, Nayeli's treasure is gone.

Jane looks around for Lupita and Dulce. There they are, near the end, burrowing cheerfully. Lupita's eyes go wide when she discovers a nearly new Barbie. Jane stifles a groan. Why a Barbie of all things? But this one at least seems to be dressed as a scientist, or maybe a doctor, with a white coat over her miniskirt and impossible figure. Lupita shows her sister the glittery high heels still attached, and the joy in the girls' faces fulfills Jane's hopes for the day.

JANE STEPS INTO THE STATELY courtyard of a three-hundred-year-old mansion. The building currently holds the offices of a high-end realty firm where her friend Gabriela works, but Jane can imagine independence hero Ignacio Allende himself visiting these grand rooms two hundred years ago to rally his neighbors to the cause. With her own mission in mind, she'd like to channel the general's confidence in the face of stiff odds.

The realtors' secretary shows Jane into a conference room where Casa Mía board members gather. As the secretary pours coffee and offers delicate cookies from the bakery across the street, trailing a mist of confectioner's sugar, Jane circles the table. "Hey, Meghan. How were your holidays, Bob? That's a gorgeous necklace, Eleanor."

Eleanor, board president, calls the meeting to order right on time, as always. She's run Casa Mía with strict efficiency for years. According to Meghan, Eleanor took over the organization pretty much the moment she arrived in San Miguel, having concluded her high-powered corporate career only a few months earlier but already finding retirement to be deadly boring.

Dispensing quickly with old business, Eleanor moves to the critical issue: selecting the ten families whose lives they will change this year. Rocío reports that they have received thirty-one complete, viable applications. She presents the twenty strongest candidate families in a parade of plucky misery. Her slideshow features children playing by grim shacks, worn-looking mothers cooking over smoky firepits, and uncomfortable fathers staring down the camera.

Jane senses the futility of her mission but pushes forward anyway. "I'd like us to consider one additional family, a holdover from last year."

"Yes?" Eleanor raises her eyebrows, at least mildly irritated at being caught by surprise.

"The Pablo López–Nayeli Pérez family."

"Didn't I just visit them?" asks Bob immediately. "Rocío was pushing them, too. Come on, girls, we've been over this. They already have a house."

"It's a temporary residence," Meghan reminds him. "They're caretakers of the husband's uncle's casita. We've granted similar cases before. And it's only one room with no bathroom, running water, or electricity."

"Temporary? They've been there for years, right?" Bob ignores Meghan's description of the structure.

Jane controls her tone and expression. "Two years, yes, but the uncle's afraid now to go to his job as a cook in South Carolina because restaurants there are getting raided more frequently. If he's deported, he'll have to reclaim his house here for his own family, and this family has nowhere to go when that happens."

Bob frowns and scratches his chin through his beard. "You've only had a seat on this board for a few months, Jane, so I understand that you're still learning how we do things, but we can't make decisions based on fear and panic. As of now, this family has a solid roof over their heads, which is more than can be said for the others."

"Wait a second," interjects another man. "I don't think their deportation fears are irrational. Our dear leader's got ICE rounding people up practically at random, and don't even get me started on kids in cages at the border, ripped from their parents."

"Absolutely horrifying."

"Beyond the pale," Jane agrees.

"At least we're on the right side of his damn wall."

Jane tries to regain control of the conversation. "I certainly don't want their fears to come true, but they very well may. If we don't help now, it'll be too late because we're going to build in a different community next year." She looks up to see Gabriela standing in the conference room doorway, her patrician face pinched. "Is everything alright?"

"Could you please try to keep it down a little? I have clients in the next room ready to make a million-dollar offer, and you're kind of scaring them off."

"Oh God, we're being obnoxious while you guys are so nice to let us use your space. I'm sorry. We'll behave."

Faces around the table look suitably contrite as Gabriela retreats.

"That's it, check your politics at the door," says Eleanor. "We'll have to agree to disagree about this family, among other things."

Jane glances around the room. Her colleagues, including Meghan and Rocío, look eager to escape the strained conversation. She failed to make a compelling argument that this family's situation is more urgent than others'. With limited resources, of course the board must tightly follow rules in the interest of fairness. Those girls and their grandmother happened to get under her skin, but that shouldn't tip the scales away from families in even worse circumstances. The others will vote for more obvious choices over 'her' family, and rightfully so.

Outside the conference room window, a man jogs down the street banging two iron bars together to announce the imminent arrival of the garbage truck. "How does he not go deaf?" Bob wonders aloud, hands over his ears. Through an open door to the hallway, Jane watches a maid respond to the summons by lugging three large bags toward the front door.

Jane concedes. They vote for the ten most compelling combinations of dire circumstances and motivated applicants, then flee the room.

Jane and Meghan walk in silence for the first block until they round a corner, where Meghan stops. "Well, that didn't go well. Sorry. I wanted to back you up, but I couldn't think of anything else that would help."

"I know, thanks, there's nothing you could have done. God, I just

"CAN I SEE?" SITTING DOWN at the dining table across from Kevin, Jane reaches for his notebook, but he shakes his head.

"Not yet."

"Just a peek?" His head swivels once more, so she changes the subject. "Hey, want to check out Burning Burro on Saturday?" Jane pictures them managing to spend a fun day together, enjoying the music and art installations, playing with the boys.

As quickly as she conjures the image, he erases it. "Burning Burro, like Burning Man? Are you serious?"

"Well, not exactly like Burning Man. One day only, and I hear it's nothing crazy, just music and art, family friendly."

"No."

"Want to think about it for maybe a second?"

"No. I have to work."

"It's a Saturday. Come on, it'll be fun."

"No." He expels his irritation in a quick blast of air. "Jane, please stop pushing this crap on me. You're enjoying your little adventures, but I have to work as hard as ever."

"So take a break and spend a Saturday having fun with your family."

"Easy for you to say when you don't have to work anymore—"

Jane feels the anger heating her cheeks. "Seriously? I'm doing basically all the parenting and managing our lives in a new country in a new language—"

"—while my job, my life, didn't get any easier."

"In your mind, none of that counts? Even though that was exactly our agreement, that I wouldn't work here, that I'd focus on the kids?"

"No, your 'managing our lives' doesn't count for much, not while I'm still sitting at my computer every goddamn day selling another software solution to another boring IT manager. You're even painting again when I was supposed to be the artist. So just don't."

She takes a deep breath. "Yes, I'm really happy to be painting again, and now you're bringing art back into your life, too, right?"

"Grow up."

Jane clenches her teeth until her molars hurt. Her patience with his martyrdom has worn thin as old denim when the white threads show and separate, but with a sickening jolt of awareness, she realizes she's afraid to challenge him further. He can upend their lives. The balance of power shifted dramatically in his favor after David. Then it slid still further when they moved here and she stopped earning an income.

The lines of anger etched into his face are starting to look permanent. Jane harbors a growing suspicion that in his mind an eventual divorce is a foregone conclusion and he's taking every opportunity to punish her first. Despite the good time they had at Christmas. She's tired of getting her hopes up for a reconciliation only to see them perpetually dashed.

Even fully conscious of her precarious position, however, why would she want to spend time staring into the abyss of divorce? There lies a move back to the States but probably not to New York, separate apartments somewhere cheaper, having to find a new job in a hurry in a new city with a gap in her resume, and looming over it all, the fight of her life for custody of her sons. Kevin told her, the night he found out about David, that if she ever left him he'd never let her have the boys. He repeats the threat every now and then when he's angry. She answers her own question: that's why she stays. Unless he decides first. She attempts to push the thought away, as if it can't happen if she doesn't let it, but a familiar weight settles on her chest. She tries to pull her next breath down to the bottom of her lungs without being dramatic about it. When she releases the air, some of the pressure abates.

"All right, fine, I just thought you might enjoy it. I'll take the boys with Gaby and Meghan and their kids."

He doesn't respond.

She sighs and reaches across the table for him. Unsure where to land, her hand comes to rest on his forearm. "Aren't you ever going to forgive me? I know I hurt you, and I'm sorry. You have to accept that I am sorry."

"Do I? Have to accept it?"

"If you're not even going to try, what are we doing here?"

"I don't know anymore." Kevin looks down at his notebook. When his gaze locks onto hers again, there's something in it that she can't read, and it scares her. "You know, I had such a brief moment as the alpha in this relationship."

"The what?"

"It was back home. You know, I was kind of a big deal. Twenty years ago. We were just kids. As soon as we got to New York, it all changed. What I want to know is, how come now, when you're not even working anymore, I still don't get to be the damn alpha? Never again?"

"That's ridiculous."

"Right, I guess it was always going to be you." He flips the cover of the notebook closed and pushes back his chair.

"No, I mean that's an ugly way to think. We're supposed to be equal partners, obviously."

"Yeah, obviously. Except in real life there's always an alpha."

"I don't know what to say to that." A thought occurs to her. "Where did you even get that idea, from your Dad? It sounds like something he would say."

"Whatever."

"It was, wasn't it? Back when he was trying to convince you to stay in that little town you wanted so badly to leave? When you wanted to be an artist, but he said you'd never make a living at it so you'd better work for him? He wanted you to take over the dealership someday, that was the big prize, right?"

"Well, I didn't want it then, but you know, it turns out maybe my folks were right. I probably would've been happier if I'd stayed home, stayed a big deal, and married some sweet girl who liked it that way, not a—"

"Yeah. Maybe you should have done that." She walks away this time.

After several days of performing an awkward domestic dance in which Jane actively avoids Kevin while trying to give her sons the impression that everything is fine, she makes the decision to go ahead and take the boys to Burning Burro. They should get out of this tension-soaked house and have some fun.

Upon arrival, Jane does a slow spin to take it all in. The amphitheater is some forty meters in diameter, the entire floor paved in a swirling mosaic. At the front looms a surreal building on which gravity-defying loops of concrete fan out from a central arch, under which the main stage has been set up. Dozens of people perch on the lower parts of the loops, some of them leaning out over flimsy railings. Next to the first bizarre structure rises a tower with a many-petaled roof resembling a half-open lotus flower.

"Mom, look." Connor points up to the lotus.

Two men crouch on a petal. They wrestle a fireworks castillo, a contraption that will shoot small rockets in all directions, balancing it over the heads of the crowd. A third man shimmies on his belly onto the edge of the petal to connect the outer brace of the castillo. For a moment, he's silhouetted against the sky, half his body extended over nothing but air. He secures the brace and slides backward to safety.

"Wow," breathes Liam, awestruck.

Jane looks around the amphitheater, taking in one architectural flight of fancy after another, until Gabriela and Meghan find them.

"You told me Gaudi-esque," she says, "but I did not imagine this. It's incredible."

Meghan grins. "How could anyone possibly imagine this? And wasn't the road to get here ridiculous? I almost wandered off back there in some pasture because I couldn't tell anymore what was riverbed and what was road. Anyway, I heard that José, the owner, designed a lot of it himself in partnership with that surrealist architect from Mexico City, you know the one, Gaby, he's super famous?"

"Oh, I should know his name." As Gabriela pauses in concentration, Jane studies her face, admiring her chestnut eyes, almond skin, and elegant features, framed by a long curtain of shiny black hair. Gabriela usually wears it up in a chic French braid, ballerina's topknot, or thick ponytail banded at the bottom as well as the top, but today she's let her hair down. Only one small section is captured in a skinny braid falling next to her cheek.

"I can't remember, sorry." Gabriela shrugs. "But it's so cool, isn't it? That complex over there is José's house and guesthouses. Gardens and greenhouses, too, and the neighbors have a private folk-art museum behind that old orchard." She points at a cluster of overgrown trees. "The installations are set up in front of the museum. Some are great, definitely worth checking out, but you might need to be on peyote to appreciate a couple of them."

"There's the burro." Meghan gestures toward an equine giant constructed of reeds around a wooden frame, then turns to Connor and Liam. "If you guys get hungry, the taco stands and bar are that way. They have aguas frescas or sodas if your mom says it's OK. Sophie and Toñio are running around, you'll find them," she adds, referring to her daughter and Gabriela's son.

Jane turns her boys loose with taco money and instructions to check in regularly. Liam and Connor disappear into the trees above the amphitheater. She hears their shouts and laughter when they encounter a pack of friends.

The three women make the rounds, greeting many people they know and offering introductions for each other when needed. A folk-rock group from Texas finishes their set, and a popular local band begins to warm up. After settling onto Meghan's picnic blanket, Jane scans the crowd for her kids. She spots Connor standing around with a group of tweens, while Liam races under the burro's belly, followed by Toñio and Sophie. She grins when they each return her wave. How much longer will her golden boys keep looking back at her? She loves this age. They're big enough to roam but small enough to still feel her gravitational pull.

"Hey girls, let's get a picture," Meghan suggests.

They pose with fanciful architecture and the growing crowd behind them. When Meghan passes around her phone, Jane smiles at the result. She is tucked under Meghan's chin, and it's hard to tell where Meghan's long, honey-blonde hair ends and her own darker blonde begins. Sure, Meghan's color is natural while hers is not, and Jane's hair has a tendency to frizz, but none of that shows in the photo. Gabriela's height splits the difference, her cheek resting against Jane's temple. With bright eyes and big grins, none of them, in her opinion, look forty. The funny thing is, she can imagine doing exactly this when they're sixty. She'd love to stay here in San Miguel on a never-ending sabbatical, and if she could, these two smart beauties would be her sisters, the core of her growing clan.

Several guys form a drum circle to fill the lull in the music while the new band sets up. Diego, a friend of Kevin's, wanders by with his three-year-old sitting on his substantial, tattooed shoulders. "Hi there," he says. "Santi, look who's here."

Jane waves to the child, who rewards her with a kiss blown from tiny fingers. His hands then start to slap softly on Diego's head.

"Do you like to drum, sweetie? Here, drum on this." She offers someone's Tupperware bowl. Diego lifts Santiago over his head to set him down, accepts the bowl, and holds it in front of his son. The child beats on the plastic, rhythmless but enthusiastic. Gabriela starts to clap along in encouragement and then to dance, drawing a huge grin from the boy.

"That's natural talent," says Meghan. "He's got a future with the band."

Diego laughs and turns to Jane. "Kevin here?"

"No, just us and kiddos tonight."

"Too bad. Lisa couldn't make it, either. She's not feeling well. We've learned that morning sickness isn't only in the morning." A huge smile splits his face.

"She's pregnant? That's fantastic!"

"Santi, you'll be a big brother, how wonderful." Gabriela swings the giggling boy into the air. "I'll call Lisa tomorrow. We have a baby shower to plan."

"Absolutely," Meghan agrees. "I love showers here. More about celebrating the woman—"

Jane's phone rings. "Sorry."

Diego says he'll catch them later and scoops up his son.

"Rocío, what? Fuck! No, thanks for telling me." Jane feels her friends' eyes on her. "I know. I didn't have the votes last time, but they'll listen now, right? We'll fix this. Call you tomorrow."

Gabriela and Meghan wait while Jane tucks her phone back into her bag. She looks up at Meghan first. "He got deported."

"The uncle? Damn."

"Yeah. Just like we warned them."

Gabriela looks from one to the other. "What's happening?"

Jane explains. "Remember that family I told you about with the two little girls, Dulce and Lupita? They and their parents, and there's a grandmother, too, live in their uncle's tiny house?"

Gabriela nods.

"At the last meeting, when your clients got an earful—again, sorry about that—we were arguing about whether or not to help them. They lost to worse cases. But now the uncle's back, along with his partner and her little kids, too."

"That poor family."

"Right? One child was actually born in the U.S., and the other arrived as a baby. The four of them got dumped in Mexico City, then made their way here. They may try to go north again eventually, but not now."

"Can't they all live together?" Gabriela asks.

"Sure, maybe if the place was a little bigger. But one seriously tiny room for two families, nine people? It doesn't work. Rocío says the uncle feels awful, so he's giving Pablo half his lot to build on, but they don't have money to build anything."

Gabriela looks sad but not shocked. "So Casa Mía will build them a house. That's what you do."

"Maybe," says Meghan. "The problem is we already selected this year's ten families."

Jane feels sick. "I just promised Rocío that I can convince the board to do extra fundraising to build eleven houses this year instead of the usual ten. But honestly, I doubt it."

"You need a mescal," determines Meghan. "I'll get three."

Jane watches her weave gracefully through the crowd. "I'm imagining the girls scavenging to build one of those awful shacks," she says to Gabriela.

"Don't they have other family?"

"In Chiapas, not here. They moved here for work, for opportunity."

"Well, maybe they'll go back to their family now. Maybe you can't solve this one. Although I love that you would even try."

Meghan approaches, stepping carefully through the crowd to protect the three shot glasses of mescal balanced between her fingertips. "Salud, chicas."

They sip, then Meghan gives Jane's arm a gentle squeeze. "You don't have to come up with a whole plan today. We're going to help you. For now, just breathe and enjoy the music—" Her voice trails off, then comes back at full strength. "That's my daughter! And Toñio and Liam. We better get them down right now because someone's going to light that thing soon."

Gabriela reacts first. "¡Híjole, little devils! They should know better."

Jane follows her friends' eyes. Sure enough, her youngest son and his two buddies are standing on top of the soon-to-be-burning burro. "How? It must be twenty feet high."

The women push through the crowd until they reach the burro's forelegs, where Meghan lets the kids know they're in trouble. "Sophie! Boys! What do you think you're doing? Sit down right now. Don't move until we figure out how to get you down."

"But first," Jane stage-whispers, "let's get pictures."

Gabriela laughs, and then so does Meghan. The children sit down on the burro's back and offer smug grins to their mothers.

"All right, no screwing around, OK? Put your arms up, king-of-the-world style."

"Queen of the world," declares Sophie.

The mothers step back for better angles.

"So how did you get up there?" Jane asks. "Did somebody help you?"

"No. We just climbed."

"Wow, but you can't just climb down. It's too dangerous."

A man approaches with a large torch and lighter fluid. "Perdón, señoritas, es la hora."

Meghan holds up an index finger and wags it from side to side in the universal Mexican gesture for no. "We have to rescue these idiots first."

The man joins them in brainstorming. "We can climb up—"

"But then what? It's the coming down with the kids that scares us."

"They must have a ladder here," Meghan suggests.

Gabriela commandeers one of the bartenders and sends him to find the owner. The kids fidget. Finally, the bartender returns with several men, including José, the owner. "Well, ladies, my only ladder won't even reach the belly, and we already took apart the scaffolding we used to build this beast, but we have rope."

"How would that work?"

They are still debating several minutes later when three spandexed and feathered acrobats appear, carrying a trampoline. Jane recognizes two of them behind their trippy harlequin make-up, a man and woman from her yoga class. Emiliano, that's the guy's name. She can't recall the woman's. "You guys performing tonight?"

"Circo Volador. We're up after the next band." Emiliano grins.

"Looks like your kids are fearless climbers. We spotted them up there and thought you might need some help."

"Thank you. We can't figure out how to get the little troublemakers down safely."

"No problem, here's what we do. I'll climb up and one of them gets on my back for the climb down." Before anyone agrees, Emiliano scales the nearest leg, muscles flexing under spandex.

"Uh, OK."

Emiliano reaches the top and sits down on the burro's back next to Toñio.

"There." He points at the ground next to the leg he just climbed up. "Secure the trampoline, just in case. Brace it, guys."

"Are you sure this is a good idea?" asks Jane, but, following the lead of the other two acrobats, she kneels and leans her weight into the trampoline. Meghan and Gabriela do the same.

Emiliano tells Toñio to stand up behind him, hold on with his arms over Emiliano's shoulders, and wrap his legs tightly around Emiliano's waist like a baby monkey. The acrobat's confident demeanor reassures the children. In a few seconds, he steps off the leg onto the trampoline. Toñio slides off his back and bounces gently, laughing. Emiliano ascends immediately to repeat the process with Sophie.

Finally, it's Liam's turn. The man whispers in his ear, and Liam grins broadly.

"What was that?" Jane demands.

Emiliano smiles. "Don't worry, mamacita."

"Yeah, don't worry, mamacita," echoes Liam.

"Too late. Be careful!"

Emiliano begins the descent but pauses half-way, ten feet off the ground.

"What's wrong?"

Emiliano holds onto the burro's frame with his left hand and reaches behind himself with his right. He holds Liam by the torso and slides him around to his hip.

"What are you doing?"

Emiliano turns his body until he is leaning away from the burro. With his right arm wrapped around Liam's chest, he holds the boy out in front of him and then releases him. Jane gasps. Liam drops straight down, looking thrilled rather than scared, and lands on his feet right in front of her, dead center on the trampoline. As Liam bounces, Emiliano falls directly behind him, narrowly missing him. At the top of his own bounce, Emiliano grabs Liam in mid-air, his hands around the boy's torso, lands, and lifts Liam onto his shoulders as smoothly as if they had rehearsed. He hops forward off the trampoline, over the kneeling form of one of his compatriots, onto solid ground.

"Ta-da," shouts Liam from Emiliano's shoulders, arms pumping the air.

"Ta-da," Emiliano echoes with a grin.

The crowd applauds and cheers.

"Wow." Jane grabs Liam from Emiliano's shoulders. "So cool. Wait right here a second." She sets him down and turns back to Emiliano. "What the hell were you thinking?"

The female acrobat leans in. "He does that move with me. We've practiced a hundred times. It was safe, I promise."

"Really? It didn't look safe."

"It was, truly. But I'm sorry I scared you." Emiliano appears somewhat repentant. "You know, your boy's a natural. You should bring him to circus classes."

"Please, Mom?"

"God, more of this? I don't know."

Connor, whom Jane hasn't thought about for some time, grumbles next to her.

"What, baby?"

"It's just, it's not fair. Liam climbed up even though I told them not to, but he's not in trouble and he got to do a trick, and—"

"Would you like circus lessons, too?"

"No."

"Excuse me," says José. "I need someone responsible to light the burro."

"Me!" shout Toñio, Liam, and Sophie.

Gabriela shakes her head. "Responsible, you guys, seriously? No. Seems to me it's Connor's turn."

José turns to Connor. "Sounds like you're the man for the job. Will you help me out?"

Connor nods, glowing.

"Thanks, José," Jane whispers.

José calls over the man with the torch and explains the process. "Tomás here will pour lighter fluid first, and then you and I will light the torch and very carefully touch it to each leg. Everyone else should stand back."

Jane starts to panic. "This is not safe."

"Shush," says Meghan. "Let Connor have his moment. José will be careful."

José has the torch going. Beside him, Connor's arm sticks straight out to grip the handle below José's hand. They walk slowly toward the burro's front legs. The crowd quiets. When they hold the torch to the left knee, the flames catch quickly, thanks to what seems to Jane an excess of dripping fluid.

"Connor, Connor," chants Meghan. Gabriela and the kids join in.

Connor and José work their way to the hindquarters. When all four corners of the beast are on fire, the duo walk forward a few steps and hold the torch high. Everyone cheers. Connor drinks it in.

"Did you see me, Mom?"

She hugs him tightly to her. "That was so cool."

"Lucky!" says Liam.

"There is something so primal about a big fire," murmurs Gabriela.

Meghan agrees. "We should all be dancing around it. Summoning the gods."

"OK." Sophie and Liam begin to dance, crouching low and flinging their arms up. Toñio joins in immediately. Then Connor does, too, with a self-conscious smirk.

8

AS THEY CLIMB INTO THE car, Jane's boys talk over each other about how high the fire flared when Connor touched the "flamethrower" to the burro's legs. They both fall dead asleep in the back seat.

While she follows Gabriela's taillights through a series of dark fields toward something recognizable as a road, Jane's mind wanders to another unique triumph. It happened during the Independence Day celebrations their first September over a year ago when they were still so new to Mexico. With two other recently arrived expat families, she and her sons had waited in the city's main plaza, known as the Jardín for its beautiful garden, for the annual Cavalcade of Conspirators. She had watched as Connor climbed a stately Mexican laurel surrounded by elaborate flower beds. At least he was careful not to trample any plants. She looked around at the strolling Mexican families and scanned their faces for signs of censure but found none. Connor climbed higher, a girl followed, and then her brother and another boy. Four heads, blonde to blonder, poked out among the leaves, golden-hour sunlight setting that hair aglow. Jane cringed at this spectacle of American kids flouting the rules, but still no one scolded them. Liam, the youngest of the group, waited at the base of the tree, frustrated in his desire to follow by too-short legs and arms.

A murmur from the crowd indicated that the riders they had come to see were approaching. She called all the kids down, and she and the other parents settled them on a stone wall in front of city hall to watch. A hundred horsemen appeared up the hill on the road from

Querétaro, their mounts holding their heads high as if they too sensed the grandeur of the moment. Re-enacting a two-hundred-year-old event that set the course of the nation, the Cavalcade of Conspirators arrived, bringing to the rebels of San Miguel an urgent message from heroine Josefa Ortiz de Domínguez that their plans had been discovered by her husband, the governor of Querétaro, and so the war for independence must begin immediately. They thundered down into the heart of the city, trading the stealth of the original act for pageantry. With a thrill of validation, Jane caught her sons' awestruck expressions in a few photos. What a cool thing for them to see. The riders circled the plaza and then settled in for the obligatory speeches. A few of the men swung their girlfriends up for a photo or posed with the woman standing next to the horse. Several young fathers had children along for the ride.

A handsome rider approached the wall, white shirt impressively crisp, new red bandanna tied around his neck, lean body held perfectly upright in the saddle. He smiled at Jane and held out his arm to Liam. Liam shrank back, but Connor and his new friends eagerly volunteered. The man chose Connor and lifted him off the wall in one smooth motion. Her son waved as the horse set off on a lap of the plaza, Jane's startled eyes following their progress. The rider and elated child crossed in front of the pink façade of the church and circled back. Inspired, other kids tried to flag down riders, but Connor was the only one pulled from the crowd that day. The man returned her beaming son with an old-world tip of his hat.

That night, when Connor proudly told his father of joining the cavalcade, Kevin berated Jane for letting their son ride off with a strange man. She understood his concern to a point, but it had happened so fast—he'd have understood if he'd been there—and everything turned out fine. She wished that Kevin had at least waited to criticize her until the boys left the room so as not to undermine their confidence in her. They should not be made to share his many fears.

So what should she tell him now about the Burning Burro drama? He'll judge her for letting the boys play on their own and for pretty much every aspect of Liam's climbing incident, and he'll certainly have an opinion about using a gasoline-soaked torch to cheer up Connor. She would like to believe that if he had been there, he would understand. But he wasn't, and the details out of context will not sound good.

She wonders whether she has to tell him everything. The boys are likely to share the story in such a way that he won't take them seriously, so perhaps there's no need to volunteer for an attack. It's a gamble, obviously, because if he hears about it from someone else, he'll be angrier. But working from home, he sees few people and listens to fewer, so he may never find out. It's a risk she'll take. No, it's not. That's crazy. There were so many witnesses. She has to tell him. But perhaps she can get away with a watered-down version.

At home, she carries her sleeping sons to their beds and climbs into her own.

When the sunlight glowing around the edges of her curtains wakes her fully, Jane gets up and heads for the kitchen, collecting Liam and Connor on the way. "Let's make pancakes, guys."

Four sticky hands are adding both blueberries and chocolate chips to the batter when Kevin enters the room in search of coffee.

"Hi Dad," they chirp.

"Hey guys, how was the concert? You went from asleep in the car to asleep in your beds, so I didn't get a chance to ask. Did you have fun?"

"Yeah. We climbed the burro, and I did a circus trick."

"You did? Wow, that's great, buddy." Kevin absently pats Liam's shoulders and leans over him to poach a blueberry.

"I got to light the burro on fire, Dad," says Connor, "and everybody screamed."

"You did what?"

"The owner helped me."

"It was fine, Kev, the guy was extremely careful. They had a great time." Jane nods toward her unharmed offspring as though it were all no big deal.

Kevin looks suspicious but lets it go. Guilty relief washes through her. Technically, they've informed him of what happened.

After scrubbing nearly every surface in the syrup-sticky kitchen, Jane decides on a happy distraction. She takes the boys to her favorite artisans' market to shop for a hummingbird feeder, following up on a suggestion from Connor. Liam chooses one with a rich green glass body and delicate red flower. Connor agrees. She buys a book, too, and they spend the afternoon learning about hummingbirds.

"They're the smallest birds in the world, aren't they?" asks Liam.

"Yes, it says here that the smallest variety are only five centimeters long. That's like two inches, right, Mom?" After looking up from the book for confirmation, Connor continues. "They live up to ten years, and they're the only birds that can fly backwards, forwards, and sideways. They hover in mid-air and even fly upside-down."

Liam leans over Connor's shoulder. "They dive at up to sixty miles per hour, and their wings can rotate in a full circle."

"That's badass."

"Language, Connor."

"Their favorite color is red," Connor reads.

"Why?" Liam asks Jane.

"I know," says Connor. "It says here they like many bright colors, but red above all indicates food to them."

Liam leans in again. "En español, se llama el colibrí, el picaflor, el chupaflor, o el zunzún."

Connor asserts control of the book. "They're found naturally only in the Western Hemisphere, especially here in Mexico and South America."

"Share, Connor." Happy to see them so interested, Jane adds, "Some of them migrate. They live here in the winter and fly north to the United States for summer. Only a few make it as far north as New York or Washington State, though, where Daddy and I grew up."

"You're learning about hummingbirds? That's nice. Your mom has always loved them."

Jane flinches slightly, not having noticed Kevin enter the room.

"They have to eat at least once every fifteen minutes, Dad, so they visit up to two thousand flowers a day. Two thousand!" Liam points at the passage in the book to prove it.

"Did you know," Kevin asks, "that some can go into torpor over-night to save energy?"

"What's torpor?" asks Connor.

"It's a deeper shutdown than sleep, like a coma or hibernation, but just at night."

"That's weird."

Liam shares another fact. "The hum is the noise their wings make from moving so fast."

Eventually, after helping her hang and fill the feeder, the boys tire of the subject and leave Jane alone with her thoughts, which return her to the first hummingbird she ever saw. It was a rare and, to her twelve-year-old eyes, magical sight.

Jane and Thomas watched for branches. That was the tricky thing about bringing the horses. They could put the tools and lunch in the saddlebags and not have to carry it all themselves, which was great, but riding through the dense forest on the edge of the ranch meant watching constantly for branches that could scrape a kid off a horse. Jane spent half of each ride lying flat over her mare's neck, feeling branches slide roughly over her back, occasionally taking a chunk of shirt or skin, once tangling in her hair. She screamed that time, which made the horse bolt, and some of her hair stayed on the branch. She learned to wear a sweatshirt with a hood after that and to pull the strings tight. Mom always told them to stay on the cleared trails, but that would defeat the purpose. The point was to build their secret forts in the wildest, most hidden parts of the forest. She and Thomas ended up getting down and walking a lot.

Thomas said he wanted to strike out on his own this time. But after they staked the horses, he picked a tree only twenty feet from Jane's.

Some of their forts were just nooks where they had cleared out the underbrush, but these would be real tree forts. They'd borrowed an old handsaw from Dad's tool shed. Taking turns, they used it to saw off the lowest branches and then nailed sections of the branches across a fork in each tree to create rough platforms.

Sitting on her platform while Thomas finished his, Jane surveyed her shadowed domain. Absolutely everything in her world was green. Jewel green cedars and dark green firs with black-green trunks loomed over alders covered in leaves of late spring green, many with trunks shrouded in still more shades of green mosses. Even the sunlight, filtered through the branches above her, had an emerald tint. Something green grew from every inch of moist earth, including wild blackberry vines with their evil thorns in the patches of sun between trees. She loved the berries in summer, but the rest of the year blackberry bushes were an impenetrable barrier to be cursed. Getting through a thicket unscratched, on foot or horseback, was impossible. Blackberries had to be gone around unless you had a machete to hack through like Dad, which still involved a good amount of swearing. She and Thomas might borrow the handsaw but never the machete. That long blade gave Jane the shivers.

She noticed the first early buds beginning to unfurl into tiny white blossoms on the blackberry vines nearest her tree and felt better about their presence. In a couple months, she and Thomas could come here and feast on the first berries of the season. The tallest vines grew to within a few feet of her platform, and she wondered if she could reach them. She lay on her stomach and had stretched her arm over the side when a flash of color commanded her gaze.

A hummingbird hovered over the most fully developed blossom. Part of the bird was green, too. The feathers on the tiny creature's chest and back flashed a gorgeous iridescent blue-green, like verdigris on copper. The head, deep rose, had caught Jane's attention, and the wings were a dusky brown. Jane watched, enchanted, until the hummingbird disappeared behind the brambles.

Thomas stood below her tree. "It was an Anna's Hummingbird," he whispered, his voice reverent. "Dad told me. Only a few humming-bird species come this far north, just for summer, and only the Anna's Hummingbird will stay here the whole year. The others fly south, like to Mexico. So it had to be an Anna's Hummingbird, I think. It's still a bit too early for any others."

"It's very cool that you know that."

"They're rare. It's lucky to see one."

"It felt lucky."

They rode home in silence but remembered to slip the handsaw back into the tool shed.

MARCHING INTO THE NEXT CASA Mía board meeting, Jane passes an elegant statue of Our Lady of Guadalupe in the realtors' entrance hall, one of a thousand traditional and pop art variations she has encountered. Carved from stone or assembled in tile mosaics, painted on denim jackets or shopping bags, crafted from sequins or corn husks, Guadalupe is everywhere. She originally appeared to an indigenous shepherd on a hill near Mexico City previously associated with Tonantzin, the mother goddess, and as a symbol of fierce motherly love, benevolence, sacrifice, and national pride, Guadalupe has come to represent the people of the Mexican nation as well as their faith. *If there's anything you can do for those two little girls*, Jane thinks, *please*.

Despite intending to wait for the most opportune moment, she blurts out the news immediately. "Did you hear about the López–Pérez family? The uncle got deported, just like they feared."

Eleanor nods. "We heard, Jane. It's sad, unexpected. I know what you're going to say, but we have already voted on the year's families."

"What would you have us do, renege on one of them?" Bob strokes his graying beard, a habit Jane finds increasingly annoying.

"Of course not." She summons her law school training. Unshakeable calm is crucial when litigating while female. "But this is not unexpected. They applied precisely because they expected it. The good news is the uncle is signing over half his lot to Pablo and Nayeli, enough to build on."

"That's great," Bob responds, "but this year's money is already allocated, and as you know, current fundraising goes to next year's builds."

"Well, as you know, next year we're moving to a new community. This family is homeless now, and they have no one here except the uncle. His side of the family has dispersed, mostly to the States, apparently. The rest of their extended family is still in Chiapas."

Eleanor speaks gently. "You're right, we made a commitment to move on to the new community. Families there are desperate, too. You can't get so attached to individuals when there is so much need."

"I understand. I'm sure you're right, but I think we should feel some obligation to this family. They applied twice in good faith and told the truth, and now they have nothing."

"I would love to help them. I really would." The sincerity in Eleanor's eyes somehow makes Jane feel worse.

"We're not helpless. Let's make it eleven houses this year. We can do this."

"How?" demands Bob.

"I don't know yet."

Meghan throws a lifeline. "Remember that concert idea we had?"

"You can get someone good to play for free right away?" Bob looks skeptical. "Then there's paying for a venue. You'd have to sell a lot of tickets and beer, girls, a lot of beer. You're right, though, in that this would have to come from outside our normal funding streams. Don't commit to this family without money in hand, or it'll be on you."

"Fine, doing the right thing is on me." Jane feels panic rise. "You'll help, won't you?"

Bob shakes his head. "Honestly, our normal fundraising is more than enough work, so no. We build for ten families a year. We voted on the ten, and that's it. We can't help everyone."

"That's your answer, when we should have already helped this family?" So much for staying calm.

"That's enough, you two." Eleanor's lips pinch together. She focuses on Jane. "Are you sure you want to take this on? The fundraising would have to happen very fast in order to get this house built along with the others this year before we leave the community. If it doesn't work out, you'll have to tell the family no—again."

"But those girls desperately need a home, and that's what we do, right?"

After the meeting, Jane won't remember the agenda items discussed from that point on. What has she done? Doing all the fundraising herself was not what she had in mind. What if she can't pull it off? If she raises the family's hopes and then fails, that will be far worse.

Meghan and Rocío, at least, will help her.

Jane wonders how to tell Kevin when they can't seem to calmly discuss anything anymore. If only he were more like David, he would understand why she has to help this family. She wishes she didn't have the thought—it's exactly what Kevin would think she'd think—but it's true. David would take on the fundraising crusade without question, while there's no way telling Kevin that she adopted an urgent, two-hundred-thousand-peso cause will go well.

"Why wasn't I enough?" Kevin sometimes asks. Each time, Jane tells him that of course he was and is enough, but he's never convinced, and she understands. It's true, she had wanted, needed, something more. Mostly, she believes, it wasn't David that she wanted, but rather the version of herself she enjoyed inhabiting when she was around him. Working with him, she felt understood and respected. She was energized and inspired by his cheerful confidence in their ability to change kids' lives for the better. Those feelings are addictive.

If Kevin has not forgiven her after this much time, will he ever? How much effort is she making anymore? Does she even want to welcome him back to her bed? Jane has been sleeping in the guest room so long, since their marital counseling went wrong, and moved so many of her things over, that the boys call it her room now. She explained the move to them by describing how badly Daddy snores, going so far as to perform snorty impressions they found hilarious. For now, her sons seem to accept this simple rationale for their parents having separate bedrooms. They will certainly develop questions over time.

When the meeting ends, Jane gets up from the conference table disoriented and embarrassed. On her way out of the building, she passes the Guadalupe statue. *Do it myself, really,* she asks the saint, *did that have to be the point?*

THE THREE WOMEN SETTLE INTO a corner table at Casa Sin Nombre's roof-top bar, a hidden treasure nearly empty despite its elegant atmosphere and Middle Eastern antiques, apparently maintained for the pleasure of the few guests in the boutique hotel downstairs. Beside their table, water trickles down a chain into a stone trough, which in turn feeds a plunge pool.

"So I'm embarrassed but also furious," Jane tells Gabriela, continuing a conversation begun in the lobby. "Except for Meghan here, and Rocío, the rest of them won't help."

"Are you sure you want to do this?" Gabriela's words, and her worried expression, echo Eleanor's from the day before. "Any ideas?"

Meghan suggests an art auction. Jane immediately says no. "That would normally be a great idea, sure, but how can we hit up artists right now when I think most of them are already donating to the Amigos del Parque auction?"

"Oh right," Meghan responds, "that's coming up soon."

"I thought of setting up a GoFundMe targeting friends back home," Jane continues, "but with everything else going on in the world, I'm not confident that it would be successful."

Meghan comes back to the concert idea. "As Bob so helpfully pointed out, we would have to convince someone good to play for free, and we'd better secure a free venue, too."

"Even then, we'd still have to sell a ton of tickets and booze," says Jane.

"It would be a lot of work. But it's possible," Gabriela concludes.

Meghan nods. "I think we could pull it off."

Jane looks from one to the other. "Seriously? You two would take on this huge project with me?"

"I brought you onto that board. I won't leave you to suffer on your own."

"And I love that you're trying so hard to help people," says Gabriela. "I'm in."

"Oh my God, thank you." Jane hugs each of them. "This suddenly feels almost manageable."

"I know a guy in a band I can ask," Meghan offers. "No promises, but they might be up for it some night when they're not already booked. Los Reyes, do you know them?"

"No, but I trust your taste. Thank you, yes please."

"They're really good," says Gabriela. "And you know, there's a house with a huge yard in Atascadero we might be able to use. The owners are friends of my parents, and they'll love the cause. They're probably Casa Mía donors already. I can ask them."

"Awesome, thank you!"

Meghan does the math. A Casa Mía house costs 200,000 pesos or approximately 10,000 dollars. She figures they can charge 400 pesos a ticket for Los Reyes, and each person might spend another 200 to 300 on alcohol. They definitely can't charge more than 80 pesos for a beer, if that. They might be able to get some alcohol donated, but most likely they'll have to pay for most of it. Volunteers can work the door, but they should hire a couple bartenders, as well as cleaning staff since guests will go into the house to use the bathrooms. They'll have to rent a simple stage, bar, and bar glasses, and print posters. All told, Meghan estimates that they'll need 400 boozy concert-goers to clear 200,000 pesos.

"No way." Gabriela shakes her head. "I know I said the yard was huge, but it can't hold 400 people plus a stage. Maybe half that at best, probably less, like 150. A venue for 400? That's the Peralta theater, bull ring, or a hotel ballroom, all expensive."

"That's OK," says Jane. "I prefer the idea of a pretty yard, for free, with bathrooms. You know what, if we can bring in even half the money we need in one night, amazing."

"We can straight-up pitch for extra donations at the end," Meghan suggests.

They're talking through the details of ticket sales when the air around them fills with the pounding noise of fireworks, the kind that don't make bursts of color in the sky, although Sanmiguelenses see plenty of those, too. This kind produce pure noise that can wake the gods to hoist the sun for another day or announce one's party to every mortal in the city. The noise says "Hey world, I am here" in strings of ear-assaulting explosions that have convinced more than a few first-time visitors the city was under attack.

Meghan flinches. "What holiday is it?"

"I don't even know." Gabriela responds. "Could just be a wedding, quinceañera, birthday, or funeral."

"They're so loud." Meghan holds her hands over her ears. "Do they have to be so loud?"

Gabriela shrugs. "I admit it sucks at four in the morning sometimes when the ones meant to wake the gods wake us, but otherwise they're ignorable."

"Yeah, you're right." Meghan removes her hands from her ears. "Just a San Miguel quirk, like getting stuck behind a wedding procession."

"Or a funeral or saint's day procession."

Jane joins in. "Kevin having to explain mariachis and church bells during conference calls."

"Running into five people you know while crossing the Jardín." Meghan grimaces as a few more booms shatter the balmy early evening air.

"And that time I was given LSD as a parting gift, that was an only-in-San-Miguel moment for me." Curious to see how her friends react, Jane seizes the opportunity.

Gabriela starts to laugh, then stops. "Really? Did you do it? That doesn't sound like you."

"It isn't me at all. I can't make up my mind, so I stashed it in my freezer, mixed with a little tequila in a vitamin bottle. The guy said I could store it that way."

"Who?" Meghan asks.

"Doesn't matter. He didn't know what a drug virgin I am."

"Are you?"

"Yeah. I've tried pot exactly once, in a backpacker hostel in Costa Rica when I was twenty, and it only made me sleepy. The huge crabs on the floor made a bigger impression."

"Huge crabs?"

"I was not imagining them. It was a hut on the beach, and crabs literally came in. Anyway, my brother did too much of everything as a teenager, which scared me straight, I guess. But I asked this guy once about ayahuasca."

"That's getting a little passé. You're late to the party."

"I know. He told me the cool kids now are taking something found on the skin of tree frogs since they can't go back in time and hitchhike to Oaxaca for a mushroom spirit journey with Maria Sabina or drink to a macho blackout with Kerouac at La Cucaracha. But I like the idea of ayahuasca because it has a legit anthropological, spiritual element to it."

Meghan grins.

"What? It does. So anyway, that led to a conversation about hallucinogens, and at their despedida he had a present for me, with instructions."

"So are you going to do it?"

"Before San Miguel, I'd have dodged the offer for sure."

"And now?"

"Now I'm not automatically dismissing it. I've met accomplished people here who just happen to take mushrooms with shamans or lick treefrog venom or whatever. My frame of reference has changed." *Maybe it will inspire me to fix my marriage*, she almost says. "So would you two want to do it with me, if we can manage a girls' weekend without the kids?"

"Maybe." Meghan smiles. "You might like it, and at least you'd know. But honey, this isn't something you have to do."

"I know. I keep changing my mind. What's actually to be gained by tricking synapses in my brain into firing faster?" Jane envisions her mind as a factory with an intense new fuel, churning to produce the answers she needs. But what if the well-worn circuitry in her brain resembles the clunky pieces of industrial equipment left behind in Fábrica la Aurora, the former garment factory on the edge of town turned into a collection of art galleries? The oldest, heaviest machines weren't worth moving, so they were simply left in place. She likes how the galleries work around them, but like the antiquated machinery, perhaps her mind is unsuited to a leap into a radically different processing style. She imagines the heavy mechanisms grinding and shuddering, steel parts screaming, chewed up in the maw of a yet more monstrous new machine.

"Tricking your synapses? I'm not sure that's what happens," says Meghan.

"Probably not. Could I actually gain a new perspective on anything important? Shouldn't I be able to access whatever insight I'm capable of in some other way?"

"You may be overthinking it." Gabriela's expression is one of gentle concern.

"Just a little. None of the answers I want are likely to be found at the bottom of an LSD-spiked tequila shot, are they? I'm worried about having it around, too. I trust my kids not to just drink something they find in a frozen vitamin bottle, but still."

"You need to make a decision," Meghan concludes. "Do it, give it away, or toss it."

"I'll probably pour it out. Disappointed in me?"

"Of course not. It's your journey." Meghan puts her feet up on an intricately tailored leather pouf she pulled out from under a nearby table. "Can you believe this place? Everything is of impeccable quality, even this little thing, and it's never crowded at all. How lucky are we?"

"So freaking lucky." Jane then adds in a whisper, "Please don't tell anyone about this place, so it can stay our secret."

Meghan sighs. "That's how I feel about San Miguel, but it's too late."

"I wanted to be the last one in and shut the door behind me, but the secret is out. We're sorry, Gaby."

Gabriela's smile is wistful. "No, it's been happening for a long time. You know I don't blame you guys. It's mostly people from Mexico City throwing their money around."

"You're so diplomatic, but I know plenty of people think the exploding number of Americans is exactly the problem. First the Texans, then us coastal types driving up prices, and now our president—"

"God, let's not talk politics tonight." Meghan crinkles her nose.

"Weren't we talking tickets before?" Jane pulls her friends' attention back to the concert. They make more decisions, and then Jane calls to update Rocío.

Eventually Meghan sits up. "Are you guys thinking what I'm thinking?"

"Probably not."

"I'm hungry, but the food's expensive here. How about tacos?"

"Great, why don't I text Lindsay, too?" Jane asks. "I know she's out tonight with a new friend she's been wanting us to meet. Hannah, I think her name is. Maybe they can catch up with us at the cart. You both like the one on the first block of San Francisco, right?"

Thirty minutes later, the women stand in line. Jane watches a man carve juicy pieces from a biblical hunk of roasted pork on an upright spit for her tacos de pastor. She loves it all, from the smells of sizzling meat and onions on the huge comal to the bowls of fresh salsas and peppers lined up on the counter, the camaraderie, mariachi music from the Jardín and dance music from the rooftop bar down the block, a couple horses' hooves making that distinctly hollow sound against the cobblestones, smiles from their riders to the cluster of women, the kid running across the street to a tiendita with Lindsay's hundred pesos for beers, and the lilting rhythms of conversations around her. Best of all, sisterhood that keeps her sane.

Hannah looks around with an expression of delight that echoes Jane's own. "These are so good," she says.

"Food of the gods, for sure," Jane agrees.

The kid is back with the beers. "Salud."

"So what brought you to San Miguel, Hannah?"

"And the big question," Meghan adds, "how long are you staying?"

"My husband and I are both on sabbatical, so a year to start, but we're already dreaming of staying longer if we can figure out remote work."

Jane smiles. "That's what usually happens. Welcome."

While the other women settle their tabs, Lindsay pulls Jane aside. "I'm going to see my bruja tomorrow, want to come with me? She's great. Reads me like a book and always gives good advice, usually just the nudge I need." Lindsay makes the offer casually, but something in her tone makes Jane wonder why the invitation is directed to her in particular.

She accepts nonetheless. "Sure, I'm curious. What time?"

"Pick you up at eleven. We can go to lunch after."

As they say their goodnights, Meghan promises to reach out the next day to the band member she knows. Gabriela says she'll talk to her parents' friends about bringing 150 guests, loud musicians, and a bar to their yard. "Don't worry, I won't say that. I'll focus on the cause."

"That's accurate, though. Go ahead, let them know what they're getting into."

On the walk home, Jane decides she'll pour out the LSD for sure. But then she doesn't.

THE NEXT MORNING, FROM THE passenger seat of Lindsay's truck, Jane studies an ugly house. Two mismatched windows stare back at her, one a murky square high up on the left, the other a stained-glass oval slightly lower on the right. A third window, a long rectangle, stretches above the crumbling sidewalk at shoulder height behind a row of bars, several of them bent, like a snaggle-toothed smile. The house leers. Or perhaps it grins, doing its best to look inviting despite the bad teeth and permanent wink.

The house's door finally opens. The figure in relative darkness beyond the threshold apparently responds positively, for Lindsay turns and beckons to Jane. In the few seconds it takes her to climb down and cross the street, the person melts back into the recesses of the house. Lindsay knows where to go. Jane follows her friend through a patio cluttered with furniture in various stages of decay as well as cheerful geraniums and succulents potted in coffee cans.

They enter a room where a young boy with a fresh scar running from the center of his forehead to a spot below his left ear greets them politely from his seat on a folding chair. The boy's eye was spared. It and its twin watch as Jane sits down, following Lindsay's lead.

A door opens to Jane's right. She can hear an old Juan Gabriel ballad announced on the local radio station that most Sanmiguelenses of a certain age still listen to. A woman in a floral skirt and navy jacket, neat but worn at the elbows, bustles out, exuding competence and a hint of cinnamon. She speaks with the boy, automatically including the two women in her conversation. Jane cannot make out much in the rapid stream, but Lindsay jumps in and soon the woman and the boy are laughing with her. Jane smiles blankly. *Someday,* she thinks, *if I do the work, I might match Lindsay's fluency in Spanish, but I will never have her auntie charm or the confidence to start a conversation with absolutely anyone.* The cinnamon woman goes back into the room armed with some bit of information from her son.

"What did I let you talk me into?" Jane wonders aloud.

The boy's calm demeanor challenges Jane to resist the urge to pull out her phone. Finally, his mother reappears and leads him away, bidding Jane and Lindsay to go with God.

"We're up," Lindsay announces. Jane follows her into the room on the right.

At first, Jane doesn't see the bruja herself amid the unsettling contents of her sanctuary. Dozens of dusty statues crowd every available surface in the room, covering bookshelves, narrow tables, and the top of a minifridge. Catholic saints Jane recognizes and many more she doesn't share space with indigenous religious offerings. Expensive works of art encased in glass mingle with more humble contributions. Here and there, saints have toppled over, landing on their neighbors in undignified positions.

Jane wonders whether their plaster hearts ever swell for truly deserving petitioners. Are some among them more intrigued by the naughty ambitions they hear, the petty, selfish desires? Does a half hour in this room ever make a dent in the plans laid out by the fates long ago?

"Buenas tardes, Doña Ximena, how wonderful to see you." Lindsay's hand brushes Jane's arm to ensure her attention. "I'd like you to meet my friend, Jane."

Jane pulls her gaze from the visual feast around her to the petite, elderly woman seated at a small table in the center of the room. The eyes peering back exude good humor.

After offering a respectful greeting, Jane finds herself again distracted, for on the floor behind the bruja lies an enormous pile of junk. The mound could almost have grown organically, an incarnate mass of clothing, trinkets, and lumpy plastic bags stuffed with puzzling contents. Household items overtaken by the pile poke out here and there, clawing for air. Perched near the top, a solitary can of Raid stands ready for battle, acknowledging the necessities of the uncleanable space. Jane wonders whether the bruja is a hoarder or takes in donations for the poor but then concludes that the collection must be related to the woman's work. The items in the pile must have been brought in by clients as physical connections to their emotional burdens, now safely contained by the witch. Seeing the incredible number of offerings must help put each person's grievance into perspective.

A small oasis of floorspace remains, just large enough to hold the two plastic chairs in which Jane and Lindsay now sit, the chair occupied by Ximena, and the table between them. Jane imagines that at any moment this space, too, could disappear, inundated by the looming masses of items holy and pedestrian.

Ximena asks for Jane's right hand and holds it over a pile of cards. She recites the first line of a prayer to San Pedro de la Misión and directs Jane to repeat it. Jane obediently beseeches the saint for insight, compassion, and assistance, and agrees to accept the negative and positive aspects of the truth revealed to her.

Jane watches for a sign, for the woman before her to know an unknowable fact. The bruja begins to lay out the cards. She pauses to ask whether Jane has headaches. No? Swollen feet? Back pain? Pain anywhere, no? The next card indicates that Jane enjoys great health and will be blessed with long life. And so it continues until the bruja assures her that her life will hold many more triumphs despite the fact that money flows too quickly through her fingers. Jane almost laughs. Her husband would agree on the last point at least.

Ximena presses her for a goal, a pending decision, a path to further, but Jane can't bring herself to tell the truth of why she's come. She imagines explaining that she's here because her marriage has gone all wrong and there's no pat answer as to why. *I didn't even really cheat. He just assumed I did, and I've tried to fix it. The problem started long before that anyway. Now I'm pathetically jealous of other people's healthy relationships, often wondering what's wrong with me that I can't have that. And why, if I'm being honest, just between you and me, witch, aren't I trying very hard anymore to fix it?*

Sometimes a marriage just withers. Many people her age can relate, can't they? Do they ever come in here talking about how when their partner gets angry, they get angry, and then things can go so dark so fast their head spins? How it's such a shock that they don't admit it for a long time, even to themselves? Even when down deep they know there's no going back? When they maybe never should have married him in the first place?

So far, she could tell this woman, there's been no real violence, just fear. She could explain how frightened she is of the latent capacity for violence lurking perhaps in both of them, as well as the varieties of non-violent damage already inflicted. She fears the reach of his anger into her future. She fears his influence over her boys. She fears losing the life she's built for them and having to start over again. Above all, she feels cold sweaty terror at the prospect of having to fight for her children against the man she once loved.

God no, she won't offer a heartsick lament for her dying marriage here in this strange room. She won't explain that she hates her own bitterness but understands also that she uses it, sculpted into a form of armor. She refuses, as though saying any of it out loud could force her hand. Ximena asks again why she has come. The awkward moment stretches on until Jane thinks to say that she shares the usual concerns of a mother for her children's health and happiness. The bruja shrugs and offers a platitude in return.

Jane enjoys, however, the closing ritual in which Ximena prays over a candle, alternating fluidly between Spanish and Otomí, the local indigenous language. She accepts the candle with both hands, feeling empowered with the feminine energy of a tradition spanning generations.

Then it's over. They're leaving. "Wait, Lindsay, aren't you having a reading, too?"

"No, I'd only booked the one appointment, and I thought you'd like to try it."

"I didn't know I was stealing your slot. Thank you, but why?"

Lindsay's eyes convey her concern. "It's felt lately like something is going on with you. I thought it might help to talk it out."

Jane wonders how much her friend has noticed. She panics at the possibility of Lindsay having sensed the ugly thoughts that just tore through her head during the reading, and she's also embarrassed for having wasted her friend's gift by not giving the bruja anything to go on.

So she deflects. "Well, there is the burning question of how I'm supposed to raise another hundred thousand pesos in a hurry—and that's once we get through throwing a big concert, right, to raise the first hundred thousand, which we're scrambling to do—but fundraising didn't seem like her area of expertise."

"No, probably not. Well, you know I'm here. If you ever want to talk about anything. And I'll help you sell a bunch of tickets, just let me know when."

"Thank you, that means a lot. So, what's up with the trolls?" Jane changes the subject while they climb into Lindsay's pickup, referring to the seven or eight naked troll dolls with fluorescent hair she saw lined up on one of the shelves nearest Ximena's table.

"Those? Nothing, as far as I know. She probably just finds them funny. I guess people bring them along with the religious gifts."

"And what about that boy we saw in the waiting room, with the scar? Do you think his mother was there for revenge?"

"No, not vengeance, for healing and understanding, I would think. Ximena's not that kind of bruja, she doesn't do black magic. She's been on the receiving end of some evil, but she won't dish it out."

"What do you mean?"

Over lunch, Lindsay tells Ximena's story. "She was off her game today. When her daughter-in-law answered the door, I remembered it's nearly the anniversary of her son's death."

"That's awful. We didn't have to go today."

"No, she wouldn't have accepted the appointment if she hadn't wanted to."

"What happened to her son?"

"It was the daughter-in-law, can you believe it? Did you see her? No? Well, he'd been sick a long time with one of those lingering, awful, expensive illnesses, but he wasn't dying. Apparently she didn't want to be stuck nursing him forever, so she fed him the tea."

"Oh my God."

"You know that plant with white, trumpet-shaped flowers? It's common here, not nightshade, datura."

"How do you know what happened?"

Lindsay shrugs. "I don't remember who told me. Lots of people know."

"And they still share a house, are you kidding?" The idea is appalling.

"No, Ximena moved in with one of her other children," Lindsay explains, "but she won't move her office for some reason. She goes back there a few times a week to work."

"She never called the police or got her own justice?"

"No, because what good would it do? Her grandchildren, who already lost their father, would lose their mother. And who knows how much longer Ximena herself will be around."

"Especially if she makes the daughter-in-law feel threatened."

"So she does nothing. But she knows, and the daughter-in-law knows she knows."

"That's insane."

"I guess."

"Speaking of insane things," Jane changes the subject again, "As I mentioned, we're throwing a benefit concert, like immediately. Meghan's working on getting Los Reyes to play for free, and Gaby has a lead on a venue."

"Los Reyes, very cool. For that house you're building, right? I heard you guys talking last night. What do you need?"

"Thank you, what we need, even before ticket sales since we haven't confirmed a date yet, is to come up with lots of booze, free or discounted."

"I'll start asking around."

"You're the best."

"I know."

At home, Jane puts the candle Doña Ximena gave her on the dresser in the guest room that's become her room. That night, she lights it and watches the flame as she gets ready for bed, replaying the events of the morning. She should have been braver when the bruja asked. Talking through her situation, like Lindsay urged, even naming it out loud, might have helped, and nothing she could share would shock that woman. Maybe she'll go back.

Jane blows out the candle and settles her body into bed. She starts to reach for Kevin even though she knows he's not there. Curling into herself, Jane tries to recall some of the words of the prayer Ximena spoke over the candle. The Spanish words, as she knows nothing of Otomi. She hovers on the verge of sleep before sinking fully.

In a foggy space, Jane sees a hummingbird. *Little one,* someone tells him as his languid wings beat only twenty times per second, *today is not for you.* His smoky gray and rich green feathers glow with the dust of the heavens he visits often on the chance the day has come. He watches jealously as other messengers are called to duty. The messages, she somehow understands, come from the soul of a loved one or, best of all, from the mother goddess herself, Tonantzin, Itom Ae, Guadalupe, she who answers to any of the hundred names the people call out to her.

12

THE DREAM LINGERS AT THE fringes of Jane's thoughts the next day, even late in the afternoon as she immerses herself in the picture-perfect world of Connor's riding lesson. A thin strip of lawn runs along a crisp double border of lavender and boxwood at the edge of the ring, and classical music floats from speakers mounted around the perimeter. Jane watches Connor practice a bareback maneuver called the prince. He kneels on a pony's back, then balances on his right knee and left hand, extending his left leg and right arm. She recognizes it as a core yoga posture, performed on the back of a moving animal. Next her son squats and then stands all the way up as the pony continues to circle the ring in a brisk, bouncy trot.

"Keep some bend in your knees," cautions his trainer, the precise, even-tempered woman who created this equine oasis and won the national trophies mounted on the walls of the tack room.

Jane considers the ninety minutes they spend here each week to be an effective form of therapy. Amid the elegance of fine animals and people who love them, she gets to unwind to the trainer's music collection and watch her son master one skill after another.

She thinks of the hummingbird watching enviously as his brothers and sisters are called for the job he wants. Before Mexico, Jane rarely remembered her dreams and was jealous of people who did, people who had a special pass to an abundant world of their own making, a world to which she was denied access. Now that she has finally been admitted, she doubts her ability to interpret what she sees.

They have saddled the pony and are working on dressage techniques now.

"Straighten up, weight centered. Hands steady, gentle on his mouth, good."

Tension reenters Jane's shoulders when her mind wanders to Nayeli's family. The contrast is obscene. Here she is, lounging in this beautiful place where privileged kids like her son take dressage lessons while Nayeli and her husband and so many others work endlessly to provide only the most basic necessities for their children. Well, she can help change things for one family at least. While Connor learns to guide the pony through the serpentine maneuver, a triple figure eight, posting rhythmically, Jane focuses her attention on what she needs to do for the concert. It all seemed manageable over drinks with Gabriela and Meghan, but now the details start to feel overwhelming, given the urgent timeline. She jots a to-do list on her phone. Poster design, tickets, spreading the word on social media as soon as they have a definite date, rentals, bartenders, cleaning staff, and thank you gifts for the band and the couple about to allow an invading army into their home. What else? She should work on getting liquor donations. It wouldn't be fair to leave that entirely to Lindsay even though Lindsay's lived here a long time and must have good connections. Jane fears she may be forgetting something, but her list provides plenty to start with. Most importantly, they need the band, venue, and date. She texts Gabriela and Meghan to ask about their progress.

A puppy wanders over, setting the trainer's cat to hissing. The music changes from Moroccan to French to Spanish and back to Moroccan. A rooster on the neighboring ranch crows insistently, the only discordant note. The sun is well into its descent and beginning to slip below the mesquite trees, glowing peach and tangerine in a beautiful but subdued-for-San-Miguel performance. Jane prefers the fierier versions in vivid pinks and reds. The air cools noticeably, and the light begins to fade.

"Heels down, Connor, always. That's your security."

A blaring back-up warning from a truck loaded with bales of hay disrupts her thoughts. Jane watches as several grooms make quick work of moving all the bales into the barn. She did a version of that work as a child.

It was always a race against the rain. Dad had to cut the tall, rich grass with one machine pulled behind his old tractor, let the grass dry for a couple days, then use a different piece of equipment to turn over the rows, let the second side dry, bale it with a third machine, and get all the bales under a roof before rain returned. The grass was usually at peak ripeness in mid-June, but a full week without rain in Lewis County before the Fourth of July was a lucky thing. The farmers up and down the valley started obsessing over weather reports in early June. Around the tenth or so, someone would make the brave decision to go first. Some of his neighbors would follow while others held off, worrying over the sky and the forecast.

Inevitably, some succeeded, some waited too long and ended up with overripe hay worth less, and some suffered the worst fate, watching heavy rain fall on their fields of cut grass. If the rain didn't last too long, they could try to dry out the grass by turning it an extra time, but that often failed. Those farmers then had to watch their hay rot in the field and live with the galling knowledge that they'd be buying that winter's supply from a luckier neighbor.

The year Jane was twelve, her father was one of the fortunate ones. His grass, especially the alfalfa, was thick, tall, and perfectly ripe. None of his equipment broke down, and the seasonal workers appeared at just the right time. On the day before he was ready to bale, a crew of six Mexican men walked up the driveway. He hired them all and asked them to come back early the next morning.

They arrived promptly as he made the second pass around his biggest field, leaving a trail of valuable bales. The men joined Mom, Jane, and Thomas in the field. Everyone helped to roll fifteen or twenty bales close together, the men stacked the bales in a pile five high, and then they all hurried to the next section of the field. They did that for hours until Mom sent Jane back to the house for the twenty chicken sandwiches she made before the sun came up. They ate quickly.

Jane couldn't understand a word the men said when they talked among themselves, but still she liked the way they teased each other and laughed often as they worked. Sometimes a couple of them sang, and they finished her rows for her when she was so tired the bales doubled in weight and her arms stopped working. They helped Thomas, too. Mom didn't need help.

Late in the afternoon, Dad drove his flatbed truck from pile to pile. He jumped out of the cab at each pile and climbed onto the back of the truck, as did one of the Mexicans. A couple of the others threw bales up to them. She could not imagine having the strength to do that. Dad and the other man on the flatbed stacked the bales higher than their heads. A couple of workers rode on top of each load to the hay shed, where they climbed down, guided Dad as he backed into the shed, and then unloaded and restacked the hay before returning to the field for more.

By nine o'clock, the light was nearly gone, but they kept going because a few more piles remained and a voice on Dad's radio predicted rain the next day. Mom asked Jane and Thomas to come with her when she headed in to make dinner, but they wanted to stick it out to the end.

They felt like champions when they climbed up themselves on the final load. They lay back on top, looking at the stars appearing in the still cloudless sky. The rocking of the stack as Dad drove to the hay shed relaxed Jane's tired muscles. She heard the men walking behind, gathering up a few hay hooks and empty thermoses.

Dad backed the truck into the hay shed. Under the roof, the night instantly darkened. Jane stretched and waited for her eyes to adjust.

The truck door swung open with a grudging whine, and Dad's boots crunched on gravel. "Thank you, gentlemen, we made it. I'll deal with this last load tomorrow. It's after ten o'clock, for God's sake. Come to the house for dinner and beer."

She enjoyed the satisfaction in his voice. She had helped bring in the year's hay. She had helped make him that happy.

She thought her eyes would have adjusted by now. "Hey, can you see?"

Thomas didn't respond.

She reached out, found his shoulder, and shook him awake. "We're done, bud. Time for dinner." He made a huffing noise and seemed to curl up, so she shook him again. Then, as she sat up, something hit her hard across the forehead. "Damn it!"

"What happened?"

She blinked and found herself staring directly at a thick beam.

"Don't sit up. I just bashed my face on a rafter, that's how high we are." She touched her forehead and felt a tiny, rough fragment of wood and then another. Her fingers came away wet. "I'm OK, just bleeding a little with splinters in my face."

"What should I do?"

"Hold still." She shivered as it occurred to her that if they hadn't been lying down when Dad parked the truck, they would have been scraped off the top of the load. She lay back, flipped onto her belly, and crawled toward the edge. She looked over, barely making out the ground below in the dark, and felt the bale under her sway outward. "Oh, shit."

"What?" he asked as she scooted back to the middle.

"We're about nine or ten bales up, right, on top of the flatbed, which is already what, seven feet high? So we're maybe twenty feet in the air."

"Yeah, we're at the rafters."

"And the pile moved when I looked over. If we try to slide over the side to climb down, some of these bales are going with us."

"Where's Dad? And Mom?"

"She went in an hour ago to make dinner for everybody, remember? And Dad just left, he's bringing the workers in now."

"He forgot us."

"Yup."

"Dad!" Thomas screamed. No answer. "Fucker."

She laughed. "Yeah, fucker."

"So what now, we're spending the night up here?"

"No. Mom will notice when we don't come back with Dad."

"Right. She'll be so mad."

They didn't have to wait long before Mom marched down the driveway, flanked by Dad and all the men. Everyone yelled their names and waved flashlights around.

"Up here, Mom."

"Oh my God." She pointed her light up at them and then told Dad to lean the long ladder he kept in the shed against the load of hay. She climbed up it, and her weight braced the pile.

"Thomas, you first."

Thomas lay on his stomach and swung his legs over. Mom guided his feet to the second rung, and he climbed down.

"Now you." Mom saw Jane's raw forehead in the glare of a flashlight. "Good Lord, what happened?"

"Nothing, I just sat up too fast and smacked a rafter."

"It's a mess, but you'll be—you were up there when he backed in?"

Jane nodded, avoiding the eyes of both her parents.

"I didn't know they'd climbed—" Dad's voice hit defensive notes.

"Because you didn't know where they were."

Jane and Mom climbed down.

A couple of the men grimaced at the sight of Jane's forehead. "Sorry, ma'am, we didn't see them up there."

"Well, it wasn't your responsibility to watch the children."

They walked together to the house, but the joy and triumph had fallen away from the evening. The men ate quickly and left. Mom used tweezers to pull out the slivers, cleaned the scratches with something that stung, and then wrapped a bandage over Jane's entire forehead.

"You're a mummy," Thomas said right before he fell asleep.

Jane pushed the back of her head deep into her pillow so that it puffed up by her ears to shut out the fighting. She didn't feel like going to her usual stair to hear them.

Jane checks her phone and finds good news from Gabriela with only a small catch. Her parents' friends are willing to open their home for the concert, but it has to be at least three weeks from now, after some guests leave. *That's ok*, she texts back, *I doubt we could pull this off any sooner. Please give huge thanks on behalf of Casa Mía. Thank YOU for getting our venue.*

No response yet from Meghan.

Finally, the trainer notices the time. "Now give him some neck, walk the perimeter. Great job today."

Connor says goodbye to each horse they pass and bounces his way to the car. On the drive home, he continues to chatter about horses and friends from school. Jane soaks it up before posing a question. "You know how I'm raising money to build a Casa Mía house? Well, the family has two girls, about the same ages as you and Liam. If I can get scholarships for them, do you think they'd be OK at your school?"

"Sure, why not?"

"Because their lives are so different, it might be hard for them to fit in. They don't have all the nice things you and your friends have. You know how some of your Mexican friends have second homes in Puerto Vallarta or Playa del Carmen and take fancy vacations to Europe and the U.S.? Well, these girls don't go on vacation at all or even play video games."

"Why?"

"They can't because they don't have a television or console or computer or phone to play on, or even electricity. And although they sometimes go to school like other kids, some days they work instead. They make bricks with their mom." She watches his face in her rear-view mirror.

"Oh." Connor absorbs the information. "That's pretty bad. But we have kids already from the girls' and boys' orphanages. They're fine. They don't get bullied, if that's what you mean."

"Well, that's a good point."

"I know, right? Like Dad says, you worry too much, Mom."

"Dad says that? It's probably true then." She wonders what other opinions Kevin may share.

Liam meets them at the door with a crestfallen expression. On his palm lies a broken hummingbird, the brown, gold, and brilliant blue feathers still gorgeous. The creature's stillness was born of violence, its wings ripped and belly torn open.

"The stupid cat, Mom, the neighbor's cat. I'm sure she did it."

"Oh honey. Where did you find it?"

"In the patio, below the feeder." Liam leads them to the spot and points out two smudges of blood on tile.

"The scene of the crime," says Connor. "I know it's nature, but that cat sucks."

"Language, Connor. I wonder how she managed to get in here?"

"Maybe she climbed the wall but then couldn't get back over with the bird in her mouth."

Liam fights tears. "Is it our fault since we put up the feeder?"

"No, I don't think so. But we'll move it to a higher branch anyway."

"Can we bury him?"

"Of course, baby. I'll get the shovel. You two choose the prettiest place in the garden." The responsibility soothes and directs them. "And mi amor? Maybe don't pick up a dead thing next time."

JANE SITS AT HER DESK, running through a concert to-do list and trying to conjure another fundraising idea, too. The concert will only get them halfway.

She has positioned the desk in front of her bedroom window for a view of her own semi-tended garden and beyond it the elaborately manicured oasis of the hotel next door, as well as the trees growing around the city's famous spring that attracted a Spanish priest to the area five hundred years ago. She enjoys the green view while weighing one unappealing option after another, from an online crowdfunding campaign to an awkward personal pitch to her wealthiest friends, a raffle for some prize she'd have to solicit, or fifty bake sales.

Her mood lifts when she sees an egret, the first of the year, and then another. She loved watching these elegant birds make their nests and raise their young last spring. Now, March again, they return. But this time, the snowy creatures circle repeatedly without landing. She senses their confusion and distress. They must wonder what to make of a landscape sadly altered since their last visit. One lands on an attenuated branch and lifts off again. Over the course of the morning, Jane watches more than a dozen arrive, hover, and fret. Most of them do not stay.

During the egrets' winter sojourn, municipal gardeners pruned the city-owned trees in the neighborhood, and for some reason, they were overzealous. Many of the once stately giants rooted around the spring and in nearby Parque Juárez stood naked for months, the unluckiest reduced nearly to stumps. Jane worried that the trees would never recover, but eventually most began to resurrect themselves. They have regenerated a portion of their formerly lush green finery, but clearly not enough for the egrets.

Jane wonders where the birds return from this and every spring. Is it an epic journey from South America or perhaps a shorter haul from a Oaxacan beach? She hopes that after summering above her garden they spend their winters somewhere magical like the islands in the middle of Lake Titicaca or the green lower slopes of a Central American volcano.

The jacaranda trees in the hotel garden next door, untouched by the city gardeners, are starting to unfurl their distinctive purple blossoms. San Miguel will soon be liberally dotted with purple domes that remind her boys of the truffula trees in *The Lorax*. Residents with allergies will suffer for several weeks while thousands of amateur photographers document the Seussian splendor.

But what will the egrets do? Apparently, they're not fans of the jacarandas or any of the other privately owned trees nearby that escaped the attack. The beautiful birds continue to arrive and one after another face the shock of their denuded homes. They wheel and swoop, circling over Jane's house and back to the spring again, trying different approaches to their trees as if from a different angle the missing branches might appear, the branches that for years held their nests each spring, to which they brought food throughout the day for their babies, the branches from which those babies learned to fly.

Jane tells herself she's overreacting. The birds will simply have to adapt by finding other branches, and the city is full of trees. On the other hand, she understands why she empathizes to such a degree with the distraught animals. Their perception of their home was suddenly undone.

Jane knew before Mom sat them down over Chinese take-out to have the talk. She knew even before they checked in to the Seabird Motor

Inn at Ocean Shores. She knew the moment Mom said Dad wasn't coming with them to the beach.

He didn't always join them on summer trips to her grandparents' lake house or come with them to visit her cousins in Seattle or Reno. Those were the kinds of vacations he skipped. But he loved the beach almost as much as she did, and he rarely let them spend money on a hotel. He wouldn't have missed this.

There were only two chairs in the room, so Mom sat on the bed. Over soggy eggrolls and sweet-and-sour chicken, she told them that she and Dad were getting divorced. They would have something called joint custody. It was sad but for the best.

"It's for the worst!" Thomas yelled. He shoved his carton off the Formica table. Lumps of chicken rolled across the floor, collecting carpet fibers and grains of sand, leaving smears of neon sauce. He sprang for the door and launched his skinny body through.

Mom chased him across the motel parking lot. Their flip-flops made slapping and scraping sounds on the sandy asphalt. Thomas appeared to be headed to the beach, and he'd have to cross the street to get there. Mom yelled at him to stop, wait, stay away from the road.

Approaching headlights glowed in the humid air. It wasn't quite dark yet, only dusk, so it was lucky the driver had his lights on.

The pickup behind that first car did not.

Mom lunged to reach Thomas on the edge of the road just as the pickup came abreast of them. She got her hands on his left arm and yanked. She fell hard there in the gravel and took Thomas with her, his coltish body landing on her sturdy one. He flung out his right arm in an instinctive reach for balance and then shrieked as the truck swerved hard. For several seconds, Jane believed it had run over his arm, but then he started hitting Mom with that hand as well as the other one. The pickup skidded to a stop a few yards past them.

Jane ran to her family, but then she just stood there as Thomas flailed at their mother. He screamed and hit until finally he sagged into Mom and started to cry. Jane still did nothing, like the people in cars driving slowly by. They stared but didn't stop.

The driver of the truck, a raspy-bearded man in stiff, reinforced jeans and logging boots, climbed down. "Thank God you're OK, but look, lady, get that crazy kid away from the road."

Mom ignored him. The words "don't look at us" throbbed inside Jane's skull but did not come out. Eventually the man stomped back to his truck.

That night, they talked and talked, at least Mom did. She explained that joint custody meant Jane and Thomas would live at the ranch with Dad and at her new house in town on alternating weeks. They would still have their horses, still ride in the woods, and still live in their fairy-tale-train-station-turned-house half the time, while at Mom's house, they would be close to everything in town, like their friends and the movie theater; won't that be fun? Most of all, they wouldn't live with Mom and Dad's fights anymore, which would certainly be better for them. This was the right decision.

The next day, Mom wanted them to play on the beach, but Jane wouldn't pretend. She walked alone along the shore a long way, as far as she felt like going, until she couldn't see Mom or Thomas anymore.

On the third day it started to rain, so they sat in the motel room. The next morning, Mom gave up and drove them home under wretched gray skies.

Jane looks out her window, squinting against the brilliant Mexican sun. Some egrets still circle their old, now spoiled, nesting ground. *Just find another tree, another branch. What's the difference, can it be so important? There are still plenty of trees with plenty of branches right here within a small radius of the old ones. Why can't you adapt?*

Her worry spreads to the monarch butterflies struggling to survive their migration, their routes interrupted by development and a warming climate. Monarchs have been wandering off track lately, no longer finding many of the plants that sustained their ancestors on the journey. Now, far too few survive the trip to their winter home in the forests of Michoacán, only three hours south of San Miguel. Fewer trees there are coated in orange glory this year.

Jane shakes her mind back into concentration and will not let her body up from the desk until she has rehearsed her spiel. "You will be changing lives by saving a good, hard-working family from home-lessness. Both parents work long hours six days a week making and firing bricks, and even the young daughters help, but they still barely make enough money to buy food. Casa Mía is their best hope of ever owning a decent, safe home—with your help."

She again urges the egrets to manage a small adaptation. Accept what has happened and make the best of it. Find a way to survive. But for their own reasons, most of the noble birds deem the nearby trees unacceptable substitutes. Only a handful appear to be staying, nowhere near last year's raucous numbers. The others circle and fly away. Where will they go, back to their winter homes? Will they die en route like disturbed monarchs?

She checks her phone. Finally, a response from Meghan about the band, and it's encouraging. They're willing, Meghan reports, and they have a few open dates in the next month. They just have to work around a possible trip to Mexico City, shouldn't be a problem. "Yes!" Jane shouts to the egrets, but they ignore her news and continue to lament their own. She sends Meghan a gleeful acknowledgement and shares the win with Gabriela and Rocío, too.

With a flash of irritation, Jane notices the time. She shoves back her chair and almost runs to Connor's room to warn him that they should leave in two minutes for his play reading. Her days are chopped up into such inconvenient increments. She spends so much time watching the clock in order to pick up the first child somewhere or deliver the second somewhere else between other errands. Then it occurs to her that Nayeli's long days in the brickyard aren't broken up at all. Jane should be grateful for her life's disjointed but vibrant rhythm.

Upstairs at La Vida Sana, a popular organic market, Jane shakes off her egret-induced melancholy with the help of the interesting collection of people one table over, where Connor sits between an effervescent red-headed playwright and a fifteen-year-old girl, focusing intently on the script in front of him. The playwright praises Connor's delivery of certain tricky lines, and he glows in response. Sunlight pours in through the market's big windows, adding a warm patina to the mural of traditional crops on the far wall. Jane scans the dozens of posters covering the remaining wall space, most of which celebrate organic farming or promote the work of various nonprofits, including Casa Mía. She feels a sense of virtue by association, although it is as yet unearned.

Connor's character must show fear. His big sister, played by the fifteen-year-old, is running away, cushioning the blow with a story of joining her ocean-father in the sea. Connor says his lines unhaltingly, producing such a believable facsimile of dread that Jane feels flickers of unease rise beneath her pride.

His face lights up again when another woman approaches. Jane recognizes her as the director of the children's theater workshop Connor attended last summer when they'd just arrived in San Miguel. Several more actors soon follow, and they arrange themselves around the table. Her son looks so small among the adults.

The script is smart and ethereal, with deep-thinking retired academics and a single mom holding the family together. Jane, enthralled, hopes the grittiest themes flow over Connor's head.

She pulls out her phone. Her enchanted mood evaporates when a text from Gabriela begins with *sorry.* The house isn't available after all, such a shame, the owners just told her. Their grandkids are coming for a surprise visit, so it's not a good time. Gabriela suspects that the more they thought about the crowd, the less comfortable they became. She can't pressure them.

Damn it, thinks Jane. We'll find another place, she tells Gabriela, no worries. But Jane doesn't know anyone else with enough space in town. Maybe they will have to rent a hotel ballroom, even though the expense will eat up a big chunk of the profits, or maybe they should move the concert out to a ranch in the countryside. Then they'd be able to invite more guests, but she wonders whether enough people would make the drive.

An hour later, Connor starts to look bored. He's probably hungry, too. The playwright leans in, coaching, keeping him engaged. At one point, something she says pushes him into giggles, pulling in the rest of the cast.

They happen to be finishing up, to Jane's relief, when Rocío calls. Jane is about to launch into the problem, assuming Rocío just received the news from Gabriela, too, when Rocío speaks first. "Hey, maybe you could check on Nayeli and Pablo. I'm worried."

"Why?"

"They had to build a pathetic shack out of garbage, and Pablo doesn't trust us. Can you maybe just swing by and reassure them that we're getting the money together? So they don't do anything drastic in the meantime? Sorry I can't do it."

"Drastic?" Jane moves to the back of the room.

"Pablo's talking about moving back to Chiapas although there's nothing there for them. Nayeli's scared he'll go north instead."

"If I tell them construction starts soon, that'll keep the family together?"

"God, who knows? He's a grown man with free will. If he wants to go, he's probably going. But it's worth a try, I think."

"Those poor girls. If we help, that's not clueless paternalism, it's being decent, right?"

"That's how I feel. Just do what you can to convince them not to give up on us. Or I can probably do it later this week if it's not too late."

"No, you have way too much on your plate already. I can handle this." After a pause, Jane continues. "But actually, I have some bad news. About the concert. We just lost the venue."

"Ay, carajo. Then maybe don't go? The last thing we want to do, seriously, is raise their hopes if this isn't going to happen."

"I know, but it will happen. We have the band, that's the most important thing, and I'll fix this, we'll find another venue. So I'm going. I'm glad you called me." Jane hangs up and turns to her son. "Connor, awesome job, buddy."

In the car, she catches his eye in the rearview mirror. "I am so proud of you. You stayed focused for a really long time and did a great job. What was your favorite part?"

"When I couldn't stop laughing and then all the grownups couldn't either."

A couple blocks later, Jane glances at her son again. "I have to make a quick stop to visit Nayeli's family, the new Casa Mía family. Do you want to come, or should I drop you off first?"

Connor looks down. "Drop me off, please."

"What's wrong?"

"It's just, what would I say to them?"

"Oh, I don't know, you'd be friendly and say hi, maybe tell them about your school."

"Wouldn't that be mean, though? What if they don't get to go?" He looks at her in the mirror. "Are you mad?"

"No, of course not. And you know what, you're right, that might not be such a good idea. You're a smart guy and a kind one." She watches relief warm his smile. "I'll drop you off. Dad and Liam are home, and I won't be gone very long. I'm making spaghetti tonight, by the way."

15

Jane pulls her car as far off the road as she can, balancing the risk of scratching it on the barbed-wire fence with the hazards of leaving it too far out in the road. She pauses with one hand on the door handle. The poverty-soaked scene in front of her strikes Jane as both surreal and mundane. Pieces of garbage fleck the yard, and a line strung between two spindly trees sags under the minor burden of the family's laundry. Jeans hang straight down, but shirts, socks, and underwear flutter like sun-bleached papel picado put up for a party weeks ago and never taken down.

Jane's heart sinks further at the sight of the tiny new shack near the edge of the property. Scraps of scavenged wood, a few bricks, plastic sheeting, and some items she can't identify have been woven together in a gravity-defying structure. A disintegrating mattress forms one wall. The door is a strip of cloth that might have had a former life as half a shower curtain. Its paisley swirls in still-vibrant shades of purple add a note of whimsy. Tío Carlos's one-room house looks solid and spacious by comparison.

Bizarrely, a herd of five-foot-tall reindeer, in various stages of completion, prance between the shack and the laundry line. Under the belly of one of the animals squats a tiny woman. She puts the finishing touches on her creation, trimming twigs from its hind legs. Jane remembers seeing similar creatures woven from green saplings and dry grass for sale on a roadside in the weeks before Christmas next to piles of oranges and handmade baskets, but it feels strange to witness the process of creation in March. She's struck by the amount of labor and artistry required.

The woman stands up, but the top of her head is no higher than the deer's back. When she steps out from behind it, Jane recognizes Nayeli's mother.

"Buenas tardes, Doña Carmen."

"¿Cómo estás, Señora?"

"I'm well, thank you, and I love your reindeer. They have so much personality."

Jane greets the girls and watches for a moment as they stir sand with water in a bucket, pack the resulting mixture into several cans and a broken mug, and then turn out the molds to add to an elaborate castle. Charmed by their absorption in the project, Jane reaches into the bucket and scoops up some sand to help.

Something is wrong. The concoction feels greasy and viscous, and brown liquid drips from her fingers. She drops the handful of sand back into the bucket and wraps her other hand around her wrist to push up the sleeve of her sweater. She rubs her sticky hand on her jeans, sacrificing them instead, and tries to hide her revulsion that the children are making their sandcastle with what appears to be old motor oil.

Nayeli approaches from the brickyard. She must have seen the car arrive. Watching her, Jane notices how low the sun is and realizes that Nayeli was probably on her way home anyway. She'd better make this quick and get going before it gets dark.

"Hola, buenas tardes, how are you?"

"Fine, we're all well, and you?" Nothing in Nayeli's stoic manner acknowledges the shack.

"Great. I just came to let you know we're making good progress on the fundraising. We'll break ground soon." The lie sits hot in her stomach.

The shower curtain flutters, and a man appears in the doorway. Pablo López, that's the husband's name. Jane had not expected him to be home.

"Buenas tardes, Señor López. Nice to meet you."

"And you, Señora." He is unsteady on his feet. "How soon?"

"A few weeks. Your walls will go up before you know it. Of course, that's after you've dug down to the tepetate hard pack for the foundation. Rocío explained the sweat equity requirement, right? You'll want to recruit some friends with strong backs." To keep him from seeing through her bravado, Jane shifts to a topic on which she can maintain authority. "So, about the school? Your girls will qualify for scholarships. It's just a matter of applying."

The girls smile shyly, but Pablo's expression darkens. Nayeli's face is a tight mask.

"You need time to think about it, I'm sure. It's a big decision for your daughters' futures. Just know I'd be happy to help with the applications." Jane smiles as though there were indeed an exciting decision to be made, although Pablo's answer is clear. "Well, good to see you all. Next time at your groundbreaking."

Jane waves to the girls and refuses to acknowledge the drops of motor oil seeping into her sweater. She turns and walks carefully toward her car, feeling them watching her. The sweater catches on barbed wire as she crouches and steps through the fence, but it doesn't matter. It's already ruined.

Nearly at her car, Jane is brought up short by a heavy sound behind her. Her mind resists. Another muffled thud. She lets her hand, which was reaching for the door handle, fall before spinning around to retrace her steps.

The family has disappeared, but she hears a child crying.

Jane lifts the shower curtain to peer inside. Nayeli lies in the dirt on her stomach, arms cradling her head, while Pablo launches a kick at her side.

"What exactly did you tell that gringa?" He kicks again, then pauses to pour out the last of his Tecate over her back. "Are you truly stupid enough to think she'll help you?"

Near the door, Dulce, sobbing, tries to get her father's attention. Lupita crouches in a corner, arms wrapped around herself, expressionless.

"Casa Mía's built ten houses here already," Nayeli says into the dirt. "This year they're building ten more. One could be ours, why not?"

"Why not? Because that man already said no."

Dulce leans into Jane. "Señora?" the child whispers.

Jane means to shout the words. Instead, they come out in a pitiful dribble. "Leave her alone."

Pablo barely glances at Jane, but when he does, his eyes make her shudder. From glassy surfaces, beams of alcohol-fueled malevolence shine.

Finally, Jane moves. She steps back, lets the curtain fall, and turns in a clumsy circle, looking for anyone who might help. There is only Doña Carmen rummaging through a cardboard box among the reindeer herd.

"Doña, is Tío Carlos home?" She looks toward the house but sees no signs of life.

Carmen shushes her with a shake of the head and bends over a second box. When the old woman straightens, she grips a lethal-looking machete in her right hand. With labored steps, she approaches the shack, moving so slowly Jane wants to pick her up and carry her. Even Carmen has to hunch to enter.

Standing just inside the doorway, feet apart, Carmen sweeps Dulce aside with one arm and lifts the machete to shoulder height with the other. "¡Basta, cállate!"

Pablo apparently retains enough sense to fear a machete swing in close quarters. He comes to the end of his rant but not before flinging the beer bottle. It hits his wife's skull with a sickening thud. Pablo steps over her, pushes past Carmen, Dulce, and Jane, and walks into the night.

Dulce kneels and wraps her arms around her mother, carefully avoiding the lump already rising on the back of Nayeli's head. Lupita still huddles in the corner, mute, unmoving, perhaps unseeing.

What the hell should Jane do? She's been no help so far. Call the police? Would Nayeli want that? Would they be helpful or more likely consider this a family matter and resent the interfering gringa? What would they, and all the neighbors for that matter, think she was doing here? Even if the officers took statements or brought Nayeli and her mother and daughters somewhere, the system, from what Rocío's told her, would almost certainly fail to prosecute Pablo for domestic violence. The ordeal would likely only serve to provoke him and further traumatize the girls. Calling the police is probably a terrible idea.

Should she call Rocío then? Or Meghan? She would be putting them in a difficult position because if she tells them what happened, they will technically be obligated to cancel the house since 'no signs of domestic abuse' is a criterion for family selection.

She could load Nayeli, Carmen, and the girls in her car—and go where? Rocío once mentioned that only two women's shelters operate in the entire state of Guanajuato and they're always full, not that Jane would know how to find either of them anyway. Nayeli has no family here other than Carlos, whom Carmen seems to have ruled out, and Jane imagines Kevin's reaction were she to bring them home with her.

Should she bring Nayeli to a hospital and pay the costs? Take the girls and Carmen, too? That would presumably mean involving child welfare authorities, something Nayeli probably wouldn't want. Could she take only Nayeli and leave the girls and their machete-wielding grandma here? What if Pablo returns, still furious?

What the fuck, why is she so useless? She's in over her head, and she's caused way more harm than good already. She should just leave.

She could simply ask Nayeli what she wants, if only Nayeli were in any condition to make decisions.

Carmen steps past her. "Help me, Señora."

Jane follows, relieved to relinquish the decision. In the fading light, they pull Nayeli up from the ground to her knees, and Carmen runs her fingers over her daughter's skull and ribs. Nayeli slumps against her. Carmen nods to the girls, so Jane sits on the ground next to Lupita and gathers the child onto her lap.

"Dulce, please help me with your sister." Dulce sits down next to

Jane, who wraps one arm around her, and together they cradle Lupita. Dulce's crying wanes as Lupita's finally begins.

Carmen moves Nayeli to the ratty mattress the entire family shares. Previously on Carlos's concrete floor, it now lies directly in the dirt. Then she mixes something bitter-smelling in a small bowl. She rubs the poultice on the back of her daughter's head, on her sides where the kicks landed, and on a swollen hand Jane hadn't yet noticed. Nayeli flinches twice but doesn't make a sound.

Jane looks around the increasingly dark room. Half the floorspace is taken up by the double mattress. She sits on the thin strip of dirt next to it. In the corners of the shack lie the few other items that prove this family's existence in the world: cooking pots, Pablo's carpentry and masonry tools, two threadbare pink backpacks holding the girls' school supplies and, she hopes, a treasure or two, and a cardboard box appearing to contain the entirety of the family's wardrobe not currently on their bodies or the clothesline.

The girls fall asleep in Jane's lap. The murkiness solidifies into an almost tangible darkness, and Jane fights a wave of panic. She should have left by now. She tries to remember exactly how far away her car is. She thinks of the obstacles in her way: Pablo perhaps, twenty reindeer, several mesquite trees, the laundry line, tools, trash, a barbed-wire fence, and then the road. Even if Pablo has gone, who knows who else might be out there.

"Doña, where's Pablo? Won't he be furious that I'm still here?"

"He won't come back for a day or two."

Jane gently shifts the girls so that she can stretch one arm, searching with her fingertips, to reach her purse and extract her phone. She calls Kevin. Nothing happens. No hopeful ringing, just a void where there should be a connection to the world. She taps out a pithy text, the phone's screen casting a cold glow. *Tried to call you. I have to stay the night with Nayeli from Casa Mía. She got hurt don't worry home at dawn. Tell the boys something reassuring.* Her phone makes the usual breathy sending noise, but the symbol that appears by the message is clear, not green. She knows that sometimes when reception is bad, texts don't show up on the recipient's phone until hours later, when the sender's phone re-enters a coverage zone. Is that what the clear symbol means? She tries again. *Please respond.*

Jane strokes Dulce's hair until she remembers the gummy residue on her fingers. She must be leaving oily smudges all over her phone, too.

Again, after another half hour. *Pls respond. I want you and boys to know I'm ok. Be home before they wake up.* Nothing. Panic rising, she imagines Kevin calling the police, but no, he wouldn't know where to send them. She told Connor where she was going, so if he remembers what she said, he will have told Kevin by now, but Kevin's never been out here. He might have a vague idea of where the neighborhood is, but he doesn't know the address, which is nearly irrelevant anyway given the unmarked roads and inky dark.

Kevin might think to call Rocío, but it's unlikely he has her number. Would he call Meghan? No, he will be too embarrassed to admit he's looking for his wife in the middle of the night. He won't call anyone. He'll just wait, worry, and hone his anger. She pushes the phone back into her purse to save what's left of the battery.

Moonlight penetrates the gloom through a gap between the two ceiling tarps. Without electric lights, the moon and stars have the run of the stage. Jane can now make out Carmen curled around Nayeli on the mattress, protectively cradling her daughter even in sleep. The old woman snores in an irregular gurgle.

Jane acknowledges the obvious: it's her fault. She can't trust her instincts out here. If she had only kept her overstepping mouth shut about the school, she might have left this family in peace. Instead, she's having a sleepover with a battered woman and daughters who saw things no child should see, courtesy of their own father, incited by her.

As if on cue, Lupita whimpers, fighting a battle in her sleep. Jane lightly rubs the girl's back and makes the shushing noises she used when her boys were babies. She prays that neither Lupita nor Dulce will wake, since her presence in the middle of the night would be frightening.

Jane reconsiders trying to call Rocío. Maybe cell service comes and goes out here. Rocío and her husband would certainly come to her rescue, and they'd actually know where to find her.

No. Nayeli, the girls, and their grandmother deserve a house more than ever, so nobody can ever know what happened tonight. Asking Rocío to keep knowledge of the abuse from the rest of the board would put her job as executive director at risk. Jane can't do that to her.

Maybe Gabriela's husband, Alejandra's, or Javier? Any of them would come if she called and stay quiet about it, too. But what is she thinking? She can't borrow someone else's man in the middle of the night and give them the impossible task of finding this place just to walk her to her car. Since she hasn't heard Pablo make noise, he's probably far away by now anyway.

What is she waiting for? She's a grown woman, a mother with responsibilities. She needs to get home. Her car is only thirty or forty meters away. She knows the general direction, and she can use her phone's flashlight. There is still a little battery left.

She thinks again of snakes and the possibility of men and can't make herself move.

David. He would come. He'd find her, and he'd write a press release before morning about how dangerous it is for a neighborhood of hundreds of people to apparently lack cell reception when they have emergencies in the middle of the night like anyone else. He'd decry the moral failure of leaving these people to live and raise children without running water, electricity, sewers, garbage collection, or paved roads. He would plan a campaign to pressure the government to regularize the ejido and fix it all. He'd raise money, and he'd—it doesn't matter what David would do. Moreover, would he really do all that, or is she turning him into a hero because it's nice to imagine someone fixing this when she herself has only managed to make things worse?

Whatever, none of her messages are going through, so she can't reach anybody to borrow their man even if she tried. She wonders how the affluent residents of La Buena Vista get reception right over there. They must have some kind of booster just for the neighborhood.

Tío Carlos and family must be home by now, or maybe they've been there the whole time. She could knock on their door. But why hasn't Carmen done that? How will they react to a stranger appearing in the middle of the night, and what would she expect them to do, anyway, especially given that Pablo is Carlos's nephew?

She tries shifting her weight toward her left side to relieve a cramp in her right leg and bring some feeling back to her butt. It's the only part of her likely to sleep tonight. Her bladder demands attention, too, but she ignores it.

The current parade of thoughts in Kevin's mind must be even darker than her own, and he has probably shared some of them too freely with the boys. Jane tries to remember how much she told Connor in the car and wonders how well her nine-year-old could have explained the situation, in turn, to his father. Kevin must be running through a range of emotions from fear of something minor like car trouble, to suspicion of an affair, to anger that she hasn't communicated no matter what, to terror that she can't communicate because of something truly awful like kidnapping or a car crash. By this point, he has probably concluded that she's off sleeping with someone or lying dead in a ditch. *God, he better not have grilled Connor about where Mommy really is.* There is no way he has come up with a graceful lie to soothe their sons, like she would do if the roles were reversed, so her poor boys must have gone to bed terrified. If only her messages would go through.

She hears a dog, another dog, a nocturnal rooster, and the work of five sets of lungs. Then a slight grinding, like boots on gravel. Carlos or his wife? Or Pablo, right outside? Her heart pounding, Jane hugs the girls tighter. Then nothing. Her arms ache. Every muscle in her body aches. Despite all the holes in the makeshift walls and ceiling, the air in the small space grows stale. She studies the sliver of moonlight beside the shower curtain. If Pablo's coming in, he's coming through that light. She'll see him and have a second to react before he's on her. She flexes her legs under Lupita's weight, ready to kick and punch and scream and bite.

Jane hears no more gravelly crunches. The stars still glow, and a moth flutters in a corner. Small, sharp rocks dig into her thighs. Dulce slips farther down onto the dirt, and Jane lets her go but tucks the bottom of her sweater under the sleeping girl's cheek.

She pictures the house Casa Mía will soon build for this family, if she can make it happen. Simple but durable, it will have bedrooms, a basic bathroom and kitchen, a roof that won't leak, a floor that won't turn to mud when it rains, and a door with a secure lock. When the construction workers finish, Rocio will bring volunteers out to paint the house whatever bright color the family chooses. She imagines Dulce and Lupita sitting at a table doing homework in the glow of one of the two solar eco-lights that Casa Mía will provide while Nayeli folds laundry on a clean bed on a sturdy frame and Carmen stirs pots that fill the house with good smells. She hopes that for the rest of their lives, scents from that kitchen and the warmth of their cozy beds in that house will form the girls' primal understanding of home. She cannot leave them in this miserable shack. She remembers the sweet aromas coming from her own mother's kitchen on the farm when she was a girl. Cinnamon rolls, blackberry pie, applesauce made from their own harvest, and pot roast so tender she could cut it with a butter knife. Nowhere else in the years following did those dishes ever taste quite as good.

Jane expected Dad to fix things when she, Thomas, and Mom got home from the beach. Mom had shown them a scary movie by mistake, but it wasn't real. Dad would turn the lights on, and everything would be OK.

On the drive home from the aborted vacation, Mom told Thomas and Jane they would spend the rest of the week at her new house. They'd stop by the farmhouse on the way to get some of their stuff. They should think about what to bring and what to leave.

Instead, Jane watched fat drops smack the windshield and tried to count how many hit between each swing of the wipers. She looked out her window, slouching far enough down into her seat that from her angle she saw only sky. Lighter gray clouds moved faster, churning and boiling, while darker ones appeared rooted to the earth by the water pouring from their swollen bellies.

She refused to think about dividing her things between two homes. She raised her hand to the window and wrote *no* in the condensation, then studied her raised arm. There hadn't even been enough time in the sun to bring out new freckles. Whenever they spent a week or two at her grandparents' place in the summer, a dozen new ones appeared. She imagined that if she ever lived somewhere sunny, so many would pop out that she'd finally have evenly tanned skin.

An hour later, the rain had slowed to a hazy mist filtering rays of weak sunlight. Mom turned the car into the long driveway. They drove past the edge of the forest, the fields, hay shed, corrals, barn, fruit trees, and Sam's kennel to reach what had always been their family home.

Jane felt herself stepping gingerly. The house they had rambunctiously inhabited her entire life had suddenly become fragile. Mom climbed the stairs with them. Jane sat stiffly on the edge of her bed, then sank back. She looked at the ceiling and three of the four walls that had always been hers, and then tilted her head to see the fourth.

The front door opened and closed. Dad's boots planted firmly on each of the narrow stairs. He reached Thomas's room first. "Hey, buddy."

Dad had to keep his strength in check, like a superhero in civilian clothes, but Jane knew it would burst out now that she needed him. She climbed down from her bed and hurried to hear his plan. When she saw him, she was shocked by the defeated look in his eyes.

"Dad?"

"Yes?" Nothing. He had no plan. This was really going to happen. The tears she had been holding down since Mom's announcement surfaced.

"My fairy princess, it's all right." He hugged her then, and she sank into the scent of him. Damp wool, coffee, aftershave, sawdust, and woodsmoke. He stroked her hair, but then he let her go.

Mom backed out of Thomas's room and returned a moment later with several cardboard boxes. Jane carried two to her room and threw things in at random until the boxes were full.

"Here?" Thomas asked in a tight voice, looking out the car window at Mom's new house. Jane's first thought was that her cousins from Seattle were definitely going to call their new neighbors white trash when the adults couldn't hear, and she wouldn't argue. Mom's voice sounded strangled, too, when she answered Thomas. It was only slightly better inside, clean but barely furnished, soulless, devoid of memory. Instead of farm and forest, the back door, the stiff sliding glass kind, opened to a concrete slab and small, patchy lawn.

Her parents' divorce was nearly thirty years ago. Her life went on just fine, and she could still build whatever future she chose, whereas these girls' lives will be brutally limited by their poverty. But she's clearly not helping them, so what is she still doing here in the middle of the night? She should just get up and leave. *How would Mom manage it?* What a strange thought, as her mother would never have blundered into this situation. But if Mom, just imagine, were somehow in her shoes, she would simply lift Lupita off her lap, work enough feeling back into her legs to stand, and be out the door in a minute, men and snakes be damned. Jane, however, still can't conquer her fear of who or what might be out in the dark, ruling the hours until dawn.

What will happen when Pablo comes home tomorrow? She won't be here to find out, that much she knows, honest and ashamed in the dirt.

Two red eyes glow from a spot near Lupita's legs. Jane lifts the girl off her lap, holding her close, and launches a kick in the direction of the eyes, but her shoe connects with nothing, only air. Her heart so loud in her ears she's surprised it doesn't wake the others, Jane looks everywhere for eyes. But the rat, or whatever it was, is gone. She lowers Lupita, mercifully still sleeping, back onto her lap.

Jane pulls out her phone. 4:37. The sun will come up in an hour and a half. Still no response from Kevin. She tries one more time. *Just kicked a rat Tried to anyway Battery almost dead home 6:30.* The second she can see, she'll get the hell out of here. Then she'll talk Kevin down by taking in his night's worth of fear and rage before the boys wake up. Unless he handled it really well, they must have been so scared last night. She won't prolong the nightmare by having them wake up to a fight.

Jane thinks of all that she wants for her boys and also the things she wishes for the girls in her arms if their parents will allow it. She wonders whether Nayeli will still push to give her daughters a bigger world or find it wiser to stop provoking her husband.

Jane wants to think of nothing. She tries to simply acknowledge the thoughts that rise and quickly let them go, the way her yoga teacher advises during meditation. Eventually she manages to slip into a light sleep.

Now. Finally, he is called. He shakes off the dust of the heavens and stretches his wings. Amid a holy chaos, he claims the message entrusted to him.

The hummingbird dives, sure of himself. He visits first the boys, easing fitful sleep, then the mother, lost within another family, and at last the girls.

Jane wakes to a gentle murmur but keeps her eyes shut while she determines whether the voice is a remnant of a dream.

"She won't help us now."

Jane barely parts her eyelids. In the nascent light of dawn, she watches Carmen, very much of this world, stroke her daughter's hair.

"Damn that pinche son-in-law of mine. Look what he's done to you. His pride is this family's curse. He is the reason we had to move to this expensive almost-desert, away from our people and our land. It may have been pitiably small, daughter, but that piece of the jungle was ours. I miss the soft, moist air, don't you? The air here is so dry it makes my old skin crack, and my nose drips blood. I wonder, mija, whether anyone believes we came for the construction job. I know and he knows the rest of the truth. Do you, daughter? We had to run from his arrogance, his mistakes—a debt, a fight with the wrong man. You cannot remain blind. Look what he's done to you. I will heal you now, but I fear for you when I'm gone."

Jane shifts her body to make a subtle noise. Carmen falls silent. The faint light grows warmer.

After feigning sleep for a few minutes, Jane stretches and checks her phone. 6:03. Time to go. She lowers Lupita to the ground beside her and gently pulls the tail of her sweater from under Dulce's head, leaving the girl's cheek resting in the dirt. She wiggles her legs gently, shifts her weight forward, and stands. She stumbles slightly on numbed limbs, a knee connecting with one of the girls' backpacks, and then regains her balance. The rasp of denim rubbing nylon provides an excuse for Carmen to wake.

"Good morning, Señorita," she whispers. "Go with God."

"And you, Doña. I am so sorry for my part in this."

Jane steps over Lupita's legs, crouches to get through the doorway, and straightens up. Her hands fly to her mouth to stifle a scream. Pablo lies asleep on the ground not ten feet from the shack. Jane runs through the maze of reindeer and laundry. Climbing through the fence, she again rips her already-ruined sweater. She doesn't stop running until she reaches the car.

"ARE YOU OK? WHERE THE hell were you?" Kevin demands as he opens the door, eyeing Jane's sweater and face. She stares back at him while dragging herself up the steps of their entry hall. Clammy skin and red-tinged eyes suggest he hasn't slept.

"I'm not hurt. I tried to call, and I texted ten times—"

"Yeah, they all popped up on my phone about five minutes ago, really helpful."

"Well sorry, but then you know where I was."

"You stayed out there, seriously? Why?" Kevin's voice rises and hardens like the taffy Jane's mother used to make at Christmas when it reached the boiling point. "You told Connor you were stopping by for five minutes. Spaghetti dinner, you told him."

"Like I said, I had to stay because she was hurt."

Kevin seems more concerned with Jane's decision to go by herself in the first place.

"Rocío called me yesterday when we were at the theater thing. She asked me to reassure Nayeli and Pablo because he doesn't trust Casa Mía and is thinking of going north."

"How the hell is that your problem?"

"It's not, but those girls, Kev. Anyway, I was talking to Nayeli when Pablo came out of the shack plastered."

"God damn it, he didn't touch you, did he?" Kevin's fingers clench into fists.

"No, nothing like that, I swear." She doesn't have the energy to push past him. Her body sags against the wall. She lets her back slide down, awkwardly walking her feet out, until she's sitting on the hall floor, the chill of the tile a welcome shock. She could lie right here and fall asleep. "Are the boys awake yet?"

"No, but I've been awake all night. I almost called the cops. Why didn't you come home, especially if this guy was out of his mind?"

"He kicked her, Kevin, hard. One of the little girls thought I could stop it, but I froze—"

"Don't be an idiot. You can't get involved in that shit."

"—so the fierce grandma, who's about a hundred, had to end it with a big machete."

"They had goddamn machetes, are you serious?" His fingers clench again against a target beyond reach.

"I know it sounds crazy. It was. But she didn't actually use it. Just showing it was enough to get him to stop stomping on her daughter."

"That's fucked up."

"I know." Jane watches residual fear course through his twitchy body. "He's a violent creep, at least when very drunk. But the grandmother, Carmen, she was amazing, and the mom is this beautiful woman who works far harder than we've ever had to. I didn't do anything in the moment, I was completely useless. But afterward, I could stay with the girls, that I could do. Not to mention that staying seemed safest since it was so dark, my car was on the other side of a barbed-wire fence, and I didn't know if he was still out there."

"Staying seemed safe? What the fuck? You could have been killed. You have to think." He comes closer, leaning over her. She slides herself a couple feet away from him. His scowl intensifies.

"I think," she tells him, "I think too much. I spent the whole night thinking about what he'd do when he came back, what else might be out there in the dark, and how I'm failing. Caring for the girls while Carmen treated Nayeli's wounds and watched for concussion or internal bleeding or whatever, that was the least I could do."

"No, coming home to your family was the least you could do."

"It's not like I was out partying. A woman was beaten—"

"Yeah, a woman was beaten, and yet you thought it smart to hang around."

"Of course I wanted to leave, but I was too scared to find the car in the dark. Didn't you hear me? In case he was out there—which it turned out he was. And I helped. You know what, never mind. I should shower before the boys wake up."

It's too late. Liam crouches on the stairs, watching them. His eyes swivel between his mother getting up from the floor and his father leaning over her. Kevin's eyes, meanwhile, are as hard and shiny as those of a bird of prey circling in upon its target. Anger rises off his body like a heat shimmer in the desert. Jane holds an index finger over her mouth for a second, willing Liam to be invisible, but he's not looking at her.

"It's OK, Dad," he whispers.

"Look what you've done, Jane. You've frightened him."

While wanting to scream that no, Kevin's the scary one, she focuses on her son. "Hey honey, I'm home. And you're right, every-thing's OK. What would you like in your lunch today? Let's go pack something good."

Taking Liam's hand, she leads him into the kitchen. Kevin takes a step as if to follow but stops. After a moment, the door to the court-yard slams behind him.

"There you are." Connor runs into the kitchen. Liam starts to cry.

"I'm so sorry, guys, I know you must have been really worried." She kneels and folds her arms around them. Not only did she leave two traumatized girls lying in the dirt behind her, but her own sons were hurt, too. If she had only had the courage to leave last night, to just stand up, walk to her car, and drive home, she could have tucked them in and they'd have had a peaceful night's sleep. Everything, for them at least, would actually be fine.

"I told Dad you had to go to that lady's house," says Connor, "but we didn't know where it was, and actually she doesn't have a house, right?"

Still holding them, she explains that the family built a shed to sleep in until their new Casa Mía house is ready and that she had to stay there overnight because of an emergency.

"What emergency?" Connor asks.

"Nayeli fell. She has a bump on her head and bruises, but she'll be fine. The dad wasn't home, so the grandma needed me to take care of the girls while she took care of Nayeli."

"That's not what you told Dad." Suspicion plays across Liam's face.

"Oh honey, you heard that? I'm sorry, there are things you're not old enough, that you shouldn't have to know. But you're right, she didn't just fall, and the dad was home. She fell because he hit her."

"Why?" Liam studies her face.

"Because he was very drunk and very angry. He doesn't believe that Casa Mía will really build them a house. But we will, I promise."

"He'll have to apologize when you prove him wrong."

She nods. "He should apologize to Nayeli no matter what."

"Yeah, he should. Did you take her to the doctor?" asks Connor.

"No, we didn't need to because the grandma is super smart and knows how to make her own medicine from plants."

"That's good." Connor says the words into her chest.

She pulls back to look at each of her sons directly. "I missed you guys so much last night, but you understand, right, that I had to help?"

Their nods of agreement are somber, but their expressions brighten when she asks what they did while she was gone. "Dad got out paper and colored pencils, and all three of us drew. He said that's what he used to do to feel better when he was scared. He's really good, Mom."

"Yes, he is, I know. A long time ago, he drew a beautiful hummingbird for me and—"

"And what?"

"He drew a sketch of me then, too, riding my horse. I loved the way he showed me to myself in that drawing."

"He should draw more," says Connor. A plaintive look crosses his face, and a wave of sadness hits Jane. He's more aware of her and Kevin's failures than she realized. She squeezes both boys tightly against her chest so they can't see her face. Liam pulls away first. "I know it's good you helped those people last night. But Mom? You smell bad."

Jane laughs, and immediately the contagion spreads. She tickles them there on the kitchen floor to keep the laughter going.

"You know what, you're right, I can even smell myself. I'd better take a shower and brush my teeth, so can you two monkeys get ready for school, please? Fix yourselves a bowl of cereal, juice, and maybe a banana, all right?"

Connor grabs her hand. "I have to tell you something first. At least I had a nice dream."

"You did?"

"A hummingbird landed right on my chest, so light and soft I barely felt it, only the tips of his wings brushing my skin, and his little claws scratched like Liam's fingernails when he was a baby. He didn't actually talk, but somehow I understood that everything would be OK. Then it was morning, and you came home."

"I saw him, too." Liam looks startled and unsettled, the way Jane feels.

"No, you didn't. It was my dream."

"I can have the same dream."

"No, you can't."

"You know what, Connor, maybe he can. Was your hummingbird shiny green and grey, with the most peaceful, soothing presence? I saw him, too. How strange."

Connor looks torn, enticed by the magic of it but protective of his claim. She moves to cut off an argument. "I know it's hard to believe, but it made each of us feel better, which is wonderful, isn't it? Now let's get ready fast, or you'll be late for school."

She hurries upstairs, praying the whole incident will be forgotten. Knowing it won't be.

When she gets home an hour later, Jane crawls into bed, burrowing like a child, hoping for the oblivion of sleep, but her mind won't stop replaying the night's most frightening moments. When she thinks of how close she came to bringing Connor with her, she shudders. Air sticks in her throat rather than reaching her lungs.

Her bedroom door flies open. Jane jerks upright.

"You're really OK?" Kevin's face is grim. "He really didn't touch you? I'll kill him."

"No, I told you, I'm fine."

"Thank God. I was so scared for you."

"Thank you. I was scared for me, too."

"So what the hell were you thinking? You could have been robbed or raped or worse."

"The plan was just to stop by, but then it all went out of control so fast, from semi-normal conversation to him beating on her in like five minutes."

"Which was your cue to get the fuck out of there. But no, you had to play hero."

"I'm no hero. I froze, I choked. But afterward—"

"Afterward nothing. Afterward leave." Liquid concern, brought to boil, transmutes into gaseous anger. "What did you think would happen when you shoved yourself into random people's lives, putting another hopeless cause before our family? Like you're some bougie Mother Teresa. What a joke."

She can see no semblance of the romantic man she married in the seething bully in front of her now. She lies back down and pulls the covers over her head, recognizing it as an infantile gesture. She wills him to leave, although even now a part of her still wants him to crawl in beside her and tell her she is safe and loved.

"Poor Jane made another shit decision." Kevin jerks the covers off. "Grow up."

Jane sits up, fury disarming her fear and erasing her need. He leans over her. She flinches, but his hand still finds a grip under her chin. He pulls up, lifting and holding until she raises her eyes to meet his. So she closes them.

"You bitch." He spits the words. "Who's the guy this time? Who's your partner in this stupid escapade? One of the board members, probably."

She opens her eyes. "Oh my God, seriously? There is no guy!"

Her phone rings.

"Oh really? Who's that?" He releases her chin to grab the phone from the nightstand. "It's Rocío. Better answer it."

"Not now."

He clicks the green button and shoves the phone at her.

She could hang up, but Rocío will just call back. She takes the phone from his hand.

"Hey, how did it go yesterday with Nayeli and Pablo?"

"Fine, I guess." Jane avoids Kevin's eyes. "I talked to them and her mom—such a character, love her—and tried to reassure them. I doubt I was super convincing, though."

"Your showing up meant something to them, trust me. You worry too much."

"I keep hearing that. So yeah, I think it was good." Jane hopes that Rocío doesn't hear anything strange in her voice.

Apparently she doesn't. "Well, thanks again for doing that. Bye."

Jane returns her gaze to Kevin's face. "So listen—"

"Yeah, you better start talking. Why did you tell her something totally different than what you told me? Is either story true?"

"Of course I told you the truth, but I can't tell Rocío or anyone else on the board because I'm protecting Nayeli. If anyone finds out what happened, they won't get the house. No domestic abuse allowed. And I don't have a goddamn boyfriend."

"Not now, you mean."

"Oh my God, not then, either. Whatever that was—nothing, really—it's in the past. We're two thousand miles away, and I've apologized a hundred times."

"Whatever, I've had enough." He drops her blankets at the foot of the bed. "Don't you ever pull a stunt like that again."

She locks the door behind him and starts down a familiar rabbit hole. *I should divorce him. No self-respecting woman would stay. Right now, book tickets and grab passports, papers, the boys' favorite things. Pick them up at school and go—and then tell her sons what exactly?*

No, do it right. Face him and fight. Half their net worth is no fortune, but it will provide some security while she gets on her feet. She's not as trapped as Nayeli. She has options.

But Kevin won't let them go quietly. Jane knows as well as she's ever known anything that it will be a nasty, all-out battle. He told her so the night she admitted feeling an emotional connection to David, and he has repeated the threat a number of times since. Now she's managed to make things worse. In a custody fight, he'll certainly present this awful night as evidence of her making bad decisions. Traumatizing her children by staying out all night.

She remembers, with a simmering nausea of regret, that night when she told Kevin about David. His reaction was worse than she expected, leaving her stunned by his immediate and complete renunciation of trust in her, his unwavering assumption that there had been sex, and his refusal to believe her denials. His suspicion and paranoia instantly metastasized, and he warned that if she divorced him, he could ensure that she lost everything, especially her kids.

Yet somehow, despite the venomous threats, Jane had still imagined that Kevin would eventually put behind them what was truly only a minor indiscretion. He had been willing to move to San Miguel, after all, in a professed desire to renew their marriage. She had believed the point of the move was to face their deeper problems together. Now it feels like he expects her to wear her guilt forever as a hair shirt of her own design.

But every time she runs through scenarios of leaving him, she ends up in the same damn place, so why torture herself? The years until Connor and Liam leave for college will evaporate all too quickly. She is better off making the most of her time with her sons rather than wasting it on a hellish divorce. She can't put them through that. She can be free of Kevin the instant custody is no longer at issue.

Her blankets still lie in a pile near her feet where Kevin dumped them. Jane climbs out of the bed to remake it, then slides under the covers again. Fatigue eventually tames her jittery mind, allowing her to escape into sleep.

She leans over him now to watch a luminous green patch grow on the pallid skin of his neck near the lump that marks him as male. From there, the sheen travels to his collarbone. Curious, she unbuttons his shirt and pushes back the fine but fraying fabric. The light is fainter now, farther from the surface, filtered by a layer of flesh. It pulses, then fades. She registers a moment of disappointment. The green was so pretty.

The glow again warms his body, stronger than before. Green spreads in all directions from its new core in his chest, with vines branching below the sternum, across the ribs, now twining their way around his hips and down his thighs. Others work their way up to his shoulders and through his arms. Around his neck. Around again, pulsing, flowering. The body elevated, flooded, reclaimed by nature, purified. Not until she looks at his face does the sense of warm satisfaction break. The face is rigid, paralyzed, a waxy mask. Only the eyes still move, aiming potent rays of hate before rolling back into their craters.

She claws at the vines, ripping them from his body, pulling, tearing, down to the bloody roots, but she's too late.

Jane wakes up fighting the need to retch, skin sticky, her heart hurting her chest with angry punches. She, who so often can't remember her dreams, sees this one with perfect clarity.

I'm a monster. I'd get caught for sure.

But maybe I wouldn't. I could be free with no custody threat.

No, he'd become the martyr he imagines he is. If I'm in jail for murder, what then? The boys betrayed, devastated. That's not who I am.

Her heart begins to slow its frenetic rhythm, jacking up again when she relaxes too much and visions reappear of those eyes staring out of a hideously frozen face.

She drags herself out of bed when her phone says it's time for school pick-up.

That evening, while she makes dinner, Kevin builds a Lego castle with Connor and Liam. His wounded air draws their protective concern.

Watching them cuddle, she acknowledges her situation's stark parameters. She can't take her sons from the father they adore.

"Time for bed, lovebugs." Jane manages to keep her tone light. She stalls as they climb the stairs. When she hears water running in the tub, she turns to Kevin. "By any chance did you dream about a hummingbird last night?"

"Did I dream about a damn bird, what? No, thanks to you, I didn't sleep."

"Never mind."

17

THEY CURL UP TO READ Harry Potter, but Liam falls asleep after two pages even though they're early in the second book and he's fascinated by Mr. Weasley's flying car. Jane slides his head off her lap onto his pillow and remembers Dulce's cheek in the dirt.

Connor takes much longer to settle. Jane wraps her stiff body around his and holds him in the dark for nearly an hour, singing softly and whispering stories. Finally, he succumbs to what she prays is unburdened rest. She folds her legs over the side of his bed, pulls herself upright, and pads out of the room in her socks.

Too wired to sleep, she climbs the stairs to her makeshift studio on the roof, where she can avoid crossing paths with Kevin. From under the protective plastic drape she's rigged to not touch the canvas, penciled outlines of Connor and Liam look out at her.

She will get back to them soon, but not tonight. Tonight, she wants to slash at something. Jane sets the portrait aside in the cleaning supplies closet she repurposed to store her materials and pulls a fresh canvas from the cramped space. Someday, she'll have a real studio.

She knows that she is not the kind of artist who can spontaneously slap paint around and make something magical appear. She's a methodical type who builds up each carefully planned work in layers from an underlying structure.

Tonight, however, Jane doesn't wait for a plan. In a thirty-minute burst of brushstrokes, a brooding monster of a man appears. No familiar reference takes shape in the background, only a chaotic sea of dark, foreboding colors. She wants to laugh—who needs therapy when you can paint?—but laughter doesn't come.

After two hours, Jane lies down on a plastic lounge chair and studies her impulsive creation, wondering whether the truth in it, so glaring to her, would be apparent to others. If Kevin ever comes up here, he for one will recognize it, so she had better hide the painting.

Far from forgiving her, he's getting angrier, his distrust ever more palpable. Their recent pattern is one of his fury growing in tandem with her disgust. He sees it, too, although in his version the disgust must be a cause, not the result, of his rage. What a horror show of a relationship they model for their sons. Jane studies the man's brooding eyes, which she has painted as two dark wells so deep they reflect vanishingly little light.

Warm air drifts on a suggestion of a breeze, enough to lift the scent of jasmine from the vines in the courtyard below. Jane intends to get up, hide the painting, and go down to bed, but the lounge chair is irresistibly comfortable after last night's dirt floor.

Another worry briefly elbows Kevin aside: the urgency of securing a venue for her neglected concert. Tomorrow she had better start cold-calling every hotel with a ballroom. She just needs one sympathetic manager to donate a space.

Despite her rich stew of worries, exhaustion pulls at Jane. She relaxes further into the chair. But when her eyes close, stranger thoughts surface.

She stirs a steaming liquid in one of the mugs made by that Oaxacan artist she admires. The tea is an unexpectedly beautiful, brilliant shade of green. Releasing the spoon, she holds the cup out to him. But then she herself is swallowing the brew. She finds it strangely without taste, but the heat is soothing. She sinks from the scene, resurfaces, and swallows more.

Pablo is there now. He kicks, dances, and plays with his girls and her boys. All of them smile as they approach, reaching out to her with motor oil dripping from their hands, staining their yellow sweaters.

A rooster or a firecracker wakes her up. Under the glow of the lamps and café lights, her watch says 5:40. Jane grabs the canvas off the easel and shoves it into the storage closet, then picks up her stiff, probably ruined brushes. Maybe she can save them later with vinegar or rubbing alcohol and some moisturizing soap, but she can't deal with that right now. When the boys wake up, she has to be right where she's supposed to be. Since these days her room is not Kevin's, with any luck, he may not have noticed that she's been up here all night. One less thing for him to hold against her.

Over the next two weeks, Jane gets turned down by every hotel manager in town. Several have ballrooms available on short notice on dates when the band can play, and they would be happy to rent them to her, but at rates that would eat up too great a portion of the earnings. Not one will donate their space. Eleanor and Rocío worry that this last-minute begging reflects negatively on Casa Mía. When Eleanor books a space for the organization's annual gala, by comparison, she does it a year in advance.

During the same two weeks, however, Jane is furiously productive at her easel. In one painting, a man brutalizes a woman, the figures resembling Nayeli and Pablo. Although the bodies push far apart on another canvas, the anger is just as palpable between versions of herself and Kevin. In the next two paintings, she doesn't recognize the strangers staring out at her. In one, the man and woman crouch face to face, and in the other she has her foot on his neck. Jane believes these are better than anything she has created before. She goes back and changes the faces that look too familiar.

On her good nights, Jane works on the portrait of Connor and Liam, building up detail, and then she adds herself over their shoulders. Sometimes she works back and forth between two canvases, the sweet family portrait and an angry couple. She puts a touch of her new freedom from her old process into the portrait, too. Contours on the canvas soften and vibrate, unlike the lines between Jane and Kevin in real life, which only seem to harden.

DURING THIS TIME, A FUNNY thing happens. Jane begins to notice a particular, luxurious shade of green in the shadowed corners of her garden, in the heavy glass of the hummingbird feeder below water level, and in the striking eyes of her elder son when he stands in certain light.

Sometimes she catches disconcerting glimpses of it in her peripheral vision but can't find the source when she turns. She blinks those moments away with a sense of opportunity wasted.

Jane finds this dark fantasy seductive. She imagines being free from Kevin's volatile moods, his blame and suspicion, his punishments and petty nastiness. She could walk confidently through the rooms of her home without pausing first to assess the level of his simmering anger. She could permanently shield her sons. She imagines no longer fearing her own anger, either, without daily provocations.

Most frequently, she encounters the green in the last moments before sleep and the first after waking, a foggy image, a tug at memory. One night after a long painting session, thinking of the greener world where she grew up, Jane falls asleep again in the lounge chair on the roof.

That Thursday night, at the end of their first week at Dad's—without Mom, it felt wrong to call it home anymore even though it had always been their home—Jane told Thomas to fill his backpack with the things he wanted to bring to Mom's the next day. She reminded him that in the morning they would take the bus they'd always taken from Dad's to school, but then in the afternoon they would ride a different bus to Mom's new house. They stuffed their backpacks full, and in the morning had to carry separately the lunches she made.

Jane chose an empty bench toward the back of the bus and leaned into the window, perversely enjoying the cold of the damp glass against her cheek. She had recently watched a documentary in science class about deep sea exploration, and it didn't seem so different from riding a school bus through the farmlands of Lewis County. The underwater vehicle moved slowly and stopped often. A scientist looked out through glass at a cold, watery world. Unlike the amazing creatures in the documentary, however, the only vaguely exotic beings on her route were the hippie farmers who lived in yurts at the organic cooperative. A couple of them waved as the bus went by, a blip of color in the green-gray depths.

She wondered whether she had remembered to pack her favorite red sweater with the fake fur cuffs. She tugged her backpack onto her lap and rooted around. Her fingers brushed denim and cotton and rayon, but not fur. When she pulled her hand out, something came with it. She watched in horror as a flutter of pink landed on the floor among muddy footprints. She lunged but another hand closed first and raised the panties to a florid face. Jane met the eyes of a beefy ninth grader with a buzz cut, the kind of kid who cut the sleeves off his jean jacket to give the world a better view of his biceps. He sniffed and mashed the fabric against his mouth.

"Give it back, you perv."

He held the underwear above his head and laughed at her. Jane climbed on her seat, so he threw her panties two seats back to another boy. She jumped down into the aisle just as the driver jerked the bus to the side of the road. The irritable vessel shuddered, and half the kids bounced off the seatback in front of them. Jane's feet slid out from under her, and she landed on the floor, furious to the point of tears. While the driver marched down the aisle, the original boy and several others continued to speculate loudly about why a thirteen-year-old girl would bring extra underwear to school. A fifth grader helped Jane up and pulled her into a seat out of the irate driver's way. Withheld tears stung her eyes.

"What the hell is going on back here?"

"They took something of mine, and I want it back right now."

"She means these," said the first boy, again holding her underwear over his head like a trophy, garnering nervous laughter.

"Good Lord." The driver snatched them. "That's detention for you and your pack of degenerates."

"Worth it," said a leering acolyte.

The driver handed Jane the humiliating prize. "Why don't you sit up front today, Janie?"

She stomped up the aisle and pushed past Thomas to claim the window seat next to him since nobody was sitting with him, either. She leaned her face against his window for the rest of the ride, determined not to let them see her cry. Her little brother patted her shoulder in a gesture so tender and protective it almost pulled the tears from her.

Jane turned her head toward him. "Don't tell Mom and Dad, bro, promise?"

As they pulled into the school parking lot, she remembered that her red sweater was already at Mom's house. This deal might have solved Mom and Dad's problems, but it was ruining her life. Probably Thomas's, too.

Jane tried to understand her parents and the pain they carried, but her anger grew with each small grievance and indignity. She also felt more and more distant from Dad without Mom around to buffer the relationship.

One night at Dad's, after filling the cows' feeders with hay, doing her homework, and helping Thomas with his, Jane cut up leftover roast and carrots to add to a pot of instant ramen.

"Where is he?" she asked Thomas. "He said he'd come in for dinner half an hour ago. If he doesn't come right now, the noodles will get mushy and gross. That's it, we're not waiting for him." She felt herself turning into Mom.

At least during their weeks at Mom's house, she didn't have to parent Thomas. Mom filled out the depth and breadth of the role in a vital way it seemed Dad would never learn.

"He'll grow into it," Mom kept saying, generously. "Be patient."

Jane doubted it, and in the meantime she worried about her brother.

19

WHEN JANE CLIMBS INTO MEGHAN'S car on a Saturday morning, Meghan's grin practically splits her face. "Guess what? Huge news. I have a venue!"

"Oh, thank God, I've gotten nowhere with the hotels. What is it?"

"Another private home, belonging to friends of friends. It's a gorgeous place with an enormous yard, and they're already used to hosting concerts for the chamber music festival, so it's no big deal. Don't worry, I told them our crowd will be a little rowdier than chamber music fans. They're fine with it, I promise. We're all set. For free."

Meghan's triumph, and Jane's exuberant relief, fill the car with manic energy. During the drive, the two of them run through every single detail that will surely make the concert a success.

When they arrive in Pueblo Nuevo for a workshop Rocío organized, Jane is the first to take in their surroundings. "I thought we were expecting twenty kids?"

"Yeah?" Meghan pulls art supplies and liters of juice out of her trunk, then straightens up. "Whoa."

At least fifty or sixty children wait in a dusty lot in front of a primary school, not just those whose mothers will attend Casa Mía's needs assessment workshop. Rocío approaches and explains that a rumor of a giveaway went around the neighborhood.

"They're going to be disappointed then," says Meghan. "We have juice and cookies and construction paper. And a soccer ball. That's it."

Jane turns to the two teenage volunteers Meghan recruited for the day. "Could you guys get a game going with the older kids? I'll pass out paper and markers to the little ones."

If the kids are disappointed, they don't show it. Rocío and Meghan ration the cookies and juice, and eager hands accept sheets of paper and a marker or two. Soon shrieks of laughter rise from the soccer players when the teenagers start showing off.

Jane spots Nayeli in the cluster of waiting women. She walks slowly over to the group, studying Nayeli as she approaches. It's been a little over two weeks since that night. The lump on her head is no longer noticeable, and the kicks targeted her torso, so that damage is hidden beneath her clothes. After greeting the other women, Jane asks Nayeli how she's doing.

"Fine," Nayeli responds with minimal affect. Her eyes convey shame but also strength and defiance. She folds her arms across her chest, and Jane notices a fading bruise on her right hand. Within a couple glances, one loaded with a question and the other a response, the two women pledge silence.

Rocío invites everyone to enter a classroom. There the luckiest women sit on folding chairs while the rest curl their bodies into child-size desks. Jane and Meghan move to the back of the room in an effort to be unobtrusive. Rocío, cheery and warm, begins with introductions. The women answer in monosyllables, their reticence in palpable contrast to the shouts and laughter of the children outside.

"Maybe we'd better go," Meghan whispers to Jane.

They slip out the door, Rocío nodding in agreement as they pass her, and join the soccer game.

An hour later, the women file out. They offer polite but stiff goodbyes, gather their children, and drift away. As soon as the last one is out of hearing range, Jane asks Rocío how the meeting went.

"Well, they all agree that their community's biggest issue is lack of access to basic services like electricity and water. As we already knew, there are a number of cases of diabetes and other serious health problems not receiving adequate care. They also acknowledge addictions and violence in the community, but each woman is quick to claim that her own family is doing just fine. It's difficult and risky for anyone to admit such things publicly. It will take time and a lot of relationship-building."

"So what do you think, is it worthwhile?" asks Meghan. "Or should we stick to what we know, building houses?"

Jane speaks at the same time. "Are we in danger of opening up a can of worms we don't understand and making things worse?"

Rocío acknowledges their concerns and puts them in perspective. "It won't be easy. We're obviously not going to magically fix everything. Of course they don't expect that. But yes, I absolutely believe that women's empowerment and community-building workshops, held during the months we're building their houses, can help them better deal with more of the issues that make their days so difficult. So their families can lead healthier lives in their new homes."

Meghan seems unconvinced. "We won't be overreaching?"

"Come on ladies, don't be too scared to even try. I know you worry, wisely, about committing the wrong kind of interventions, but there is such a thing as a positive intervention. Don't forget, most of the time I'll be the one out here working with them. The nurses and other experts I bring in will be locals, too. You just need to raise a little extra money to fund the program, on top of all the house money. Please."

"Yeah, because I'm so good at raising extra money, clearly." After a couple seconds, Jane's grimace turns into a grin. "Have you always been such a hard person to say no to?"

Rocío shakes her head. "Actually, it took me a long time to get here."

In the car on the drive home, Meghan's phone rings. Even hearing only half the conversation, in Spanish, Jane understands that it's bad news from the band. When she hangs up, Meghan explains. Los Reyes just got booked for a big festival in Mexico City the same weekend they were going to do the Casa Mía concert. They're sorry to back out, but it's too big an opportunity to turn down. After that, they have some other gigs in the city, then they're committed to several dates in the States, and then something else. "They're still happy to do it, but not for like four months, and I'm afraid that's too late."

Jane nods. "Yeah, if we're going to build this house, I have to make it happen now, before the board and family lose all confidence. So it can be built along with the other ten."

"I'm sorry. I mean, I'm glad their careers are taking off, but the timing just sucks," says Meghan as she stops her car in front of Jane's house.

"It's not your fault. We'll figure something out." Jane opens the car door but turns back toward Meghan before climbing out. "I'll see you tomorrow at the Amigos del Parque event, right? We can brainstorm. We'd better have a new plan before we tell Eleanor the news."

20

JANE DESCENDS SLOWLY, CAUTIOUSLY PLANTING her feet in spike heels. She likes this grand hotel staircase, a vertical art gallery featuring a revolving collection of works by contemporary Mexican artists. She pauses to scan the walls. Her favorite Jorge Maríns are still there, remarkable sculptures of Adonis-like men wearing bird beak masks, current homages to local indigenous beliefs that somehow look classical. Then, with a thrill of recognition, she discovers a new painting, a self-portrait by a friend of hers. Several more hang nearby.

"It's Javier." She points with the beaded clutch in her right hand while her left continues to grip the railing.

"Oh wow," Kevin responds. "It's like they're melting."

A portion of each face is rendered in exquisite detail, but other parts, such as the chin, the eyes and forehead, or the entire right or left side, are liquified, distilled into lurid black ink that pours down the canvas.

"When will we see your work for sale on this wall?" Kevin's smile and tone of voice seem sincere if wistful.

Picturing the violent images in her recent paintings, Jane feels a surge of guilt. She imagines his pain and fury were she to display them publicly. They can never be seen. "Maybe someday. Yours, too."

He does not respond. At the bottom, they pass a series of grottos, several used as wine cellars and others as art galleries, before reaching a ballroom where gliding waiters offer champagne or tequila. Jane spots Gabriela, Meghan, and Javier, the artist whom they've just been talking about. She and Kevin cross the room to congratulate him.

A sleek young man in a tuxedo announces that the auction is about to begin, so the friends find seats together. Jane wishes she'd had time to study the auction items displayed around the perimeter of the room. Javier's wife, Araceli, steps onto the stage with another woman. The auctioneer introduces them as co-chairs of los Amigos del Parque and the reason the crowd is here tonight. Araceli glows in a red gown. She presents plans for a safer, better-maintained Parque Juárez with a new, state-of-the-art playground and refurbished paths and green spaces, then hands the microphone to her partner.

All eyes focus on the second woman, who wears a black cocktail dress and expensive boots. She introduces the first artwork, a large canvas exploding with color, all psychedelic swirls and Ganesh images. She acknowledges the artist, a Santa Claus figure in the front row, if Santa ever tired of the red suit and decided instead to wear tie dye in every shade of the rainbow. As the bidding begins, a waiter brings the woman an elegant little glass of tequila on a silver tray. She sips first, then tosses it back to the crowd's approval. The auctioneer uses the rising energy in the room to drive up the bidding, and the piece fetches an impressive sum, as does one of Javier's portraits next.

Assistants then carry a large canvas draped in a black velvet cloth onto the stage. With a flourish, Araceli pulls off the velvet to reveal a nude portrait of a young man from behind. The man reclines, his back, buttocks, legs, and arms sensuously captured. Jane wants to reach out and run her fingers through his glossy hair.

"He should roll this way, right, girls?" asks Meghan.

Kevin grimaces. "Don't go there."

Meghan gives him an innocent look. "Oh, is this making you uncomfortable, Kev?"

An elegant woman whom Jane knows from yoga class bids on the nude. When she raises her paddle, a heavy gold cuff on her wrist slides a few inches toward her elbow. Jane admires how glamorous and confident the woman is, not in the least embarrassed by the subject matter she admires. Jane wants to know her better. Hell, she'd like to be her.

"Ándale, Regina," she calls. Regina smiles over her shoulder, then lifts the paddle one more time. She wins.

Later in the evening, after all two dozen pieces have been sold and an impressive total is announced by a jubilant Araceli, Regina passes by the circle of friends.

Meghan congratulates her. "What a handsome man you're bringing home tonight."

"Pues, sí, I just had to."

A flash of recognition crosses Araceli's face. "You already have the front of that man, don't you? The portrait in your guest room?"

"Exactly. Now he's all mine. And my husband's," she adds generously, nodding to a handsome man in well-cut slacks and a crisp guayabera shirt deep in conversation with other obviously wealthy men near the bar.

Gabriela suddenly turns to Regina. "I have an idea. If you're buying half a man tonight, why not half a house?"

"What?"

"See, Jane's on the board of Casa Mía, and there's this family that's homeless. They were living in an uncle's casita, but he just got deported and needed it back for his own family. So Jane's on a mission to build a little house for them, for two hundred thousand pesos."

"Jane, what good work you do. I've been a fan of Casa Mía for years. Of course, yes, we'll help. A hundred thousand?"

A grin takes over Jane's face as her brain processes the words. "Fantastic, thank you!"

"I'll tell hubbie to write a check." Regina kisses Jane and then Gabriela on the cheek and walks away, every motion an unconscious expression of power and glamour.

Jane turns to Gabriela. "That was incredible. How did you do that?"

"Hey guys, we can't let Regina, and Gaby here, take all the credit.

I'm in for ten thousand." Javier's face lights up with an impish grin that Jane finds sexy in the moment. "Kevin, how about it, man, you'll match me?"

"Of course." Kevin's jaw clenches visibly.

Jane wonders how they all manage not to see it, and she hopes they remain equally oblivious to her irritation with Kevin and to exactly how moved she is by Javier's gesture. "Muchísimas gracias, gentlemen. We just went from zero to a hundred and twenty thousand pesos! Is there anybody else we should ask? What about those men with Regina's husband?"

Gabriela shakes her head. "I don't think so. They're not the sort who give something for nothing. Tonight, they're getting valuable art."

"Regina just gave a hundred thousand for nothing."

"She's different, and she was on a high from buying that painting. Her husband won't be happy about it, trust me. You better charm him when you collect that check."

"Good to know."

"With the concert, that should be enough, though, right?" Gabriela asks. "So why don't we go celebrate? La Terraza? Everybody in?"

"About the concert." Jane and Meghan share the news that the band has postponed indefinitely, but even that can't dampen the communal glee over suddenly being 120,000 pesos closer to the goal.

They decamp to a chic rooftop bar and run into more people they know. Jane and Gabriela, near one end of the expanded group, get pulled into a debate between Javier and Araceli over the relative merits of the auction's bestselling paintings and then, when someone they haven't seen since Burning Burro joins the conversation, into a retelling of their children's burro-climbing adventure.

Jane spots Kevin chatting with Meghan three tables away. She can only see the side of his face but recognizes the sweet, melancholic look he's wearing. A twinge of jealousy surprises her as she remembers the impact that look once had on her. Then she notices how animated his gestures have grown. A waiter hands him a tequila, and it clearly isn't his first or second. She can't hear what he's saying, but she fears that people at the tables between them probably can, so she excuses herself to Gabriela, Araceli, and Javier, and walks toward the bathroom, pausing near Kevin's table to edge her way around a group of twenty-something guys with hipster beards conveniently blocking her path until she's almost directly behind him. Meghan, spotting her from across the table, shakes her head nearly imperceptibly.

"—we came together young and promised each other we wouldn't get stuck in that town, that we'd get out together." Though not spoken as loudly as she feared, his words, maudlin and confessional, are headed in a humiliating direction.

Meghan shushes him and smiles, clearly to lessen the sting. Kevin evidently misreads the smile as an invitation to continue. Jane hovers, wanting to rescue her friend but fearing the volume of Kevin's reaction were she to intervene.

"—we did it, too, got out, built careers, had great kids. But it takes more than that amount of success and money to cure the coming-from-nowhere imposter syndrome, you know? For me anyway. Then she met someone, another lawyer, who better fit her new vision of herself."

As Jane watches, Kevin looks down at his hands, which are gripping the edge of the table. The fingers must be pale at the tips from the pressure and red below the knuckles where the stiff hairs sprout.

"She sees me now as something she's outgrown and should have left behind." He makes the admission quietly, but Jane's certain that she heard him correctly. Why is he sharing so much with her friend? Hitting on her or trying to convince her to help him somehow? Jane watches as Meghan starts to raise a hand to his shoulder, to console a man in pain, but Kevin misses the gesture because he is looking off to the side, toward the table where Jane had been sitting. She tenses, afraid he'll look around for her and find her eavesdropping right behind him. She slips farther behind the cluster of guys. When she peeks again, Meghan has pulled back her hand.

Too dumbfounded to help her friend, Jane saves herself instead. She returns to Gabriela before looking back at Meghan in time to see her smile graciously at Kevin, stand up, and walk toward the bathroom. Jane wonders what her friend must be thinking and what her husband thinks he was doing. She dreads the inevitable conversations with each of them. Arranging her features in what she hopes is a normal expression, she tries to pick up the thread of the story Gabriela tells.

She can still remember how that tender, vulnerable look of Kevin's could change her, how his desires would become hers.

Jane let the screen door slam behind her. Without a plan, she found herself at the barn. She slipped a bridle on her mare and swung her body up. Bareback was fine for a quick ride. Maybe she'd actually stick to the trails today.

She was fifteen already, and all her friends were going. Mom would have said yes. Why did he have to be so controlling? It wasn't fair that her social life was at the mercy of a custody schedule.

Because her parents failed, that's why she had to fight Dad to do obvious things like go to the solstice bonfire. The uptight dinosaur hadn't known that Mom let her go last year, when it happened to fall during Mom's week, so he was furious. He seemed to want to stuff her teenage self back into a child's constraints.

On top of that, she had to take care of Thomas every other week, and she was a pathetic substitute for Mom. She'd been doing it for two years and still wasn't good at it. Despite Mom's early confidence, Dad had not grown into his role. He didn't know what a twelve-year-old boy needed now any more than he had known what a ten- or eleven-year-old boy needed then.

Jane followed the main trail, moving steadily into the heart of Dad's timber. The trail parted the forest, creating a line of light like the one that appears when someone pulls back a heavy curtain an inch or two late on a summer morning. Old-growth evergreen trees lined both sides of the ribbon of sunlight, the kings of a world draped in heavy shade, carpeted with huge ferns, wild rhododendrons, black-berry vines, and other varieties of dense brush.

Maybe Mom could talk some sense into Dad. Maybe she didn't have to give up on going to the bonfire.

The sound of branches snapping made Jane pull up on the reins. She scanned the woods in the direction of the noise, trying to determine what type of animal would behave so strangely in daylight. A wounded deer or elk? A wolf, mountain lion, or coyote would never make so much noise. Please, anything but a bear.

The chaos of breaking branches and pounding hooves drew nearer. A distinctly human noise became discernible, too. "Whoa! Whoa! Fuck!"

An impressive palomino bolted into view. The angry horse's ears were folded back, mouth foaming. Reins hung loose beyond the reach of the red-faced rider flopping in the saddle.

The rider saw her, too, to his misfortune. A second after his face turned toward her, a thick branch struck his chest an alarming blow. The horse shot out from under him. He hit the ground heavily.

Jane slid off her mare. The dethroned rider lay flat on his back. As she approached him, startled but focused eyes looked up at her from an attractive face. Strong, precise cheekbones, jaw, and brow, with clear skin that wasn't usually so flushed, framed by wavy hair the warm color of toasted almonds. She recognized him from school, two years ahead of her. Kevin, that was his name.

Kevin smiled. "I hate horses."

"That one doesn't seem to like you, either."

He started to sit up. "Everything hurts."

"Wait, we should check for broken bones."

"No, nothing like that, I'm fine. Although you're welcome to check." He grinned again.

Her day had definitely improved. "Was that Cindy's gelding?" Cindy Cooper's family had the big ranch behind the hill where their timber met Dad's. Cindy was also two years older than Jane. They must be dating.

"Yeah. She loves that beast, but horses and I never get along."

Jane laughed. "So what were you doing?"

"Learning my lesson. Again."

"What spooked him?"

Kevin grimaced. "Cindy's punk brother shot a pellet gun, the little shit."

"Oh, that figures. Well, you'd better find him before he gets hurt."

"You mean the horse, not the kid, right? Can't go back otherwise, can I?"

"I wouldn't," she agreed. "Cindy and her dad will kill you once they're done with the brother."

He offered her another smile. "Will you help me?"

They followed an easy trail of broken branches and crushed plants. She liked the athletic way he moved even though he was sore. His improbable presence in her woods felt like a gift.

The palomino hadn't gone far. He'd apparently stopped fighting once the big irritant in the saddle was removed. They found him standing with his head down and sides heaving. Jane approached, held out a hand for him to sniff, and stroked his neck. She reached for the dangling reins while murmuring sympathetically about what the poor horse had just been through thanks to a couple of idiot boys. She looked over his rump, legs, belly, neck, and chest, and found no sign of pellet wounds or other damage.

"You're amazing," Kevin said, and the respect felt genuine.

She led the gelding back to where she'd tied her mare, then handed him the reins.

"I saw a hummingbird near here." She immediately regretted saying it out loud.

"You did?"

"They're rare," she explained.

"Cool. Well, thanks, you're my hero for real. So, going to the bonfire tomorrow?"

She shook her head. "Probably not. My dad won't let me."

"Who says he has to know?"

"He does."

"Don't you have one of those super long driveways they have out here? On the main valley road? There's a mailbox with your family's name on it, right?" This grin was overtly sexy.

Jane grinned right back at him. "Yeah, so?"

"So, sneak out and walk down to the road. I'll pick you up there."

She didn't know whether to take him seriously.

"Tell you what, I'll be there at ten. If you don't show by ten fifteen, I'll bail."

The look on Kevin's face made her want whatever he wanted. "What about Cindy?"

"What about her?"

It was as easy as he suggested. After she said goodnight to Dad, Jane put on makeup and changed out of her pajamas into jeans, boots, and her favorite sweater, which was starting to get tight, even better. For once she was grateful that Dad imposed a strict nine-thirty bedtime so her brother would be asleep before she left. She listened for Dad to turn off the television and close his bedroom door, then checked the time and made herself wait a little longer before slipping down the stairs and out the back door. She brought a flashlight but didn't turn it on until she was far from the house, past the barn and hay shed, so they'd block Dad's view if he happened to look out a window.

There had been no need to call Mom and drag her into an argument with Dad. Jane had made her own decision. But as she neared the end of the driveway, her doubts grew. It was a joke. Kevin wouldn't be there. She was an idiot to ever believe that beautiful, popular boy had asked her out. She almost turned around.

There he was, parked beside the mailbox. She didn't notice the make of the car in the dark but, judging by the growl of the engine when he turned it on, Thomas and maybe even Dad would be impressed. She climbed in, and his easy smile made her doubts evaporate.

Talking to him felt natural. She forgot to obsess about how mad

Dad would be if he caught her, how badly she was getting along with him, or how worried she was about Thomas.

Kevin parked on the edge of the field below the bonfire. Half the kids from their high school were climbing out of cars and unloading beer coolers. Jane felt a jittery thrill letting Kevin take her hand for the walk up the hill. They left a trail of surprised teens in their wake. Nobody would ever have predicted them. She was the good girl, the too smart and therefore slightly strange girl, while he was infinitely cooler and certainly above caring about school. His dad owned the only local car dealership, which explained the string of cool cars he drove, and girls also seemed to come effortlessly to him. Everyone knew him or claimed to.

The raucous scene around the fire was his world much more than hers. He was greeted by all the people she'd never had a reason to talk to, while she knew the kids from her honors classes who understood what the solstice was and could explain to a visitor that this local version of the Midsummer celebration was started by the nineteenth-century Swedish settlers who established their town. Not that even the honors kids particularly cared. It was simply a solid excuse for a party in the woods.

She expected him to realize at any moment that he'd made a mistake. To preempt that, it was her idea as much as his to walk farther into the trees. The urgency and joy in their voices, their first kiss, her back pressed against a mossy trunk, and their giddy flaunting of fresh couplehood in front of the kids by the fire, all of it dripped with undiscerning magic.

Around three in the morning, he parked by the mailbox and walked with her as far as the hay shed. She floated over the last stretch of driveway alone and took off her boots to sneak up the stairs.

21

JANE TRIES TO HIDE HER nervous energy from her friends on the drive to Pueblo Nuevo the next afternoon, but when Rocío parks her Jeep in front of Tío Carlos's house, a shudder runs through her shoulders and Meghan notices. "You OK?"

Jane nods at Nayeli and Pablo's shack. "I can't imagine having to live like that."

"Well, cheer up. You're about to make their day."

Rocío and Jane show Meghan the best place to duck through the fence. Jane's wearing boots, so she's the one to push down the middle strand of wire while pulling up the top one.

The shack looks even worse. One wall has developed a pronounced bulge where a salvaged mattress frame is buckling. The still-bright shower curtain covering the doorway, which struck Jane as cheerful the first time she saw it, now just seems tawdry.

Jane wills Pablo to be out. She won't be able to hide her fear. Anger she can camouflage, but fear is transparent.

Meghan marches toward the shack.

Carmen's head pops out around the shower curtain. "Hola, señor-itas," she chirps as she steps into the sun.

Jane lets her breath out, unaware until that moment that she'd been holding it in.

Rocío gives Jane a sideways look before turning her attention to Carmen. "Buenas tardes, Doña. We have exciting news. Are your daughter and son-in-law still at work?"

Carmen calls to a small boy playing outside the partially finished but fully inhabited house next door. "Run to the brickyard, please. Tell Señora Nayeli to come quickly." The boy's plastic sandals slap the earth, trailing puffs of orange dust.

Carmen explains that it would be difficult to contact her son-in-law at the kilns, so perhaps it would be acceptable to just talk with her daughter and herself? Rocío agrees.

"Love those warrior princess cheekbones," says Meghan, indicating Nayeli, who approaches the group. Even in muddy work clothes, the woman is striking.

"Buenas tardes, Señora," Jane calls. "We're sorry to interrupt your work, but we have good news."

"Jane did it." Meghan blurts. "She found a big donor last night who gave half the money, just like that." She then looks sheepishly at Jane. "Sorry to steal your moment."

Nayeli looks to Jane, too.

"It's true, although really it was my friend Gabriela, and we still have to raise the rest, but I promise you we will. We can start building almost immediately, by mid-April."

Before Nayeli can respond, her mother speaks. "You women are a gift from God, an answer to our prayers."

The weight of the promise settles on Jane's shoulders through the featherlight touch of the old woman's palms. Rocío launches into construction details, such as the requirement that the family help dig the hole for the foundation and recruit friends for the day of the roof pour, when bucket after bucket of heavy wet concrete must be carried up a ramp. The neighbor boy runs giddy laps around the women, aware that something momentous is happening, and an underweight mutt joins the race, barking enthusiastically.

"Will this help convince Pablo to enroll your girls at Academia Cervantes?" Jane probes.

"Perhaps, I hope so." Nayeli's smile does not portray confidence.

Rocío helps. "You know, there's a Cervantes family with girls about the same age as yours who live right there in La Buena Vista."

The other women look where she points, toward the high wall around the impressive homes that are less than a kilometer but a world away. "They're lovely people. I bet they'd be willing to give Dulce and Lupita rides, and sometimes the scholarships cover not only tuition, but also uniforms, supplies, activities, and lunches, so it will probably cost less, actually, to attend Cervantes than you spend now on their public school."

Rocío's pitch works. Nayeli looks increasingly optimistic. "I'll talk with Pablo tonight," she promises. "He's going to be so surprised about the house."

"He didn't believe it would happen, did he?" Rocío's knowing grin is that of one wife to another.

Lying awake that night, Jane wonders if the family Rocío mentioned will actually agree to drive Dulce and Lupita to school every day. That's a huge commitment. They need a backup plan, like a transportation fund to take the city bus when necessary. Not that it will matter if Jane can't convince the scholarship committee to give them full rides. She and Rocío spoke today as though that were a near certainty when it is not. Even assuming she succeeds, how can the girls possibly fit in at Cervantes, despite Connor's innocent confidence? Some kids are always cruel.

Worse yet, what if she can't come up with the rest of the house money? The concert isn't going to happen for months. It may not ever happen. God, Kevin's right, she's intervening recklessly in these people's lives. Look at how many promises she's made. They will suffer if she can't deliver. If construction stops, they'll end up moving into the half-built house, rigging tarps over the top, and trying to eventually finish it themselves, but since they live hand-to-mouth, that could take the rest of their lives.

Well after midnight, anxious thoughts still chase each other. The only order Jane manages to sort them into is this: she promised to raise the money, so she will. She promised scholarships, so she'll do her best to make that happen, too, but then she has to disengage. She knows how fragile the trajectory of a child's life can be, and putting kids on a healthy path is everything, but she has gotten far too involved with this particular family and it's already backfired with brutal consequences.

Knock it off, Jane tells herself. *Focus on either getting the concert locked in as soon as possible or coming up with a better, faster idea.* Maybe she can talk the board into fronting the money, borrowing it from next year's budget, just until the concert money comes in. Probably not, with Bob holding so much sway, but it's worth a try. Or could she move her family's money around and somehow hide a missing five thousand dollars from Kevin for a few months, until she can replace it? No, impossible. Borrow from a friend? No. Her mother, a retired schoolteacher? Obviously not. Her brother, no.

Her brother. God, maybe that's what she's really doing here. Claiming a second, or third, chance. Trying to protect those girls since she failed him and may be letting down her own sons, too. But the one thing won't undo the others.

She tries again to empty her mind for sleep, but memories have started swirling of her brother and mistakes made long ago.

Things were so messed up. She shouldn't have to mother Thomas or cook and clean for Dad. She'd like to live in just one house and see her boyfriend every weekend, not every other. Jane told Kevin these things, the things she didn't tell anyone else, not her friends, not Mom, definitely not Dad, and not even Thomas. Kevin took her seriously.

She wasn't sure, however, why she told him about the bully on the bus grabbing her underwear when she was thirteen. It was such an embarrassing story, from two years ago. Those guys were his age. They were driving by this point, too old to ride the bus anymore, so it's not like it could happen again, but the day after she told him, he punched the ringleader and threatened the others anyway, behind the carpentry shop where no teachers would see. She'd never told Mom or Dad, and even if she had, they wouldn't have done anything about it. Kevin did something.

For good measure, he started driving out to the ranch every morning during Dad's weeks to take her and Thomas to school so she wouldn't have to ride the bus ever again. He parked by the mailbox at the end of their long driveway, so Dad never saw, and Thomas understood not to mention it. He loved riding in Kevin's car. It gave him street cred with the other seventh graders.

Jane told Kevin she was frustrated with Dad for being so distant and old-fashioned and going off on political rants some nights after a couple of whiskeys. She admitted to him that she didn't want to live with Dad anymore, that she resented Mom for putting her in this position, and that she worried about Thomas and what he would do without her if she stopped going to Dad's.

"Maybe he'll stop going, too, or maybe he'll be fine with your dad. You're not his mom, it's not up to you to solve this for him. He still has parents. He'll be OK."

Kevin's confidence was liberating. Mom and Thomas liked him. She was going to have to introduce him to Dad eventually.

Jane invited Kevin for a picnic at the ranch one Saturday when she knew Dad and Thomas would be away at a cattle auction. She offered to show him one of her forts.

She told him to park his car behind the tool shed at the edge of the forest, even though Dad wasn't home, just because it felt exciting. They hiked up the main trail, he carrying the picnic basket and a small backpack, she a couple of rolled-up blankets. They slowed at a sunny spot to pick ripe blackberries until their hands were full. He unzipped the outer pocket of the backpack, and they gently set the berries inside.

Ten minutes farther up the trail, Jane paused and patted the trunk of an alder. Then she stepped off into the underbrush. "This way."

"How do you know?"

Jane pointed to a small length of rope knotted around a low branch on the alder. Gray and frayed with time and rain, it still clung, serving its purpose. "I tied it there when I was ten."

Off the trail, it was slow going. She slipped carefully through the brush with hard-won skill, but he had to stop twice to untangle his legs. She used those moments to orient herself, as more than a year had passed since her last visit.

There it was. The summer she was ten and Thomas was seven, they had scavenged big chunks of broken lattice from Mom's vegetable garden and hung them between four almost perfectly spaced trees in the middle of an alder grove. Over the next two springs and summers, they trained woodbine vines to weave through the lattice. The vines had cooperated by growing in thickly. At this point, five years later, she wasn't sure whether the lattice still held up the vines or the vines supported the disintegrating lattice. Either way, the effect was magical. They had created living walls and a ceiling, an entire little room made of green leaves.

Kevin bent to peer inside, and Jane realized how important it was to her that he see the room as she did, as a work of art embraced by nature and therefore special, maybe sacred.

He straightened up and turned to her. "You built this? By yourself?"

"With Thomas. You don't believe me?"

"It's incredible, that's all. So beautiful. Like you."

He kissed her then.

They spread her blankets over the little plants and grasses that grew within the room. Light filtering through the vines and lattice created intricate shadows, patterns of natural lace, on the floor and on their bodies. Jane knelt to set out the picnic, first carefully retrieving the blackberries, but he stopped her. She looked down at his hand on her arm. Under the shadow lace, the simple intimacy of his fingers resting on her forearm became truly beautiful.

"Wait, I have something for you." From his backpack he pulled a book and opened it to extract a heavy piece of paper. "I drew it that first week. I've been waiting to show you."

Jane pulled her eyes from his to the paper and gasped. Accurately and evocatively rendered in charcoal, a hummingbird hovered over a blackberry blossom. "It's so good. You're crazy talented."

"Is it right, though? I looked up hummingbirds, and not many come this far north. This is the only kind that stay all year, apparently. Is that what you saw?"

"Yes, it's right. An Anna's Hummingbird. He was just like this."

The relief on Kevin's face revealed how important this was to him. "I have another one." He pulled a second paper from the book and pressed it into her hands, his eyes holding hers again. Finally, she remembered to look down.

He had drawn her. In the woods that day, sitting bareback. Perhaps it didn't exactly look like her, but she liked this version of herself. The girl on the horse was confident and brave. He'd given her extra curves, sure, but not to the extent of the comic book heroines that Thomas liked to draw. This girl looked beautiful, powerful, and real enough. Jane wanted to be her.

"This is how you see me?" She kissed him. Kevin pulled her against him, still kneeling. She drank in his desire and let it flow through her and mix with her own until her body pulsed with it. The slipping off of t-shirts and jeans was not as awkward as she had feared. His strong body, however, was exactly as she had imagined, or even better. She slid her hands over him, exploring. As he lay her on her back, her right hand grazed the pile of blackberries she'd unpacked. Jane pinched one, reached up, and pushed it between his lips. She tasted a hint of it a second later. Kevin took a couple berries in his own hands then. She was confused when he only brushed them across her lips. He continued down her neck and torso, leaving smears of blood red juice. He followed the trail with his mouth, until she felt as ripe as the berries. He lowered himself into her then, and she had no fear, only one brief moment of sharp pain, and the hunger still grew. They moved together until it was met.

Jane studied the quilt of leaves above them, grounding herself as her body still tingled and throbbed. She felt it had never been awake before.

On the hike back, she told Kevin she'd been warned that it usually wasn't good for the girl the first time, but it had been for her. He let out a whoop, threw his arms around her waist, and spun her around until they landed in a heap on the trail.

"Jane?"

She froze. "God, that's my dad. I guess you're meeting him now."

They climbed to their feet. Dad stood fifty yards below, peering up the trail, shading his eyes with a hand. Thomas hunched a few feet back, the reluctant accomplice.

"Hi Dad, it's me," she called.

They reached him. "And not just you, I see. Who's your friend?"

"This is Kevin."

Dad nodded. "Son, that's quite a car down there behind my tool shed."

"Yes, sir, thank you."

"We were just having a picnic—" Jane began.

"You might have asked permission before bringing boys into the woods."

"Dad."

"And clearly you understood that since you chose a time I would not be home. I'm disappointed, princess."

"Dad—"

"We will talk about this later."

Even as her conviction grew, Jane dreaded telling him, and she resented having to make the decision. Mom should have already done so in her and Thomas's best interests. But according to the law and her parents' agreement, she was old enough to decide for herself, so she was going to have to be the one to tell Dad that she wanted to live at Mom's full-time.

Gnawing self-doubt and fear for Thomas almost dissuaded her. Maybe this wasn't the right thing. Maybe she was a petty, short-sighted, selfish teenager who would regret this decision for the rest of her life. Maybe she shouldn't second guess Mom and Dad, who appeared to honestly believe that the alternating schedule was the best thing for their children.

The crux of the problem was leaving her little brother behind. If she couldn't convince him to come with her, how would he get through Dad's weeks without her? He and Dad would sit in silence every night, just the two of them, and the kid would bear alone the concentrated weight of Dad's anger and loneliness. Her brother would have to tiptoe around her name, or maybe he and Dad would talk openly about how awful she was to leave them. She feared Thomas would blame her the way Dad blamed Mom.

She had to convince him to come. "Want to walk to the hay shed?"

They started down the driveway. "What's going on? I know something's going on."

"You're right. I think we should stay at Mom's all the time, at least for a while."

He didn't ask why. "No. Can't leave Dad by himself."

Jane stopped walking and put her hands on his shoulders. "It's not our job to take care of him. He's the parent, not you and not me."

"But he needs us." Thomas shook off her hands. "Maybe he'll pay more attention to me."

"I don't know. I'm afraid he'll always be distracted by whatever has to be done on the ranch or by stupid politics, and I don't think anything we do will ever change him."

"Maybe."

"Please come with me. It's better at Mom's."

"No."

"I can't leave you behind—"

"Then don't go."

This degree of defiance surprised Jane. "Are you mad at me?"

Thomas finally looked at her. "Actually, yeah."

"I'm sorry, I have to do this." She hugged him hard. "You don't have to keep coming out here, either. You can—"

He pushed her back. "Yes, I do."

"Then I promise I'll make sure you're OK."

He was rightly skeptical. "How exactly, if you're not here?"

"I don't know, somehow—no, you're right, it won't work, so just come with me."

"I can't."

"Thomas, yes, you can."

"No."

Jane tried over and over to convince him. Did he really think he'd be ok out there without her? Didn't he understand how much she'd been doing to take care of him? Although she understood his wish for more of Dad's attention, she didn't believe he'd ever get it, so his loyalty to Dad mystified her. He would be left alone often and probably have to take over her chores. He would have to make his own lunches and many dinners and be the only audience for Dad's rants.

Jane didn't understand why Mom wouldn't help her convince him. Mom said they had to respect the custody agreement unless Thomas decided for himself to ask for a change. Jane disagreed. Sometimes, she argued, we have to stand up for people who can't yet stand up for themselves. Neither Mom nor Thomas listened to her. In the end, her frustration with Thomas's stubbornness made it easier to push down her guilt at leaving him behind to fend for himself.

Telling Dad she was leaving was even worse. She didn't mean to, but she crushed him, her big, tough, invincible father. Then she had to watch as his pain congealed into disappointment in her.

Weeks later, when Dad sold her horse, Jane tipped from guilt to anger. She felt free of him then and his farm chores, his kitchen, his awkward silences, his tirades, his control.

At Mom's house, sprawled on the sofa together, Kevin made her feel better. "You're doing the right thing. Here, you have more time to study, you big nerd."

"True." Jane curled more tightly into him.

"And time for the most important thing in your life, me. We'll get out of this hick town and go places, you and me. You'll be something smart, like a doctor."

She propped herself up on one elbow to look at him. "Lawyer."

Kevin grinned. "See, you already know."

She grinned back. "And you'll be a movie star?"

"What, don't think I'm pretty enough?" His flirty tone covered something else.

"Oh, you're pretty enough." Jane ran her hand around the back of Kevin's neck and pulled him toward her to feel his lips on hers.

"So a movie star." He looked at her hopefully. "Or an artist."

So that was it. "An artist, yes. You're so talented. You probably need to start taking grades a little bit seriously, though, don't you, to get into art school?"

"Too late. My folks worry I'll never make a living that way anyway. So movie star it is."

"Solid plan. If they're worried about you being an artist, I'm sure they'll consider making movies a much more reasonable option."

"What they really want is for me to stay and take over their car dealership, but that is not going to happen. So Wall Street, maybe. A guy needs more balls than brains there, right?"

"You've got both."

"Don't tell anyone or you'll ruin the low expectations I enjoy."

"I have high expectations. You'll be an artist."

He pulled her closer and his tone grew serious. "I know that was hard, but you did the right thing, and Thomas will be fine."

JANE ARRIVES AT SCHOOL ONE afternoon a few days after the art auction to pick up her boys from Survival Club, their favorite extracurricular. A grinning Liam runs up to her to offer a clump of tiny legs and torsos in his palm. "Here Mom, try some chapulines."

She pulls her lips into a semblance of a casual smile, reaches out, and scoops up a few of the small bodies from his hand. Intense April sun roasts her skin, and her stomach pulls in on itself, already rebelling. She tries to think of something else, such as the child before her, filthy from Survival Club exploits, proudly sharing his snack, or the fact that soon, in June, the rainy season will begin, cooling things down. That will be nice. Slowly she raises her hand to her mouth, sliding as many of the chapulines as she can into hiding under three folded fingers, allowing only a couple to pass between her lips. Her teeth close on their unwanted prey with a disturbing crunch. Her mouth has gone completely dry, but mercifully she tastes only chili and salt, nothing overtly meaty or otherwise obvious as grasshopper. She forces herself to chew and swallow. Legs stick in her throat.

"Cool, Mom," says Liam, making it all worth it. "Want some more? Coach gave us lots."

"They're good. Crunchy. But no, that's OK, honey, they're your treat. Now you two can survive in the jungle on bugs and rainwater if you have to."

"Like Bear Grylls."

"Bear who?"

Connor joins them. "Grylls, Mom. He's this amazing survival guy with his own TV show. Coach showed us a video. They drop him off in the jungle on a deserted island or whatever, with only a knife, and he has to survive all by himself."

"But with a TV crew?"

"Don't ruin it."

Jane half-listens to her sons' glowing descriptions of the man's exploits, which continue for much of the walk home. She is proud of them for not being squeamish about the grasshoppers and chalks it up as another Mexican win, right up there with their Tolantongo trip a few months back when she and her boys climbed in semidarkness, because nobody but Coach had thought to bring a headlamp, through waist-deep water and over piles of slippery boulders to reach the back of a long, narrow cave. It felt like they were tunneling to the center of the Earth. Connor and Liam were fearless while she was terrified that one of them would crack his head open on the slick rocks. They all made it out with no more than a few scrapes, and the boys loved it.

Motherhood is a series of gambles anywhere, and motherhood in Mexico, in her experience, means higher stakes. Her sons regularly receive opportunities that they wouldn't in the U.S., either because the cost would be prohibitive or the safety regulations more strictly enforced.

Jane thinks of the time they hiked through a forest near Xilitla to see the Sótano de las Golondrinas, the world's second largest sinkhole. The entire Empire State Building could fit inside. Tens of thousands of swallows arrive there each evening at dusk. Hundreds swoop out of the sky every second in a high-speed aerial ballet and dive-bomb into the hole to roost for the night.

The natural spectacle was mesmerizing enough, but Liam immediately spotted the guy taking tips to tie a rope around people's torsos and hang them over the edge. The other end of the rope was tied around a big rock, and the man fed it out slowly as her child approached the edge. He instructed Liam to sit on the lip, lean forward, and hang.

Jane crawled toward the drop-off for a photo. The man told her to lie on her stomach and wiggle forward like a snake the last few inches. When her head cleared the edge and she looked straight down into the abyss, her body went rigid with fear. She couldn't see the bottom thousands of feet below in murky shadows. Her hands shook, but her iPhone met the challenge, capturing stark images of her baby hanging over nothingness, surrounded by streaks of diving swallows. By the time it was Connor's turn, her heartbeat had slowed and her hands were steadier.

After some years in Mexico so full of exposures to natural wonders as well as cultural events covering the spectrum from homespun to elegant to surreal, her boys should be able to handle any weird thing the world throws at them. Even if as adults they're only half as up for adventure as they are now.

God, she would extend their childhood a few years if she could. There's so much more they should see, but she doesn't have the time or money to show them enough of the magic in the world—and were she to leave Kevin, she would have much less of both. She wants to spend every minute she can building them up before they go out on their own. Her sons have to have more resources than Thomas did when they inevitably face the world's dangers.

Thomas kept slipping through the cracks of her parents' lives into a small-town trough of alcohol and then drugs, but Mom and Dad refused to see it. At Mom's house, he'd sneak out at night and often go back to bed after Mom left for work in the morning, and the school only sometimes managed to report his absence. Jane had no idea anymore what he did at Dad's house.

She heard scary rumors about him, that he'd been partying with wild older kids. Kids who stole things, like car stereos, and then sold them. Kids who as often as not didn't show up at school. Jane felt her brother slipping away.

She needed to share the blame. "Thomas is not fine! You told me he'd be fine."

"How is this my fault?" Kevin shrugged.

"It's not, it's mine. I left him."

"No. He makes his own choices."

"He's still just a kid."

"Well, he's almost an adult."

"Kev, I have to help him."

"How?"

At first, whenever she tried to talk to Thomas about any of it, he offered breezy reassurances and non-answers. Later, the denials her sweet, smart little brother gave her turned ugly. He said he'd never speak to her again if she ratted him out one more time to either of their parents.

Kevin knew much more about that world than she did. He took her to the right parties to drag Thomas home a few times, but it never made an impact. Thomas just shrugged them off.

"Get it together," Kevin would say to him. "Don't you want to get out of here and go somewhere interesting? *Be* someone interesting?"

"Sure, Kev, I'm getting out." Her brother laughed at them. "Nobody gets out."

Jane and Kevin were getting out.

"What's the opposite of here?" He asked her late one night after they'd tried and failed to bring Thomas home.

She took the question as seriously as he intended it. "New York City."

"New York then." He pulled her close.

"I think it's the best place for you to be an artist. Law school for me. But what about your parents?"

"I know, you've heard them go on about me running the dealership, but that's not me. Stuck here forever, selling cars my entire life? Screw that."

"They'll hate me for stealing you away."

"They can't blame you. I mean, sure, I'm going wherever you're going, but I was already getting out of here no matter what. They'll accept it eventually."

At bedtime, after the boys have washed away Survival Club grime and regaled their father over dinner with Bear Grylls's exploits, and after they've curled up with Jane to begin the next Harry Potter, she brings out her painting of the three of them. "What do you think?"

"It's good, Mom," says Liam. "I like it."

Connor is less certain. "Isn't it a little messy, though? We're sort of blurry. Your old paintings were clearer, you know, sharper. This isn't done, is it?"

"It's almost done. You're absolutely right, the old ones were sharper, but I'm trying this new style now, and it's more exciting, I think." Jane tries another angle. "My teacher reminded me that modern art developed at least partially in response to the invention of the camera. Painters used to make portraits as realistic as possible, but then cameras were invented, and since they're better at capturing reality, fewer people were willing to pay a lot of money for a painted portrait. So artists had to get creative to attract patrons. At least that's a piece of the story."

"Now you're getting more creative, too." Connor's approval is sparing, but it is enough.

"That's the idea. I hope at least some people will agree and want to buy my new work."

"This one of us?" he asks.

"No, this one's for us to keep. I mean other new paintings in my new style."

"But Mom?" Now Liam looks concerned. "Aren't you going to add Dad?"

She gives him the answer he wants, "Sure, honey," and hugs them both goodnight, thinking about the fact that she hasn't yet confronted her husband over his confessions to Meghan at the bar. As much as she would like to know what he thought he was doing, she should probably bite her tongue. Bringing it up seems much more likely to cause a fight than a breakthrough. She has to find some way to reconnect with him, but that is not it. Better to keep the peace for the boys' sake, although she likes the painting the way it is.

THE EVER-PRESENT SYMPHONY OF CHILDHOOD noises has gone silent. When her sons aren't in their rooms, the living room, or the patio, Jane's curiosity ripens into fear. She climbs the stairs to the roof.

Two faces etched with shock stare up at her. They've pulled out all of her hidden paintings, now strewn over the tile floor. She instantly wants to take it all back, to blot each of the ugly scenes from their memories. "Boys, no, why did you get into my things—?"

Liam lowers his eyes in guilt and confusion. "We were looking for something."

"We wanted to make art." Connor's reaction is closer to anger. "What are these even about?"

"I didn't want you to see them, not yet. They're not done. I know they're scary. I've been painting monsters, too, like that comic book artist you like."

"Why is this one all green?"

"I'm playing with color. Green can be powerful and pretty."

"That is not pretty." Connor points to a painting in which a man strikes a woman and then to another in which the woman's booted foot rests on the man's neck.

"I know." Jane pulls her sons into her arms, feeling sick at her own carelessness. She holds them quietly for a long moment. Then she lets them go and starts picking the canvases off the floor while weighing her next words.

Kevin appears in the doorway. His eyes sweep from the boys'

faces to the paintings in her arms to those still on the floor. "What the hell? What lies, what is this garbage? So this is what you've been doing at night for hours on end?"

"Let's talk later."

"Like you're worried about what they see." He turns around, but not without shooting a venomous look over his shoulder, and marches down with such heavy steps that she expects the stairs to show permanent footprints.

"Dad?" calls Liam, but it comes out too softly.

"Boys, don't worry." She gathers them into another hug. They pull away.

"We're going down now, OK, Mom?"

The soft slaps of their footsteps recede. Of course he didn't like the paintings. He was caught off guard and had a right to be angry, but he could have handled it so much better for the kids' sake. He shouldn't have given them the message that they should be frightened, that she'd done something wrong. He could have assuaged their fears instead of intensifying them.

Maybe that's too much emotional control to expect from anyone in the moment. She should have hidden the canvases better or not have painted them in the first place. But she needed to. They are her best work. Not here, though, not in the house where her children could find them. Now she has to somehow make it right with the boys as well as deal with Kevin's anger. What will be the half-life of this transgression?

It takes three trips to move the paintings to her room. Jane removes her shoes from her closet, leans the canvases against the back wall behind her clothes, and then returns the shoes to the closet floor. While making dinner, she thinks about how to undo the stricken looks on her sons' faces. Distracted, she overcooks the pork chops. At the table, Jane tries but fails to engage her subdued children in something approximating their normal chatter. The meal becomes a miserable ten minutes of conversationless chewing while looking at her plate to avoid Kevin's accusatory glares and the fight he's primed for.

After dinner, she watches for a chance to talk with the boys, but Kevin hovers, so it doesn't happen until bedtime. Liam comes out of the bathroom in Transformers pajamas, face still flushed from the shower. He climbs onto his bed, where she just sat down, and curls into her.

"You guys OK?"

Connor doesn't look up. "Sure," he says, still taking apart a Lego rocket.

"Daddy said—" Liam begins, but Connor shifts his gaze to stare down his brother.

"What did Daddy say?" she asks gently.

"Nothing," Liam mumbles.

"Oh." She takes a deep breath. "Guys, I'm sorry my paintings scared you. I know they're creepy. They're not meant for kids."

"Why did you make them?" asks Connor.

"Well, for me, when I'm upset, a good way to feel better is to get my bad feelings out by painting them."

"What bad feelings?"

"I was angry that sometimes people hurt each other."

"That man who hit his wife the night you didn't come home," says Connor.

"Yes, exactly. I painted them. Well, I changed them according to my imagination, but the point is that my anger came out through the paint. Now I feel better."

"That's good."

Connor allows her to hold him tightly for a long time. Only when his body and his brother's relax into sleep does Jane let go. She's relieved that they have forgiven her, but she can't stop wondering what Daddy said.

Kevin finds her in the kitchen while she's putting water on to boil for tea. "How could you make them think I hit you? They shouldn't see that shit. I had to tell them you're a liar."

"How could you do that? I'm not a liar. The physical ones are

Pablo and Nayeli, not us. I told them they're all Pablo and Nayeli. They weren't meant to see anyway, the paintings were hidden."

"Not well enough, obviously. What did you expect? They're kids, they get into shit."

"I know, I'm sorry. But why would you leap to the conclusion that I painted you hitting me? You couldn't even ask me first before telling them something so vile?"

"You sure seem to want to give the world that impression."

"No, why would I?" The kettle starts to whistle. She turns off the gas, but a shrill sigh lingers as though the pot is angry with her, too, for not immediately pouring out a cup. "You do scare me sometimes, though. You seem no closer to forgiving me now than you were a year ago, and your rage, it feels like it's actually growing." She tosses onto the counter the towel she'd been holding at the ready because the old handle gets too hot.

"Don't even try. I am not the problem here. You were so wrong to paint that trash."

"It's not—why did you have to make things worse? You could have been reassuring and calm, but no, you tell them something horrible and totally untrue."

"Was it?" He absently picks up the towel and pulls it taut between his fists.

"That's what you warned them not to tell me, isn't it? That you called me a liar, that you said I was painting lies of you hitting me? What the fuck? That's so damaging—"

"I'm damaging? You're damaging." His hands twist the towel as though to wring out water, but it's bone dry. "And you call that art? That shit so violent it's hard to look at?"

"Yes. Art. I had to get Pablo and Nayeli out of my head. And you, out of my head."

He plays his trump card. "You saw the horrified looks on our sons' faces when they saw your 'art'?"

"I saw their faces, and their fear destroyed me. But you accusing me of lies—"

"That's the problem, is it, my imperfect reaction to the shit you do? No way, this is on you." Kevin stabs his finger in her direction, throws the towel back onto the counter, and walks out of the room.

Jane wonders when exactly, over the course of so many years, she should have known better, when she should have understood and had the strength to go. Should she never have married him in the first place? Or have been smart enough to leave before kids? She was in love and had so much will to make it work. Which only led here to the brink of divorce with her children at risk. Half their lives could slip from her control, and then anything could happen to them, like Thomas, outside of her protection. She won't let that happen. She won't fail them.

WHEN JANE MEETS GABRIELA AND Meghan for coffee, she knows a quick, cheerful catch-up is the communal expectation. But five minutes in, she tells her friends about her paintings, her boys' shock, and Kevin's ugly response.

"Before, I might have said he just really overreacted in the moment." Meghan pauses, wrestling with something. "But he was so strange the other night at the bar."

Jane meets Meghan's eyes. "I know. I heard part of what he said to you, and it was some serious oversharing. I'm afraid to imagine what else he told you."

Gabriela pushes back her chair. "It's such a beautiful day, how about a walk in the park?"

Meghan's look is quizzical. "Here they're all beautiful days. That's kind of the point."

"Especially today." Gabriela sweeps her eyes around the cozy café. Every other table is within hearing range.

The women pay for their coffee at the counter and step out onto the cobblestones. As they stroll a few blocks toward Parque Juárez, saying good morning to people they pass on the narrow sidewalks, Gabriela chatters about her son's school project and guitar lessons. Meghan follows suit, leaving Jane free to nod along.

When they reach the park, Gabriela leads the way to a secluded bench where a pattering fountain further shields their conversation. "Sorry to be dramatic." She sits. "But you guys know what a small town this is."

"You're right. I really shouldn't have been venting back there. And Meghan, I'm sorry. I should have rescued you that night and called you the next day. I didn't out of sheer embarrassment."

Meghan waves off the apology. "It's fine, stop. I'm worried about you, though."

Jane is embarrassed, but now that they're having the conversation, she will not wimp out. "So what did he tell you, besides the part I heard about me outgrowing him?"

"The whole thing was so awkward. Out of nowhere, on the wings of his second or third paloma, he started talking about how you basically grew up together, he still loves you, and he fears that 'what was passion for him was only security for you.'"

"I know that theory, I've heard it. But why tell you, of all people?"

"I don't know." Meghan looks thoughtful. "He didn't ask me to do anything, but maybe he was working up to it. Has he done this before?"

"Poured out his sob story to my girlfriends? God no, not that I'm aware of, anyway."

Gabriela puts words to the question forming in Jane's mind. "I wonder if he thought that as your friend Meghan could somehow fix something."

"At first I didn't really mind," Meghan continues. "He was a little drunk and moody, oversharing, but no big deal. He was kind of sweet, honestly, right up until he wasn't."

Jane nods. "I think I saw that moment."

"That's when I caught a scary glimpse beneath his pretty surface. He was half turned away, staring at where you'd been sitting with Gaby. He probably thought I couldn't see his eyes then, but he looked like he could kill somebody. I know I flinched." A shiver plays through Meghan's shoulders. "This was like two seconds after sounding all sad and nostalgic, so it made me feel manipulated."

"Yeah, he can be manipulative. I'm sorry. And embarrassed that you got stuck with him."

"Jane, don't be. This is on him. But are you all right? It was a scary vibe."

"You have no idea."

"Buenos días, doña." Gabriela greets an older woman who walks past the fountain with a tiny but supremely fluffy dog trailing her. Then she turns sharply toward Jane. "Do you mean he hurts you? Is that why you painted those scenes?"

"No, I swear. He'd kill me—metaphorically—if he thought you believed that. He's angry and depressed for sure, but no, he doesn't hit. That was someone else."

"What are you talking about? Who?"

"I shouldn't be telling you. You have to promise you won't tell anyone. It's a long story and a really shitty one."

"Tell it."

So she does. While squeals carry from the playground and people walk their dogs along the park's shaded paths, Jane tells Gabriela and Meghan about that night and its aftermath. She describes what she witnessed and why she stayed. She admits that given everything that happened and how useless she was, a part of her wishes she had simply ignored the sickening noises. She could have kept walking, climbed in her car, and driven away. Or not have shown up in the first place—then it wouldn't have happened at all.

"Don't you dare blame yourself for that asshole's violence." Gabriela is vehement in her conviction. "You had good intentions. You were trying to help. What happened is not your fault."

"My good intentions and that woman's trust in me got her beaten." Jane continues by reporting that Kevin didn't cover for her with their scared sons. Finally, while staring at a brittle, graying leaf on the ground instead of meeting her friends' eyes, she tells them how he reacted when she got home.

"Oh my God." Gabriela sounds frightened. "I had no idea he was like that."

"I never let you have any idea, you or anyone else."

"You swear he's never hit you? He's not like that other creep?" demands Meghan. "Whom we technically, you know, should not be giving a house to."

"I know. Please don't tell Rocío or anyone else. I can't ruin things more for those girls. And no, like I said, Kevin's never hit me." She pauses. What do they think of her now? But humiliation is outmatched by relief, so the admissions keep coming. "He's so angry and insanely negative in private, but he fools everyone by acting normal in public."

"Normal?" Meghan looks disgusted. "Not the other night, he wasn't."

"Right, but usually. Meanwhile I have to be on guard all the time. Sometimes he makes me feel like I'm going crazy, and I'm always trying to hide the drama from the kids—"

"Why do you stay?" Meghan wonders.

"For them, and to be completely honest, for all the good things I wouldn't have time or money for if he weren't taking care of us financially. But mostly because divorcing him would be far worse, trust me."

"Jane—" Gabriela tries.

"I truly loved him in the beginning. It dissolved slowly at first, like when those tiny insects eat your old furniture from the inside out but you don't notice until it's too late. I suppose he's right about what I think, what he told you at the bar, that I believe I've outgrown him. I don't know, sometimes people just become not enough anymore. My career became important, then my kids even more so. He wasn't my hero anymore, he was less and less of my world, and then there was this guy at work—"

"Did you?"

"Cheat? Physically no, but emotionally, I guess. David cared about what I cared about. I was obsessed with a case, and so was he, so we spent a lot of time together."

"Ah, he was your work husband. Not a sex thing?"

"No. But Kevin doesn't believe me. It would have been easy to fall into, but I didn't. I've denied it a thousand times. Sometimes when he's being horrible, I almost wish I had."

"So that's where the controlling and what sounds like a little gaslighting come from. He feels he needs to keep you in check," Meghan concludes.

"And how do you prove the negative?" Gabriela asks.

"Exactly, and I shouldn't have to. A little honesty about the problems we had long before David would have helped, too. David was just a symptom, not the root of anything."

"And now? Sorry for asking, but are you guys still—?" Meghan asks.

"Having sex? No, well, rarely. Only a couple times in the last year, after big parties when I got drunk enough to remember how attracted to him I used to be. We had a good sex life, but we've had separate bedrooms practically since we moved here, after a failed attempt at marriage counseling. I told our boys it's because he snores like a freight train, which is true but trivial."

"He's a frustrated ticking time bomb." Fear tinges Meghan's voice. "He could blow up your life."

Yes, he could. "My poor boys. I wonder if they'll be able to have healthy relationships." Jane jabs a knuckle at a tear that had the nerve to escape her eye. "And don't just tell me kids are resilient. This has to be doing real damage, and he takes on about as much responsibility as guilt: none."

"Jane, you should leave him." Gabriela's words form a directive, not a question.

"I think I never should have married him in the first place. He should have just been my high school boyfriend who helped me through my parents' divorce. Why have I stayed so long, convincing myself that everything was fine, or if not fine, normal? The more years I invested, the more horrifying it became to admit I was wrong, so I just kept going."

"We do that." Gabriela nods. "Telling ourselves we're doing the right thing by making the best of a less-than-ideal situation, because how many people get dealt ideal situations?"

"Over time he sensed my ambivalence. That festered, of course. I created the monster."

"No, you didn't. He could have left, or gone to counseling, or done something, anything, rather than become such a bully." Meghan's eyes gleam with anger, but when her hand squeezes Jane's shoulder it does so exceedingly gently.

"Jane." Gabriela waits until she looks up. "It's time to stop pretending it'll get better."

"I know, you're right—except for the vicious custody battle he threatened. I can't put my kids through that, and I'm not losing them. I know how bad this is, but the alternative of him using some nasty maneuver to win custody would be worse. When he found out about David, before we decided to fix things by moving here—which has worked out so well—he threatened to do whatever it takes. He brings it up again sometimes when he's angry enough."

"Sshh." Gabriela scans the paths nearest them.

"So what will you do?" Meghan holds Jane's eyes. "We're worried about you. You're going to stay in this godawful marriage? Liam's eight—so ten more years of this?"

Shaken by her friends' horrified expressions, Jane regrets sharing so much. Would she be as supportive in their place, or would she resist getting involved in someone's mess? To Gabriela and Meghan's confusion, she suddenly gasps and begins to laugh. It's not a hypothetical question. Here she is in Nayeli's life, interfering on behalf of the girls' education and the house, but the abuse Nayeli endured is the one thing she's not addressing, despite having her own eyes as witnesses. To smother her shame, Jane tells herself that she would help if Nayeli asked her to, but Nayeli never will.

Jane looks at her friends' unsettled faces. "I don't have a choice."

"Yes," Meghan insists, "you do."

"I don't because I'm not risking my kids."

Gabriela squeezes Jane's hand. "I hate that I never saw this."

"I didn't want anyone to know."

"Well, I'm still an idiot. In retrospect, I think Lindsay saw more."

"Maybe. She took me to see her bruja."

"And you know what?" Meghan interjects. "I caught Javier,

of all people, looking at you strangely a couple times, but I didn't understand."

"Yeah, he asked me the other day if I was doing OK."

"What did you say?"

"That I was a little tired but everything's fine. If anyone asks, everything's fine."

"If that's what you need." Gabriela's worry warps her face, and Jane suffers a stab of guilt for her unworthy bargain. All her venting has provided only minimal and certainly temporary relief, while her friends can't ever unknow what she told them.

"For now, fine," Meghan agrees. "But ten more years of this, you can't be serious."

Will it be easier or harder now that they know the truth? Jane doesn't have to pretend everything's fine anymore, nor *can* she now. As often as the pretending made her feel trapped or crazy, going through the motions of being part of a normal couple sometimes provided comfort.

Something occurs to her. "Could I keep those paintings at your place, Gaby? I'm afraid he'll find and destroy them before I can decide for myself whether to paint over them."

"Of course, and don't paint over them, I'm sure they're amazing." Gabriela wraps a warm arm around Jane's shoulders. "You know you can always stay with me, whatever you need."

"Same here." Meghan's body radiates a fierce, protective anger.

Guilt tugs again at Jane for burdening her friends this way. "I know, thank you. For the offer, for listening to all of this, everything."

Meghan and Gabriela offer uncertain reassurances. The three women get up from the bench, each one trying to look normal and failing.

Jane gets through the rest of the day and goes to bed early, but sleep evades her. She can't stop seeing her friends' fear. Well past midnight, exhaustion finally wins.

From her garden, Jane climbs a silvery ladder up, up, over lush boughs of bougainvillea, luxuriant rosemary, deep cups of calla lilies, and stands of blood-red cana in full flower. Up, through cotton-candy clouds. She reaches out and runs her fingers through the froth, grasping the ladder with only her toes curled over one rung and the fingertips of one hand oh-so-lightly touching another.

She maintains the slenderest of connections as though she has no need of support, as though she could step off onto the clouds themselves and stroll away. Jane arches back. Her spine is made of plastilina, clay so soft only a child would sculpt it. She looks straight up at the universe above her, then directly behind herself. She bends back farther, farther.

Then she is falling.

Disoriented in the dark, to Jane the vertigo feels real.

She stands on the now-familiar ladder watching two hummingbirds dance in flits and darts and blurred wingbeats. The brown one suddenly falls out of the sky, dropping straight down with incredible speed. Her wings must no longer work. Jane grows furious at the green one who appears oblivious, or worse, unbothered. She remembers reading with her sons that hummingbirds do not mate for life. Far from it. They join for a few seconds, and then the female does all the nest-building, incubating, and caring for the babies while the male looks for more females.

But right before she would slam into the ground, the brown one's wings flap intensely. She hovers just above the earth in front of an old woman who stares, awestruck. What does the woman see in her, a message from a husband, parent, or God forbid, a child?

The green one had no cause for worry.

25

JANE DOESN'T MEAN TO EAVESDROP, but the changing room at the yoga studio is tiny, and when she enters it, she can't avoid hearing Meghan's half of the conversation, as well as some of the words coming out of Meghan's phone.

"It's been three days, I don't understand, wouldn't you want everyone to know?" Meghan asks. "Right, broad daylight, horrible—hi Jane, I'm talking about Vero, it's so awful."

"What? Which Vero?"

"You haven't heard? Kidnapped—look, I'll call you back, ciao—Verónica González. You know, she has a son in fifth grade, and she owns that terraza bar you like."

"No, I don't know her." Jane feels relief along with horror. "How?"

"They forced her car off the road on the Carretera a Dolores. She lives out that way, a hacienda-style place in the countryside. Took her and left her son in the car on the side of the road."

"Oh my God." Jane imagines the boy huddled alone, in shock, in the car. She hopes it wasn't long before someone found him. She has a sudden memory of a lonely girl on a park bench. A girl she failed to help.

More women, including Gabriela, enter the dressing room and catch the gist of the conversation. "What are they doing about it?" "Do they know who took her?" "Why?"

"They were targeted for their wealth, presumably," Gabriela answers. "They own restaurants here, bars in Los Cabos, and I don't know what else. Family money."

"You've seen that car she drives," someone says. "Too flashy."

"I know, the car. But Vero's not like that," Gabriela insists. "She's laid-back and a good mom."

"So what's being done?"

"The husband and their friends have asked everyone to be hush-hush, which doesn't make sense to me. Shouldn't we all be outraged?" Meghan certainly looks the part.

"Yes, but the family know what they're doing. They're trying to protect her." Gabriela sighs. "Word will get out anyway. In this town, of course it will."

Another woman speaks up. "My husband was called into security meetings. They're working on it. We'll have roadblocks and guards at the school for a while."

That's the last thing Jane wants.

They finish their breathing exercises and move into sun salutations. The older kids at school must know by now, but maybe the little ones don't. Jane would prefer that Connor and Liam never find out, that they never have that kind of fear introduced into their lives. Surviving their own parents' failings should be more than enough of a burden for any child to bear.

The teacher seems to be rushing them through the poses too quickly today. Maybe it's the news, or maybe she's still riding the high of her recent stint in India where she lived on lentils for three weeks and did five hours of yoga a day. She looks great, though.

Jane would like to wait until Verónica's been rescued to tell her sons anything if she has to tell them at all. But no, the way rumors fly, she'd better sit them down tonight. They should hear a calm version of the truth from her before inevitable exaggerations spread on the playground.

Jane lies back in shavasana and wonders whether the woman will ever come home.

Sitting with her Spanish teacher a couple hours later, Jane comments on the news that has everyone rattled.

María Fernanda shakes her head. "Tell your friends not to worry. This is not a problem for everyone. This is very specific. When you are as wealthy as that family, you have many business dealings. Some of them are with people who do not like to lose." She says the family has certain business connections in Michoacán. She's too polite to spell it out, but the subtext is obvious. One of Mexico's deadliest drug cartels is based there.

"Verónica and her family went away last year, out of México," María Fernanda continues. "They must have had something to fear." She clearly sees this as further evidence of shady deals gone bad, nothing that should scare anyone else, as awful as it is.

The next afternoon, over a quick lunch before pick-up, Jane shares María Fernanda's suspicions with Gabriela and Meghan, which help to assuage their fears and have the added benefit of distracting her friends from her own problems that she's increasingly embarrassed to have revealed.

"It never happens to Americans or Europeans," says Meghan.

Jane pauses with her fork poised over her citrus salad. "Except for that American guy who disappeared a couple years ago. They found his body in some sleazy hotel in Acapulco, remember?"

"But they proved he was working for a cartel, right?"

"Yes." Gabriela nods.

"Kidnapping is never supposed to happen in San Miguel because tourism is too important here," says Meghan.

"You're spinning, girl," says Jane.

"Yep, chasing my own logic, trying to convince myself—"

Jane finishes the sentence. "That we're not crazy to be here. Well, we're not. This is awful, but in terms of murder rates, probably kidnapping, too, and crime in general, San Miguel's safer than New York, Washington, Chicago, LA, lots of places." She waves her hands, and the fork, to indicate not just the pretty sidewalk café where they sit but also the tranquil street beside them and the whole city. "At least our kids don't need to do active shooter drills," she adds, then finally lowers her fork to spear a chunk of grapefruit with more force than necessary.

"True," Meghan agrees. "The news back home has my family convinced that we live in a war zone, but that's so wrong. Usually. How are we supposed to raise children anywhere these days without fear?"

"Who's ever been able to do that, honestly?" Jane shrugs.

"Well, I grew up here without fear." Gabriela sets down her own fork. "We played in the streets. We were free all day long in the summer, going from house to house or wherever we wanted. As ten-year-olds, we'd walk out to the club to go swimming."

"Malanquín? That's a couple miles."

"A little farther, I think. At least five kilometers. Our parents just told us to come home by bedtime. Everyone knew everybody else, so it was safe."

"Was it, though?" Jane probes. "That sounds wonderful, like an even better Mexican version of my mom's 1950s suburban American childhood, roaming the neighborhood with a pack of kids. But bad things did happen when they were unsupervised. You know, dirty uncles, that kind of thing. They just didn't talk about it back then."

"I suppose we must have had a little of that here, too, even then, but it's really different now, with so many more people and all these new things to be afraid of. I'd never let ten-year-olds walk that far by themselves today, no way."

"I know what you mean," says Meghan.

Jane shakes her head. "I actually don't think the world is that much more dangerous now. I think it always was, we're just more aware."

"I don't know," says Gabriela. "It felt safe back then, and having that freedom made us capable and confident. Maybe a touch of willful ignorance was a good thing. I'd take my son back to that time if I could."

ON THE SIDEWALK AND STONE steps in front of a small chapel, several dozen mostly upper-class Mexican women, a sprinkling of foreign women, and a few men gather. As Jane approaches the group, she first runs into Araceli and Javier and then spots Lindsay, Gabriela, Meghan, and other friends, all wearing white as instructed. She hears several people commenting to each other about the threatening clouds overhead. Rain would be strange at this point in the spring. Rainy season doesn't begin until June.

The organizers line them up in pairs, hand out candles, and remind everyone to be silent for maximum effect. Jane thinks of Verónica, the kidnapped woman for whom they will march. She clings to Gabriela's reassurances that women kidnapped in these circumstances are sometimes treated reasonably well and tries not to envision the stories of brutality they've all heard. Those horrors are for rival cartel members and the brave journalists who cover them, and sometimes, nightmarishly, for migrants already suffering every sort of deprivation. Despite María Fernanda's suggestion that Verónica's family is connected to narcos, most people seem to believe, or at least to say, that she was kidnapped simply for money, and that kind of kidnapper wants victims' families to trust that if they keep quiet and pay, the hostage will be returned alive, relatively unharmed.

Jane looks up as they turn a corner. A dramatic double line of white-clad figures with wobbling candles stretches out in front of her in the cloud-shrouded dusk. She feels growlingly irritated at the few participants who didn't bother to wear white, spoiling the effect. They march another block and another, while drivers wait patiently.

Her phone breaks the silence. She fishes it out of her bag as fast as she can to decline the call. Eleanor. Jane sighs. She knows the Casa Mía president wants not an update but an answer. When she calls back, she'd better offer something truly reassuring to buy more time.

They pause on the final block before the main plaza known as the Jardín. Jane wonders why they would stop so close to their destination, especially when the clouds look more pregnant than ever. She's near the back of the line and can't see the cause of the delay.

Music reaches her, but not the usual festive kind performed by mariachis in the Jardín, nor does it sound like one of the frequent free concerts, either. No, this is a saccharin dirge, a hymn sung slowly for a congregation to follow.

The marchers around her look at each other for clues, but none of them know what is happening. They try to keep their candles lit as the breeze picks up and light drops of rain begin to fall. Finally, the line moves forward again.

When they reach the plaza at last, Jane sees the problem: it's already full. In addition to the usual throngs of photo-taking tourists, a religious procession led by four priests in brown cassocks circles the Jardín. Several young women carry huge floral arrangements, and behind them rides the main attraction, a meter-high statue of the Virgin of Guadalupe, in a glass box on a flower-covered platform shouldered by six middle-aged devotees. Hundreds of worshippers follow the statue. Their music pours from speakers set up in the center of the plaza, an arrangement typically reserved for concerts and major holidays.

Next to Jane, Gabriela reacts with surprise to the banners of the first groups that pass them. "They're charismatic Catholics, from rural communities far from here."

This startles Jane, too. Her vision of charismatics is a tentful of American evangelicals speaking in tongues.

The effect of their silent vigil is clearly lost, but Jane and her comrades carry on with a single lap of the plaza. They have to pause midway to let the religious marchers pass again. When their group finally reaches the open area in front of the famous pink church, they arrange their candles on the ground to form huge letters. Jane isn't sure what they're spelling, but she bends and sets her candle in line with the previous person's. As she stands back up, she smiles at various faces around the circle, including Araceli, who looks as graceful as ever while she squats to relight candles, battling the breeze. The finished word is PAZ.

The Virgin statue draws near again. Jane and her companions contract their circle to clear enough space for the procession to pass. The many onlookers, they conclude, must think their group is part of the religious ceremony. They give up and say their goodbyes while hymns continue to blare over the loudspeakers. Their actual message was certainly drowned out.

Once beyond reach of the speakers, Jane dials Eleanor, who responds on the first ring. "Hi, glad it's you. Tell me you have good news."

"Yes. Several hot prospects—who? Oh, friends from home, you wouldn't know—"

"Jane, you've got this, right? We can't afford the blow to our reputation if we stop in the middle of the build, and you know we're burning through the first half of the money, and now that your concert has been postponed until who knows when—"

"Yes, of course, I've got this. But actually, I wanted to talk to you. Just as a back-up, to avoid stopping, you know, could we possibly borrow against next year's budget if necessary? No more than eighty thousand from the general fund. Just until the concert happens or my other prospects come through first."

"Oh Jane, you know Bob would scream. It's risky."

"Only as a last resort."

"Very last. You have four weeks at the most before it comes to that. Don't let it."

The next morning, Jane takes her boys to an event at an upscale equestrian center and vineyard that she and Gabriela like. Searching the parking lot for a space this time entails touring a collection of exotic cars. The boys shout their approval for each one they pass, making extra noise for a red Ferrari that purrs and roars as its driver also looks for a parking spot.

They locate Gabriela and her son in the crowd. The three boys set off to explore. Jane sits down across from her friend at one of many small tables elegantly set for brunch on a manicured lawn. From her seat, she has a great view of the paddock where a sleek horse flies over elaborate jumps carrying an equally polished rider. "It's like a Ralph Lauren ad come to life."

"What?"

"This." Jane gestures around them. "All these beautiful people and their beautiful animals, and the place itself." There is so much money at the tables, in the parking lot, and prancing on four legs that the air practically shimmers with it.

Gabriela smiles. "I see it."

"I bet any one of these people could fund Nayeli's house without even feeling it." Jane scans the tables. "Who are they?"

"Most aren't from here. They're in from Mexico City, Monterrey, and Guadalajara, plus probably a few from the States, even Madrid."

"Hey, who's your friend who runs these shows? Would he let us make an announcement? 'While you're in town, help a local family in need.'"

"No, trust me, he won't give you the microphone. Nobody wants to hear something dreary between the jumping and dressage, amor. Also, they probably already have an affiliation with a charity cleared by committee months ago. So no, sorry."

Jane sighs and asks Gabriela about something else on her mind. "So what happened yesterday? Just a scheduling error, or did our group not ask permission or something?"

"No, it was intentional. It had to be."

"Seriously? We were supporting a kidnapped woman, how could anyone be opposed? Who would go to that much effort to silence us with those huge speakers when we were literally already silent?"

"Appearances. Marches like that don't usually happen here over kidnappings. You know, we were talking about this the other day, it's normally super hush hush. The government doesn't want tourists freaking out and canceling their reservations, and also the families are usually afraid of provoking the kidnappers. So we're all supposed to act normal, like nothing's wrong."

"So why did we even march then?"

"Good question. Some of her closest friends, the ones who organized it, must have talked with the family and gotten their approval. I don't know, maybe they decided to pressure the government after all for more resources, and the government didn't appreciate it."

A horse stumbles upon landing a long double jump, its rider flung far forward over the animal's neck. Jane watches the horse recover its footing and the rider slide back into the saddle. Instantly, the pair gather themselves and launch forward toward the next obstacle. "Wow. But anyway, won't that drama last night end up raising more eyebrows?"

"No. Well, maybe. But I still say it had to be the mayor's office. Those were very rural people bussed in. You must have heard about the kinds of manipulation that happen, especially during election campaigns, but it's hard to believe until you see it for yourself, no?"

"I'm still having trouble believing it, actually. You know, I couldn't get that scene out of my head last night." After a pause, Jane continues more quietly. "Which was an improvement over other dreams I've had lately."

"What dreams?"

"I think I've been envisioning murdering my husband. With a poisonous plant."

A glance at Jane's face stops Gabriela's laughter.

"It's happening because I heard about a wife who got away with it although everyone knows. Her mother-in-law is even a bruja, the one Lindsay goes to."

"No way."

"You haven't heard about this? Here's the kicker, the mother-in-law never turned her in. For the good of the grandchildren, so they still have a mother. Señora Ximena, in Colonia Guadalupe?"

Gabriela shakes her head.

"Anyway, the seed of the story has grown in my subconscious, producing pretty little poisonous blossoms like the tansy I protected my horse from as a child. Except here it's datura."

"What?"

"They're small white flowers, I'm told, but I fixate on the green of the plant itself and the tea it would make, a gorgeous emerald green, but maybe rotten-smelling, fetid."

"Yeah, I know what datura is. So let's keep you away from poisonous plants, as well as medicine cabinets and kitchen knives and maybe cars for a while."

Jane manages to laugh. "The obvious options don't tempt me, I promise, but that green has woven itself into my nightmares."

"What do you mean?"

"These insane green vines strangle him from the inside."

"That's dark. But datura looks more like an herb or a weed, not a vine."

"I know. My crazy brain somehow turns it into a powerful vine that grows through him. It's pretty grim, but—" Gabriela's expression tightens in warning. Jane pauses, and they both smile as a waiter sets menus on the table and offers champagne, Bloody Marys, or micheladas.

"You were saying, the vine?"

"Just that it's awful, obviously, but also beautiful. This glowing green presence passes through his body. Except for the eyes. They're the last to die, filled with hate. That part is not pretty at all. Then I wake up with my heart pounding. It's happened a few times now."

A long moment passes before Gabriela speaks. "Let's assume you're not actually homicidal. This is just your brain processing anger in a safe way while you sleep."

"Sure, this is totally normal. But now that I've told you, I can't poison him. You'd know it was me. So he's safe, don't worry." Jane forces another laugh.

"Are *you* safe?"

"Yes, I think so. Like I said, he's scary but he doesn't actually hurt me, and I won't hurt him, I promise. I ignore him, work around him, and enjoy everything else in my life."

"How is that a sustainable strategy?"

"It is because it has to be." The waiter returns to set flutes of champagne in front of them. "Honey, thank you so much for listening, but I think that's enough therapy for today. Let's talk about something else and enjoy this beautiful place and all these pretty people."

"All right, corazón, but I'm here, always."

"I know. Just letting me talk like this is a gift, so I don't go completely crazy." Jane lifts one of the glasses. "And thank you for not thinking I already am."

27

"WHAT DID YOU DO?" KEVIN demands when Jane and the boys get home from the horse show. Connor and Liam gape at him. Jane watches the joy of the outing drain from their faces.

"Boys," she says quickly, "you can have extra screen time in your rooms. Go on up, I'll bring snacks in a minute." She walks them to the stairs and waits while they climb before turning back to face Kevin. "What are you talking about?"

He doesn't lower his voice to match hers. "You pledged our money to build that house."

"No, I didn't." She moves away from the stairs toward the kitchen.

He follows her. "Yes, you did. I ran into that guy, Bob. He said he admired your 'commitment' but definitely put quotes around it. Of course he doesn't understand your obsession. He hasn't had the pleasure of seeing your savior complex in action before."

"It's not a savior complex, stop it. Anyway, we're more than half-way there, thanks to Regina at the auction."

"And me."

"Yes, you and Javier. We're not committed to anything except matching Javi's ten thousand because you agreed to it that night." She pulls out a cutting board.

"Bob said they'll stop construction if you don't provide the rest of the money very soon, and I am damn sure not forking over a hundred thousand pesos to save your ass."

Her voice grows as loud as his. "Yes, I have to raise the money—but not personally pay it. I'm working on it. How are you not hearing me?" She starts to walk away, then turns back, picks up an apple from a basket on the counter, and starts slicing. "You know, I'm terrified of what might happen if I fail. The husband will believe he was right not to trust me, and he'll probably beat his wife again the next time he drinks. Those girls saw it all last time. I can't let them down again. But yeah, I know perfectly well not to use our money."

"Good. But why make this your problem in the first place? Why do you have this need to fix people? Can't you ever mind your own fucking business and focus on our family?"

"That's not fair. I do focus on our family. And why do I try to fix other people's problems? Oh, I don't know, Kev, maybe because I can't fix us. Maybe that's why."

"That's it, Jane, I'm done with this shit. We're going home." A toxic stew of emotions plays across his face, thickening his voice like curdled cream in coffee. Stubble bristles around his contorted mouth.

She registers, cloaked but discernible, the note of triumph. She wants to stay in Mexico, but he doesn't, and he's had all the power since David, even more so after she stopped earning money when they moved here. How can she possibly convince him? She has to get it right after overreaching last time.

"You go," she'd said, around the time last year they stopped going to marriage counseling and she moved into the guest room. "We're happy here, and you've decided to be miserable wherever you are. Please don't pull us all down with you."

Kevin had sneered at her. "If I go, Jane, the boys come with me. Because how would you support them? You don't have a job anymore, remember, and you can't get one here without a work permit. Your residency probably wouldn't be valid anymore, either, without me."

He apparently remembers the same moment. "What? You want to tell me again to go without you? Fine. Say goodbye to your kids, crazy lady."

Jane can think of no response that will help. Nothing comes up in her mind but rage. She puts the apple slices on a small plate with a second plate beneath it, grabs napkins and a bag of Goldfish from the pantry, and heads for the stairs. At the top, she feels the quiet. He hasn't followed her. Still, she steps into her own bedroom rather than one of the boys' rooms and locks the door behind her, a maneuver that requires tucking the bag between her elbow and her ribs to free the fingers of one hand to turn the flimsy metal ridge on the knob. Jane lets the roar in her brain dissipate, then moves half the slices and adds a mound of Goldfish to each plate. She unlocks the door to deliver the snacks.

Jane seriously considers running away with her kids. They wouldn't understand. They love their dad. She can't risk them wanting to go back to him, choosing him over her, as she once chose her mother over her father. Moreover, if she flees with them and then he finds her, which he would, she'll have seriously undermined her case in a custody battle. There is also the pathetic reality of her lack of money beyond his control to consider.

How did she let this happen? Jane looks back, trying to trace the origins of the choking vines that grew up around her when she gave them the slightest purchase. They emerged unnoticed and spread gradually at first, expanding with each small, individually trivial incident in which she ceded power, every time she was resolutely cheerful and willfully blind.

WHEN THEY REACH THE NEW applicants portion of the scholarship committee meeting, Jane is ready with photos of Lupita and Dulce standing in muck. When she explains that the girls work long hours making bricks to help their family survive, sympathy grows. Once she announces that Dulce, Lupita, and their parents are about to be the newest recipients of a Casa Mía house and will have the organization's logistical and emotional support, several committee members' heads start nodding. She notes that these will have to be full scholarships, but Casa Mía's executive director has already successfully approached a current Cervantes family about providing daily transportation. She brings it home by adding that the girls' current teachers believe they have academic potential, something she heard from Rocío.

"You've certainly done your homework, Jane," says Ana Paula, the school's director. "I think we can commit to full scholarships for the coming year."

Several others murmur their agreement.

"That's fantastic, I'm so glad. But just next year? They'll need support beyond that. Even with a Casa Mía house, their parents will never be able to afford our tuition, and we can't just send them back to their underfunded public elementary after a year here." She'd better get this locked in now in case she's not here next year to fight for them.

Ana Paula sighs. "You know there's a new private school opening in August. If our numbers drop, how will we pay our teacher salaries, let alone provide so many scholarships? Until we know what's going to happen with enrollment . . . I'm sorry."

The mood in the room shifts from triumphant to glum.

"I understand. The rest of this year and next, then reevaluate. Got it."

"This year? It could be disruptive to move this late in the year."

"The sooner the better, though. Every day they're not here is a missed opportunity, don't you think? It's still April, so more than two months are left. They can get adjusted for next year."

"All right. If you truly believe they can handle it and Casa Mía supports them."

"You aren't really concerned about that new school, are you?" asks a man a few seats away from Jane. "I hear kids at their other branches in Celaya and Querétaro are glued to screens half the day, everything progressive experts warn against. I seriously doubt we need to worry."

Jane telegraphs her thanks to him as Ana Paula's expression softens. "You're right."

Jane tries once more. "So perhaps we can commit to a longer scholarship?"

"No." Irritation returns to Ana Paula's brow. "We'll continue to revisit all scholarships annually, with renewals dependent on academic performance and financial availability."

On the way out, while crossing the school's central courtyard, one of the parents on the committee brings up Verónica, the kidnapped woman. The conversation always turns to her these days. After all, she's a parent at the school. But nobody has solid news to offer.

Jane has almost reached the imposing front doors when an older woman from the meeting pulls her aside. "I can see how much you care about those girls," the woman says. "Be careful not to get too wrapped up in their lives. I've watched it happen before."

"I appreciate your concern."

"When someone falls into that role, who wouldn't ask for more?

They'll take advantage of your sympathy. You'll start to see yourself as their savior, and that's when the whole thing can go sideways."

"Really, I'll be fine."

The older woman smiles. Jane detects a streak of condescension. Worse, if she's honest, the advice hits uncomfortably close to the mark. Jane nods to end the conversation and steps through the doors.

Nayeli's family isn't taking advantage of her, but of her own volition she's become overly involved in their lives. She got herself into this, and she needs another eighty thousand pesos to get herself out. She has to fulfill the promises she made, and that will be the end of it.

29

DULCE AND LUPITA'S FIRST DAY at Academia Cervantes dawns bright and clear, like most San Miguel days. Jane waits on the school steps after she walks her own children to the door. Students brush past her to enter the building. The sky is a cloudless, brilliant blue, and two hot air balloons float over the city. They skim so low over rooftops that Jane imagines one day a balloon will snag on a steeple.

She still can't believe Pablo came around. As Rocío predicted, the thoroughness of the scholarships convinced him in the end.

"Look, three." A small boy on the bottom step points at the sky. Jane looks up. A third balloon has appeared. The first two float so close together that she can almost picture the passengers having a conversation between baskets.

"Have you seen four at once?" she asks the boy.

"No, six. My record is six." His legs stretch to carry him over the last step.

Her girls have arrived. The older students they've ridden with urge them out of the car. They look charming in their crisp, new uniforms, with pleated knee-length khaki skirts, neat white blouses, and black sweaters with their names freshly embroidered beneath the school logo. Dulce recognizes Jane and smiles tentatively. The car drives away, waved on by a harried teacher on drop-off line duty.

Jane releases the older girls from their task. "Thank you, girls, you can go ahead." She turns to Dulce and Lupita. "It's so nice to see you, and don't you look pretty in your new uniforms. This is going to be a fun day."

Neither of them seems convinced, but Jane sees Carmen and Nayeli's strength in them. Their hands in hers, they walk up the steps for the first time.

At the top, the director introduces herself and takes over. Jane lingers at the door, straining to see their first contact. She wishes she could stay with them all day to smooth every interaction. She wants assurances that none of the other kids will behave in that casually cruel way some always master at a young age. This, of course, is impossible.

At pick-up that afternoon, Jane watches for the girls again. Liam pulls on her arm, but she waits until they appear at the door looking dazed but happy. A girl she doesn't recognize chats to Lupita. Dulce walks at her sister's side and directs her toward the correct car.

Jane introduces herself to the mom at the wheel. "Hi, I'm Jane from Casa Mía. Thank you so much for doing this. Did Rocío tell you we have a small fund for the bus whenever you can't drive?"

"Yes, but I'm happy to do it. It's no trouble. They're sweet girls."

"They are, aren't they?" Jane looks in the back seat. "How was your first day?"

"Very good, Señora," Dulce responds politely.

"Well, nice to meet you, Jane, but I'd better move along."

"Right, sorry. Bye." She waves until the car merges into traffic and the next parent pulls forward.

"Are you going to be like that every day?" asks Connor as they begin the walk home.

The question makes Jane see her behavior through her sons' eyes. "Sorry if I embarrassed you. It's just that I feel responsible, so I want to keep an eye on them for a while. We talked about this. They don't know anyone, and they don't speak English yet. Luckily, since you two are in the same grades, you can help."

"Oh, they're fine," says Liam. "Lupita has a best friend already."

"Really, who?"

"Sarah, the other new girl, from Portland. She already knows Spanish, and all the girls like her. You saw her."

"Oh yeah, I think I did. Curly blonde hair?"

"Yep. Lupita's fine, I told you."

Jane reaches for Connor's hand now that they've rounded a corner and are out of sight of the school. "How about Dulce?" she asks him. "How was her first day?"

"Fine, I think. She was quiet."

"Quiet scared or quiet sad?

"I don't know, just quiet."

"Tomorrow could you please pay a little more attention? Be friendly. She's already in fourth grade, and the older you are, the harder it is to learn a new language, remember? You two had just finished kindergarten and second when we moved here, so it was easier for you."

"It was a new country, Mom," says Connor. "They're just going to a new school that's bilingual, that's not such a big thing."

"Actually, it is. Their experiences are very different from the lucky, rather spoiled lives of most of the kids you know. In a way, their adjustment will be bigger than yours."

"How?"

"Well, for one thing, their parents probably can't help them with their homework because they didn't finish school themselves when they were kids, because they had to work."

"Oh."

Jane wonders whether Nayeli and Pablo can read. She knows some Casa Mía recipients can't, but it doesn't seem wise to share that with her kids. Maybe she's already said too much. Truth can inspire empathy, but too much too soon defines an unbridgeable distance.

"Now they're happy that their daughters will receive a better education than they did and be able to have more choices in their lives. We should help if we can because they deserve a chance like anyone else, right?"

"Yes, Mom," Connor answers dutifully.

The next afternoon, Jane arrives early again. Children pour down the steps with grinning urgency. Jane smiles, too, when she sees Sarah and Lupita holding hands and laughing. Then she spots her own boys chattering to their friends.

A head among the crowd, belonging to an Argentine friend of hers, turns toward her. "Impressive, Jane, your boys really don't have an accent anymore. They sound like Mexicans."

"Thank you. I, on the other hand, don't seem to be a natural."

"Yeah, you still have an accent," the woman agrees, laughing. "It's harder as an adult, but don't worry, you'll get there."

Jane smiles with satisfaction as she listens to her sons and watches Dulce and Lupita climb into the car.

A BABY SHOWER IS A bad place to be jealous. Especially this one, which will clearly be different from any Jane has attended before. The midwife-shaman begins by explaining that a 'blessing way' is based on indigenous traditions, and material goods are not the focus. The point of the ceremony, rather, is to mark the transition in a woman's life, to celebrate the enormous significance of becoming a mother.

Jane remembers that transition to parenthood in her own life and Kevin's. Like her, Kevin could not have been more excited the first time. While she pored over parenting books and lists of names, he researched ergonomic strollers and every video monitor on the market. He attended many of the doctor's appointments with her, put the crib together, and stayed home to paint the nursery while she was at work so she wouldn't breathe a single fume, even though the paint was the low emissions kind that cost twice as much. While she dreamily bought tiny clothes and children's books and felt the magic of her son stretching his body inside her own, he read the first chapters of *What to Expect*. He stopped only when she asked him to because the book made him crazy with worry.

His attention fell off sharply for the second pregnancy, as often happens, but he was a proud dad and loved his babies fiercely. For a while, as their common purpose, she thought the kids would keep them happy together.

That was far too much weight to place on tiny shoulders.

The midwife tells everyone it's time to enter one by one into the sacred circle she's constructed with cut flowers among re-arranged living room furniture. She instructs each entrant to smudge the woman behind her with copal. At the front of the line, a tall, striking older woman with close-cropped platinum hair waves the smoking stick through the air above Jane's head, in front of her face, over her shoulders, arms, and belly. She bends to attend to Jane's legs and feet, walks behind her to smudge her back, and then hands her the incense. Jane turns around. The woman next in line, whom she's just met, is tall, solid, with piercings and tattooed arms, all curves and the shiniest black hair Jane has ever seen. It shimmers when she turns her head. The potential for intimidation is softened by the childlike smile that plays on the woman's lips as she enjoys the moment. Feeling like a fraud but not wanting to cheat this woman, Jane performs the task conscientiously, sweeping the copal in generous circles. Then Meghan, Gabriela, Alejandra, and Lindsay, along with several women Jane doesn't know well, smudge each other and take their places within the circle.

The midwife seats the mother-to-be, Lisa, whom Jane met through Meghan and Lindsay months ago, in front of them within a second, smaller circle of flowers, and places a flower crown on Lisa's head. She then demonstrates how each of them should introduce themselves to the group by honoring their matriarchal line and their womanhood. Following her example, in which she shares the names of her mother, grandmother, and great-grandmother, and her roots in the earth, sky, and water, Jane announces that she's the daughter of Margaret, granddaughter of Mary Jane, great-granddaughter of Patricia, and she hopes to become a daughter of Mexico, too. The Mexico line goes over well, and Jane realizes she's scored a lucky break. Seated next to the midwife, she will be the first to follow each direction, so whatever she says will at least be fresh. In contrast, by the time a third woman proclaims she's the daughter of the moon, the poetry has faded.

Each of them braids a ribbon into Lisa's hair. They share their love and admiration for the young woman before them, who looks more and more like a wild forest sprite from some ancient fairy tale as a dozen messy braids take form in her long, wavy hair.

They continue with a community necklace. Each woman explains the significance of the bead she brought to string together into an unusual, highly personal adornment that Lisa will wear while in labor. Jane tells Lisa that her contribution of an amethyst bead is from a necklace her own mother gave her, and she believes a significant part of motherhood is sharing the strength of a meaningful, supportive sisterhood. She's relieved to then just watch several of the others massage Lisa's hands, head, and feet. Not everyone can fit around her at once, so Jane doesn't get an extremity. She's raw, feeling not just excitement for Lisa and appreciation for her own journey as a mother, but also an ugly kernel of jealousy.

It is not for the new baby boy soon to come into the world. She has two amazing sons of her own. No, she covets the atmosphere of love surrounding this woman. It's not just a pregnant glow, it's not even the great hair and makeup job Lisa's sister gave her early this morning before taking her out into nature for a belly photo shoot. Lisa already had that love and peace glow before she was pregnant. From what she has shared, she didn't have an easy childhood, and she and her husband struggle a little financially, so it's not a case of ignorance or an especially cushy life breeding bliss. Certainly the explanation lies in part in the warmth of the home she's prepared for her baby, amidst kind friends, in a city she chose.

Jane admits the core of her jealousy. A huge reason, obviously, for Lisa's happiness must be a healthy relationship with her husband, Diego, who is so good with the son they already have. Jane recalls that stage of her own marriage when she was pregnant for the second time and there was still so much anticipation and joy between them and an expansive trust that she can't, at this point, imagine ever rebuilding. A trust, already corroded, which she definitively destroyed by growing close to David.

Jane brings her attention back to the ceremony and forces a smile but worries that everyone has already read on her face the regret and bitterness that eat away at her mind.

They light candles around the circle and offer gifts of wisdom, strength, wonder, stability, beauty, and love to Lisa and her baby. They toss a ball of red yarn back and forth across the circle. When someone's errant toss almost sends the ball into a flame, they blow out the candles. The midwife instructs the women to light them again on their home altars when Lisa goes into labor as a means of sending her all the positive energy they can. Jane is charmed by the assumption that all the women already have year-round home altars, not just for el Día de Muertos, and she resolves to create one of her own.

Finally, the midwife tells Lisa to release each woman from the web they have created together, so Lisa works her way around the circle. She cuts the red yarn and ties a small segment around each woman's wrist. They are to wear their new bracelets continuously during her last three months of pregnancy to remind themselves of Lisa's need for their support and to celebrate the new spirit she's about to bring into the world. It's all so beautiful that Jane can't wait for someone to ask her about the yarn on her wrist so she'll have an excuse to talk about it. She wants to share this experience and feed on Lisa's glow to burnish her own.

"Before you all leave, I have something to tell you." Lisa looks anxious. The room goes quiet, and the women pull closer.

"What's wrong?" demands Meghan. Lisa doesn't answer.

"Is everything good with the baby?" Gabriela asks more gently.

"The little guy's fine. He has a bad habit of sitting on my bladder lately, that's all."

"So what is it? You look spooked."

"Well, nobody knows this yet, but this was actually a farewell party, too. Diego got a job offer in Silicon Valley, near where my family lives, and it's a great opportunity."

Meghan looks as blindsided as Jane feels. "Congratulations, but do you have to go?"

Lindsay protests, too. "I'm supposed to be baby's cool aunt, remember?"

"That's the other thing, it will be nice to be close to my folks and my sister again."

"Ah, Baby and Santiago will have their real aunt."

"Don't make me cry, this is so hard. It's not that I want to go, but we have to."

Lindsay stands up and enfolds Lisa in a hug. The others pile on. "Of course we understand; we'll just miss you like crazy."

"When?" asks the woman with the tattoos whom Jane smudged. "After the baby's born?"

"Diego has to report for the job in three weeks."

"So soon, are you serious?"

"Sooner, so we can get settled before he starts. Next week."

"Next week? Does Santi know yet?"

"No, this just happened, and I wanted to sort out a few details first, so it doesn't feel so chaotic. But he needs time to say goodbye."

"He was born here, right?"

"This is the only home he's ever known." Lisa gestures around her, and Jane takes in with fresh eyes the high white walls covered in quirky art and the tile floor currently piled with flowers and flustered women. She looks out one of the tall, arched windows at Lisa's traditional Mexican courtyard. In front of the fountain half buried in potted geraniums, Santiago's tricycle takes on a poignant air.

"Yeah." A tattooed arm wraps around Lisa's shoulders. "That kid has lived in a pretty magical world full of people who adore him."

Meghan agrees. "Exactly, so he loves it. This is happening too fast."

Gabriela elbows Meghan. "No, Santi will be fine."

"Tell him you're moving because it's time to be close to his other grandma and grandpa now," Jane suggests. "That will help him accept it."

In the center of the nest of women, Lisa stops holding back her tears.

Later, as they all gather their things to go, Lisa generously asks about Dulce and Lupita. Jane performs an instant, questionable mental calculation: could she raise the topic? Won't these women want to help another mother in need? "They're doing great, they've made friends at school. They're behind academically, but the teachers work with them privately, so they'll catch up, and their scholarships cover everything." Now's her chance. "All they still need is another eighty thousand pesos to build the rest of their house. If anyone would like to help, every little bit—"

She looks around the room while the number hangs in the air. A dozen women peer back at her. Their expressions range from startled to annoyed. Jane wishes the midwife had an herb to make her disappear.

"It will all work out," says Lisa. "Way to go, sister. You're doing good in the world."

On the walk home, Jane tries to convince herself that the moment wasn't too awful. She had to try, didn't she, when handed the opportunity? But she won't keep forcing it. It looks like she will in fact have to convince the board to borrow against the general fund until she can finally hold the concert or find another angel like Regina. *Fine.*

31

LIAM TAKES THE STAGE WITH serious swagger, resplendent in a full charro costume. He leans slightly forward, thumbs tucked in his belt, as his booted feet hammer a syncopated rhythm across the stage. Baroque gold braiding accents his black jacket, trousers, and sombrero. He approaches the bull, another second-grader with an elaborate horned headdress, and circles around him, swinging a lariat. The bull twists and parries, then bolts across the stage. Liam charges after him, they spin together, one approaches and the other feints, first to one side and then the other.

Then, since this elegant gentleman has failed to tame the bull, the prettiest girl in town is asked to try. A gorgeous child dances onto the stage, swaying, twirling, beguiling the crazed animal. He's charmed for a few moments, but then thrashes about wildly once again. Next a wise elder is called to the task in the form of another seven-year-old dancer who advances slowly in a shuffling step, his posture convincingly hunched under the traditional mask of the viejito. A maternal character with a rebozo around her shoulders and another over her hair performs a graceful, authoritative turn around the stage. Jane smiles when she recognizes Lupita. She learned the steps so quickly. They've only been at the school a few weeks.

Jane looks behind her to where Nayeli and Pablo sit two rows back. She spotted them earlier, before the lights went down. Smiles and glints of pride in their eyes acknowledge their daughter's success. Jane is impressed that they both came, since they would normally still be working at this hour, and it couldn't have been easy to leave their posts. She turns back to the stage to watch several more village archetypes have their moment, culminating in the turn of the lowly borrachita, an angelic girl playing the town drunk. It's Sarah, the other new girl in Liam's class, whom Liam has reported is kind and popular and has taken Lupita under her wing. She does a loose-limbed dance in the general vicinity of the bull and falls theatrically.

Still not despairing, the entire population of the village dances onto the stage. They work together now, but they can't control the bull no matter what they do.

Finally, Death appears. He lurches about wielding his scythe until the stage floor is covered in dead villagers. Even the cruel bull, the source of all their troubles, is brought down. For in the end la Muerte conquers all. This surreal spectacle is met with full-throated cheers from the parents. *These kids just laid down some truth,* thinks Jane. Death is always in the game, and he will have his triumph. But what is there to do about it? Ni modo, keep dancing.

On to the next act. Connor appears on stage in not much more than a loincloth and armbands. He and his classmates begin a dance representing the lives of the Chichimecas, a fierce, nomadic people indigenous to this region of central Mexico. The Chichimeca men once dressed in that manner, apparently, so the boys among these nine- and ten-year-olds matter-of-factly do the same in front of several hundred people.

Jane relaxes into her seat to enjoy the older children's performances, ending with ballroom dancing by the high school students, and then claps like crazy for the curtain call. After collecting and congratulating Connor and Liam, she looks for Nayeli's family and finds them in the bottleneck of the theater lobby. Pablo stands with a hand on a shoulder of each of his daughters as though to keep them from getting swept up in the swirling currents of proud parents and adrenaline-fueled children.

"Great job, girls."

"Gracias, Señora." They answer almost in unison.

"And how are you enjoying your classes?"

"Very well," says Dulce.

Before Jane can think of a better question, Pablo says good night and ushers Nayeli and the flushed, happy girls toward the exit. She watches them go.

Across the lobby Jane glimpses Sarah and recognizes the woman next to the girl as the new friend Lindsay brought to the taco stand that night. What was her name? Hannah. She's been meaning to reach out for weeks, but they have barely gotten past hurried hellos at pick-up. Now's the time. "Let's invite Sarah and her parents to join us at the restaurant."

"Wait, why?" asks Liam.

"Why not?" she says over her shoulder, already crossing the lobby. "Sarah, well done, you are a dancing queen. Hannah, do you guys have plans? Would you like to join us and a few other families for dinner?"

While the kids run around the restaurant's courtyard, all still in their costumes except Connor, for whom Jane brought jeans and a sweater, she and her friends get to know Hannah and her husband, Gavin.

Jane thanks them for how kind Sarah has been to Lupita. "I'm on the board of Casa Mía, a local nonprofit similar to Habitat for Humanity. Lupita's family is about to receive a Casa Mía house." Provided she finally raises the second half of the money by like yesterday.

"I heard about that," responds Hannah, "and I think it might be a harder transition to the school, a bigger culture shock, for Lupita and her sister than for Sarah."

"That's exactly what I told my kids. From what I hear, Sarah's been a huge help to Lupita."

"Well, Sarah adores her, and being new girls together is more fun."

Over the course of the evening, Jane discovers how much she likes Hannah and Gavin. "I wish I'd reached out sooner. My excuse is that it gets hard to say goodbye to the families who come for short sabbaticals, so it's tempting after a while to just stick with old friends. But we still need to look up sometimes and welcome the new arrivals."

Just then Sarah and Meghan's daughter, Sophie, approach the adults' table. They each whisper a question in their respective mother's ear. Hannah and Meghan smile at each other.

"Sure, that sounds like fun. Our house or yours?" Meghan asks Hannah.

"They want to have a sleepover," Hannah explains to the others. "We'd be happy to host."

"Sarah is so friendly," says Meghan, as the girls head back to the kids' table. "What a sweet girl."

"We should hang out again, too," Lindsay proposes. "Hannah, have you two been out to Santa Mónica or Viñedo San Tomás yet? They serve food from their own gardens, and you'll probably be surprised, Mexican wines have come a long way in the last few years."

"Sounds great. We haven't been to either one."

"Absolutely," Gavin agrees. "We'd love to put those wines to the test."

"What's that?" Kevin rejoins the group after sitting with Enrique and Alejandra.

"Recent improvements in Mexican wine."

"Good luck with that." Kevin grimaces. Jane nudges him under the table, but he doesn't change course. "It's a low bar."

Gavin ignores the unpleasantness. "We're up for the adventure."

Meghan follows Jane to the bathroom. When Jane assures her that she's doing OK, Meghan looks doubtful, but another woman enters the room.

Back at the table, the adults' conversation turns to Verónica. After weeks of uncertainty, Jane assumes the worst.

Gabriela shakes her head. "No, this is normal. It can last for months. The last guy was taken for a year and a half."

"He was released alive after a year and a half?" Kevin is incredulous, and the others stare at Gabriela, too.

"Yes."

"What about the women? Are they—?"

"Probably. Although some people say they're treated better than the men, so I don't know. No matter what, that much time in a small room, or even a cage, must destroy a person."

32

"How rude," says Liam, shocked, as the bull's body slams into the ground. The powerful animal lies unnaturally still, stretched taut by a rope around his horns and another restraining his hind legs. The opposite end of each lariat is controlled by an expert cowboy, wound around the pommel of his saddle. Both men sit astride their horses with practiced ease, looking like perfectly cast extras in a Marlboro commercial from the late eighties.

Next to Jane, her friends Enrique and Alejandra chuckle at Liam's indignation.

"Yes, how rude," Enrique agrees. "But the bull will be fine, I promise. I know some of these cowboys, and they don't want their animals to get hurt."

Liam is unconvinced.

In one well-choreographed moment, a third lithe cowboy steps over the bull and settles onto his back while the first two release the ropes. The animal is on his feet in an instant, furious and determined to remove the nuisance. The cowboy clings as the bull leaps, kicks, and shimmies his way across the corral, emoting anger with every muscular ounce of his body. Liam's eyes can't possibly open any wider as he takes in this contest, and he appears to Jane to be holding his breath.

Only when the cowboy lands in the dirt and both bull and man walk away unharmed does air finally burst from Liam's lungs. "I guess that was fair."

Jane relaxes, reassured that her son is not about to launch a protest. Now she can take in the scene from her perch on an ancient set of bleachers that leans decidedly to the left. A large corral has been constructed in the middle of nowhere. An expanse of pasture in rainy-season green stretches wide, dotted by mesquite trees, and a clear, narrow river empties into a small, probably seasonal lake. Beyond the lake, hills rise in dusky blues and grays, with stone outcroppings creating dramatic silhouettes. Cowboys in jeans and starched button-ups await their turns, sitting tall on patient horses. Their families secure vantage points from the beds of pickup trucks backed up to the corral, and a brass band in peacock blue and yellow uniforms adds a festive soundtrack. One of the horns is consistently off-key, but this inconvenient fact is overshadowed by the enthusiasm with which it is played.

As the only foreigners in attendance, Jane and her family draw curious looks. They are here because one day last week their housekeeper happened to mention to Jane that she was worried about a cousin blessed with more confidence than skill who planned to compete in the bull-riding event. Jane expected to see her here but hasn't yet. She may be boycotting the man's reckless performance. Jane wonders which of the competitors is the cousin at risk. Alejandra and Enrique know a couple of the cowboys, too, so they decided to join the outing.

Jane finds it fascinating that the rodeo is taking place on the same day and only a few miles away from a very different, even more memorable spectacle. Not two hours earlier, she and her boys had been in the center of town cheering the Día de los Locos parade, an event entirely unique to San Miguel. She'd heard stories of how each year on the Sunday following June 13, the feast of Saint Anthony, the town goes cheerfully nuts, but last year they hadn't gone to the parade for some reason she can't remember. Reading about it and listening to some friends enthuse while others rolled their eyes had not fully prepared Jane or her kids to see twenty thousand people dress up in the most bizarre, whimsical, or satirical costumes imaginable and dance in the narrow streets. Each participant slipped on a new identity and inhabited it fully. Martians, cartoon heroes, Vikings, zombies, political figures beloved and reviled, teen beauty queens and drag queens, monsters, herds of papier mâché animals, and thousands of other imaginative creatures strutted and preened for hours. Each group of characters followed a float carrying huge speakers pumping out dance music.

Her kids were overwhelmed by the noise and chaos at first, but then they'd been lucky to find a window seat in a restaurant on the parade route. There they could see perfectly, but the noise was muffled and so were the odds of getting stung by a piece of candy tossed by the dancers into the crowd with too much enthusiasm. From this safe spot, Connor and Liam had a great time soaking up the spectacle and pointing out the craziest costumes to each other.

After walking home to collect their car and Kevin, a thirty-minute drive took them out of the city over a brief stretch of highway and a winding country road onto a dirt path that couldn't possibly be right but was. Jane bounced the car over ruts and through a stream bloated by recent rains before parking in a field behind the bleachers. They opened their doors to the earthy aromas of horses, cattle, and fresh earth churned up in the ring. Jane finds the differences between the origin of that quick trip and its destination pleasantly disorienting. As she watches the cowboys take on the bulls, she continues to savor the earlier performance as well.

She had tried and failed to drag Kevin to the parade. He hates crowds. It's time to accept that he will never love Mexico, either, not the way she does. The move hasn't reawakened his youthful joie de vivre any more than it has repaired their relationship. *Well, the boys are happy that he's here at the rodeo at least.*

Alejandra asks Jane how the Casa Mía house is coming along. "Remember, mi amor," Alejandra nudges Enrique, "that family she told us about at Christmas when we were all on the terraza after the present exchange, before your sparkler extravaganza? Well, a month or two later, they ended up getting kicked out of the little house where they were living because it belonged to an uncle and the uncle got deported—tell me if I'm messing up the story, Jane—"

"No, that's right."

"But it was too late, the Casa Mía board had already chosen their ten families for the year, so the other board members said they couldn't help this family, but Jane wasn't having it, no way. She decided to raise the money herself, and she did it."

Jane smiles in acknowledgement of Alejandra's enthusiastic recap. "Well, we've raised half of it so far. A bit more than half. But now we need the rest in a hurry, so if you have any brilliant ideas, I'd love to hear them."

Enrique and Alejandra have money. Just as Jane resolves to launch into a pitch, a tap on her shoe distracts her. She looks down to see a small hand snake up a second time from under the bleachers. It prods her foot again. Connor looks straight up at her. "Mom, Dad! Liam fell."

"What do you mean? Fell from what? Where is he?" Kevin's voice shakes.

"Mom said we could look around."

Jane ignores Kevin's glare. "Connor, where is he?"

She's moving, working her way to the end of the row. Connor follows beneath her and Kevin behind. She jumps off the end and so does he, both of them landing heavily. Alejandra and Enrique climb down the normal way and catch up to them.

Connor grabs Kevin's left hand and Jane's right and pulls. "This way. I think he's OK." Connor leads them a short distance toward a spot where women sell tortas, sopes, and cans of soda and beer from their tailgates. Liam sits on the ground, his back against a fence post, head hanging down.

"Liam?" Jane drops to her knees and pulls him into her arms.

"Don't worry, Mom."

Relief floods through her. But when Liam lifts his head, she sees that a lump already grows above his right eye.

"Honey, can you see normally? Is anything blurry? No? Good. And your stomach?"

"I'm fine, Mom. My head's fine. So's my stomach."

"You didn't black out, did you? This just happened?"

"Yes, it just happened, I'm fine, I told you."

Jane looks up at Kevin. "He's not disoriented. I'm pretty sure it's not a concussion."

"God." Kevin runs his hands over Liam's skull. "What happened?"

"Ice. We need ice," Jane interrupts. "Connor, please ask those ladies selling soda."

Before Connor even turns around, someone pushes a towel-wrapped bundle of ice cubes into Jane's hands. She gently rests the ice on the lump before looking up to acknowledge the ice giver. When she does, she's face-to-face with Pablo.

Jane freezes, looking directly at his eyes. Deep-set and dark, they're calm. Nothing in his demeanor acknowledges that night. She detects no hint of suppressed aggression, no expression of anger, bitterness, or shame. How is that possible? Does he not remember? He must. Even if he blacked out, he would have been reminded the next morning by the damage to his wife's body and his daughters' spirits. Those emotions must be there, of course, beneath the surface, and whether or not she can read him is beside the point.

Today his manner is contained and helpful. Jane glimpses the confident, handsome young man Nayeli must have fallen in love with. She forms the expected words. "Thank you, Señor."

Pablo nods. "He should stay away from the bulls, Señora. Gracias a Dios, he fell outside the pen, not into it."

"What did he say?" Kevin looks at Connor.

Connor translates for his father. "He said Liam should stay away from the bulls."

"The bulls? Liam, what were you doing?"

"I—just climbing on the fence. Then one of them, a big one, freaked out and kind of hit it. The fence. So I fell, and I guess I banged my head on a rail."

"Good God, what were you thinking?"

"Gracias por su ayuda, muy amable," Jane says again while cradling the ice against her son's skull.

"No fue nada, Señora. Señor." With a nod to Kevin, Pablo walks away. Jane shudders, seeing Nayeli in the dirt with her arms shielding her head.

Kevin leans in. "Thank God it's just a goose egg. You could have been killed."

"I'm sorry." Then, a moment later, "Can I have a soda?"

"Sodas on me," offers Enrique. "Will you help me, Connor?"

Jane hugs Liam as another wave of fear-tinged relief hits her. Kevin follows Enrique and Connor toward the nearest woman selling sodas from an ice-stuffed cooler, grilling Connor on what he saw. While they're gone, Alejandra strikes up a conversation with Liam about his latest Survival Club adventures, providing a welcome distraction.

Ten minutes later, however, Liam's patience with the icepack runs out. "Can we go now?"

"Good idea." Kevin stands up. "Let's get out of here."

He marches ahead, cutting a path through the crowd. After saying a quick goodbye to Enrique and Alejandra, Jane and the boys follow. Jane sees Pablo approach Kevin near the edge of the parking lot. She hurries to catch up.

"There was a night, Señor, when I was not at my best," Pablo begins.

Kevin looks at Connor, who translates.

"Your wife, she stayed with my wife and daughters then," Pablo continues. "She has a good heart."

"Now I know who you are."

"I thought she'd forget us after that—my mother-in-law was sure of it—but she didn't."

"Yeah, I guess Casa Mía's so important to her that she chose to stay there with the woman you beat instead of coming home to her own family."

"Dad?" Connor's voice shakes. "Do I have to translate that?"

"No, honey, you don't," says Jane as she puts her hand on Kevin's arm. "Please don't start a fight."

He shakes it off. "Connor, go ahead. Tell him exactly what I said."

"Kevin, what are you doing?"

Pablo watches them impassively.

"Connor, now."

Connor looks at the ground as he speaks.

Pablo turns and walks away. Jane assumes he's holding back the urge to punch Kevin, just like she is. Connor is in tears. Jane folds him into a quick hug. Then she takes his hand as well as Liam's. They walk well behind Kevin toward the car.

"Sorry," Connor whispers.

She leans down to him again. "Not at all, you were just helping Dad. A translator has to say everything exactly. It's a hard job, and you did it really well. And you're only nine, wow."

"But—"

"It wasn't you saying those things."

"It felt like it was."

"It wasn't."

Liam leans in. "But Mom? You told Dad you wanted to leave that night but you didn't because you were afraid of that man. Why? What would he do?"

"You've been worrying about that this whole time?"

"No. I just thought of it now."

"Well, I didn't know what he might do since he wasn't thinking straight because he was so drunk. Also, I worried that I wouldn't be able to find my car in the dark. So I waited until the sun came up. That's when I saw him. On the ground, just sleeping. He didn't hurt anyone else."

Connor grips her hand. "What if he's angry at me?"

"He won't be, no way. You are a child, a wonderful, smart child who can translate. You were doing a job and doing it well."

"Is he angry at Dad, though?"

"Well, he must think Dad's a bit rude, but I know he's only a little angry, because I saw what he looked like when he was super angry that night, and he looks completely different today. It was kind of him to bring ice, remember? There's nothing to worry about, I promise."

That night's fight grows particularly ugly.

"That stunt you pulled, making Connor translate your macho shit, what the fuck, Kev? He's only nine! What do you think that did to him? And Liam?"

"So you wanted me to act like it's totally fine that asshole beat his wife?"

"What I wanted you to do is stay civil in front of your children and not make them afraid that a violent man is angry at them. You keep exposing them to ugly, scary things."

"The fuck I do, that's on you." His jabbing finger comes close to her face. She instinctively takes a couple steps back. He rolls his eyes as though she were being needlessly dramatic.

"No, it's not. Yeah, I'm the one who got myself stuck out there that night, but it's you who keeps making things so much worse."

"Look who's talking. You're batshit thinking you're some kind of hero."

"I don't think I'm any kind of hero. Do you ever actually listen anymore?"

"Keep giving me attitude. See where that gets you."

They begin to move through the house without acknowledging each other. She knows they've reached a new low when they start to communicate through the kids.

"Liam, could you please run up to Dad's room and tell him dinner's ready?"

"Tell Mom I'm not hungry."

"Connor, please go tell Dad we're getting Lucha Libre tickets with Gaby's family Friday night."

"Tell her I'm not going. Tell her we're out of milk."

Jane wonders whether this version of them was always there, awaiting an inevitable rise to the surface. The thought is morbidly comforting. But no, it didn't have to be this way.

KEVIN SITS JANE DOWN BY the fountain in their courtyard, where the steady patter of water lends vibrancy to the otherwise still space. Her nose catches just a hint of jasmine from the vines on the back wall. Their heady scent is stronger at night.

"I'm up for a promotion," he tells her.

The look of pride makes sense, but there's something else, a note of triumph in his tone, that makes her nervous. "Congratulations. What is it, exactly?"

"The next step up the ladder. At headquarters, in Houston. No more working remotely."

There it is. "Oh."

"Don't look like that. It will mean more money."

"More money sounds great, but our lives here—"

"You mean your life here. I work all the time, just like I did back home. I'm the troll in the basement toiling away to make life in the castle more perfect. You hate it when you're forced to acknowledge the troll or maybe even say a fucking *thank you* to the damn troll."

She gapes at him.

"It's the truth. I work while you play, princess."

"Why do you have to act like I'm a leech sucking down your life-blood? You make all the money now because that was precisely the plan, remember? We chose this together. Being the full-time parent and organizing everything, mostly in Spanish, is work, too. You wouldn't recognize their teachers, coaches, or doctors if one of them slapped your ass on the sidewalk."

"Classy. And we didn't exactly choose this together, now did we? No, this was our desperation move after you chose all by yourself to cheat on me."

"I didn't. You know I didn't—" She switches tactics. "Our boys, Kev. It took time to adjust, but now they love it here."

"Awesome."

"Their Spanish is amazing; they've made friends. Liam has soccer and Connor has his dressage lessons and guitar lessons, plus all the little adventures I make happen. They're thriving. The last thing we should do is uproot them again so soon."

"Don't try to make it about them. You're focused on what you want, like always."

"No. I'd have left you a long time ago if that were true." She wants to suck the thought back in, but it's too late. Her words hang in the thick air between them.

"Nice, babe, real nice." As he spits the words, his face ripens from a pink flush to full, throbbing red.

"What timeframe?" Jane asks while choking back another response.

"It'll happen fast, assuming I get it. So start getting quotes from movers and all that. We should move over the summer so the guys can start the school year in Houston. Stop looking shocked. I told you weeks ago we were going home. You just refused to accept it."

"Home, you said. Houston is not home. We don't know a single person there." Jane hears her voice turn screechy. She tries to rein in her emotions in order not to lose all leverage. "I know you deserve a promotion. I just want you to consider all of us. I still get a vote."

"No, you pretty much forfeited your right to tell me what to do. I have a decent shot, so get ready."

Her resolve to de-escalate weakens. "That's your answer? This is what you want, so it's obviously the right thing? I better fall in line and sell it to the kids, too?" She hears how out-of-control she sounds, but she's too angry now to bother with sugarcoating.

"That about sums it up, thanks. And you know what else? You better find the money fast for that Casa Mía house or it won't happen."

He's right, although she refuses to give him the satisfaction of admitting it. Without her here to ensure that the concert eventually happens, the board won't loan the money from next year's budget. Construction will stop.

No. Meghan, Rocío, Gabriela, and Lindsay would finish the job without her, with Eleanor's support. The thought is comforting, but she'd rather not leave this mess for them to clean up. She should do it herself before she leaves. If she has to leave.

"Let me know when you find out." Jane stands up and controls her walk across the courtyard. She doesn't let out a stream of curses until she has reached her bedroom and locked the door behind her.

That evening, after the boys are asleep, she tries a different angle. "What if, please hear me out, you were to go without us? Come down every second or third weekend, and we'll come up during school vacations—"

He turns off the football game with a jab of the remote. "You're trying that on me again? Oh, you're welcome to stay here and do whatever the fuck you want, like you always do, but my sons come with me." Red splotches grow on his face again, the anger toxic to his skin. "Any judge will agree I deserve custody. How would you support them here?"

"That's not how it works." The floor suddenly unstable under her feet, Jane sits down on the edge of the sofa and turns her body to face him. "I've been the constant parent, and of course I'd take care of them financially as well as all the other ways. I'll go back to work online; I'm still a lawyer. And you'll have to pay child support."

He leans toward her. "They're coming with me." The combination behind the words of hard, unreadable eyes and taut, solid body unnerves her. There it is again, the raw fear washing through her belly.

She has to win, and the fear tells her she will lose this way, so she says it just to end the conversation. "I'll start working on quotes tomorrow. For movers."

THE ENTIRE SQUARE IS A maze of celebrating bodies. Three mariachi groups try, good-naturedly, to outdo each other. People sing along, and some dance. Others stroll, stop to flirt, or buy balloons for the kids. Shouts and laughter fill every inch of remaining space.

Liam's in there somewhere. Jane's eyes race over faces in the crowd. He was right here at her side a few seconds ago. She could tell he was getting bored as she chatted with Alejandra and Enrique, so she made motions to go, but then Araceli and Javier happened by, so the conversation went on just a little longer. *He couldn't have wandered off more than a minute ago. He can't have gone far. More than that, he wouldn't go far. He's such a good kid. He probably just spotted a friend. There's no reason to think something's happened to him.*

Jane works her way to the center of the plaza by the bandstand and circles around it. She checks every bench and looks up into each of the trees. She squeezes between revelers, searching for the slender frame of her son. He was probably oblivious at first and then brave, but panic may be building by now. He wouldn't try to run all the way home, would he? If he did, could he find it?

Since they may not be in San Miguel much longer, Jane has vowed that she and the kids will make the most of their time before they go. That's why she brought Liam to the Jardín for the festival today, but now she wishes they had just stayed home. If only Connor were here to help her look, but he's at a classmate's birthday sleepover.

From behind her, Araceli grabs her arm. "What's wrong?"

"It's Liam. I can't find him."

Javier takes charge. "Amor, walk that way around the outside of the plaza, I'll go in the opposite direction, and Jane, why don't you focus here and on the area right in front of the parroquia, which seem most likely."

Jane agrees. She does another circle around the bandstand, and then, increasingly frantic, run-walks toward the church, sorting through the tourists taking selfies in pairs, families, or packs of friends. Some pose on the huge, docile Clydesdale that pulls the ice cream wagon while others snuggle a burro wearing a flower crown whose owner, dressed as a revolutionary, is also available for photos. Most need no prop at all beyond the glorious pink building itself.

She imagines kidnappers offering candy or a balloon to draw Liam close and then grabbing him, her son too shocked to scream. She searches among every cluster of children around the fountain near the parroquia's entrance. She hunts among the vendors of corn, candy, ice cream, and especially balloons. Liam loves the long, skinny mylar ones shaped like crayons taller than himself that can be launched into the air by slamming the flat end against the ground.

He's not here. She runs back toward the center of the plaza again, the panic a living thing buzzing inside her chest.

"Mom."

"I win." A grinning Javier walks toward her, Liam's hand held loosely in his.

She scoops up her son. "Where were you?"

"I was right there with those kids from my class. I wasn't lost. You didn't need to worry."

"But I do worry when I can't find my child."

"You were talking for so long."

Javier intervenes. "Dude, you know you scared your mom, right? Moms get crazy when they're scared. They start imagining things like chupacabras and stuff."

"Those aren't even real."

"Well, you know that, and we know that, but when we're scared, parents start worrying. We can't help it. You don't want to make her go crazy again, do you?"

"No." Liam's grinning now.

"So how about you keep that from happening by not wandering off?" They fist bump to seal the accord. "All right, my man."

"Thank you both." Jane gives Araceli a hug and then Javier.

"Any time," he says. "How's Kevin, by the way? Haven't seen him in ages."

"Fine, just working too much." She glances at Liam and wonders, as she often does, how much he understands. "I'll tell him you said hi."

"Mom, can we get ice cream?"

On the walk home, double chocolate and salted caramel drip onto their fingers. "Dad would like this," says Liam. "Poor guy couldn't come."

"Poor guy?"

"Yeah, like you told Javier, he has to work too much."

She hopes that's how he really sees it.

Jane weighs whether to tell Kevin what happened. Deciding not to, she tries to ignore the resulting stab of guilt. He would only use the episode against her as proof of bad mothering or evidence, somehow, of the evils of Mexico, one more reason to leave. There's no upside to gifting him ammunition.

Rocío invites Jane for coffee the next morning. They get it to go, and Rocío steers their walk toward the natural spring around which the city was begun five centuries earlier. The water dried up long ago, but it remains a pretty place, right by Jane's house. They sit overlooking a plaza with stone washbasins where women still bring laundry, although the water is provided now by city pipes rather than the flow of the spring.

Nearby benches are empty. *Now*, thinks Jane, *we'll get to the point.*

Rocío tells her that she noticed something was wrong during the most recent workshop at the elementary school when Nayeli leaned sideways in one of the child-size desks. She had gripped the side of the desk with one hand and extended the other to reach a dropped pen on the floor. The move was bound to be awkward in the cramped space, but something else about the way she held herself pulled Rocío's attention.

"As she stretched, her shirt rode up. I could see purple bruises spill off her ribcage to her hip. She must have heard me gasp. When she sat up, she tugged her shirt down hard."

But when Nayeli raised her head a moment later, her eyes were steady, and Rocío continued her lecture on childhood nutrition. Afterward, as the women filed out of the classroom, Rocío asked her to stay behind to help organize materials. Nayeli didn't bother to dodge the question. She explained that although Pablo does drink and get loud, and he's occasionally been a little rough, he never beat her before these two times, and she knows he'll never do it again now that they're getting a house.

"Two times, I told her, that's a pattern. Once someone proves themselves capable of abuse, you can never fully trust them again."

"What did she say?"

"She swore Pablo's not like that. She said it was the stress of suddenly having nowhere to live and having to build a shelter, a pen hardly fit for animals. He wants to go north, but she doesn't want him to. Then she admitted that he didn't like that extranjera pressuring him," Rocío holds Jane's gaze with her own, "and that's when he snapped the first time."

Jane squirms. "Yeah, that's pretty much what happened."

"What the hell? You said it went well."

"I couldn't tell you. I didn't want Nayeli to lose the house."

"Híjole, it's my fault. I sent you out to interfere."

"No, your intentions were good, and so were mine." Jane now catches Rocío's eyes. "You won't tell the other board members, will you? It's a terrible rule that punishes victims."

Rocío has one condition. "No more slumber parties."

"No argument here." Jane shudders as certain details from that long night replay in her mind. "So she told you I stayed. Honestly, does she blame me for what happened?"

"No, and she said you stayed because Carmen asked for help with the girls."

"Well, that, and because I was afraid of the dark." God, it happened again. "Did she say why he did it again?"

"Last Friday, without the girls' help, since thanks to you they're in school now every day—which is a good thing—she didn't make her quota, so the pinche boss wouldn't pay her."

"And for that, Pablo hit her?"

"Well, later that night he got drunk, and then, yeah."

"I *am* doing more harm than good. I just wanted those girls to get an education."

"She wants that, too."

"But she's getting beaten—"

"This is why Casa Mía ensures that the wife's name is on the deed. If she ever has to kick him out or he goes north, she'll still have the house for herself and her children."

"That's good, but—" Jane feels tears threatening. "Please tell her I'm so sorry."

"No. You didn't hit her. It's one hundred percent his fault." Rocío then shrugs. "Well, you can also blame an unequal society that still leaves so many people trapped in poverty, impotent, unable to improve their lives no matter how hard they work. Some big apology from you won't help anything. Better to leave her alone."

"All right. But I am sorry."

"I know, corazón, but don't wallow in it or let it discourage you from helping others. Buck up, babe. I just learned that one from Eleanor." Rocío changes the subject. "Speaking of her, you're cutting it really close. The money you brought in will run out in less than ten days, you know that, right? Bob is having a meltdown about stopping construction next week, and Eleanor's starting to lose it, too. We really need the rest of the money, querida, like immediately. You're out of time."

"I know. Eleanor's been on me. I've been—really distracted. But I've convinced her to borrow against next year's budget if necessary, which it pretty much seems it will be. Didn't she tell you? Just until we finally do the concert, which should happen in a couple months. If the concert falls through again—I know everyone is worried about that—I understand that I'll have to find another way fast to pay back the money. Believe me, I get it."

Rocío heads back to the Casa Mía office, but Jane lingers on the bench, watching a woman turn an oversize tap to fill one of the stone washbasins. The woman empties the contents of two plastic shopping bags into the water, then reaches in and pulls out a shirt to scrub with a bar of soap and a plastic brush.

Nayeli continues to pay a horrible price for trusting her, and they're running out of time.

That night, the ladder dreams change.

A demon appears far above Jane, propelling his limbs down the ladder one languid step at a time. He moves so slowly that she is not afraid. But that is wrong. In an instant, he's beside her. He leers, he smirks, he winks with dead eyes.

With a flourish, the demon offers a hand. Jane flinches and leans away but grips a rung of the ladder more tightly with both of her own. Thrusting his hand even nearer, the demon fans open his fingers to reveal a tiny black lump in the center of his palm. The lump appears to move on its own, and he indicates that Jane should look closely.

Perversely fascinated, she does. Two shapes take form. Two miniature figures pose in a tableau vivant on the demon's palm. Nayeli huddles on the ground, and Pablo looms over her. Beer bottles rain down while Nayeli ducks and writhes. Jane jerks back, and her left hand slips. The grinning demon closes his fingers around the tiny humans and then, with the resulting fist, shoves against Jane's chest. Her right hand, too, tears away from the rung.

She wakes up screaming. But no sound comes out.

"Diego and Lisa are in town this week, with her brother and sister-in-law," Jane tells Kevin.

"Back already? They just left like two weeks ago."

"Yeah, she said they had to come back to wrap things up with their house and pick up the dogs. The family's here to help them, I guess, or to get in a visit before the house is no longer theirs. Anyway, they want us to have dinner with them tomorrow. Up for it?" Dissonance clangs like a church bell she's way too close to. The invitation feels especially treacherous because Kevin has made it clear that he sees Diego and Lisa's choice to move to the States as a validation of his own desire. He'll use the opportunity to affirm his position. Moreover, an intimate, adults-only evening, without the boys as a buffer between them, is a situation she's avoided for months. She and Kevin have hardly been speaking, let alone going out together. But she likes Lisa and Diego, and it will likely be her last chance to see them for ages.

"Sure," Kevin answers. "We can find out how their re-entry is going, you know, see if they have any tips for us."

The job is great so far, Diego tells them over dinner at Lisa's favorite Italian place.

"We just came back to wrap up loose ends. I won't be allowed to fly pretty soon." Lisa pats her belly. "And then I probably won't be traveling with a newborn, either."

When Kevin asks, they assure him that Connor and Liam will do fine academically in American schools. Jane wonders how they can possibly know that since their son, Santiago, is a toddler, but she sees no point in questioning their confidence in her boys.

Beyond the job, the proximity of Lisa's family, and the wonders of Whole Foods, Lisa and Diego don't say much about their new lives but instead spend most of the evening waxing poetic about Mexican life and telling funny stories for the brother and sister-in-law's benefit. One story Jane has heard before centers around the annual festival in the Valle de Maiz.

"The Valley of the Corn?" the sister-in-law asks.

"Yes," Diego explains, "it's this neighborhood that used to be a separate village, not far from where Kevin and Jane live. They celebrate a local festival throughout nearly the entire month of May—you just missed it—with fireworks, drumming, and traditional dancing. It can go on all night."

"Sounds beautiful," says the sister-in-law.

Kevin groans. "It's not so beautiful when the drums keep you up for hours and then fireworks go off at four in the morning. It's ridiculous."

"The drumming doesn't do anything for you?" Jane demands a concession.

"No, after the first time, it's just noise."

"Seriously?" Her voice grows shrill. "You don't love seeing the gorgeous costumes and the athleticism of so many dancers young and old? How almost mystical they look in that fog of copal smoke? The fact that they uphold indigenous traditions in this day and age, that doesn't impress you? Have you no soul?"

They stare at her. Jane excuses herself to the ladies' room. She lets the water flow through her fingers and wonders whether they're all talking about her. Hopefully Diego is telling that story he was building up to.

When she returns to the table, Jane focuses on Lisa and the sister-in-law for the rest of the evening. She ignores the disgusted looks Kevin sends her.

37

GABRIELA RESTS HER HAND ON Jane's forearm as a cue to pause her story for a moment. "Is your daughter here, Meghan?" Gabriela asks.

"No, it's fine, she's at a sleepover," Meghan responds. "We have the house to ourselves."

Jane looks sheepish. "Sorry. I should've asked you that before unloading. I shouldn't have lost it at dinner last night, either. I seem to be losing it all over the place these days. But how can he not appreciate the drumming? Everyone loves it."

Meghan agrees. "It's hypnotic."

"I think it was just another way to make me crazy, dismissing the drumming and dancing like he dismisses me. To be honest, he's getting in my head with all his talk about his awesome new job. It makes me wonder, you know, am I still doing enough with my life during this career hiatus? Because if I think I am, his opinion of me shouldn't matter so much."

"You're doing plenty." Meghan refills their wineglasses and brings a salad bowl to the table.

"We're that generation, though, you know," Jane continues. "I bet your mom was like mine, Meghan, working to pass the ERA and change the world."

Meghan nods. "She was, actually, exactly like that."

"They told us our generation could have it all, right? Equal relationships, serious careers, and kids."

"Phases of life seem more realistic to me," says Gabriela.

"For sure, and I already had the career superwoman phase, but now I get these humiliating feelings that I'm letting down the sisterhood by not making money, not using my education. One of my law school classmates just got an appointment as a judge, and some are raking in cash or doing amazing human rights work, and what am I doing now?"

"Hey, you moved here to get away from some of that pressure, right?" Gabriela's voice is firm. "You're being really present as a mom, plus you're doing Casa Mía, painting, learning a language, and, it turns out, surviving a psycho husband. That's more than enough for anyone."

Meghan ladles pozole into big soup bowls. "Our mothers couldn't actually fix the whole world in one generation, you know."

"Right," Jane acknowledges. "That smells incredible, by the way."

"I can't take credit. I picked it up at that place on Calzada de la Luz." Meghan sets steaming bowls in front of each of them.

"Oh good, they make it spicy."

"I think you're not really that upset about your career break," Meghan continues. "It's more about the equal relationship part of the package, right? You guys doing any better?"

"No, not at all. We're broken, and Mexico hasn't fixed us. He'll never forgive me, and honestly, at this point, I'm not sure I'm capable of forgiving him, either. But I don't need to keep grieving the marriage. The problem is that when I try to talk honestly about what we're doing now, which is obviously just staying together for the kids, he gets so angry."

Gabriela pauses with a spoonful of pozole halfway to her mouth. "You've said that explicitly?"

"Yeah, big mistake, apparently. To him, the responsibility for fixing everything is on me, and he's not just a glass half empty kind of guy, he's more of a 'this cheap glass will shatter because nothing works in this stupid fucking country and the water will kill us anyway' guy."

Meghan laughs. "Well, that's not toxic or anything."

"He wasn't always like that, and on some level he knows it's wrong because he doesn't behave that way in public. He brings out this gentle 'aw shucks' vibe and has everyone fooled."

"No, he doesn't," says Gabriela. "Not us, we've seen the cracks in the façade."

Meghan snorts. "Not cracks, bloody holes."

"When we met as teenagers, his rebel without a cause thing worked on me. He was passionate and gorgeous back then, which didn't hurt."

"Never does."

"He was right, too, about things that were important to me then. Our small town was as backward and boring as he said it was, so we got out and made something of ourselves together. It was exciting for a long time."

"That's what he was telling me about," says Meghan, "your good old days."

"The problem is he never really stopped being that angry teen. He just hid it better for a decade or so. Now he feels entitled to feed that side of himself again, to sulk and rage."

"Do the kids see it?" asks Gabriela.

"Sometimes, and too often they hear him blame everything on me or Mexico and then see me react badly. I feel so guilty every time. He doesn't seem to, but I do."

"How long has it been like this?"

Jane isn't sure how to answer that. She's tried and failed to pinpoint the beginning of the dissolution. It was long before her connection with David. How long before, years? When was the last time they were truly happy together? Because they had been happy. When they were very young, when they got married, when they traveled, when she was pregnant. When exactly should they have realized that their problems were more than the normal tensions of a marriage? When exactly did it become intolerable?

If only she'd cashed in on her law degree and made real money, he wouldn't have resented her work and student loans. If only he'd gone to art school or done his art anyway without school or found another career he loved, he would have been so much happier, and he might have better understood her passion for her job despite its low pay. If only they'd gone to counseling much earlier. If only she'd been brave enough in the first place to leave him behind when she went off to college, she'd likely have met someone who'd have been a better fit. If only her parents had provided a healthy example, she might have been better at marriage. How far back should she go?

"I don't know. It happened gradually. I felt he saved me at first, so I tried to save him in return. In these last few years, whenever he had a streak of good days, I'd start hoping yet again that maybe the surliness and self-pity were just temporary byproducts of midlife stress from work or parenting. I can be a naïve perennial optimist, like you once said, sort of, or a complete idiot, because that hope was always dashed. Then with David, I thoroughly quashed it. But part of me still somehow believed this grand Mexico plan could actually work."

"Jane—" Gabriela tries.

"Now I realize how crazy that was, so I just try to protect myself and focus on other things."

Gabriela squeezes Jane's hand to get her attention. "I know what you told us before, about what he might do in a custody fight, but are you really sure that with the right lawyer divorce isn't the best option?"

"Believe me, I've thought it through a thousand times. In my case, it's the worst of two lousy options." Jane gazes into her soup. "I know I'm shaped by my own experience on the receiving end as a kid. My parents divorced when I was a little older than Connor is now. My brother and I lost. Sure, their failing marriage was bad for us, but their divorce was worse."

"How?" Meghan asks.

"Well, for one thing, my dad was older and completely unprepared to be a single father. Mom thought the custody arrangement would force him to step up—we did that modern-for-the-eighties thing, one week at Mom's and one at Dad's—but he never did."

"Jane, was he abusive?"

"No, no, just ill-equipped and old-fashioned. After a couple years of doing that back-and-forth, I was old enough to choose to live with Mom full time, and I still feel guilty for breaking Dad's heart. I shouldn't have had to make that decision, see? Mom should have made it for us. I bet she could have won primary custody, but she agreed to fifty-fifty."

"I'm sorry," murmurs Gabriela.

"It was so much worse for my brother out there alone on the ranch with Dad after that. When I bailed, Thomas felt he had to take care of Dad even though Dad was hard on him. That's when Thomas started drinking like a fish, among other things."

"What happened to him?"

"It threw his life off course for a while. That's a long story, and anyway, he's fine now, pretty much, he has his own big ranch and everything, but my point is that for us kids, divorce made things worse. I know marriage to my dad must have been miserable, but it would have been better for us if Mom had either stuck it out or fought for full custody."

Gabriela points out that Jane probably didn't know everything her mother was going through.

"Right, I'm sure I still don't. Nor can I know the alternate reality, what actually would have happened if she'd stayed. But I've had to live with betraying my father and especially my brother. I left him behind." Jane wipes tears from her cheeks with unnecessary force.

"It wasn't your fault," Meghan insists.

"Well, I could have stayed. I realize that a childish part of me has been angry at Mom ever since. I will not put my kids into a version of that story."

"So do what she didn't, do what you wanted her to do, get full custody or close to it. How could Kevin possibly win?"

"He flat-out told me he'll do whatever it takes to win, no holds barred, and I believe him. He always convinces himself that he's in the right, even that he's the better parent."

"A judge won't believe that. How the hell can he believe it?" Meghan wonders.

"No idea, but he does. And now with the possibility of moving back—"

"Wait, what?" Meghan interrupts. "You said something earlier about a job offer, and I meant to come back to that—it involves moving?"

"Yeah. I haven't told you that awesome bit of news yet. He's up for a promotion. In Houston." Jane sighs and pushes away her half-full bowl. As much as she loves the spicey pozole, with its chunks of tender pork, hominy, shredded cabbage, radishes, chiles, avocado, and onions, all swimming in a rich red broth, she can't seem to summon an appetite.

"No. You can't go." Gabriela shakes her head rigorously. "You'd be all alone, starting over again, with him like this."

"I know. So I proposed that he move without us. You know, he could come down some weekends, and we'd go up during school vacations. He lost it."

"Leave him, Jane," says Meghan with a certainty enhanced by fear.

"You don't understand the prospect of fighting him. I'm so afraid we'll end up not only bankrupt but with traumatized children. He's made it exceedingly clear that I should expect a ferocious battle. That might all be bullshit and bravado, but how can I take the risk?" Jane rests her face in her hands. *If only he would let the boys go gently. That's all that matters.* She wouldn't fight for much of the money if he conceded primary custody.

When Jane looks up, her friends have aged.

Gabriela straightens her shoulders. "Counseling?"

"We tried, finally, last year. Here, with that therapist from New York. After only three months, the guy offered to mediate our divorce."

"Not a good sign."

"Why don't I hold the kids' passports for a while?" Meghan offers, and nobody asks why. "There's a box of old clothes under my bed, we'll stash them there. Let me show you. You already have my spare key in case you ever need to come by and grab them in a hurry."

Meghan stands up and walks into her bedroom. She returns a

moment later with a plastic tub full of jeans, peasant blouses, and slim dresses, all of excellent quality but each with a rip, stain, or frayed hem.

Jane manages to smile. "These are beautiful."

"Too nice to throw away, right? I want to patch the jeans with leather or something, and embroider over the stains on the blouses, or have them made into new pieces, but I never get around to it."

"Someday. They'll be even cooler then, vintage."

"I promise it's the perfect spot. Nobody will ever look there."

"Thank you. It will help to know he can't run for the airport. I'll drop them off tomorrow." Jane drops her forehead into her hands again. "I can't believe I'm hiding my children's passports from my husband."

Gabriela brings cups of tea from Meghan's kitchen.

Jane dreams that night of faces melting in the style of Javier's self-portraits.

Her own face surfaces first, vaguely defined, then sharper in black and white until she sees every wrinkle, the depth of the bags under her eyes, and the harried expression within them. As she melts, Kevin's face takes over, and the ink brightens from black to green. Half his face screams his anger while the other side despairs. It's the angry half that dissolves, ink pouring off in chunky globs, leaving the pain.

When her sons' contorted faces begin to liquefy, too, and warm to green, that's when she wakes up, clawing at her sheets.

"LET'S GO," SAYS ELEANOR AS Jane approaches. "We should plan our pitch before the meeting starts."

Jane, Rocío, and Meghan follow Eleanor into an elegant hotel and through the lobby. The four women descend a wide stone staircase to the hotel's ballroom, chatting about the progress of various participants in Casa Mía's workshops. Jane usually loves checking out the rotating collection of impressive art on the walls of the stairwell, but now, glancing up at Javier's dripping portraits, she has to turn a shudder into a cough. They reach the ballroom and sign in, greet friends, collect glasses of wine, and settle into a row of available seats.

"So how exactly do these Women Funding Progress meetings work?" asks Eleanor.

Jane explains. "Three nominated organizations will be drawn from a hat. If drawn, we get five minutes to present. Then all the members vote. Meghan and I are joint members, so we share a vote for our thousand-peso contribution. I'm sure most of these women are already familiar with Casa Mía, so we wouldn't need to spend much time explaining our mission. Instead, we can focus on exactly how we'd spend the money."

"How much are we talking about?" asks Eleanor.

"It depends on how many women are here tonight," Meghan jumps in, "plus how many submitted contributions ahead of time. The goal is a hundred thousand pesos, but it's never actually been that much. I think it's typically around seventy-five to eighty-five."

"So," Jane declares, "I think we should propose funding six months of our new women's workshops—they don't cost much—and put the rest toward a house. This group will love the angle of helping families by empowering women. With the majority of the funds going toward our core mission."

Eleanor nods in agreement. "Very well. You speak for us, Jane. Rocío, go up with her."

"Let's all go in a show of force," Jane counters. "But are you sure you don't want to do the talking?"

Eleanor glances around the room. "No, most of these old broads have heard from me before, many times, in other settings. Your youthful energy will be more effective."

Jane smiles. This is her chance. "Then if I do this and it works—if we get drawn, first of all—"

"There are twenty-two names in the hat," says Meghan. "So a one in seven shot."

"—the money should go to Nayeli's house specifically, not the general fund. This certainly counts as outside our usual fundraising sources. Bob and the guys had never even heard of Women Funding Progress."

"I agree," says Meghan.

"The approximately eighty thousand we'd win," Jane continues, "is exactly what we need to finish the house, minus a few thousand for the workshops. And I got the first hundred and twenty right here in this room after the art auction for Amigos del Parque."

"So it's fate, clearly." Eleanor's tone is dry, but she smiles.

"Please, I cannot handle those girls sinking up to their knees in mud making bricks for the rest of their lives."

"That's a strong pitch," says a voice behind them. "Good luck up there, I'll vote for you." Four heads turn to locate the source. The speaker is an imposing woman of about fifty with a lush crop of corkscrew curls.

"Really," says Eleanor with a polite chuckle although she seems irritated by the interruption. "Thank you."

Jane grins at the woman. "Thanks."

Eleanor reclaims her attention. "All right, Jane, fine, if we get drawn and you manage to win. In that case, we wouldn't have to face Bob this week about borrowing from next year's budget, which would be a huge relief for both of us."

"Yes!" Jane crows. Somehow she's not surprised a few minutes later when Casa Mía is pulled out of the hat, along with Las Líderes del Futuro and Hope for the Children.

"Yes." Eleanor squeals this time, while Rocío and Meghan cheer.

Jane is more circumspect. "Tough competition."

"How do you mean?" asks Eleanor.

"You know them, Las Líderes helps teenage girls stay in school and go to college. Hope for the Children does art education and literacy projects. This will be a tough vote."

But when it's time to make the pitch, Jane's confidence grows as she talks. Most of the women already know and respect Casa Mía. When she tells them about the new workshops, how her team is not only building solid, cost-effective houses for desperately poor people but now also providing a year of empowering, community-building workshops on topics from nutrition to addiction to family planning, many of the women smile back at her. The room is with her. When she describes Nayeli and her daughters working from dawn to dusk in the brickyard, the girls missing school to do so, her husband breathing in toxins at the kilns, and all of them having only a horrible shack to come home to, some women grimace in sympathy or nod along.

By the time Jane sits down, she's on a high. Eleanor nervously pats Jane's hand while the votes are counted. Meanwhile, the director of a nonprofit nursing home makes a pitch to recruit volunteers, someone announces a spay and neuter campaign for dogs in rural communities, and other groups invite the crowd to their various fundraisers. Jane stands to greet an acquaintance just as there is a call from the podium for everyone's attention. She sits back down.

"First, I have some great news," announces the director of Women Funding Progress. "We have a new record. Give yourselves a hand, ladies, you contributed 93,000 pesos tonight." The large room swells with clapping and cheering. "Now, the big moment. Our winner is Casa Mía! Come on up here, congratulations."

Jane and her colleagues jump from their seats while the ballroom again fills with the clapping of satisfied women. She actually, finally, did it. Nayeli's house is paid for. Jane feels tears of relief welling. She blinks them back and does a silly dance with Meghan instead.

"Way to come in under the wire." Eleanor smiles at her.

Registering the relief in Eleanor's eyes, Jane feels more than a little guilty for putting her through this. "Now the money we raise from the concert can go into the general fund," she says. The promise assuages her guilt.

As they make their way down the aisle toward the front of the room, a voice calls out behind them. "Let's make it an even hundred."

"What was that?" asks the director. "Hush, everyone, things just got interesting. Am I to understand you will personally kick in the remaining 7,000 pesos right now? We just met our goal for the first time?"

"Yes, ma'am." It's the woman with the abundant curls. The room erupts again.

The director invites the woman to the front of the room along with the Casa Mía team and the treasurer of Women Funding Progress with the big envelope of cash. They line up, and a dozen camera flashes go off. When the mayor's wife congratulates them, cameras flash again.

Several people approach with proposals for joint projects. When Jane finally looks around for the woman with the curls to properly thank her, she's gone.

ARRIVING AT SCHOOL THE NEXT morning, Jane and her boys cross the street in front of a four-wheeler. She waves at the dad at the wheel in a hot pink wig and cowboy hat, his daughter leaning around him, her grin matching his. In honor of the last day of classes, the school is swathed in pastel balloons and banners celebrating the year's successes. As Jane enters the building with her sons, elaborately costumed payasos, niñitos, and animalitos wish her a good morning. She has to look closely to identify each teacher beneath the make-up. Some parents have stepped up, too. Alejandra appears to be a magician, and Jane laughs when she sees Enrique dressed as el Chavo del Ocho, the title character from a hugely popular old sitcom in which adult actors portrayed kids. He's about the same age as the middle-aged star who played the role. "Nailed it," she tells him.

The parents swap greetings and summer vacation plans until the principal calls them out to dance for the students in a reversal of the usual routine. Teachers lead the parents in the chu-chu-wa, a dance children learn in kindergarten. Jane finds a spot next to Nayeli. The dance ends with each parent turning circles, brazos extendidos, dedos arriba, cabeza atrás, lengua afuera y pompis atrás. They laugh at each other as they willingly make fools of themselves for their kids.

When the song ends, words pour out of Nayeli. "Señorita Rocío called me last night. She said you made a speech to a hundred rich ladies, and they all helped. Is it true?"

"That's what happened." Jane grins.

"Dios mío, I can't believe it."

"To be honest, I can't, either. Nothing can stop your house now. Construction will continue straight through. We'll be celebrating at your housewarming in a few weeks."

"Come on you two, sing," commands el Chavo del Ocho. The rest of the adults have begun Las Mañanitas, the traditional song for birthdays and other sentimental events. Afterward, the parents are dismissed, knowing the fun will continue.

On the way out, Jane introduces her kids to Nayeli. "I'd love for you to meet my boys. This is Connor, and the one trying to run away over there is Liam."

"It's good to meet you. What handsome boys. Connor, Dulce says you have been kind to her. She can be shy, so having friends like you helps. Thank you." She turns to Liam. "And I hope you haven't been wrestling too many more bulls, little warrior."

"Oh no, Señora, not too many." Nayeli chuckles as Liam bounces away across the courtyard, clearly pleased with himself.

Jane spots Gabriela and Hannah near the door. "Guess what? We won the rest of the money for the house last night."

"I heard," says Gabriela. "At Women Funding Progress, right? Eleanor told me your speech was powerful stuff, chica. I ran into her this morning at the coffee shop."

"Did she tell you what I did?"

"She may have mentioned it." Gabriela grins.

"What did you do?" asks Hannah.

"Well, when Eleanor said I should make the presentation if our name got drawn, I said sure, on the condition that if we won, the money would go to Nayeli's house. She didn't totally love it."

Gabriela shrugs. "But why bother to argue about such a long shot, right?"

"Exactly. And then we won. It's such a relief."

Meghan approaches. "You guys, it was so cool. Jane was amazing."

"Want to celebrate?" asks Hannah. "I'm meeting Lindsay out at La Gruta in an hour. The hot springs and then margaritas for lunch."

"Thank you, sounds fabulous," says Jane, "but I can't today. Tell Lindsay I want a raincheck with you two."

As thrilled as she is about the house, melancholy descends as Jane leaves the school. Her babies, growing up so fast, are happy and settled here. They shouldn't have to face starting over again so soon in another new school. They shouldn't have to learn yet another culture.

"Hey, can we walk with you?"

Jane turns. Gabriela and Meghan catch up and fall into step with her.

"Any word on the promotion?"

"Not yet."

"Good, here's hoping he doesn't get it." Gabriela holds her crossed fingers up to the sky.

"I could call the company and make a complaint against him." Meghan looks serious. "Like that he's a scary motherfucker."

"Don't."

"It seems like a good sign, though, that he hasn't had an answer yet."

"Keep us posted. We're always here." Gabriela wraps an arm around Jane's shoulders. "You know that, right?"

"This wasn't the direction either of you needed to go, was it?"

"Nope, not at all," Meghan acknowledges. "We just wanted to check on you."

"I love you guys."

They hug her and turn back.

Walking through Parque Juárez, Jane spots Chinese bead dancers. The women, all appearing to be Mexicans in their sixties and seventies, have gathered in a circle around a fountain in a quiet corner of the park. They execute slow, graceful tai chi movements while Chinese music tries to escape from an ancient boombox. Each woman has a long rope of beads slung diagonally across her chest, ammo-belt style. After the warm-up, they get down to the serious business of swinging the ropes to one side and the other at the command of their leader, a poker-faced, pot-bellied matron who keeps time and barks instructions. Today two teenage boys have joined them, presumably someone's grandsons. The Chinese music and the whole scene are utterly out of place and time and therefore seem somehow universal and comforting.

At home, Jane faces a long list of errands and a glaringly blank canvas, but church bells chime and the chu-chu-wa and scratchy Chinese music echo in her head. She settles down to work, trying to keep the move out of her mind. There is no point in panicking while it's still only a possibility, and if it is really about to happen, she should fully enjoy her last days in Mexico.

The annual film festival is coming up, and Kevin used to like that kind of thing. Perhaps he would see an invitation as an olive branch. Maybe it would get them talking again, at least. Whatever happens, they have to communicate. Perhaps they can survive an evening together if there's a screen to stare at most of the time.

THE LIGHTS COME UP IN the theater, but the image of a father shouldering his errant son's coffin doesn't fade. The man's poignant physicality remains with Jane, his grizzled, deeply lined face in striking contrast to his still muscular, lean torso. The scene in which the man asks the funeral director for a discount but still can't afford to bury his son replays in her mind. What dignity in the face of shame and unbearable loss.

Jane glances at Kevin. She speaks first to set the tone of the conversation. "I read the director was German. German angst meets Latin passion, right? What did you think?"

"I don't know." He shrugs.

"Oh." She tries to focus on the positive. At least he came. They're trying to get along for an evening, and it's important that they manage to be civil, but she feels herself slipping into a comparison of the sullen man beside her with the young romantic he once was. That man would have talked about nuances of the film all night, preferably in bed with her, nothing but a bottle of wine ever coming between them.

They need to get through the evening at least. She has to try. "Want to walk around the Jardín and stretch our legs before the shorts? Hopefully the rain has stopped."

"You really want to stay for those?"

"If you don't mind. We have a babysitter and everything." She carefully keeps her tone light as they emerge into the rain-scented air. "Look, just a little drizzle."

They make footprints crossing the soggy red carpet and then step onto the glistening stones of the sidewalk. At the end of the block, they turn from Calle Mesones onto Hidalgo, where the buzz of the Jardín reaches them. She can always feel it at least a half block out, further at night. Rather than the cheery rhythms of the usual mariachis, though, this evening's hum is a deeper, pounding call. She recognizes the Conchero dancers' drums, the ones she loves that seem able to control her heart's rhythm. A rock anthem rises, too, layered over the drums.

"So what have you been drawing lately? I'd love to see what you're working on."

"I haven't had much time." He continues after a pause. "It's not turning out."

"Give yourself a chance. Maybe take a class to get back into it? That helped me."

"I said I don't have time."

"Come on—"

"Jane, give it up. That ship has sailed."

They reach the Jardín. Four shaggy young musicians on a temporary stage seize their hour of glory undeterred by the rows of empty, dripping chairs stretched out before them. Equally unstoppable, Conchero dancers at the other end of the plaza whirl and stomp. The two streams of sound prove strangely compatible.

She channels her nervous energy into capturing the spectacle with her phone, thinking about how the German director would do it. Standing on a park bench, she finds a good angle to pan over each dancer, hover on the drummers, and then sweep across the puddled plaza and empty folding chairs to the rockers on stage. The neo-gothic grandeur of the parroquia looms over the entire scene. Jane wonders, as she has before, how such a huge pile of stone can look so light and airy. Right now, in the last moments of sunset, the church is bathed in warm, rich rays, as though the whole edifice has caught fire. The mist left behind by the rain only seems to amplify the colors.

The Jardín should be full of people at this hour, but only a few diehard friends of the band are rocking out in the wet, and only a few determined tourists film the dancers. The locals who would normally take an evening stroll and populate the benches haven't come out yet. A little later, however, if the sky clears and the puddles begin to dry up, the mariachis will appear as if by magic, as will the vendors of hot roasted corn, tacos, ice cream, and balloons.

Kevin makes it clear that he has neither the patience nor the desire to sit through a collection of arty, cerebral short films. Jane debates turning back alone and slipping into the theater, but in the end she plods beside him away from the plaza. This date night, she concludes, was as futile as nearly every other they've attempted in the last two years. The romantic might still be in there somewhere, but her fishing for him, always unsuccessfully, has become an absurdist exercise worthy of its own short film. She should have gone to the festival with Gabriela or Meghan instead.

As they walk home, she redirects the movie's funeral procession, imagining it here in the streets of San Miguel. The slim, powerful old man shoulders a side of his son's coffin and turns this corner here, then that one. A woman follows, her steps heavy with grief, fingers working the beads of a rosary. They pass a flower vendor sitting on the sidewalk next to a pyramid of white roses protected by a sheet of plastic. Jane adds a few extras: people she knows join the mourning or simply pass by. A block further, the scene turns inappropriately festive. Mojigangas show up, and then a band in parrot blue jackets. That tequila burro from Rocío's wedding procession last year arrives. His handler takes a bottle from the basket on the burro's back and starts pouring a nice reposada into small ceramic cups that people wear as clunky pendants on ribbons around their necks. They dance.

She starts to feel guilty, as though she were defiling the memory of someone real, so she blinks them all away.

41

GABRIELA SMILES AS JANE APPROACHES the table in their favorite coffee shop. "Hi, I ordered you a latte. So how's the house coming along?"

"Thank you, and great, the walls are up. The roof pour is still a big deal, that's next, but in a couple more weeks we can bring volunteers out to paint and then throw the best housewarming ever. Half the school wants to come because of the girls."

"How can I help?"

"You already did. We wouldn't be here if you hadn't convinced Regina to donate the first half."

"But what do you need now?"

A sudden thought lights Jane's face. "You know what would be amazing? Mariachis. We wanted them for the hundredth housewarming but couldn't justify the cost. This turnout may be even bigger, with lots of potential new donors to impress. If you were to chip in and get some friends to help, it wouldn't be at the organization's expense."

Gabriela agrees. She offers to hit up Lindsay, Araceli and Javier, and Enrique and Alejandra.

"Gracias, corazón, what would I do without you? When are we finally going to convince you to join the board?"

"Hold up there, I don't think I have time. Lately you and Meghan seem to live and breathe Casa Mía. For a volunteer board position, it takes over your lives."

"You're right, I've gone a little overboard, but that's not required or even encouraged. You can put in only as much time as you want, I swear. The actual requirements are minimal."

"You don't give up, do you?" Gabriela laughs. "I'll think about it, I promise, but I won't commit until we know for sure you're staying. I've been afraid to ask."

Jane glances around the café. "I don't know yet because Kevin still hasn't heard about the promotion. Let's talk about something else, though, so as not to ruin this beautiful day." She is not in the mood to reveal, even to Gabriela, just how hopeless she's feeling about the impending move. Moreover, it was Gaby herself who taught her not to overshare in cozy coffee shops.

"Actually, did you hear? Verónica's back. She came home last night."

"Oh, thank God! She's all right? Her family paid?"

"They must have. I don't know the details." Gabriela shrugs. "We may never know. They'll probably move abroad and never come back. That's what I would do."

"Right, how can she ever feel safe again?"

"It's horrible. Fucking Mexico."

"Gaby."

"It's my country, I can say that."

JANE SLAMS THE CAR DOOR. She slumps into the driver's seat, rests her forehead on the steering wheel, and lets her anger dissipate from the hundredth round of the same fight.

As awkward as it is to go to events by herself, the truth is she'll have more fun without him. At least she won't have to be his incompetent translator the whole evening, and he won't start pressuring her to leave the party a half hour after they arrive. Rocío, Meghan, and their husbands will be there, so she won't be alone. It'll be fine. She sits up, starts the car, and backs out of the garage, slipping her sunglasses down from the top of her head. A strand of hair snags in the hinge, and she swears.

Her left elbow pokes out through the open window. Warm wind licks her skin and makes her hair dance. She turns her music up and swerves around the occasional pothole while wondering what to expect. This party will be very different from the last quinceañera she attended a few months ago in which the birthday girl, whose parents are real estate developers, wore a ballgown with an enormous skirt to the religious ceremony and then, during the lavish banquet that followed, went through three costume changes while performing sophisticated and jaw-droppingly sexy dances with her six male attendants. When all the guests were invited to hit the dance floor after dinner, two ten-foot-tall club robots appeared. It was the most elaborate coming-of-age party Jane had ever been to, beating out several swanky bar mitzvahs back in New York. Tonight, however, will be the no-frills version.

Just before she reaches the turn for Pueblo Nuevo, a burst of light doubling itself in her rearview mirror blinds her momentarily. Police flashers. She's being pulled over. Alone. By Mexican cops. Her heart makes up for a missed beat by pumping at double speed. She brakes and brings the car to rest on the narrow shoulder.

The policeman taps his knuckles against her window. She lowers it and looks up at him. He's fifty-something, graying at the temples, fatherly, his expression serious but gentle.

"Buenas tardes, Señora. Do you know why I stopped you?"

"Buenas tardes. No, Officer, I don't." She wonders when she's supposed to offer the mordida and how much it should be.

"Your environmental inspection sticker expired three months ago. This is a pretty new car, so it should pass easily, but driving around with an expired sticker can get you into trouble. It's a hefty fine. You should take care of that tomorrow."

"Yes, Officer, I'll do that." This must be the moment. She probably missed some nuance. Her Spanish still needs so much work. She reaches to the passenger seat for her purse. Better a small bribe than a big fine. But the officer is already walking back to his car, offering over his shoulder a polite reminder to drive safely and have a pleasant evening, leaving Jane to wonder whether she knows anything at all about this country yet.

43

JANE ARRIVES IN PUEBLO NUEVO a few minutes later, still wondering how getting pulled over by a member of a famously corrupt police force wasn't the worst part of her day. The interaction with that man was far more civilized than most of the communication that goes on within her marriage at this point. She slaps the steering wheel. She may have to walk into this party alone, but she won't do it with ruined mascara.

Before getting out of her car, Jane scans the scene across the road. She's surprised to see a stage framed by huge speakers and a wooden dance floor elevating the partygoers a few centimeters above the dusty vacant lot that serves as the neighborhood's communal plaza. Twenty tables covered in crisp white cloths surround the dance floor. Half the ejido must be invited. Guests enter through pink balloon arches, and more balloons spell out "Gloria 15" over the stage. A bouncy castle off to one side sways under the impact of a dozen of the smallest guests. Jane wonders how the family can possibly afford all this.

She joins the Casa Mía contingent, and Rocío greets her. "Hey there. Some party, right?"

Jane poses the obvious question. "How in the world did Gloria's parents pull this off?"

"We were just talking about it. Don't worry, her mom told me an uncle went north five years ago and started his own gardening business in Annapolis, Maryland. Doing very well, apparently, with fifteen gardeners under him now. Gloria's his favorite niece, and he still has no kids of his own, so he's the padrino."

"He's footing the whole bill? Thank God. I was scared they'd gone to a payday lender."

"The sad thing is the uncle couldn't even come. It's high season for him, so there was some fear of losing clients."

"And the risk of not making it back across the border to his business."

"Exactly."

"That's so sad. Well, I'm sure they'll send him lots of pictures."

Jane spots Nayeli and works her way through the crowd. At the same moment, each woman mentions that the next big party in the neighborhood will be Nayeli's housewarming. They laugh and acknowledge that it will be a much simpler affair than the extravaganza unfolding around them.

"I have a surprise, though," says Jane.

"Are you going to tell me?"

"No, then it wouldn't be a surprise. I shouldn't have brought it up." She is immediately embarrassed. She's getting more passive aggressive by the day and leaking anger all over.

Nayeli doesn't look upset. "You're so mean," she jokes as a faraway look passes through her eyes.

"What is it?"

"Oh, nothing. It's just, do you see that girl over there in the red top, all sparkly? She's sixteen or seventeen?"

"Pretty girl, and yeah, gorgeous blouse, too."

"Well, I saw it first, when you brought those clothes to the church. But someone got to it before I could, and then that girl's mother grabbed it out of the first woman's hands, remember? She's smart, she saved it for tonight. That could've been me if I were clever. But with so much coming into my life right now—a house, my God—how can I be jealous over a shirt?"

Jane feels honored by the intimacy of the confession. "We may be middle-aged mothers, but it's not wrong to still want a little glamor in our lives, to be beautiful, even desirable."

Nayeli's laugh is small and wistful but without malice. "It's fine. That girl wears it better than I ever could have."

Jane notices several of Dulce and Lupita's old classmates asking them questions with hard edges about their new school. At the beginning of the evening, the two girls are warm and friendly to Jane, but after weathering the second such barrage, they begin to keep their distance from her, and she understands their need to make peace with the neighbors. They're right not to flaunt their abundance of luck in front of the many children who still enjoy little of it. So rather than invite them directly, as she had planned to do, she instead tells Nayeli quietly about an upcoming trip to a water park.

"It's not an official school trip or anything, just some moms looking for fun things to do now that school's out and our kids are driving us crazy. Most of Dulce's class will be there, I think, and some of Lupita's friends, like Sarah, and a few younger ones."

"It sounds nice but expensive, Señora."

"I would like to invite your family if you will allow me. Dulce and Lupita will have so much fun, and you and Pablo can get to know some of the other parents."

"How kind. I'm sure my girls would love to go. I'll talk to Pablo."

THE CURLY FRIES FROM THE water park's cafeteria are soggy, but the tacos look good. Jane's fingers start to cramp from pinching the corners of the flimsy, red-checked cardboard trays containing her boys' greasy lunches. She walks back toward the main pool dodging shrieking toddlers and shuffling grandparents. Several teenagers run past her, laughing and cheering for two of their own who tap a beach ball back and forth between them, never dropping it, as though they were one hormone-drenched but coordinated organism.

In the poolside crowd, Nayeli and Pablo talk to another couple from the school. Jane is impressed that they came. They both had to have taken several hours off work, which is a significant sacrifice since they won't get paid for the missed hours, for the bricks they didn't make and didn't fire. She will check on them again just as soon as she can get her boys to climb out of the pool long enough to eat the lunches currently dripping onto her hands.

She spots a teenage lifeguard lecturing a group of Cervantes fourth graders. His earnest eyes reflect irritation and concern as he repeats an injunction against dunking. Some of the kids look at their feet, while others, with jutted chins and crossed arms or hands on hips in shows of bravado, argue that they were just playing and didn't do anything wrong. Is that Dulce? Great, she's part of it. Jane spots Connor hovering nearby, too. Before they left the house this morning, she asked him and his brother to make sure Dulce and Lupita were included. She had imagined them inviting the girls to play a round of

Marco Polo or freeze tag. This is not what she had in mind. She alters her route, heading toward the culprits.

Pablo walks in the same direction. He must have noticed the line-up at the same time she did. She flinches, then tries to cover it with an eyeroll at the naughty children. He cracks a smile and walks around the group toward his daughter.

Jane touches Connor's shoulder and asks what happened. Was he part of it? No, because he'd gone to buy a lemonade, but he would have been otherwise. "I'm supposed to play with Dulce, right?"

"Right, play with her, not get her into trouble."

"I didn't."

"Well, find something fun but safe to do, all right? After you eat these tacos and fries. Now where's your brother? I have his lunch, too."

It begins with a keening. Horrible, inhuman, a sound Jane has never heard before and prays never to hear again. Her stomach clenches as she looks for the source. A woman has fallen to her knees by the pool, and several faces around her contort in horror. Jane understands before she knows. The platter of tacos for Liam slips from her grasp first, splattering her sandals, and a second later his curly fries tumble into the grass beside the path. Connor's right here, but where's Liam? Her eyes frantically scan the pool.

Blonde hair, darker in the water, billows and sways like fronds of seaweed. She can barely make out the rest of the child in the blinding glare of the sun on the pool's surface.

A long body launches into the water. Strong arms find the girl's torso and gather her up. Jane still can't see the child's face, only slack limbs hanging as the lifeguard cradles her. Empty space grows around him as children pull away, instinctively putting distance between themselves and a terrible thing. The screaming spreads. More adults freeze, eyes searching for their own children. Several who don't immediately spot their offspring turn and run toward other pools. Jane glimpses the face of the first screamer now manically hugging her own children, a small girl and smaller boy. The blonde girl is not hers. A chill envelops Jane as she admits to herself that she recognizes that hair. Tiny hairs on her own arms and neck respond.

Someone's running through the crowd, shoving people out of the way. Alejandra, thank God, she's a doctor. Jane feels a flash of electric hope. Alejandra's there now, breathing into the child's mouth while the lifeguard counts out chest compressions.

Jane looks around for Liam but instead sees Hannah, who at that moment, along with many others, registers the commotion and turns around. Her features instantaneously harden into a mask of terror. These screams are guttural. Choking, searing anguish. Hannah lurches forward, taking a dozen clumsy steps, and latches onto Alejandra's shoulders, pulling her friend away from her daughter.

"Get her off me," yells Alejandra. When no one moves, she barks, "Now!"

Jane forces herself forward. She crouches next to Hannah, wraps her arms around her chest, and yanks. They both tumble backward. A blanket of arms behind them cushions their fall, catching and lifting. Jane holds Hannah as tightly as she can. More arms hold them both. Then Lindsay is beside her, wrapping her arms around Hannah, too.

"Shhh, Ale's doing CPR. You have to let her do it," Lindsay says into Hannah's ear. "You can't be in her way."

Hannah writhes. When she looks at Jane and Lindsay, her eyes are wild. Jane can't bear to hold her gaze, so she pulls even closer and tucks her chin over Hannah's shoulder. She tries to make soothing noises but hears her own terror, so she shuts her mouth and rubs Hannah's back.

Lindsay's voice is more controlled. "Try to stay calm, honey, Ale's helping her."

Hannah shudders, calls to her daughter, and fights again to pull away from Lindsay and Jane. Jane stops rubbing and hugs harder, while Lindsay's strong arms encompass them both. Other hands push down on Hannah's shoulders, other arms embrace, other faces murmur.

Alejandra turns Sarah's head to the side and scoops away vomit. A cheer goes up, but others squirm, those who know enough to realize it may only have been an involuntary reflex.

Suddenly Ale and the lifeguard are up and running, the girl again cradled in his arms. She hangs limply, like the broken hummingbird Liam once held. The other arms pull Hannah up from Jane's lap. Men on either side of Hannah half carry her as they follow the lifeguard. Jane and others follow, too. "An ambulance?" Jane asks.

A man running near them answers. "No, it would take too long to get here." His expression is grim. "Park van."

Jane stumbles as the realization hits her that even the one-way trip to the hospital will take too long. Her right elbow takes the brunt of the fall, and her bare knees also lose a layer of skin on the asphalt path. It's several miles down a slow gravel road to the highway, and even then, too many more miles. Too much time passes. She thinks of brain damage, of that vivacious child barely existing in a hospital bed for the rest of her days, she who was always smiling and chattering, always moving. A still hummingbird is unnatural, unimaginable.

Then Jane's up again. She reaches the parking lot as the van shudders away, trailing a storm of red-gray dust. She runs after it a few more steps, then stops, limp-armed, defeated.

Her car, her keys, her boys. Oh God, she never located Liam. Jane spins back toward the park and runs again, pushing through the gates at an adrenalin-fueled clip. Two confused attendants eye her bloody knees and don't attempt to stop her. Inside, hundreds of people haven't noticed the trauma in their midst. Kids still splash in the other pools, cheery ranchero music still blares from large speakers, and families lounge on blankets in the shade of enormous trees here long before the park was built. Tinfoil packets of vegetables and slabs of arrachera still sizzle on grills, and a fútbol game unfolds among sweaty teens on a sunbaked field. All around her, people still talk and laugh, unaware.

Jane nears the main pool and starts to encounter parents from the school. She hears them offering false reassurances to their children.

"She'll be fine," mothers tell daughters and sons. "She threw up the water she swallowed. Her body is protecting her." "A doctor has her," say fathers. "They're taking her to the hospital." With smiles of forced calm, nannies round up their charges, explaining that they need to go home. Now. "But we just got here," whine the littlest ones.

There, Gaby has her boys.

"Thank you." Jane pulls Liam and Connor into her arms. She hugs them too hard. They don't complain. Over their heads, she looks at the now-empty pool, which stretches placid and inviting, its surface glittering in the brilliant sunlight.

Connor pulls back and eyes her. "Mom? Sarah's gonna be OK?"

It dawns on her what those other parents must be thinking, what lies behind their false cheer. Now is not the time nor the place. Get the kids home first. "I really hope so."

"I guessed you'd go in the ambulance," says Gabriela. "I was going to take Connor and Liam with me."

"I tripped and fell on the path, so stupid. They couldn't wait. Lindsay's with her, though."

"That's good, I think Lindsay's the closest to Hannah of anyone here. I'm sure she could use some help, though. Do you want to go in your car and catch up to them at the hospital? I'll take Connor and Liam home with us to watch a movie."

Jane studies her sons' faces. "Does that sound good, guys? Go watch a movie at Toñito's house until I get there to pick you up? Sarah's mom needs some help right now."

Connor looks hesitant but nods. Liam dips his chin, too.

"Mom." Connor tugs at her hand. "You're bleeding."

"I'm OK, I just tripped on the path."

"Doesn't it hurt?"

"Not really, just stings a little." Then she remembers. "Nayeli's family. I brought them here. Gaby, can you give them a ride home? We can't leave them stranded."

"No problem. It'll be a packed car, but the three boys can ride in the way back."

"Thank you. I'll just tell them and go."

It doesn't take long to find the family. They huddle on a bench, Lupita curled tightly into her mother's chest, while Dulce slumps against her father.

Before Jane can produce any comforting words, Pablo speaks. "They will blame our children, won't they? That young man, the lifeguard, wasn't watching because he was dealing with our Dulce and your Connor and the others."

"Not my Connor." It's a kneejerk reaction. Then the horrible truth of the statement lands like a blow. "No, it wasn't the kids' fault or the lifeguard's, either, it just happened, and we don't even know—"

"Yes, we do."

Dulce's shoulders shudder.

"They'll blame them, Señora," Pablo insists. "They'll blame us, you'll see."

Dulce looks at her father. "Sarah wasn't playing with us. She's too little, she wasn't part of our game, I promise."

"You and your friends weren't supposed to dunk. It's dangerous. While you were getting in trouble, she was drowning. He didn't see her, so he didn't save her."

Dulce's anguish rips through her face. "Papá, no."

Jane wants to slap her hand over Pablo's mouth, but the words are already out and, in their truth, have life. If the kids hadn't played that stupid game, if the lifeguard hadn't had to deal with them right then, he would have been watching. He would have seen whatever happened to Sarah. Connor was thirsty. For that alone, he escaped lifelong guilt. Her relief at the preservation of her son's innocence is absolute but wrong before the pain in Dulce's eyes.

Right now, maybe she can be useful to Hannah if not to Dulce. "I have to go to the hospital, so my friend Gabriela there will drive you home."

"All right, Señora, thank you," says Nayeli.

Jane hurries back to Gabriela, wraps each of her boys in another too-strong hug, grabs her bag, and runs again to the parking lot. On the way, she steps in taco mess and smashed curly fries and ignores the startled looks several people shoot at her as she brushes past them. Once she reaches her car, she drives as fast as the gravel road will allow.

How is it possible that nobody saw it happening? There were thirty kids in the pool and nearly that many parents standing around. How did no one notice?

She sat through a video when her boys were toddlers taking their first swimming lessons. The video taught that drowning doesn't look the way we imagine it does. There is less thrashing and screaming, more slipping and quiet gulping. But still, how could not one person see it?

Pablo's right. Human nature dictates finding an explanation, a guilty party. People won't let this be something that just happened, although it's not the lifeguard's fault nor should they allow the kids to take on a mantel of guilt. They can't handle this. No child should have to. Of course they didn't mean to distract that boy at the wrong moment, they were just playing, for God's sake. He was doing his job.

FINALLY, JANE REACHES THE FREEWAY. The road deserves her full attention. It's a two-lane highway treated as four since there's no good reason to let unusually wide shoulders go to waste. She passes a semi loaded with tall stacks of chicken cages, getting around it just before a car coming from the opposite direction passes a pickup pulling a horse trailer. Approaching the city, she reaches a traffic circle and flies onto the first exit. Ten minutes later, she arrives at the hospital.

Jane marches past the emergency waiting room attendants, following the sound of Hannah's voice. There is no need to ask where to go. No need to ask anything.

In a wide, white hall, the vanload of Cervantes parents and park staff huddle in front of Sarah's room. Several cry openly, and as Jane approaches, the nearest mother acknowledges the worst. The young lifeguard sits on the floor, the eyes in his ravaged face staring at something Jane can't see.

She steps into the room. Because Hannah's back is to her, she has a moment to take in the sight of Sarah lying too still on the gurney. One of Hannah's hands rests on her daughter's chest, and the other finger-combs Sarah's now dry hair. The crisp sheet, precisely folded, reaches to an inch below the tops of Sarah's shoulders, where pink and teal swimsuit straps glare against pale skin. Alejandra and Lindsay stand on either side of Hannah.

Hannah's voice has sunk into a scratchy, arrhythmic moan. At the touch of Jane's hand to her shoulder, Hannah jumps. The noise stops.

"My baby." Hannah chokes on the syllables. "How could this happen?"

"I don't know. I'm so sorry." Jane tries to hug her, but through the open door, Hannah sees the lifeguard slumped on the floor in the hall.

"You." Hannah spits out the word, steps through the door, and lunges at the guy. "Where were you?"

The boy does nothing to defend himself when Hannah claws at him. It takes two fathers to pull her off him. Thin lines of blood glisten where she's scratched his face, neck, and shoulders. Tears rinse some of it from his cheeks.

"Señora, why don't you sit down?" With calm authority, a police officer points Hannah back toward Sarah's room. Two more officers approach behind the first. The fathers already holding Hannah ease her back through the door and into the only chair, an institutional, white plastic thing.

"We are sorry for your loss. I know this is difficult, but we need you to tell us what happened."

"Do you have to do this right now?" Alejandra crouches and folds a protective arm around Hannah's shoulders. "As you can see, she's not doing well."

"Yes, Señora, it must happen now. Privately."

"Can I stay with her?"

"You're not family?" The officer looks at Lindsay and Jane. "You two?"

"She doesn't have any family here. Only her daughter." Jane's voice breaks. "Her husband is traveling."

"One of you may stay."

The three friends look at each other. "It should be you," Jane says to Lindsay. "You know her best."

Alejandra murmurs her agreement.

"Ok. So you call Gavin. I've been trying, but no answer. He's on a business trip."

"Chicago," whispers Hannah.

Jane squeezes Hannah's shoulder again before shuffling with

Alejandra out into the hall, where one of the officers instructs the parents and park staff. "Everyone, please go to the waiting room. Don't leave the hospital. We will speak with you individually."

Jane follows the other parents down the corridor, then opens her contacts on her phone. Gavin's number isn't there. Alejandra doesn't have it, either, so Jane goes back to hover by the still-open door of Sarah's room, waiting for a chance to get the number from Lindsay.

Jane watches Hannah stare at the floor while Lindsay looks up at the two impassive officers, a young male doctor, and an older female doctor. Something in the demeanor of the doctors, although professional, reflects their shock.

"Please, ma'am, tell us what happened."

"I don't know." Hannah answers in a jagged whisper.

"Where were you?"

"By the pool with the other parents, of course. It's the lifeguard you should ask. Where was he while my baby was drowning?"

"We will talk with him. But first we're asking you."

"I was watching the pool. I was talking, maybe my back was turned for a moment, I don't know, there was a lifeguard."

"Where was the lifeguard, Señora?"

"That's the question, that's what I'm telling you."

Lindsay stands up but keeps her hands on Hannah's shoulders. "I know," she volunteers. The policemen's eyes shift to her face. "He was dealing with kids who were playing rough. He was by the pool, but his attention was focused on them, telling them to behave so nobody gets hurt." Hannah's body shakes under Lindsay's fingers. "Is that enough, officers? What more do you want from her?"

The male doctor clears his throat. "Will there be a request for an autopsy? Additional information may be obtained, such as whether the child had a seizure or something else occurred to instigate—"

"An autopsy?" Hannah turns as pale as if all the blood in her veins had just frozen. "No." Her sobs ratchet up an octave, and her face loses its angles.

"You don't have to decide now, Señora, but we need to know

within seventy-two hours whether the family or authorities direct an autopsy."

Hannah's head hangs out over her knees. Lindsay steps around to the front of Hannah's chair and gently pushes her back. "Can I get some help here?"

In response, Alejandra marches back into the room, just as one of the other doctors, the woman, asks "Would you like a sedative, Señora? Would you like to sleep now?"

Hannah looks up and nods, her face streaked with tears.

Alejandra agrees. "That's a good idea."

The doctor looks at the policeman who seems to be in charge. "May I administer a sedative?"

"Yes. We'll speak with the witnesses." The officers file out of the room.

The doctors, including Alejandra, settle Hannah into a hospital bed next to Sarah's gurney. As she receives the injection in one arm, Hannah reaches the other under the sheet covering her daughter's body to hold Sarah's hand. Jane, still peering through the open door, wills herself not to make a sound so as not to intrude on Hannah's final moments with her child, but to her later shame, she doesn't step away from the door. She watches as muscles in Hannah's face slacken and her gaze falls away from Sarah. The sedative pulls her into a sleep so still it mirrors the child's aspect. The female doctor pulls Hannah's hand from Sarah's, the male doctor tugs the sheet over Sarah's head, and the two of them wheel Sarah away.

Jane slips back into the room. "I'm sorry, I need the number."

From the plastic chair, Lindsay looks at her blankly.

"Gavin's number."

"Right." Lindsay digs her phone out, pulls up the contact, and hands the phone to Jane.

Jane walks out of the room and down the hall so there's no chance Hannah can hear her should she be somehow conscious beneath the drug-induced sleep. Hands shaking, she pushes the button to start the call. No answer. It goes to voicemail. She hangs up, but her relief is short-lived. She has to reach him. He can't find this out from someone random. What the hell, she hardly knows him, she's someone random. She can't do this.

She goes back to Lindsay and Alejandra to regroup. "He didn't answer. It went to voicemail."

Lindsay looks up. "You left a message?"

"No. I couldn't."

"For God's sake, give me the phone, I'll do it. You locate the rest of Hannah's family. Get online, call the school, figure it out."

Jane leaves the room determined to be useful, but she doesn't know anything about Hannah's family. Where are they from? Chicago, New York, LA? Portland sounds familiar for some reason.

She pulls out her phone. A dozen messages. She answers Gabriela's. *Sarah is gone. Can you pls start group for Hannah? Someone with her 24/7. 4-hour shifts? Lindsay and Ale with her now. I will find her family. Do you know where they're from?*

Gabriela responds immediately: *God. On it.* And *No, sorry, I don't know.*

Our kids ok? Dulce and Lupita?

Ours are fine, Toy Story and pizza. I don't know about the girls. That dad was worked up.

Jane's heart sinks further, but she can't deal with that right now. She'll check on the girls later. First she has to find Hannah's family. She starts by calling the school secretary, but the emergency contact in Sarah's file is a San Miguel neighbor, and no additional family information was provided. So Jane starts scrolling through Hannah's social media posts. There, among birthday messages a few months earlier, she finds her mother and a sister. She clicks the button to private message the mother. *Hello, I am a friend of Hannah and Gavin in San Miguel. There has been an accident. Please respond as soon as possible. Here's my number. Thank you.* She copies the same urgent but vague words into a message for the sister, then looks back into the room. In drugged slumber, Hannah's expression is peaceful.

Jane scrolls through two years of Hannah's posts but can't identify anyone else as family. Gavin apparently isn't on social media at all. Jane slips back through the door and sits next to Alejandra and Lindsay. At some point, someone had brought in two more of the white plastic chairs.

An hour later, Meghan arrives. "Gaby has arranged everything. Four-hour shifts for the next three days here or at the house, longer if need be, and people will bring food."

"That's great," says Jane. "I messaged Hannah's mother and sister, but no answer yet. I can't find phone numbers. We'll have to ask her when she wakes up if they don't respond soon."

"And Gavin?" asks Meghan.

"He's traveling somewhere on business. Chicago, if Hannah was in her right mind when she said it. Lindsay left a voicemail asking him to call."

"My God, that poor man. So he doesn't know yet?"

"Not until he calls her back or I get a response from the mother or sister and they tell him." Jane shudders. "Sorry, I have to go get my kids now. When Hannah wakes up, tell her we're contacting her family. Then get the doctors to sedate her again if necessary."

Meghan nods. "Go get your kids, I'll be here. Ale, Lindsay, why don't you two go home and see your kids and get some rest, too? This could be a long haul."

Alejandra agrees, but Lindsay, no longer needing to advocate for Hannah, looks stunned for the first time. "Lindsay, you were amazing," Jane tells her. "I'm so glad she had you with her. You, too, Ale."

On the way out, Jane passes the three police officers each interviewing a different parent. The questions sound strangely mundane. How can anything about this be routine? Several parents still sit in the waiting room, waiting to be questioned. She should wait for her turn, too, but she doesn't. What's the point? She doesn't know anything. Nobody stops her.

Jane goes home first to clean herself up and is surprised to find that Kevin is not there. He's golfing, she remembers, a rare indulgence. Alone in the kitchen, she fills a glass with water, but some slops onto the floor. Bending down with a towel, she notices smears of something on two cupboard doors. The generic smudges take shape as small fingerprints. Then a glint under the lip of the corner cabinet catches her eye and pulls her down further, onto her knees on the fraying kitchen rug. Her hand follows the flicker of light. Fingertips brush against something small and slick. A speckled marble rolls out and comes to a stop in the fringe at the edge of the rug. Jane picks up the marble and brings it close to her eyes. The little glass ball holds sticky echoes of the smudges on the cabinet doors, evidence of her children's messy, vibrant lives.

Hannah will never again find her daughter's fresh handprint on anything. Maybe she'll find an old one and instead of cleaning it, leave it until it dissolves over time. She will check it one day and find the last smudge vanished, the last bodily evidence of Sarah lost. Jane lets herself cry there on the kitchen floor.

From this unusual angle, she spots Kevin's drawing pad, the one she gave him at Christmas, shoved between cookbooks on an open shelf. She pulls it out and flips through sketches of the boys, a plaza scene, and several people she doesn't recognize. Some of the drawings are scribbled over, and several loose pages tucked in the back have been crumpled and smoothed out. Two of the crumpled ones are her. Younger versions of her.

Jane puts the notebook back on the shelf exactly where she found it and flops down again on the rug. She should get up and get her boys from Gabriela's, but she can't seem to move. Her body weighs a thousand pounds, and her muscles have liquefied, pooling in the flabby bits.

The ring of her phone forces her to move. It's a U.S. number she doesn't recognize.

"Hello, is this Jane?"

"Yes, and you are?"

"Hannah's sister."

"Oh." Jane's pulse jumps ahead. "Thank you for calling me back. Hannah needs you as soon as possible. I'm so sorry to tell you this—"

"What?" the voice demands.

Jane bites her lip hard. Just say it. "There was an accident this afternoon. Sarah. Sarah drowned. I'm so sorry. Can you get on a plane today? Or tomorrow?"

"What did you say?"

"Sarah drowned. I'm sorry."

"What? What do you mean? That can't be, no—"

"At a pool party today, at a water park, it just happened. I'm so sorry." The words are terribly inadequate. Jane cringes. She should have done this better.

"Oh my God."

She has to keep going. "Can you come? And your parents or other family? For now, we have friends staying with Hannah at the hospital in shifts, and we're trying to reach Gavin, but he's traveling and hasn't returned the call." There is silence on the line. "Hello, are you there? Is there someone else I should call?"

"Of course I'll come, and I'll bring our mom. What's the name of the hospital?"

Jane tells her. "I'm so sorry." The dial tone drones in her ear. The woman is gone.

"Someone drowned?" Kevin squats down beside her on the rug.

"What? I didn't think you were home."

"Just got here. Are you all right?"

"Not even a little bit. A girl drowned at the water park. Every parent's worst nightmare. I have to go get the boys now."

"Where are they?"

"Gaby has them. She took them home with her so I could help Hannah."

"Hannah?"

"The mother of the child. You sat across from her and her husband for a while the other night after the school show, remember? Their sweet girl, Sarah, Liam's age? She was planning a sleepover with Meghan's daughter, remember?"

"Oh God. Them."

She stands up and starts toward the garage.

"Jane," he calls after her.

"What?" She doesn't slow her pace.

"Jane, seriously."

"Seriously, what?" She spins around.

He points at her, his finger angled down, and she remembers. Her knees and elbow are a bloody mess. It will scare Connor and Liam if she shows up still looking like this. "Thanks."

She climbs the stairs and lets water run in the bathtub while she grabs a pair of jeans, a shirt, underwear. She pulls off her clothes, climbs into the tub, and sits to rub away the blood and bits of asphalt. Her raw skin stings under soap and hot water. She turns down the heat and rinses away the soap, climbs out, dries off. Neosporin and three band-aids on each knee are hidden under the clean jeans, with two more on her elbow.

"I can get the boys," he says from the bathroom doorway.

"Thanks, but no, I should."

On the drive to Gabriela's house, Jane replays her conversation with Hannah's sister. How horrific to receive such news out of nowhere from a stranger on the phone. Now the woman has to inform her parents that their granddaughter just died and then share the nightmare with the rest of her family. Worst of all, someone has to tell Gavin.

Hannah and Gavin came to refresh their lives and give their daughter something wonderful, a San Miguel chapter in her childhood. Now what should they do, stay here without her or go home without her? Both options are unthinkable. Jane wonders whether in their place she'd have the strength to resist following her child into the next world.

At Gabriela's house, Jane squeezes her way onto the sofa between Liam and Connor and pulls them onto her lap. Gabriela's son Toñio pauses the movie, and then he and his mother pile on. Eventually the kids squirm, and they all sit up.

"She died?" asks Connor.

"Yes, mi amor, she did. It's so sad."

"She drowned." Toñio says the words tentatively, as though testing their finality.

"That's right," says his mother.

"Why?" Liam breathes the word quietly into Jane's stomach.

"Well, we know her body took in too much water instead of air, and it filled her lungs, so she drowned. But nobody knows why it happened."

"She's going to heaven," says Toñio.

"We're going to miss her," adds Gabriela.

"Liam, are you all right?" Jane lifts her son's chin so that she can see his face.

"I should have helped her. You asked me to be her helper." His whole body shakes.

"Liam, no, there's nothing you could have done. This isn't anyone's fault, especially not any child's fault. Lots of adults were watching the pool, but nobody saw it happen, nobody knows how or why. It was just a terrible accident, honey."

She hugs her baby for a long time. His brother and friend pat his back. Eventually Liam's tears ebb, and Toñio lobbies to continue the movie. They curl again into a life-affirming pile. Gabriela makes popcorn, and Jane suddenly remembers to call Meghan. She asks her to let Hannah know when she wakes up that her sister and mother are on their way.

"What took so long?" asks Kevin.

"We finished the movie. It was actually the sequel by the time I got there. Cuddling up together was nice after what happened."

"Do you know what happened, Dad?" They collapse into him.

Kevin finds Jane unloading the dishwasher after the boys have gone to bed. "How did it happen, anyway? Were you all drinking?"

She stifles the urge to throw silverware at him. "Don't start. Almost everyone was sober. Connor's friends were screwing around—"

"Connor?"

Her slight smile is one of relief, not connection. "Not Connor, thank God, but just by luck because he'd gone to buy a lemonade. The others played a stupid dunking game, and he would have joined in if he'd been there. The lifeguard made them get out of the pool, and while he scolded them, Sarah drowned. Somehow, nobody knows, but if he hadn't had to deal with them—"

"He could have saved her."

"Probably. The poor kid, he's sixteen or seventeen and he'll live with this for the rest of his life."

"And where were you?"

The desire to throw a fork returns. "Bringing lunch to our boys. God, there will be enough collective guilt, trust me, without people like you pointing fingers. Maybe show up sometime and show us all how you would do parenting so much better."

"Fuck off."

"So we're not one of those couples who come together in tragedy?"

"Guess not. These moments reveal character, don't they, princess?"

"Why do you have to be so condescending? At a moment like this?" Reading the fury on his face, Jane leaves the dishwasher half emptied, walks directly to her room, and locks the door for good measure. She tries to sleep, but Sarah chatters to Lupita, Hannah lunges at the lifeguard, Lindsay scolds her for her failure to leave a message for Gavin, and Kevin glowers at her over the heads of their distraught sons.

RUMORS RISE AND FLOW THROUGH the community like silt carried in flood-blackened waters. People who previously talked about what must have happened to Verónica before the kidnappers let her go start speculating instead about what must have happened to Sarah. *Pablo's right*, thinks Jane. *We're driven to seek answers and assign blame.* Parents question their children's actions, their own, and the actions of other people's children. According to one report, a boy held Sarah under. No, it was a girl. The lifeguard wasn't paying attention because he was texting a girlfriend. He was flirting or not even there. It was Hannah's fault or some troubled kid's fault or an inappropriate adult's fault.

Sarah wasn't part of the dunking game. All the kids swear it. Connor came back with his lemonade just as the lifeguard was telling Dulce and the others to get out of the pool. The kids in the game were all friends of his, all fourth graders. Sarah wasn't with them.

Several witnesses confirm that she was playing toward the shallow end of the pool, but nobody seems to know with whom or exactly what she was doing. No child acknowledges swimming near her during the final moments of her life, not Lupita nor any of the other girls in their class. All parents profess belief in their children's innocence. Any who might have horrible suspicions never admit it. On the tide of grief and guilt, still more ugly rumors fester.

Some parents suggest a lawsuit against the water park. The park owner fires the lifeguard. Others try to calm the furor. Someone sends around one of those articles: "Drowning doesn't look like drowning." Everyone starts explaining to each other that victims rarely wave their arms and yell like in the movies. They just sink and bob and swallow. If you're not trained, it's hard to recognize it happening right in front of you. It is not our fault, they say. It was God's will.

Many people deliver food and flowers to Hannah and Gavin's house, where Jane, along with Gabriela, Alejandra, Meghan, Lindsay, and a dozen others try to organize everything. There are too many of them. They get in each other's way or stand around unable to find anything that needs doing. They fill the kitchen with soups and tamales and large casserole pans and fill the rest of the house with the bouquets and cards that keep arriving. Someone offers to read the messages to Hannah and Gavin, but Hannah's mother stops them. They will read these later, she says. They're tired now.

The mother and sister do the most difficult tasks. Lindsay and Jane and other friends help to pack up the house, but the mother and sister take Hannah and Gavin to collect the ashes. They prop up the couple to sign the paperwork and try to convince them to eat. They keep Hannah sedated most of the time, and Gavin, too, and Jane doesn't blame them.

Kevin agrees to pick up the boys from art class on the third afternoon so Jane can do another shift at Hannah's. When she gets home, she heads straight to her boys on the sofa, but Kevin pulls her into the kitchen.

"What did you tell everyone about me?" he demands to know. "Those moms and dads at the class, from school I guess, were weird with me."

"What? Nothing. You barely come up."

"Good one."

"I'm not being funny. Whenever anyone asks how or where you are, I always say fine, working a lot. What do you want me to say?"

"Fine. Working."

"Then could we not do this? The kids can hear us."

Meghan provides sporadic updates about the rumors, but not until Rocío tells Jane that Pablo has pulled his girls out of the school for fear of reprisals does she pay much attention. Jane doubts that anyone could truly blame a child. She has to convince Pablo that his daughters are still welcome at the school. Summer's almost over. When classes start again in two weeks, what a shame it would be for Dulce and Lupita not to be there.

49

"Mom? I heard they're asking kids to share poems and songs at the memorial."

"You want to read something? That's great, Connor."

"No." He shakes his head. "I want to play something, 'Hallelujah.' It sounds good when we play together, for real," he says, referring to his guitar teacher.

"I'm sure it does, and I am happy that you want to honor Sarah." Jane puts her hands on her sweet boy's shoulders. "But kiddo, I'm not sure it's appropriate for a funeral, with lyrics about tying someone to a kitchen chair and all." She suggests that he choose a different song.

Connor won't hear of it. "I don't want to play any other song, only that one. It's the best song I know. I don't know that many. We won't sing it, just play it. Except the hallelujahs, we can sing those."

"Just sing the hallelujahs, oh." Jane considers that. An instrumental version. "OK."

What an achingly beautiful day for a funeral. It's early August, still the rainy season, so the weather could have been suitably gray, but no, it is a gorgeous day.

When they pull up to the school parking lot, a FULL sign bars the entrance. Cars double park down the block. For a moment, Jane wishes Hannah and Gavin could see how many people have come to mourn their child, but no, Hannah's sister and mother made the right decision to fly them back to the States so quickly. Some people argued that it would be cathartic for them to stay and attend the memorial, but Jane imagines three hundred parents, most of whom they didn't yet know, looking at them with pity. Wouldn't it be unbearable for them to watch people whose pain is an incomparable fraction of theirs grieve their daughter with momentary tears? All these parents who still get to raise their children. No, they were right to go home to conduct their own memorial. Today is for the school community, the children here who briefly knew Sarah.

"I guess we park in the middle of the road like everyone else." Kevin shrugs. "There's no going forward or back now."

At the door, Ana Paula, the director, welcomes them and invites Liam and Connor to go to the art studio. "We're making things for Sarah's altar."

Connor and Liam nod in solemn acceptance of this responsibility and head toward the studio, Connor lugging his guitar.

"It's art therapy," Ana Paula explains. "We have psychologists available for private appointments, too. Parents are gathering in the courtyard. There's coffee. We'll start soon."

Jane and Kevin pass through the elegant vestibule and step down into the central courtyard. They work their way around clusters of parents toward the raised dais near the kindergarten classroom where the kids sometimes perform and where Jane expects to find the altar. Her breath catches at the sight of it. A heartbreakingly accurate portrait hangs above the altar. Sarah's expression is one she recognizes, curiosity and friendliness leavened by a touch of new-kid caution. Below the suspended painting floats a layer of pale pink roses, simple in design and elegant in their abundance. A cross of white flowers, a meter high, rises up from the center of the rose sea. Jane recognizes the elaborately carved table leg visible at a corner of the altar. Some poor souls lugged Ana Paula's huge antique desk down a flight of stairs from her office. In front of the desk, two benches of different heights form additional levels, draped in white cloths. Displayed there are children's art and snapshots of Sarah.

Gabriela and Lindsay greet Jane and Kevin. Then Gabriela flicks her eyes toward the portrait. "Stunning, isn't it?"

"Javier?" asks Jane. "But how? He couldn't have completed it in the last few days?"

"No, Hannah commissioned it months ago."

"She did? She's only been here a few months."

"I heard she and Gavin discovered Javier's work at their first ArtWalk, loved it, and immediately commissioned a portrait of Sarah. I didn't know her that well, not like Lindsay, but I almost get the sense that on some level Hannah knew, if that makes any sense."

Jane doesn't respond.

"Are you all right?" Gabriela asks.

"It's just that no, it doesn't make any sense at all. That couple had to lose their child, their perfectly healthy child? Hannah didn't mystically know, and they were in no way prepared. If you tell me it was part of some plan, I will lose it."

"Oh honey, we're all just trying to make sense of the senseless. The truth is it's a stupid horrifying tragedy and the world feels evil sometimes."

Jane leans into Gabriela's shoulder. "I'm sorry."

Nayeli's family arrives. Pablo leads, his body maintaining the rigid posture Jane remembers from their last conversation at the water park. She wonders how many of the week's ugly rumors he has heard. She has to reason with him soon, before school starts, but not today. At least they came.

Ana Paula asks for everyone's attention. Teachers lead the kids in from the art studio to form the first concentric half-circles around the altar. Parents arrange themselves behind the children, filling the courtyard.

Instead of a Catholic priest, Ana Paula introduces a shaman whom Jane recognizes from somewhere, maybe the inauguration of the peace pole in Parque Juárez or that temazcal she attended last year. A striking woman in an elaborately embroidered dress, the shaman leads everyone in prayer to Mother Earth and Sky and acknowledges the four directions. The audience responds with a refrain that sounds like "o mateo." Jane says it, too, even though she doesn't know what it means.

Two pairs of Mexican parents whom Jane knows to be very conservative Catholics seem a little tense, and some of the Americans look lost, but most of the parents appear comfortable with the syncretic mixture of local indigenous practices, Catholicism, and a dose of Eastern spirituality. They follow the shaman through the motions of the ceremony with varying degrees of familiarity.

Sarah's teacher invites students to the front to share. Connor steps forward with his guitar and then waits while his music teacher works his way through the crowd. The initial chords are tentative, but then Connor settles into the song. During the first chorus, the teacher's strong, modulated voice sings the hallelujahs, Connor's echo small but pure. At the second, a lone voice from the crowd joins in. Then more. Soon everyone is singing hallelujahs or crying or both. When the last note fades and Connor walks back to his friends, hands reach out to pat him.

Some older students sing a hymn, and then Sarah's teacher reads a farewell letter, its eloquence undiminished by her hoarse voice or the heart-wrenching seconds when she has to fight for composure.

Finally, four girls from Liam's class come forward. They whisper something to the teacher, who nods and glances around until she spots Lupita. Looking first to Pablo and Nayeli for permission, she reaches for the child's hand and leads her to the girls, who surround her.

Before they begin, the teacher explains to the crowd what's happening. "Lupita here was Sarah's best friend, so the girls want to dedicate this poem to her as well as to Sarah."

She nods at them to go ahead. They make their way through the lines slowly with excruciating pauses. By the end of the ode to friendship, when the girls have become so tightly entwined that they are one many-legged creature, people cry again. Nayeli's expression crumples, and Pablo looks dazed. The couple gather themselves as Lupita emerges from the huddle.

Beside Jane, Gabriela has her arms wrapped tightly around Toñio. "Earlier I thought Hannah and Gavin should have stayed for this. Now I think it better that they didn't."

Lindsay agrees. "I mean, it was beautiful, and I love this community more than ever, but it would have been too much for them."

Families start to move toward the exit, clumping as they encounter friends on the way out. Jane gathers her boys and Kevin.

"Jane, wait." Ana Paula waves her over.

"Yes? First, can I say thank you? That was so well done."

"It was the kids who made it powerful. Connor, wow." Ana Paula pauses. "I need Nayeli and Pablo, too, just a sec." She calls to the couple, and they turn back, along with their girls. "Have you all heard that Sarah's family endowed a scholarship fund?"

Jane nods. "I can't believe they thought to do that in the midst of their grief."

"The grandmother came in to make the arrangements before they left," Ana Paula explains. "Between their initial contribution and the community donations that have poured in this week in Sarah's name, it is a significant amount. The family has promised an annual gift, too. I believe it fitting that the scholarships go to your girls, Señora Pérez, Señor López. Sarah would have wanted that, don't you agree? So girls, your places here are now guaranteed through graduation. We are so glad you are part of our school."

Dulce, Lupita, and Nayeli share startled expressions.

Pablo clears his throat. "Thank you, Directora." His eyes convey profound shock.

"How wonderful," says Jane. "These girls will make you proud."

Ana Paula smiles at Lupita and Dulce. "I have no doubt."

Kevin, waiting at the entrance with Liam, beckons impatiently.

A DAY AFTER THE MEMORIAL, Jane stands at the door of Kevin's home office, once again trying to keep anger out of her voice. "The boys need us to show them how to handle all this."

"You could ask for my help." He sets down a coffee cup, her favorite, the four-sided one she bought at that gallery in Mexico City, the cup with an etching on each side of a different wild-haired woman with hooded eyes. Created by an artist she admires from Oaxaca. Her cup.

"So I should ask you to show up and parent? Like as a favor?"

He absently spins the cup, rotating it by quarter turns, so the four women greet her one after another.

Something in her breaks. "You know, your capacity for empathy is stunted. You have a range of about ten feet. It covered me early on and now the boys, but that's it."

"What are you talking about?"

"That's why you seem untouched by what happened to that poor child, and that's why you've been so resentful and condescending about me building the house."

"Yeah? That's why? You have everything all figured out? Screw you." His hand, having yanked the cup up, slams it back down. Coffee sloshes onto his desk. "God damn it. Meanwhile, you have all the feelings, don't you, for every stray kid and half the town, except me." Then his tone changes, becoming broader and warmer, in striking contrast to the tension in his hands and arms. "Well, you won't be doing whatever it is you're doing here much longer anyway."

Jane feels her shoulder and stomach muscles constrict. "What do you mean?"

"I got the promotion."

"Congratulations."

"Ah, you can do better than that."

"Good for you, truly." Jane pauses. "But don't expect me to turn cartwheels when a move to Houston isn't good news for me or the kids."

"Of course you're not happy for me. When was the last time that happened? But this is a big break. I need to prove I'm still hungry, not some loser taking the slow track from Mexico."

"I understand, but for the kids, starting over again so soon—"

"That's on you. This is all on you. We'd still be in our real lives if you hadn't ruined us."

"I didn't ruin us. I just made a mistake when we were already broken. I'm done apologizing for something I can't fix alone. And this is our real life now, for better or worse."

"Worse." Kevin shoots the word from his mouth like a bullet from those stupid paint guns the boys tried at a birthday party. Connor liked them, but Liam was too young, and the pellets hurt when they hit any part of his little body not covered by the plastic armor the rental place provided. "For sure. Nothing works here, and who knows how many parasites we have now."

Jane doesn't bother to hide her disgust. "That's how you think of our San Miguel lives? Parasites, that's what comes to mind?" How can he not see how good this has been for their sons? Doesn't he feel a thrill every time he hears them chattering in Spanish with their friends? They have become truly bilingual and bicultural. Plus the pyramids, beach trips, and all the other opportunities they've been gifted here, like dressage lessons they could never afford in the States, el Día de Muertos and el Día de los Locos, all of it. Most importantly, she and the boys have become part of a community stronger than any they ever had back home.

She is darkly confident that she can read his thoughts, and they are not pretty. She forced them all into this, he's thinking, and now the ridiculous episode is over because he says so. She stares at the triumphant expression lighting his face.

Jane feels the shift coming in the slight release of tension in her neck, so she is less astonished than she might have been when she looks up at Kevin and some of the fear slips away. She can't make sense of the words pouring from his mouth, but she takes in the mouth itself. Wide, pink, and gray, leaching hot sour coffee breath.

Not just anger and the familiar anguish rise within her this time, but also something more. It starts in her chest, then spreads into her limbs, heat charging every cell. It's time. "We're not going with you. I want a divorce."

He gapes at her, his face a caricature of disbelief. "What did you say?"

"You heard me." Jane doesn't quite believe herself either, so she grips the doorframe and says it again. "I want a divorce."

"You don't have the balls. You need me, I'm the troll in the basement, remember?"

"Stop it, nobody has to be a stupid troll."

"Right, because money will just fall from the sky for you, princess."

"I will raise the boys here. You'll visit, and I'll bring them up for holidays. Moving to a new city, with you working all hours because that's what you always do, is not what's best for them. I have spent the last two years building a great life for them here."

"No way."

"They're not going to suffer through this sick excuse for a marriage anymore. I know it has affected them more than we admit."

The physical sensation is overwhelming. Jane's body feels light and insubstantial. Her voice is nearly steady, but a part of her is so scared that she wants to stuff the idea back into her mouth. She doesn't let herself run away or even lean on the doorframe but stands as tall as she can. When she sees her hands shaking, she crosses her arms over her chest.

Kevin rages for an hour, but the torrent conveys diminishing confidence, and each time he provokes her, she regains her equilibrium more quickly. She makes herself look out the window at the clear, bright sky. She focuses on the bougainvillea climbing the walls of her Mexican garden, and somehow she doesn't believe Kevin anymore when he threatens to throw her in the street and leave her with nothing. Lawyers and a judge will have a say in that now.

A hummingbird, similar to the one the neighbor's cat killed but with an aquamarine breast rather than a golden one, hovers at the feeder. Jane remembers splotches of blood on tile.

An icy wash of fear floods her body when he promises to hire a cutthroat attorney to take the kids from her, prompting an urgent plan to lock in her own fierce lawyer. She'll get referrals immediately from law school friends, as divorce law is far from her own specialty. When he threatens to pack up the boys in the middle of the night, she thinks of their passports folded into an old dress under Meghan's bed and tells her lungs to take in the air that sticks in her throat.

Kevin turns her cup again. Jane realizes the second before he lunges that he's going to, but she fails to react. The cup drives through the air, trailing coffee dregs. For an impossibly long second, she watches the handle flip toward her face. She squeezes her eyes shut, expecting impact, pain, pottery shards, blood. The cup shatters against the doorframe next to her, pieces falling at her feet. Her eyes open, and from Kevin's expression, she concludes that he meant to scare but not actually hit her. Fear is damage that doesn't show.

In two strides, Jane crosses the room. Her arm sweeps toward his desk, and her fingers close on the first object they encounter, a thick book. Then the arm reverses its sweep until the cover connects with the side of his face. She recoils from the fleshy noise, dropping the book, and steps back hard, in the process driving into her flesh several bits of pottery lodged between her right heel and sandal.

She loses her balance and falls heavily on the tile floor just as his fist flies toward her. The trajectory of the punch is off now. It passes well over her head. Kevin freezes, face ashen. She glares up at him, then without a word, unbuckles her sandal, cradles her right foot, and digs three gravelly bits of coffee cup out of her sole. From the largest piece, a cup woman's inscrutable eye peers at her, weeping blood. Judging her as well as him.

From the bathroom, he brings a dripping towel and a fistful of band-aids. He holds these things out to her until she accepts them.

Jane wrings out the towel and presses it to the holes in her heel. Finally, she looks up at him. "I can't believe we just did that."

"Sure you can. You've been holding it in for a long time, and so have I." They stare at each other again. There are no words. Until he finds some. "You know why I'm this angry. Don't pretend you don't. I hate that."

"I'm not pretending anything. I'm telling you I'm exhausted by your rage and self-pity. It's way out of proportion to what I did, and you haven't even tried to move on. I don't understand it, I sure as hell don't excuse it, and I can't live with it any longer."

"It's not complicated. I still love you. But you haven't loved me for years."

"Kevin—"

"I've known that for a long time, so I'm angry. How is that hard to understand? I wanted to fix it, sure, but how, when we're stuck in this death spiral? The more you pull away, the angrier I get, the less you love me, and the more you pull away. For a while you tried to force yourself—"

"You're skipping over a hell of a lot of bad behavior on your part."

Kevin jerks one shoulder in a dismissive shrug. "Despite what you think, I'm not an idiot. I know you have felt yourself too good for me for a long time. You stayed only because you thought it best for the boys, and because you're afraid of me, which is just stupid."

Jane gestures at the pottery shards. "Is it?"

"Yes. This is pathetic on both our parts. I've known this moment was coming. That's the core of the anger, knowing and being unable to stop it."

"You haven't even tried to stop it."

"Not recently," he acknowledges. "It was obviously too late."

Jane goes stiff to hold in her fury at this confirmation of his refusal to reciprocate the efforts she made. Those date nights she attempted, especially when they first arrived, the marriage counseling, the whole move to Mexico. "Well, this must be a relief for you then."

"No." His voice seems to come from a distance. "It's not."

Kevin claims that her falling out of love came first and for no good reason and that her dalliance with David just proved it. Jane argues that his negativity, his lack of self-confidence to pursue his dream of being an artist, and his dark view of her intentions and the world in general were insidious poisons curdling their relationship from the inside.

At this point, they agree that it no longer matters whose fault it is.

"It was my decision," he says.

"Fine." She agrees, understanding his need to salvage his pride.

Jane talks for hours with Gabriela and Meghan, their patience generous. "This is going to require professionals, isn't it?" she acknowledges one night around Gabriela's kitchen table. "We did try couples therapy, right after we moved here, but it was already too late."

Meghan remembers. "With the guy who offered to mediate your divorce."

"He told us it was important to continue individually."

"But you didn't?" asks Gabriela. "Why not?"

"The failure of our joint effort turned me off, and if Kevin wouldn't keep going, when he needed it more, why should I? That was my mature response. But I'll start now."

"Good girl." Meghan offers a gentle smile. "It will help."

"I need to call my mom, too. I realize I owe her an apology for years of anger over my parents' divorce. Now that I'm in the same damn place."

Kevin insists that Jane and the kids follow him to Houston. She tells him no. "Remember all the paperwork I did last year to get our Permanent Resident visas so we wouldn't have to leave and come back every few months on tourist visas? I have the right to continue living here with my children, and I've checked, after being 'legally domiciled' in Mexico for six months, let alone two years, we're eligible to file for divorce here, too."

"You've got to be kidding."

Jane concedes the unimportant part. "It probably makes more sense to file in the U.S., sure. But the kids and I can keep living here. The point is you can't drag us to Houston."

"The point is you should move willingly to keep your family together, at least to keep your children with their father." Kevin's voice is icy.

"Please try to see this from my perspective. You expect us to leave the rich lives we've built here to follow you somewhere where the kids and I have no support system, everything is more expensive, and they would hardly see you anyway because you work so much?"

Kevin ignores all of that. "This was just a sabbatical, remember? We were only supposed to be here for a couple years. What are you doing, planning to live here forever?"

"Maybe. But I don't have to figure out forever right now."

"They're American, they should be with their father in America, period." Kevin crosses his arms. The agitated fingers grip and release, digging into upper arm flesh.

Jane backs up a couple steps. "I will bring in money again, you'll be happy about that at least. I'll do online legal work, U.S.-based, no work permit needed. Better to make dollars and spend pesos, right? Here I can afford to keep my hours limited so I will still have plenty of time for the boys, and like I said, here we have the support of an amazing community."

"My sons—" Suddenly he's crying.

Jane's resolve weakens but only slightly. "I'm sorry. I know how much you love them and they love you, but what about all the actual work of parenthood? Shuttling them to school, practices, and lessons, dealing with homework, playdates, doctors' appointments, birthday parties, and school meetings? I do all of that. You have no idea how much time it takes because even back in New York when I was working crazier hours than you, I was still always the one who coordinated with the nanny and the school and took care of those things. If we come to Houston, you'll suddenly start doing all that whenever they're with you?"

"Sure, not a big deal—"

So much for staying calm. "No, you won't. I know I'll still do nearly everything, but if we follow you to Houston, it'll be so much harder because I'll have to work more hours to pay for life there. You'll just see them sometimes on weekends, and they wouldn't see enough of me anymore, either. We've done that before. No way am I going back to it. When Liam was two and I returned to work, remember? I got sucked into the work culture even though I hated that the nanny spent more time with our kids than we did—"

"Yeah, that's what you let yourself be sucked into."

Jane ignores the jibe. "It's like I've found the secret key to work-motherhood balance: work part-time online from Mexico for U.S. clients." She failed at creating that balance in the States before, and it would only be more difficult if she were to return now as a divorced mom, but in Mexico, for her, it's doable. Jane can't help but see the glaring irony in the situation. Many women in Mexico have no choice but to work long hours, often at multiple jobs. She will be gaming the system by earning in dollars and spending in pesos, benefitting from the lower cost of living and the rather luxurious quality of life it affords her, while knowing that same quality of life is unattainable for many Mexicans.

"Good for you. But under my roof, I know my sons are safe."

"Of course they're safe under my roof, too, and they need a lot more than that."

"Jane, they're Americans. So are you. You can't stay here."

"Yes, I absolutely can. We can. We have permanent residency cards that say so. Listen to me. The quality of our sons' lives is significantly better here; you know it is. So we're staying. Maybe not forever, but for now."

"My boys." The fingers, which had for some moments hung loosely, curl into fists. Kevin turns abruptly and walks away.

They fight through ten variations of this conversation. Eventually, to Jane's astonished relief, Kevin stops insisting. "I'll bring them up to you for alternate holidays," she promises. "You can visit them here. Video chat whenever," she offers. This does little to soften the blow.

Kevin also stops demanding that they sell the house. He lets her keep it. For now.

51

"Why can't you and Daddy love each other no matter what, like you tell me and Liam to do?" The loss etched on Connor's face makes Jane feel ashamed. Her failure to keep the family intact, to keep the marriage alive for Connor and his brother, carved that loss into him.

"Baby, I'm so sorry." Jane scoops her son into her arms on the bed and tries to shield him with her body from this blow to his world. She searches for words that will help, knowing that any criticism of Kevin will only inflict more pain and draw resistance. Pain already has a vise-like grip on her own lungs. "I tried for a long time, and so did Daddy. But we can't stay married because we're making each other too unhappy, and we don't want that unhappiness to hurt you and Liam anymore, either." Her sons will no longer live drenched in their parents' rank soup of resentment. That has to be the right thing. "It will be better for you, I promise, to have two happy parents living apart than unhappy parents together." Jane hears her mother saying the same words, invoking that same hopeful incantation, all those years ago.

"Why can't you fix it?"

"I tried my hardest, but sometimes a marriage gets so broken it can't be fixed. Nobody wants that to happen, but it does. You have friends with divorced parents, right?"

He nods miserably.

"And you know that parents' love for their children is special and unending. Nothing can ever break it, not divorce or anything else."

Liam walks into the room. He lets Jane pull him up beside Connor.

They stay there together, huddled in her arms on the bed, for a long time. She would do anything to take away their pain, anything except continue her poisonous marriage.

A sense of childhood events repeating is so strong that Jane's head aches with it. She vows that Connor and Liam will have stability, unlike what divorce meant for her and Thomas. Her boys will live with her most of the time. There will be no alternate weeks riding different school buses to split lives, just occasional holidays in Texas.

Right now, her babies drown in a pain Jane has long known. They're angry with her in a bitter echo of the way she's been angry at her own mother. She owes Mom that apology. She may still disagree with her parents' custody decision, but she finally understands just how horrible it is to have to decide at all when there's no right answer, only shades of wrong.

Jane and Dad were always going to have a reconciliation. Dad would forgive her for leaving him. After her freshman year of college, Jane considered going home but decided it was too soon. The nascent process of becoming someone who mattered felt fragile, and she didn't want to leave New York, almost as though she feared that if she left, the city wouldn't welcome her a second time. As the already fully formed grownup, why couldn't her father take the initiative anyway? Well, eventually she'd have the confidence to go home for a long visit. They'd get to know each other again as adults, and everything would be fine.

During the fall of her sophomore year, too soon became too late when Dad had a heart attack at fifty-nine. He'd never trusted doctors.

Thomas found the body.

"How are you?" she asked him. "Will you be OK?"

"I won't go on a bender over this, if that's what you're asking. And I'll probably even graduate."

"Thomas, I—"

"Jane, just book a flight. Get here. What I don't know is how to plan a funeral."

GABRIELA AND MEGHAN KEEP CHECKING on Jane, and Jane keeps talking. Seemingly every shuttered feeling and censored thought from the last several years demands to be heard.

"Moving to San Miguel was a drastic step, but it wasn't enough," she tells them.

"This city can break couples. I've seen it," says Gabriela. "It's the overblown expectations."

"Yeah, no, the blame is on us, not San Miguel, for failing to fix what was already broken. Like you kept telling me, I had to stop convincing myself I could stay with him ten more years for the kids' sake. I've failed them anyway. Connor just told me he'll never get married."

"Jane, he's just young." Meghan's tone is uncharacteristically gentle.

"He shouldn't know our marriage was so bad that it turns him off the prospect forever." Jane fights tears. She's sick of crying. "Liam has said things recently, too, that reveal just how much they knew and internalized, despite the fact that they followed my example, always trying to act like everything's fine."

"They will be OK." Gabriela pulls Jane into a quick hug and then releases her but holds her gaze. "Listen, you tried to save your marriage for your kids' sake. That's admirable. Also for their sake, you tried to stay long after it died, but that's not healthy, so you're getting out now. You're doing the right thing for them."

"It's not wrong, by the way, that this is for you, too, for your own happiness and your future," Meghan adds, her voice back to its normal strength.

Gabriela nods in agreement. "Right now, all you need to do is survive the transition. Just do the next thing and the thing after that, and love on them like crazy, like you always do. It will get easier."

"I'm sure you're right, it will, eventually. But first I need to get the divorce done with primary custody. That's non-negotiable."

"You said you know he'll play dirty, so do whatever you have to," urges Meghan.

"Actually, no, I can't believe it, but as far as I can tell, he's not fighting the way he threatened to. I guess that was just a way to control me, and I fell for it out of fear. He must realize that he would never in reality make time for daily parenting."

"Of course you'll get primary custody." Meghan flings a hand with such vehemence that Jane expects a ring to go flying. "You do most of the parenting, that's obvious. We'll testify to that if you need us to."

"Thank you, but he'd tell you parenting is providing, so he's had to work so much. Since he never loved the job itself, his sense of achievement comes from the hours he puts in and how much money he makes for his family."

"I understand that to a point," acknowledges Meghan, "but I'd tell him there's always an element of choice in showing up for your kids."

"He loves them like crazy, of course, but he's not wired for the multi-tasking that parenting while working full-time requires, and I don't believe he'll change. I learned that lesson when my mom thought my dad would grow into it after their divorce. He didn't." Jane stares unseeingly through her friends. "The thing is, the boys worship him. They light up under his attention. I'm the consistent one, but he's the shiny object, the one who just plays with them while I nag about homework, picking up their dirty laundry, and getting out the door. He gets to be the exotic attraction. They talk 'man things' with him. I know it's healthy for them to have that. They hate me for leaving him."

"There's some hero-worship going on, sure," says Gabriela.

"They'll be angry for a while, but they won't hate you. The boys being with you—and none of you stuck in that toxic marriage any longer—is what's best for them. You'll get custody. But it is true," she adds, "that he's a good provider. That's something."

"He can be a good provider from far away." Meghan's disgust coats the words. "You deserve to keep the best parts of this rotten marriage, the kids and enough money."

"Did I tell you he's letting me keep the house for now? Although I will have to sell it eventually and split the proceeds. He'll pay child support, too, hopefully enough for tuition."

"He had better at least cover tuition."

"I'll get myself hired by one of those on-line legal services. I'm still an attorney in New York. I've kept up my license. I probably won't be able to work as a child advocate like I used to—can't do much of that remotely—but I can work on some aspects of labor and employment law, I think, which I liked in law school. I'll figure it out. I'll be OK even if I have to churn out simple divorce agreements, which can definitely be done online. But I need to get Liam and Connor through the worst of this first."

"Sounds like a good plan," her friends assure Jane, offering their support each time.

Jane hermits with her boys. She goes out for necessities and brings home treats. They clump together on the sofa to watch movies and move to the dining table to play board games. She tries to stay off social media.

Kevin holes up in his room. When he emerges, she makes herself invisible. The boys pounce on him and then return to her. It's a temporary holding pattern. Let him have a little more time with them. Let them have more of him.

When they get cabin fever and burst outside to play, she climbs to the roof to paint. Inspired by Javier's portrait of Sarah, she decides to paint Nayeli's family as a housewarming gift, or at least to try. She borrows family photos from their Casa Mía file.

Her style evolves further. These figures are more alive and infused with light than some of her recent creations.

One afternoon while she's focusing on Nayeli's eyes, Kevin joins her on the roof. He doesn't say anything at first but walks to the railing and looks out over the city. Finally, he turns around and breaks the silence. "It's time. I have to be at work on Monday."

She sets down her brush. "In Houston? That's five days from now."

"Yes, Houston, and I know it's five days. I'm the one who has to say goodbye to my sons, my reasons for living, so I know exactly how many fucking days I have left. My flight's on Saturday. I've rented a loser's apartment near the office. Send the stuff boxed up in my room. I'll text you the address."

"When will the kids see you next?"

"When I can get back here, that's when. One ticket down is less than three up. When I can afford a nicer place, I'll bring them up once a month or whatever the judge says, right? You did this, so you tell them. You be the one to break their hearts."

"Kevin—"

He takes a few steps toward her. "This really worked out for you, didn't it, princess? You're walking away with our kids, our house, and your magical mystery Mexican life."

"This is not what I wanted."

"Not originally, but it sure is now."

"I'm sorry. You have to know that. I tried to fix things a lot harder than you did."

"I don't want to hear it." Kevin's stare grows icier. "You know what? My dad will remind me that I could have been the happily married owner of his dealership, the king of our hometown like he was, not some pathetic guy moving alone to Houston while his stubborn, pretentious ex keeps his kids in freaking Mexico. The thing is, he's right. If he hadn't sold the dealership when he retired, I'd probably be heading there now."

"You're not serious? I think actually doing your art, if you could have just believed in yourself a little more—I guess that's my fault, too, for failing to build you up enough—would have made you happy, not running the damn dealership with some woman at your side who was content never to leave that town. That's not you. You desperately wanted to get out of there, don't you remember that? You're an artist."

A memory surfaces. Kevin, wrapped in a sheet on the bed in their Brooklyn apartment, sated and proud, showing her a sketch he had made of a man on the subway. The man had a dreamy, poignant, utterly convincing expression. She loved it, and Kevin loved her reaction. She remembers spending the rest of the afternoon in that bed.

"So you know who I am?" His wounded expression still has the power to break her heart.

"I thought I did. I tried to."

"I'd say you failed."

"Seriously? Fine, go find one of those grateful hometown girls now if that's what you want. I want you to be happy."

"Do you?" Kevin laughs.

"Yes. I still do."

"Clearly."

"Oh my God, why do I try?" Jane starts to walk away but turns back. "Hey, when you're around the boys, don't take out your anger on Mexico, OK? It's been good for them—"

"Yeah, right. Watching their parents' marriage die has been good for them."

"That's not fair. Our marriage was dying anyway. It had been dying for a long time, we both admit that now. San Miguel was our crazy idea of marital life support, but that was never realistic because wherever you go, there you are, right? And you know what I meant, learning to speak another language and navigate another culture. Having all these cool experiences."

"Whatever. This is the place I lost my family. You can't expect me to like it."

Jane searches Kevin's eyes for some hint of the man she fell in love with all those years ago. He's either no longer in there, or he won't come out for her again. Either way, she's done. "You can have the LSD in the freezer." It's all she can think of to lighten the mood.

They almost laugh, but then his face sets again. "Fuck you. Throw it away."

"OK." After a moment, she looks up again. "One of your drawings of the boys, in your sketchpad, Kev, it's really great. If you're not doing anything with it, I'd love to frame it."

"What the hell, you were snooping?"

"No, but I saw the pad there on the shelf when I was sitting on the kitchen floor the day Sarah died. I meant to talk to you about it. You should really keep drawing. You're seriously talented. I hope you know that."

"Fine, you can have that, too." More heavily, he adds, "I'll tell them I'm leaving on Saturday."

He announces it right before he goes to the airport. Liam clings and cries while Connor argues. Kevin shoots knifelike glances at Jane over their heads until finally he kneels, buries his face in Liam's chest, and cries, too. Even knowing it was coming—having caused it to happen— Jane is horrorstruck by the wreckage of her family.

At the door, Kevin takes one last anguished look at his sons. "I'll be back to see you as soon as I can, guys." He lets the door shut hard behind him.

"This is your fault." His body rigid, Connor glares at Jane. "I hate you."

He won't come out of his room. Jane sits on the floor with Liam in her lap and talks through the door. She tells them stories of themselves as babies and toddlers. She talks about her many favorite days with them and all the adventures they will have as they grow up. She tells them in every way she can how much she loves them. She explains again that she tried for a long time to fix the marriage, without going into detail, and implies that Daddy did, too. She says she will always love Kevin on some level because he is their father. They just can't live together anymore without making each other too unhappy. She tells them how sorry she is.

When Connor opens the door, Jane falls into his room. Liam spills from her lap onto her chest and head. With his ribcage heavy on her face, the chalky feel of his t-shirt in her mouth, even though she fears their reaction, she can't help but laugh. To her relief, they both erupt in giggles, shattering the tension. Connor flops onto the floor and curls into her.

Old fears lift. Jane does not step cautiously through her home anymore. She no longer has to dodge Kevin and fear his moods. Instead, she fields plaintive questions and sporadic storms from Connor and Liam. Without Kevin, she is the only foil for their pain.

Over yet another cup of tea at Gabriela's kitchen table, Jane tries to understand what happened. "In my fear I built him up too much. I let him have such power over me."

"Don't judge yourself for being scared."

"I'm not explaining it well. What I think is that I ceded more control than necessary. I became paralyzed, like holding my breath to avoid provoking him took all my strength. Now I can breathe and think and start imagining a future."

"Thank God."

"I'm still panicking about custody, though, and how he may fight me."

Gabriela shakes her head. "He wouldn't know what to do with them if he got them. But still, hire a lawyer right this second."

"I'm working on it, getting referrals."

"Good. How are the boys?"

"Better. Flashes of anger and withdrawal between longer stretches of normalcy." Jane tries to smile but judging by the look that comes over Gabriela's face, she is not successful.

"You're a fantastic mom, and they will be fine. I promise."

"I hope so more than anything." Jane finds that she wants to change the subject. "Guess what? I'm turning his room into a studio. It has good light. I won't have to work on the roof anymore."

"A real studio, great."

"And I finally threw out that vitamin bottle in my freezer. Remember?"

"The one with the magic potion?" Gabriela laughs. "Sounds like you're cleaning out everything you were hanging onto for the wrong reasons. So, will you call David?"

"No," Jane says simply.

53

ONE FIDGETY AFTERNOON, LINDSAY STOPS by with apples and zucchini from her garden.

"I picked these for Hannah this morning before I remembered that she and Gavin already left. I'm losing it in my old age, aren't I? I guess I was only half awake. Since I can't very well mail vegetables to Portland, I thought you might like them."

"Thank you, and that must have been awful. I hate those moments when it hits me all over again. You'll stay? We'll make zucchini pasta and apple crisp. So how are you doing?" Jane rinses the zucchini and apples and sets them on a towel on the counter.

"I'm OK, but I keep thinking about Hannah. I wonder if she ever has even a fraction of a second, maybe when she wakes, of pure joy or pleasure or even boredom, any kind of normalcy, before the pain slaps her under again."

"I don't know. But honey, you were amazing that day and those that followed. You were good to her."

Lindsay takes a peeler from Jane's hands and begins on the apples. "I'm not sure I reached her at all."

"Yes, you did." Jane starts on the zucchini. "She knew you were there, taking care of her. She and Gavin hardly knew anyone here, but thanks to us, mostly you, they weren't alone."

"Her mother and sister did all the hard things."

"Of course they did. People turn to family during trauma."

"What about poor Gavin? He didn't really have anyone. We focused on Hannah, but Gavin—"

"You're right. I hope he's with his family now, too, not just hers, and I hope they're getting counseling and whatever else they need to stay alive and married. But you showed up every day for that week that felt like a year. It mattered."

"Thanks for saying so. How are you holding up?"

Tears form immediately, and Jane laughs at herself. "Well, that didn't take long. I'm a mess, to be honest. Terrified."

"This isn't about Sarah, is it? What's going on?"

"I told Kevin I want a divorce."

"You did?" Lindsay sets the peeler on the counter. "Come here." She pulls Jane to a chair at the kitchen table. "Is that what you truly want?"

"I'm scared, but yes. I can't do it anymore."

"What exactly are you scared of?"

"Lots of things, like how I'll manage financially, but most of all losing the boys."

"You won't."

"That's what he always threatened me with. When I finally had the courage to tell him I wanted out, it got ugly. He's gone now, thank God. He took that promotion in Houston."

"Oh honey."

"He insisted that I had to move, too, but then he caved. At least he seemed to. I told Gaby and Meghan it looked like he wouldn't fight me for custody after all, and I meant it. But I keep spinning. I'm scared he might come back and try to take them. Either his threats were all just a means to control and punish me or he simply hasn't carried them out yet. I know I sound nuts. He makes me paranoid."

"You're not crazy. You might want to stash their passports somewhere, just in case, like a safe deposit box. Wait, why are you smiling?"

"I already hid them in a basket of old clothes at Meghan's house. I did think to do that. Well, it was her idea."

"And you've hired a tough lawyer, some badass classmate of yours, right?"

"Yes, I just did."

"Then I think you're ready. I didn't know. I mean, I knew it was bad with you two, but I didn't understand how bad. Why didn't I see it?"

"Because I didn't let you. That's on me."

"I'm still sorry. How are the boys?"

"Confused and angry, mostly at me for the divorce, and also at God or the world for taking Sarah. But a lot of the time, they seem OK somehow. It's like they can't bear to inhabit a grieving space for too long."

"That seems healthy." Lindsay reaches for Jane's hands. "You know no parent, nobody, learns to deal with trauma until we're forced to."

"I just pray that with what my boys are going through now, the damage isn't permanent. Divorce can do that. I should know, look at me."

"Jane, no."

"I asked one of those grief counselors after the funeral, and she said I should stay open to talking about Sarah's death whenever they want but not force it. Good, fine. But then five minutes later, we hit them with divorce. That's too much for any child. It wasn't the right time."

"Honey, you can't control everything, no matter how hard you try. Sarah's death was a lightning strike, random and cruel, but it's not a reason to stay in an awful marriage any longer. There's no perfect plan, no right time, good luck with that—"

"Yeah, good luck with that." Jane is near tears yet again.

"No, I meant of course divorce is hard no matter when it happens. But you're such a good mom; you're doing the right thing. I know you are because you would never do this lightly."

"I probably should have done it a long time ago."

"Right." Lindsay squeezes Jane's hand. "You'll stay here, won't you?"

"Yes. I have a stronger community here than I've ever had in my life. Same for my kids. Plus it's more affordable, and they have so much going for them here."

"You know I never liked him?"

When Jane starts to laugh, it rolls through her body with cleansing force and washes over Lindsay, too. The two women return to peeling and chopping at the counter.

After a few minutes of comfortable silence, Lindsay looks up from the apples. "It's good that Día de Muertos is coming up in a couple months. Having a structure for grieving, a ritual, will help us all process Sarah's death." She pauses. "But really only time will heal that wound, and the same will be true for you and your boys in grieving the divorce."

"Last year, I had a tourist's vision of Día de Muertos as a celebration. I thought I'd had some sort of Mexican epiphany, so I'd be more comfortable with death, but I'm not." Jane shakes her head.

"Of course not. Having an annual observance for the dead doesn't blunt the impact of a death, especially a child's. There's a reason there's a whole separate day that comes first, el Día de los Angelitos, for children who die. It's always a god-awful tragedy to lose a child. And you know what? I'm pissed at the way this newer bunch of foreigners, along with some local business owners, have commercialized the whole thing."

"Commercialized it?"

"Made a festival out of it, a tourist spectacle. It's meant to be a private time of mourning, although with a brave face for the outside world. Some older women still wear black to the end of their days for a husband, a child, or even a parent. I'm sure you've seen those black ribbons hanging over doorways for years, drooping with age, faded by the weather."

"Someone put one up over Hannah and Gavin's door. It made me cry again, which scared Connor and Liam."

"I think it's good for them to see you grieve." Lindsay pauses in her chopping to wrap an arm around Jane's shoulders. "Anyway, people find comfort in building altars, and entire families like my in-laws will spend hours by the grave of a family member, talking, eating, crying, and hiring mariachis to play their loved one's favorite songs. But although it's happening in a public cemetery, it's personal. They're not performers at a festival."

"I get it."

"Now all these tourists get right up in the mourners' faces to take pictures and even trample over the graves. It's offensive. The city had to close the main cemetery last year, when it used to be open all night."

"That's awful, I totally see that. But just to be fair, some local artists and businesses seem to be embracing this more public version with all the installations and performances."

"I suppose there's an upside, too."

"Well, speaking for my family at least, we'll have a more sober attitude this year."

The mother of one of the friendship poem girls calls Jane for Nayeli's phone number. Her daughter wants to invite Lupita to a playdate.

Jane crosses her fingers that Nayeli's cheap pre-paid cell still works, has recently been charged somewhere, and has available minutes. "If you can't get through on the phone, let me know. I can get a message to her."

On the day before classes start, Jane and Liam stop by the school to pick up the boys' new uniforms.

"Look Mom, it's Sarah."

In an alcove in the school's entrance hall hangs Javier's painting. Jane is surprised he hasn't yet shipped it to Hannah. Then she leans in and realizes that he must have, as what's hanging here is a high-quality print.

Two mothers walking by with piles of uniforms in their arms stop when they see Jane. "Oh, it's so awful," says one of them. "How's Hannah doing?"

Jane offers a tight smile for lack of words. The women look

embarrassed, and the one who asked shifts gears. "Your Casa Mía family, how are they?"

That Jane can talk about. "Well, their father wanted to pull the girls out of school because he was scared they'd be blamed somehow."

"Oh."

"But Sarah's family set up memorial scholarships—did you hear?—and the school is awarding them to Lupita and Dulce because that's what Sarah would have wanted. They can stay through graduation, whereas they only had a year guaranteed before. So now the father trusts that his daughters are accepted here and nobody's blaming them."

"Of course."

"It wasn't obvious to him, apparently. Anyway, their Casa Mía house is almost done. The housewarming party's a week from Saturday if you'd like to come. Out in Pueblo Nuevo. There are directions on our website."

"I'd love to. How nice to have something to celebrate."

The second mom agrees. "We'll be there."

Lately whenever Jane's eyes close and she hovers in a place before sleep, a watery world appears. Brilliant light shimmers on the surface, dancing with every ripple. Under these prisms, tendrils of hair undulate, beautiful, hypnotic, horrible. Fearing she will lie awake again for half the night, Jane takes a sleeping pill. It releases her.

After anchoring its legs in wet sand, Jane climbs the ladder. Waves splash against the second step as the tide advances.

The demon appears a thousand rungs above her.

She draws him down, but as he closes in, he sprouts enormous hummingbird wings. A brutish beak grows from his face, which he aims at her chest. At the last second before he reaches her, she leaps to the opposite side and kicks the ladder as hard as she can. It falls toward the desert floor, slamming the demon, whose new wings fail him, into hard, sunbaked earth. He lies still, oozing inky blood to be drunk by cacti. The wings and beak dissolve, leaving his true form to feed desert scavengers.

Jane splashes alone into a cold, tea-green sea and starts to swim, flailing her arms before settling into an effective rhythm.

A long time later, she reaches clear water.

JANE SHOWS UP EARLY TO Nayeli and Pablo's housewarming. She wants to present her painting to the family before anyone else arrives.

Lupita gasps when her mother unwraps it. "That's us! Mamá, Papá, Abuelita, Dulce, and me."

"Phew, I'm glad you can tell."

"Señora, it's beautiful."

"We'll hang it here, won't we?" Pablo indicates the most prominent spot, the center of the main wall in the living room. Nayeli nods her agreement, so he collects a hammer and nail from among his tools.

As Jane watches Pablo pound the nail, she looks through the polite, dedicated husband to the desperate, drunk man who beat his wife. This was the right thing, wasn't it? Won't he, as Nayeli says, be less likely to do it again now that they've escaped the shack? But maybe he resents that the house isn't something he accomplished for his family himself. It took accidental tugging by his muddy daughters on the guilty heartstrings of this bumbling foreign woman, urged on by his mother-in-law, first funded by one very wealthy young Mexican woman and then by an army of other women, largely foreigners, and two men. How understandable it would be to find that emasculating. He might half hate Jane and everyone involved. How natural it would be to find a human focus for his pain and resentment rather than trying to pin it to the impersonal, amorphous structures of systemic poverty he's been swimming against his whole life.

He did have to put in all that sweat equity. He spent many hard hours digging the hole for the foundation, laying bricks with the crew, hauling buckets of wet cement to the roof, helping to build a cistern, attending some of the workshops along with his wife, and more. *Please let that be enough to create a sense of earned ownership, enough, somehow, to keep Nayeli and the girls safe.*

As they all step back to admire the painting in its place, Carmen rests a hand on Jane's forearm. "They are amazing likenesses, but did you have to include all my wrinkles?"

"Oh, but I didn't," Jane responds. Carmen chortles. "Well, we'd better get ready. A lot of people are about to come through that door."

As if on cue, Eleanor pokes her head in. "Hello, happy homeowners. Let's get all the tables set up out there, shall we? I have the cake in my car, and we'd better bring it in before the frosting melts." Then she notices the painting. "Oh my God, look at that. You did that, Jane? It's marvelous. I heard you painted, but I had no idea. You do realize what you've done? Now they'll all expect a formal portrait to go with their houses."

Everyone comes to the party. The usual board members, volunteers, donors, and construction crew members attend, along with neighbors, Casa Mía families, and people hoping to become Casa Mía families. Representatives arrive from the water conservation nonprofit they recently started partnering with to build rainwater catchment systems, and so do the cheerful retirees who crochet bright bedspreads for every Casa Mía family. They like to see the children's delighted reactions when their works of art are spread out over new mattresses. And this time, twenty families from the international school show up, too, bearing housewarming gifts. Every time Jane looks up, someone is pressing something into Nayeli's arms.

Nayeli soon finds her. "It's too much, Señora. We would like to share some of these things with other families in the community."

"How generous. I'm sure Rocío will be happy to arrange that." Jane spots Rocío nodding her approval.

"Did you put her up to that?" Jane asks later, taking advantage of a few moments of privacy while she and Rocío carry bags of trash out to the trunk of Jane's car.

"It was her idea, but yes, I agreed. She knows it's not smart to incite more envy. They're already getting a house when some of their neighbors weren't quite poor enough to qualify, and now you have all these rich people bringing them gifts."

"You know it's for the most terrible reason. Because that girl died. Most of the people with presents are families who were there when it happened. Giving purges some of our guilt."

"I can imagine. All the same, it's better that Nayeli share the bounty."

"All right, but please, not in front of the school families. We want them all to leave happy and become regular donors. Can you wait until after the party?" Jane pauses. "Doesn't it sometimes seem like we're playing God?"

Rocío's eyebrows hover halfway up her forehead. "That's extreme."

"I guess, but it just feels to me that sometimes we treat these people like children."

"I don't see it that way at all. Is this because I think it's right to redistribute a few gifts?"

"It feels paternalistic. We sort of take over their lives for a year."

"Yes, we make them go to my workshops, which are valuable, if I do say so myself. How terrible. But from the day a family moves into their house, it's all on them to do the rest of the work to build their own futures. There's absolutely nothing wrong with what we're doing. So what's the problem?"

"Nothing. You're right," says Jane, chastened. "Sorry, I guess I sometimes question my own motivations and whether I personally am doing more harm than good, but I realize those are my hang-ups, and my fuck-ups, to be clear, not your problem or the organization's. I know we're doing good work."

"Well then, you go ahead and work out your angst or whatever you need to do. But hey, guess what? Remember Juanito, the super cute little guy with Down's? You met him one of your first times out in the community, remember?"

"Yeah, of course."

"The grant came through. He'll start speech therapy and some other classes next month. Within a year or so, he should be able to go to regular school with a teacher's aide."

"That's fantastic. Great job."

"And did you hear about Pablo?"

"What do you mean?"

Rocío shakes her head at Jane's obvious wariness. "No, it's good news. He found a better job doing construction again, so he's not at the kilns anymore. It's not just more money and safer conditions, but also shorter hours. He wants to be able to keep going to the girls' school events."

"That's great, good for him. But why aren't we doing anything about the violence? How can we trust him?"

"We can't. But Nayeli doesn't want to leave him or kick him out, so what can we do? She swears it was just those two times and now that they have a house it'll never happen again. Despite my warnings. Also, to be real, how would she support her daughters without him? She's already working as many hours as anyone can, and it's not nearly enough to live on. We're working on empowerment in the women's workshops—"

"Which will take years, maybe lifetimes. Generations."

"Yes. But it's a start."

"So turn him in for her. Call the police."

"For something she won't swear to?"

"But—"

"What? Seriously, Jane, what would you have me do?"

"I don't know. But we're not going to do anything, really? Just walk away, knowing it'll probably happen again?"

"I've told her we're here to help if she ever wants to drag him to a therapist or a priest or a social worker like me, but don't hold your breath. That's all we can do."

Jane accepts that she is not going to change Rocío's mind. *And I of all people,* she thinks, *should acknowledge that it can take a long time for some women to be ready to leave. But we should do something for the kids' sake.* "Then for the next community let's change that rule about no signs of domestic abuse. We got away with not sharing with the rest of the board what we knew in this case, but that might not work next time. Think of it from the child's perspective. Your dad hits your mom, so you can't have a decent home, either? Why punish the victims?"

"I know previous board members made that rule out of fear of getting the organization involved in messy situations."

"But haven't we addressed that by requiring the wife's name on the deed? You know, we could keep the rule for worst-case scenarios but look the other way in cases like Nayeli's."

Rocío nods in agreement. "Let's bring it up at the next meeting. We should probably talk to Meghan and Eleanor and get them on board ahead of time."

As Jane and Rocío return to the party, Gabriela and Eleanor approach them from different sides at the same time. Gabriela speaks first. "Are you guys OK with Grandma's side hustle?"

The other women give her blank looks.

"Doña Carmen's reindeer. She's back there behind the house selling them to guests."

"Is she really?" Eleanor's laughter pulls them all in. "What an entrepreneur. I think everyone needs a reindeer, don't you?"

"Bob keeps sending people, all innocent, to see the back of the house," Gabriela explains, "and then they return a few minutes later lugging a big reindeer. It's hilarious."

"Bob, really?" Jane can't picture it.

"Jane, he's not a bad guy, you know," says Eleanor. "He's poured his heart into this organization for years. You just got under his skin by coming in and immediately insisting on this family. Not playing by the rules is how he saw it."

"That's fair," Jane acknowledges.

Eleanor smiles gently. "Well, girls, it's time for the ribbon-cutting ceremony."

As the family's board sponsor, Jane gives the first speech and then holds an end of a shiny red ribbon while Eleanor holds the other and Dulce, beaming, cuts it with an oversize pair of scissors. Jane helps Nayeli dish up carnitas and thanks the mariachis for their performance and Gabriela for paying for it. Over the course of the celebration, she brushes off three friendly inquiries about why Kevin is not in attendance. Although pleased that news of her separation apparently hasn't spread around town yet, Jane still finds herself irritated to be asked. Finally, she passes out dozens of slices of cake. One goes into the hands of the woman with the curls from the Women Funding Progress meeting.

"I remember you. I never got a chance to properly thank you for getting us to a hundred thousand."

"We were so close to hitting the goal, it just had to be done, and I can't imagine a better cause than this." The woman motions to the house and a group of children bouncing balloons.

Gabriela walks up and hugs Jane. "It's your party, too, chica. This house wouldn't exist without you."

"Or you. So will you finally agree to join the board?"

"I don't know."

"You're perfect for it. You understand these communities better than I ever will, you have the biggest heart, and your loaded friends are potential donors. We would be grateful for whatever amount of time you can put into it, honestly."

"Well, I am in awe of what you guys accomplish. So if you believe I can help, I suppose, yes."

"Eleanor, she said yes!"

Eleanor excuses herself from another conversation and approaches the two of them, smiling warmly. "That's wonderful. We will be so lucky to have you, Gabriela. I suppose your first official duty will be working on that concert. It's coming up soon, next month, and Jane tells me it wouldn't be happening at all without you and our Meghan here."

An hour later nearly all the guests have left, more than a few with a reindeer strapped to their cars. Jane imagines the looks on passing

JANE'S PHONE RINGS A FEW days after the housewarming. The caller introduces herself as the owner of an art gallery in the Fábrica la Aurora, a converted garment factory on the edge of town that now houses dozens of galleries, some more successful than others. "I saw your portrait of the Casa Mía family. Those souls practically stepped off the wall into the party."

"Wow, thank you."

"Eleanor gave me your number. So why haven't I seen your work before, are you new in town?"

"I've been here two years, but I only recently returned to painting after a long hiatus."

"That explains it. So when can I see more?"

"Well, I can show you my Anger series and a self-portrait with my boys. Oh, and a portrait of a woman and her daughters standing in mud, the same Casa Mía family, actually."

"OK, interesting. And the Anger series sounds promising."

"It's really dark."

"That's fine."

"Domestic violence."

The "Oh" sounds disconcerted. A pause grows for a beat too long, but then the voice comes back stronger. "You know what, I would like to see that. How many paintings in the series?"

"Maybe four, plus the two portraits."

"You don't have anything else here? I'm asking because I have an unexpected opening for the November ArtWalk, but it's the whole gallery. You'd need ten or twelve strong works at a minimum, and I'd like to choose them myself from as many pieces as possible."

"I can produce more. My process has really sped up lately."

"By the first Saturday in November? It's the middle of September already, so that's only six weeks. Not much time, even if you do nothing but paint all day."

"Which I can't." Jane feels the offer slip away.

"Why don't you call me in a few months? March is still available. No promises, but call when you think you're ready, and we'll see."

March, the time of the egrets' return. The trees the city over-pruned last year have recovered much of their former lushness during the summer rains, so hopefully the graceful birds will come back to her to reclaim their place. By March, she'll have built up a roster of legal clients online. By March, her boys will hopefully have worked through the worst waves of pain and anger over the divorce. And in March, she might even sell some paintings.

Rocío and Jane meet for coffee. This time they stay at the café, but they take their steaming cups up a spiral staircase to a small terrace where customers can enjoy a view of the city's spires and roof gardens. The space allows for only two tiny round tables, so Jane crosses her fingers that one will be available.

They're in luck. "Oh good, it's all ours."

Rocío gets down to business. "I have a new family for you to sponsor. Don't worry, this one we voted on, so the funding's already there. No need to go all vigilante fairy godmother this time."

"Ah, this is how it's supposed to work."

"Yes, so maybe try not to get so emotionally invested? It's great that you care, but you know, things went off the rails last time. I'm not saying full ice queen, just dial down the fairy godmother a smidge."

"I get it. It doesn't take a psychology degree to see I overinvested in Nayeli's family to avoid my own stuff. I'm supposed to empower them, not obsess."

"Do you though, really get it, I mean? Sorry if that sounds harsh, I'm just worried about you. It could be, like you're saying, to avoid something else."

"I'm getting divorced."

Over Rocío's shoulder, Jane watches a head crowned by a sleek silver bob and then a set of shoulders wrapped in a woolly shawl appear at the top of the spiral staircase. The eyes widen, and then the lips form a slight but sympathetic smile before the head and shoulders retreat.

Rocío looks stricken. "Oh my God, I had no idea. Sorry for going off like that."

"The waiters will hate me. I'm scaring away their customers." Jane manages to laugh, even as Rocío is confused by the comment. "No, it's fine, you're right, what you said was true. Also, I have to get used to talking about it. Now that school's started, more moms find out every day. Some are super supportive while others just want the gossip. You know how it is, the school steps can be treacherous."

"If I'd known, I wouldn't have said those things. Are you doing OK?"

"Yes and no. I'm confident that I'm doing the right thing, but sometimes I'm still a mess, like I'm afraid every time I go to the ATM because he could cut me off at any moment. I'll make my own money, I'm still a lawyer, but it will take a while to build up a new client base online."

"I seriously had no idea. I am so clueless."

"Not at all. I didn't give you any idea." Jane looks again at the stairs where the woman appeared. No one is there now. "This is a positive change in my life, I promise. But I won't be able to really exhale until the divorce is final with primary custody settled for good."

"Do you have a lawyer?"

"Everyone asks that. Yes, I hired an old law school classmate. She's brilliant. I'm afraid the process will take forever, though, and I just want it over."

"It doesn't have to. Take forever, that is. And of course you're struggling, of course you're lost. There's no other way it could be. Just get through this part."

"You're right." Jane suddenly can't wait to change the subject. "You know what? I got an offer for a gallery opening. Sort of."

Rocío looks equally relieved to seize on something positive. "Out of the blue? That never happens; that's amazing."

"The gallery owner was actually at the housewarming, and she saw my portrait of Nayeli's family. She doesn't believe I can be ready for an opening she has in November, but she told me to call her again in a few months if I produce enough. Which I will, for sure. She has another available slot in March."

"But do you need more pressure right now?"

"This is good pressure. I have so much support here, and I've also invited my mom for a long visit. My brother, Thomas, even offered to come, and he's great with the boys."

"That's wonderful, but let's take something off your plate. You don't need to sponsor another family right away. One of the retired guys with lots of time can do two, no problem. Your big concert's coming up. That's more than enough Casa Mía in your life right now."

"But—"

"No."

As they pass the tables on the main floor on the way to the door, the woman with the silver hair reaches out and pats Jane's arm. The sincerity of the simple gesture moves her.

On the school steps the next afternoon, Lupita tells Jane she saw a hummingbird outside her new house, and it had a message.

"What was the message?" Jane asks, basking in the girl's confidence.

"I think it was from Sarah. She wants us to know she's fine where she is now, and also probably to do our homework and get along and be happy."

"That sounds about right."

On the walk home, Liam brings it up. "That does sound like Sarah. She always wanted people to be happy. It's working, I think."

"I think so, too," says Jane.

Connor slides his hand into hers.

She goes home with her boys to paint a girl flying with an egret, although she has never painted birds before. The inspiration came on strong, and she trusts it.

In Jane's garden, the neighbor's sleek calico stalks a hummingbird. The cat circles beneath the feeder while Jane wills the tiny diva to fly beyond reach. He does, shifting directions, gorgeous wings beating incessantly in blurs of sun-gilded metallic greens, without ever acknowledging the threat. He hovers above the garden wall, and, seemingly out of sheer pleasure, adds a few beats per second.

Epilogue

"Liam, would you like to find the best spot for Sarah?"

"Next to Grandpa." He positions the photo Jane hands him, framed in Mexican silver, on the top level. "Her parents must be happy that she's still remembered every year."

Connor places low candles in front of the portraits, and then Jane wraps an arm around each set of broadened shoulders.

She remains at the altar after her sons move on. *What do you think, Dad? It took long enough, but I am finally standing on my own, fear in check. Wings unbound, unbroken. And my boys? You would be proud of them.*

Hummingbird, a last journey. Go to the north and find her people. Assure them that a person's memory lives on throughout all the years someone places her picture on an altar for el Día de Muertos. Every year she receives such an invitation, she can return to visit those who honor her.

We remember.

Hummingbird wings have curious magic, for they move at an impossible rate. Certain hummingbirds cover impossible distances, equivalent in proportion to an eagle flying to the moon. Such a hummingbird's power, improbable and marvelous already, grows still greater when he is assigned a message to deliver. We must hear and interpret those gifted to us.

We listen.

Painting of Ann Marie Jackson by Kate Van Doren
Yo Sí Te Creo (Yes, I Believe You) 60 x 90 cm, oil on canvas

International Women's Day 2020, San Miguel de Allende, México
These women performed a flash mob for Ser Mujer, a women's advocacy organization, and collaborated with the Healing Words Project.
Author at center in white t-shirt with skull.

The Healing Words Project was created by artist Kate Van Doren during the national strike *Un Día Sin Mujeres* (A Day Without Women) in March 2020. In support of this national protest against an epidemic of femicides in Mexico, Van Doren documented over a thousand women and children using photography, videography, and painting, culminating in a powerful installation at the Fábrica la Aurora in San Miguel de Allende on International Women's Day 2020. The names and numbers written on the arms of the women and girls pictured below are the names and ages of victims of femicide in Guanajuato State in the preceding year.

Since 2020, the Healing Words Project has grown to spread awareness about domestic violence and femicide worldwide. Van Doren has photographed hundreds more women with words of reclamation and empowerment inscribed on their arms, torsos, or backs. To learn more, visit healingwordsproject.com. Ann Marie Jackson is an advisor to the project.

Acknowledgments

To the people of San Miguel de Allende, thank you for welcoming me, an immigrant. *Muchísimas gracias con todo mi corazón. San Miguel es verdaderamente un pueblo mágico debido a su belleza, su magnífica historia, sus tradiciones que se han mantenido vivas por tantos años, el arte y su gloriosa arquitectura, y más que nada, su gente tan amable y generosa.*

To the whole team at She Writes Press, especially Brooke Warner, Samantha Strom, and Julie Metz, thank you for believing in this book. Two wonderful editors helped me whip this story into shape. Kerry Muir, thank you for your passion, humor, and deeply excellent advice. Ellen Lesser, your insights were golden. I also had fantastic beta readers: Jessica Claire Haney, Lucie Frost, Sarah Bringhurst Familia, Alex Montgomery, Beth Getchell, and Katie O'Grady, thank you so much.

To my writers' group, in all its forms: Without you, I would not have begun, let alone finished, this journey. Even as the group scattered across the hemisphere, your inspiration kept me going. I thank from the bottom of my heart Jenifer Phillips and also Shannon Stepan for your unflagging support. You were always willing to read another draft, which is the ultimate test of friendship. Moni Wessel, Kim Slote, Erika Hernández Barasoain, Christie Long, Harmeet Kaur Sidhu, Jessica Patterson García, Susan Cobb, Katie Van Doren, Kimberly Bernstein, and Teddy Kellam, thank you for your feedback and sisterhood. I honor the ever-fabulous Lisa Carol, an early member of our group who lived powerfully and beautifully and was taken from this world far too soon. She was writing a spectacular one-woman show, and truly, she lived it.

Judith Guille, Maia Williams, and Willa Madden, I am grateful to you for the early push through *Solamente en San Miguel.* Judyth Hill, poetess-priestess, thanks for your early enthusiasm. To literary agent Anna Knutson Geller, for orienting me to this peculiar industry, thank you.

Muchísimas gracias to stellar early readers Laura Rodríguez, Natasha Herron, Kristi James, Diana Markel, Martha Vega, Hadley O'Regan, Muriel Quinn, Zoë Siegel, Amber Nieto, Scottie Elliot, Katja Smith, Rachel Ballard, Violette Feldt, Ana Dimen, Kathy Crewe Kelly, and Lindsay Oldenski.

To the whole Casita Linda family, you inspire me more than you know. It was an honor to celebrate the hundredth house with you, and I look forward to the two hundredth. Louise Gilliam, who has given her whole heart to this noble cause, Magdalena Pérez López, Gabriela Rodríguez, Amber Nieto, Ilian Barrera, María Guillermina Reyes, Lyn Gawron, Gregg Blackburn, Guadalupe Alessio Robles, Kim Slote, Rachel Ballard, Agustín Solórzano, Valerie Fischer, Zoë Siegel, Aleysha Serrato Garfias, Jessica Patterson García, Mario López González Garza, Tracey Kitzman, and Teri Kavanagh Guerrero Armendariz, I salute you all. Daniel López, your Modern Mexican Political History lecture series benefitting Casita Linda was epic. Alex Trapp & Laura Rodríguez, thank you for taking Casita Linda donors to dine like kings in the shadow of the pyramid.

To my Mano Amiga team, thank you. Our little microlending nonprofit has made a world of difference in the lives of many Sanmiguelense women. Cheers to you, Magdalena Pérez López, Nory Contractor, Tracey Kitzman, Janan Asfour, Rachel Ballard, Amber Nieto, Hadley O'Regan, Migdalia Camacho Denike, Jessica Patterson García, Kim Powell de Olivares, Aleysha Serrato Garfias, Alexandra Silén, Rocío Barrera García, Magdalena H. Copado, Elizabeth Davidson, and Kim Slote.

To the teachers and community of the Academia Internacional

San Miguel de Allende, thank you for welcoming me, as well as my sons, so warmly. *Nos ayudaron mucho a adoptar las hermosas raíces mexicanas.*

To the many friends and neighbors who helped my family build a life in San Miguel, *muchísimas gracias.*

To the astonishingly talented artist Kate Van Doren, being your occasional muse is an honor.

Jessica Patterson García, you are the sister I never had and always will have.

I offer armloads of gratitude and love to my first reader and lifetime fan, my dear mom, Theresa Ann Greiner Downey, to my steadfast brother, Pete Downey, and to the memory of my father, James Edward Downey.

Philip, thanks for Mexico and good memories.

Tristan and Rowan, my loves, you are everything.

About the Author

photo credit: Lander Rodríguez

ANN MARIE JACKSON is co-founder of microlending organization Mano Amiga and former Vice President of Casita Linda, which builds homes for families living in extreme poverty in San Miguel de Allende, Mexico. Early in her career, after earning degrees from Stanford and Harvard, Jackson joined the U.S. Department of State to promote human rights in China and other East Asian and Pacific Island nations. She has worked for several NGOs, including Human Rights Watch, A Better Chance, and Internews, and traveled widely on five continents. This is her first novel. A portion of the proceeds from *The Broken Hummingbird* will benefit nonprofit organizations serving women and families in central Mexico. A native of Seattle, Washington, Jackson resides in San Miguel de Allende.

SELECTED TITLES FROM SHE WRITES PRESS

She Writes Press is an independent publishing company founded to serve women writers everywhere. Visit us at www.shewritespress.com.

Luz by Debra Thomas. $16.95, 978-1-63152-870-5
When Alma Cruz, a young Mexican woman, journeys across the US border to look for her missing migrant father, she encounters love—but also encounters profound cruelty—along the way.

Lost in Oaxaca by Jessica Winters Mireles. $16.95, 978-1-63152-880-4
Thirty-seven-year-old piano teacher Camille Childs is a lost soul who is seeking recognition through her star student—so when her student unexpectedly leaves California to return to her village in Oaxaca, Mexico, Camille follows her. There, Camille meets Alejandro, a Zapotec man who helps her navigate the unfamiliar culture of Oaxaca and teaches her to view the world in a different light.

A Drop in the Ocean: A Novel by Jenni Ogden. $16.95, 978-1-63152-026-6
When middle-aged Anna Fergusson's research lab is abruptly closed, she flees Boston to an island on Australia's Great Barrier Reef—where, amongst the seabirds, nesting turtles, and eccentric islanders, she finds a family and learns some bittersweet lessons about love.

A Matter of Chance by Julie Maloney. $16.95, 978-1-63152-369-4
Guilt, hope, and persistence propel New York fashion editor Maddy Stewart in her search for her daughter, abducted from the Jersey Shore—a quest that takes her through Brooklyn's dangerous underworld and eventually to Bavaria, Germany.

A Wife in Bangkok by Iris Mitlin Lav. $16.95, 978-1-63152-707-4
After moving with her husband and children from a small Oklahoma town to 1975 Thailand, Crystal is confronted with a strange culture and a frightening series of events. She finds beauty in Thailand but also struggles to fight loneliness, depression, and, ultimately, betrayal, even as she tries to be the good wife she thinks she ought to be.

After Kilimanjaro by Gayle Woodson. $16.95, 978-1-63152-660-2
It was just supposed to be a break, a respite from the rigors of training to be a surgeon. She would fly to Tanzania, climb a mountain, do a little feel-good medical work. She didn't realize that she would fall in love with the place—or that it would change her life forever.